DEN OF THIEVES

BOOK ONE OF PANTHEON ONLINE

S.A. KLOPFENSTEIN

BOOKS BY S.A. KLOPFENSTEIN

THE SHADOW WATCH SAGA

The Shadow Watch
The Rage of Saints
The Darkling Queen
The Well of Shadows

PANTHEON ONLINE

Den of Thieves
Rogue Assassin

Pantheon: Den of Thieves © 2022 by S.A. Klopfenstein
Published by Guardian Grey Publishing

Cover Illustration by Ömer Burak Önal
Edited by Tamara Blain

ISBN: 9798419446137

This one's for the Forge

[PART 1]
GRID EIGHT

WELCOME TO PRISON

[2046 AD - Somewhere in Washington State]

JAKE DARROW's mind was shrouded in fog as the guards shoved him through a set of cold steel doors, then dragged him down a long white corridor. It was the sort of stark hallway that felt straight out of a horror movie set, the sort of hallway that never led to anything good.

But his body was exhausted and his eyes were heavy, and so he did not resist.

He couldn't remember why he was here, or where the hell here was. It was as though his body had been dropped into the middle of a strange dream.

But his mental faculties were sharp enough to understand that he was in deep shit.

The guards hurried him along so fast he could barely keep his feet under him. Both men were dressed in black uniforms with no decorations save for a patch on the right breast—an emblem of an octagonal maze with a red circle at the center. Both were tall and muscular, one Hispanic and bald, the other a very pale redhead. Neither man so much as looked at him.

They gripped him tightly by the arms and led him through another series of corridors.

"Wha's going on?" Jake slurred.

And immediately regretted it.

The redheaded guard slapped his face. "Shut up!"

Jake grimaced. *Yep, very deep shit.*

"Go easy, Connors," said the other guard. His badge named him Officer Marco Reyes.

Connors glared, but complied.

The impact awakened Jake's mind further, and he realized he must be coming out of some sort of sedation. Likely the reason his legs felt so wobbly and the guards gripped him so tight. A queasy feeling filled his gut, perhaps a side effect from whatever drug he'd been given.

But there was something more.

An image flashed in his mind. It was not entirely clear, but he vaguely made out the form of a young girl on the ground beside him. No older than his own twenty-three years. Blood poured from a gaping wound in her head, pooling on the concrete, covering his hands and clothes in her blood.

Terror gripped him. He blinked hard and glanced down at his hands.

They were clean.

But the sudden movement sent his head spinning. He dropped to his knees in the middle of the corridor and retched on the ground.

"Dammit!" Connors shouted.

"Forget it," Reyes said. "The orderlies will clean it up."

The two enormous men jerked Jake back to his feet.

"Lucky you missed my shoes, asshole," Connors said. "Cost me two hundred credits. I'd've kicked the crap out of you."

"Ain't worth getting writ up over," Reyes said.

"You make me wish they never banned the death penalty,"

Connors muttered. "What you did to that girl. I would happily watch them kill thugs like you. Hell, I'd sign up to do it myself."

Jake said nothing, but the sinking feeling in his gut only worsened, and it took everything inside him not to vomit again. That girl had been real. A memory. Him on the concrete beside her.

Oh god! I killed her?

His breathing grew frantic and shallow.

Who had she been? Had he known her?

The image was still hazy in his mind. She had blonde hair, when it wasn't covered in blood, but he couldn't quite picture her face. His memory was consumed by the gaping wound and the blood. He knew it made him a coward, but if he was honest, he didn't want to picture it. His heart thundered in his chest.

This can't be real!

Jake didn't bother asking the guards about her, for fear he would only get slapped again. The pair led him through a final set of steel doors, which opened into a smaller hallway. A tall black man with a mustache stood in front of a solitary door.

The man wore the same dark uniform as the other two guards.

It was only then that Jake realized how strange it was that he wasn't wearing any handcuffs. But then again, Jake was short and scrawny, and all three of these guys looked like they lifted all day. He was no match for any of them.

And where the hell would he go anyway?

The man gestured to Connors and Reyes. "I'll take him from here, boys."

The two released their grip and backed away.

The steel doors opened into another corridor, this one made of stone, lit by dim yellow lamps. A rush of cold air shot into Jake's face, jolting him fully out of his haze. He glanced back. The two guards were already gone.

"Let's go, kid," the third guard said. According to his badge, he was Officer Shad Matthews. He walked through the doors.

"You just expect me to follow you?" Jake asked.

The man laughed, a deep-throated cackle that shook his whole body. "If we were worried about your resistance, you'd be cuffed, boy. Besides, where else do you think you're gonna go?"

Jake glanced back again and realized that another set of doors had closed silently behind him. Apparently, he'd been standing in some sort of holding cell.

With no options and no answers, he obeyed. The ground was made of concrete, but the corridor went on and on and made Jake think of a tour he had gone on once during a family vacation to Mammoth Cave, when he was in high school. Their guide had been a cute college girl, and Jake hadn't paid very much attention to the cave. His mother had been really upset at him. She was the nature-loving type.

He felt a sharp pang of guilt at the thought of his family. Did they know what had happened? Would he ever see them again?

With the level of surveillance technology in use, the jury trial system had been abandoned before Jake fully understood what it had ever been like. The evidence spoke for itself now.

Which meant there was no doubt about whatever it was he'd done. The government had footage. The girl's bloody face entered his mind again and tried to stick, but he pushed it back.

The cavernous corridor continued for some time. Shad kept a quick pace ahead of him, saying nothing. Jake guessed it was ten minutes or more before they reached a gigantic vault door. Shad punched a code into the keypad to the right, and the door shot up and another rush of cold air struck Jake in the face.

The room beyond was empty and stark white. There was a stainless steel table at the center, and two steel chairs. Upon the table was a single plate set with a juicy rib eye steak, mashed potatoes, and buttery green beans. Beside the plate, there was a bright red can of Coke.

It was a silly thought all things considered, but he was relieved it wasn't Pepsi.

Shad gestured to the seat.

Jake stared at the food stupidly.

"Your favorite meal, isn't it?" Shad asked.

"Y-yeah, but how did you know?"

Shad shrugged. "The law knows things, boy. Same way they don't need a trial."

"What the hell is this?" he asked, pointing at the food.

"Back when I was a boy, I had an uncle. Ran with a rough crowd and got himself into all kinds of trouble. One night, my mama got a call in the middle of the night. My uncle had killed a man. Swore up and down it was self-defense, but there was no way to prove it. That was back before the satellite cams were built. Back when they'd kill a man for that sort of shit. Well, on the day they executed him, he got a meal. For the last meal, they'd cook up something real special. Whatever you wanted. Same as we got here for you."

Jake started trembling. "M-my last meal? But they don't—"

"Nah, they don't execute folks no more. But from now on, you're going to be eating a bit differently."

"What do you mean?"

Shad took a seat in the chair on the other side of the table. "You better eat before that steak gets cold."

Jake was starving, now that he thought about it. He tore into the steak, cutting off large chunks and dipping them in the creamy potatoes. He guzzled it down with a large swig of Coke.

"Why's this the last meal? Because the prison food is so terrible?"

Shad smiled, and Jake thought it might actually be genuine, if a little patronizing. "Your head still feels a bit hazy, don't it?"

Jake paused his eating and nodded. "How did you know?"

"You all come down like that. You got a headache too?"

Come to think of it, he did. It wasn't the blazing pain of a migraine, it was more like a strong, constant pressure at the base of his cranium, where the neck met his skull.

What part is that again? The occipital bone!

His Intro to Anatomy professor would have been proud. Jake reached back to the source of the discomfort, then jerked his hand away in horror.

There was something metal embedded in the back of his spine.

[2]
GRID EIGHT

JAKE PUSHED himself away from the table, seizing the steak knife from his plate and backing against the wall. With his free hand, he felt at the protruding metal.

Shad remained seated, not seeming overly alarmed about the knife in his ward's hands.

"What the hell is this?" Jake shouted.

Shad just nodded casually. "Check the ones on your arms too."

Jake frantically pulled up one of the sleeves of his navy jumper. Three more metal disks were embedded in his forearm. It was the same with the other arm. Each disk was circular, maybe an inch in diameter, with fine ridges spanning from the center, where there was a small divot.

His fingers shook, barely able to keep hold of the knife. "W-what did you people do to me?"

"Now, see here, boy. You best get a few things straight real quick. First, we didn't do nothing to you. That was the folks upstairs. The Suits and Ties. Second, you don't get to question how anyone treats you. You're a damn felon. You're scum. You killed an innocent young lady."

"B-but I—"

"Shut your mouth, boy," Shad said, rising to his feet. He crossed over to where Jake was standing. "Third, even if you could take me with that knife, it wouldn't do you any good." Shad reached for him, and to Jake's amazement, the man's hand passed right through him.

"What is going on?" Jake asked.

Shad laughed. "A hologram, boy. If you really think anyone would be stupid enough to give a knife to a convicted murderer while he was alone with one guard, then you won't last a day down here."

Jake paused, taking in the information. All the holograms he'd ever heard of had to be projected from something. He glanced up at the ceiling. No drones. No flashing lights in the ceiling. No obvious source at all.

"Where the hell am I?"

"Sure you don't want to finish your meal first?"

Jake eyed the steak and potatoes. There were still a few bites left, but he had lost his appetite. "I want to know where I am. And I want to know why. What happened to that girl?"

"You sure about that?"

Jake pictured the blonde girl one more time, and this time he let the image linger. She'd had flush cheeks and deep brown eyes that made him shudder as he pictured the life fading from them. "I need to know."

Shad leveled his gaze at Jake, not hiding a hint of disdain. "You were at a party, Jake. You were drunk out of your mind, and you drove. She was crossing the street, coming home from a late shift at a restaurant downtown. I'm guessing you never even saw her, you were so blitzed."

Jake definitely did not want to eat anything else. A new image filled his mind—of blonde hair flying through the air, her head smacking the concrete. He pictured himself stumbling out of the car, the hood splattered in blood. Dripping hands as he slipped in the crimson pool on the road and realized with horror what he'd done, as those beautiful brown eyes settled on him, as he watched her chest rise and fall for the last time.

Was it a memory? Had the truth jerked him out of his mental fog? Or was he just imagining it, his mind filling in the blanks to help make sense of the unfathomable?

He just could not believe he had done something like that. Sure, he had never been one to shy away from a few drinks, but it just wasn't like him to drive. And the one time he did...

"What was her name?" Jake asked, unsure why it mattered. But somehow, he felt he owed her that much.

"Alex Keynes," Shad said evenly. "Pretty girl. Wrong place, wrong time. All on surveillance. Open-and-shut case. You got offered a deal for a shorter sentence in exchange for coming to this particular prison. And here you are."

"A deal?"

Shad chuckled. "That sedative really does a number, don't it?"

The airlock doors behind Shad's hologram shifted open with a whooshing sound, and the sight outside the holding cell took Jake's breath away.

Beyond the doors, a broad window looked out over a massive underground dome that must have stretched for a couple of miles at least. Enormous pipes jutted from the ground into the stony ceiling hundreds of feet above. Wires and thick cables stretched above short buildings, and all around there were huge turbines and power stations. A mechanical droning sound filled his ears.

"Welcome to Grid Eight. Powering the world above, one prisoner at a time."

For a minute, Jake said nothing. He merely stared out through the window at the strange expanse.

"Get used to that view, kid. This is your future. Well, the real one anyway."

"What do you mean?"

"This is where you will work, sleep, eat, take a dump. Call it the mercy of the great state of Washington. You did the crime, now we take your time and make it worth something."

The holographic guard made his way down the hall, but Jake didn't follow.

Surely this couldn't be real. *A labor camp? That has to be illegal.*

Shad reached another door and turned back.

A shock surged down Jake's spine, and he fell back against the window. He grabbed onto the small sill, barely managing to avoid falling on his ass.

Shad smiled in a satisfied manner.

"Y-you did that to me?" It was difficult to speak. Jake's tongue felt like a bloated fish in his mouth.

"No," Shad said. "That thing in your neck serves a few purposes. Lets the folks upstairs know where you are. Lets us track your work. And if you do something stupid, like attack another prisoner or refuse to do what you're told... Well, I think you understand just fine."

Did he ever. Jake's arms were raw and shaking, and he wasn't sure he could feel his legs. But his feet moved, which was a huge relief. His thighs began to tingle, and slowly, sensation returned.

When he was able to get back to his feet, Shad waved him over, and this time, Jake followed without hesitation.

They passed through another set of doors, which reminded him of the blast doors in sci-fi films. Jake had always preferred VR games, but his dad had been a huge cinephile, and growing up, Jake had spent many a night watching old sci-fi movies with his family.

A dark pang coursed through him at the thought of them. Oh, what he would give for this to be a dream. To go back and visit his parents' house and watch those old films.

He pushed the thought to the back of his mind, or he thought he might fall apart right there in the hallway. And he didn't think Shad, or the Suits and Ties upstairs, would take that well.

After passing through one last holding bay, they emerged in the station upon a busy lane lined with stark white buildings. People moved quickly past them, all wearing plain navy uniforms just like the one Jake was wearing. No one seemed to take notice of them.

"How many prisoners are there?" Jake asked.

Shad's hologram shrugged. "Hundreds in this station."

"How many stations are there?"

"No idea. One in most cities, I suppose. Come on."

Shad led the way down the thoroughfare. Both sides of the lane were lined with two-story buildings made of concrete painted with large blue numbers on the front. They walked past dozens of them before entering Building 69.

Jake couldn't help himself. He smirked. Shad rolled his eyes and carried on down a white hall lined with doors every ten feet or so.

They stopped at Number 17.

"Welcome to your new home. And believe it or not, this will be the best part of your day." With a whooshing sound, the door opened, sliding into the side of the wall.

What lay beyond was not at all what he expected. There was no bed. No furniture.

Just a terrifying contraption that reminded Jake vaguely of a dentist's chair. Tubes hung from a large robotic arm, and the room was lit by the soft glow of a display screen beside it.

"This is the best part of my day?"

Shad laughed. "Your waking life will be spent doing nothing but work. Tomorrow, you will be shown to your position. But when you sleep, you will be hooked up here to the Virtuality Core."

"Virtuality? Like the gaming company?"

Virtuality had made some of Jake's favorite VR games when he was in high school, though they hadn't released any new titles in a couple years. Not since a scandal involving stolen tech tanked their flagship MMO. There were rumors that they were going under.

Looks like those rumors were a bit premature.

"Like the gaming company," Shad said. "Virtuality is owned by the Mercer Corporation, who also own this prison. Should have all been in your NDA."

"NDA?"

"Installing that hardware takes its toll for a bit, but it'll all come back."

"So prisoners here get to play video games?" Jake asked, rubbing his hand across the disk on the back of his neck.

"Call it an incentive. You do your job. You behave. You get to have a semblance of a life, even if it's fake. While you're in, you'll be nourished with these." Shad ran his hands over the tangle of tubes on the robotic arm.

"Like an IV or something?"

Shad nodded. "Saves us all the trouble of cooks and a mess hall and time." Shad gestured to the seat. "Go on, climb aboard."

"Now? Before I've done any work?"

"Like I said, it's an incentive. They work best when you've had a taste. Believe me, every time you leave, you'll be dying to work and earn your next trip back."

The robotic arm began to shift. The tubes began to orient themselves at one end of the chair arm, while the other end of the arm shifted toward the headrest. With a whirring sound, a large needle emerged precisely where Jake's neck was supposed to rest.

"I-I'm not so sure I want to. This isn't like any game I've ever heard of. Where's the headgear for virtual immersion? Where's the hand controls?"

"This is something new altogether," Shad said. "You might say they're beta testing it."

"What do you mean?"

"Kid, this is unlike any game you've ever played. You won't just see it as if you're in the game. You will actually be there. Now, climb aboard before that shock comes again. The first one was light, but in the future, you'll really feel like hell afterward."

Jake shook his head, but he knew there was no point in resisting. The last thing he wanted was to experience that shock at a higher level.

He climbed into the cushioned seat. The robotic arms whirled around, and the tubes attached themselves to the three metallic disks in each of his forearms.

"All right, now lean back."

Jake obeyed. The Virtuality Core whirred, and there was a sharp pain and a rush in his neck.

He couldn't hold back his scream as his vision went black.

THE REALMS OF PANTHEON

THANK ALL that was good and holy, the pain only lasted a few agonizing seconds. The haze seeped away like a flow of water, and vibrant colors peeked through Jake's vision, a stark contrast to the sterile environment of Grid Eight.

He stood in the midst of a lush green meadow at the edge of a towering wood. He had never seen trees so gigantic in all his life, and his family had visited the redwoods when he was a kid. But these trees were something else entirely. To his right, they towered hundreds, maybe thousands of feet, like a tangled web of skyscrapers.

On his left, a wall of cliffs shot into the air, and in the distance, he could make out a rushing plume of mist at the base of the largest waterfall he had ever seen in his life. It cascaded from a cleft in the cliffs with a distant roar.

The meadow was alive with sound, the buzzing of bees and the chirping of birds and the rush of a soft wind through the grass. Jake had spent the majority of his life in the city. Of course, there were parks, but they were always crowded. Nothing he had ever experienced could compare with the unadulterated beauty of this place.

It felt like a dream.

His mind began to slowly understand that he was in the midst of a game world unlike anything he had ever experienced.

These graphics are incredible! This can't be virtual.

The cerulean sky was filled with soaring birds. By the size of their wingspan, Jake guessed they were eagles or condors or something, but they were too distant to tell.

A black one veered with a smooth arc and headed in his direction, growing larger and larger as it neared, spanning at least ten feet. It swooped down, just above the meadow, and headed straight toward him.

As it neared, Jake realized it was not a bird at all. It had dark leathery wings, long talons, and a dark and hideous humanoid face. Just when Jake realized this gigantic ugly creature was attacking him and he should probably drop to the ground, he also realized he could not move.

In fact, he had not moved an inch since he'd arrived. It should have been obvious, but he was too distracted by his new breathtaking environment. He was stuck, and this flying demon-thing was going to claw his eyes out!

But just as it reached him, the creature lurched back, slowing its descent, and came to a hard and slightly clumsy landing in the meadow, directly in front of Jake.

The thing was even more disgusting up close. Two large yellowish fangs protruded from its upper jaw. Its eyes were bloodshot and there was a distinct smell about it. Not quite pungent, but like the smell of food left too long in the fridge on the verge of decay.

It opened a blood red mouth, and to Jake's amazement, it spoke.

"Welcome to the realms of *Pantheon*, whatever you are." Its voice sounded like gravel in a meat grinder.

"Er, I'm Jake. I'm human."

Does this game not have humans in it?

"Wrong. You are nothing. Not yet, anyway. Or haven't you bothered to look at yourself?"

Jake looked down at his hands and feet, and to his shock, he found that there was nothing there at all.

Well, that would explain why I couldn't move.

"Before you soil your nonexistent pants," the creature said, "I will remind you that you are nothing. Yet. You must choose."

"Choose?"

"Do I need to spell this out for you?"

Of course! Jake thought. *It's a game. I haven't created my character yet.*

"*Pantheon* is a product of Virtuality Game Studios, and it is the greatest advancement in MMORPG gaming." The creature's voice shifted to a duller tone, as though it were tired of repeating the same information over and over for every new player. "To enter the realms of *Pantheon*, you must first create your character."

A holographic display emerged from the air, hovering before him.

In even the best virtual games Jake had played, the display had come as a pop-up in front of his vision. It was distracting as hell until you got used to it, but this...

One by one, a series of avatars displayed themselves, hovering in three dimensions:

First, a dwarf with a smithing hammer. Then an elf drawing an elegantly carved bow. Followed by a gray-skinned orc, nearly as ugly as the flying monstrosity that had welcomed him to the game. There was a human man, a cherub, a hideous reptilian chimera, and the list went on.

Each avatar looked so lifelike. Jake could even make out the weave of the fabric of their clothes. Skin and hair had as much distinction as any real person, maybe more. Their skin did not shimmer unnaturally the way it did in all the VR games he'd played.

This is incredible!

In fact, it seemed far too impressive to be true.

"You are probably wondering why they let prisoners like you play a game like this," the flying creature said.

Jake jolted, having forgotten it was right beside him. If that was even possible, considering he had no physical body.

"Er, yeah," Jake said. "That's creepy. How did you know?"

"Your kind always want to know," he said in a monotone. "The prison camp you work in is owned by the parent company of Virtuality Game Studios."

"Yeah. So?"

"So, anytime a new technology is introduced, it needs testing. And who better to test than prisoners no one cares about anymore?"

Jake felt a pang of guilt at the reminder of the terrible thing he'd done. But he pushed the image of the girl away for now.

"You really are one of the slower inmates to arrive here," the creature said. "In more ways than one. I am running out of time. You're not the only new arrival, you know. Now, choose your race, will you?"

The holograph cycled through the races again: dwarf, elf, orc, chimera, halfling, human, merman, cherub, and on and on through creatures Jake was not fully familiar with, until the final being—god.

God? That sounds badass!

As though responding to his very thoughts, the image of the large and muscular luminescent being flashed red, and a loud beep filled his ears.

A prompt hovered in front of his vision in the form of a glowing red orb. It flashed, and an animated male voice spoke.

[*What are you, a total dunce? God status can only be attained by the most advanced forms of all races. Whatever race you are, your current achievement status lies somewhere between an earthworm and the dirt it shat out behind it. Better luck next time!*]

The notification vanished with an echo of laughter that seemed to rain down on him from the heavens.

The dark flying creature crossed his wings in front of him. "Oh, don't mind me," he said sarcastically. "I've got nowhere I'd rather be or anything."

What is with the snark in this game?

"Any way we can limit this to things I can actually play?"

The beast nodded, and the display narrowed, removing god and several of the more impressive monstrous races, including werewolf and dragon shifter, which he assumed required in-game achievements.

Jake focused on the choices before him. It was unfortunate they didn't provide any background information about any of these races.

It would be nice to know what strengths they have for skills and whatnot.

Impressively responsive, a new window appeared beside the avatars and the cycling races paused.

Dwarf

Description: Before you start to imagine yourself an ax-wielding warrior riding a battle hog, you should know that the dwarves of *Pantheon* take more after the diminutive craftsmen of old Norse tales. They are cantankerous and rather useless in a fight, but they make up for it in their ability to craft items of unmatched quality.

Development Ratings: Strength - 30%, Dexterity - 50%, Agility -

20%, Constitution - 25%, Charisma - 20%, Creativity - 50%, Wisdom - 30%, Intelligence - 40%

Jake was not sure exactly what those ratings meant, but all the lowest ones seemed to relate to physical abilities. Between that and the general description, it told him enough to know this was not the sort of character he was looking for in his new life. Being able to construct powerful weapons was a handy skill, but Jake had never been one to sit still in a dark shop for hours on end, nor if he was honest, had he ever been someone able to work well with his hands.

"Go ahead and remove races poorly suited to combat."

The creature rolled his eyes. "Should I remove *you* while I'm at it?"

Jake glared at him. "Next."

The selection cycled. The human reminded him of a Roman soldier, dressed in bronze-plated armor. He had ripped muscles and wielded an enormous broadsword.

Human

Description: While generally weaker than orcs in terms of brute strength, and while they are usually slower and less agile than elves, humans make up for it with their cunning, their ability to acquire an abundance of skills, and their unmatched ambition. Humans are capable of great sacrifice and great cruelty. Wherever they gather, remarkable things are bound to be accomplished for the Glory of the gods. Whether for good or evil is up to you to decide.

Development Ratings: Strength - 45%, Dexterity - 30%, Agility - 40%, Constitution - 50%, Charisma - 35%, Creativity - 30%, Wisdom - 35%, Intelligence - 30%

Jake admired the soldier for a moment. He had always liked

playing a melee warrior in these types of games, though in truth, he'd spent more time playing games with assault rifles than swords.

The elf was appealing too. The tall olive-skinned man was athletic and imposing.

Elf

Description: Sure, the elves are lovers of nature, and there is no doubt that their isolation from broader society has often left them with something to be desired in the personality department. But their affinity for magic and speed, along with their ability to bond with wild creatures, offers plenty of opportunities for Glory.

Development Ratings: Strength - 35%, Dexterity - 50%, Agility - 50%, Constitution - 30%, Charisma - 25%, Creativity - 30%, Wisdom - 40%, Intelligence - 40%

"Anytime now," said the flying creature.

"You know—er, what's your name, anyway?"

The creature rolled its dark eyes. "Azmar. I am a servant of the goddess Nymoria, tasked with preparing her newest servants for entry."

A goddess, hmm?

"Well, Azmar, what are the stakes of this decision exactly?"

"I thought you'd never ask." Azmar groaned as though he'd rather die than answer the question. "The race you choose will dictate the sort of quests you receive in order to win Glory for Nymoria."

"How about some specifics?" Jake was getting a little annoyed with Azmar's standoffishness.

"It appears you've already passed on the dwarf, so I won't bother wasting my time further on them. Elves are reclusive by nature. They prefer to exist with their own kind, and generally only get involved in greater quests when it serves their people. They win Glory in many ways. Through a devotion to the natural world, through magnificent hunts, and through territorial conflicts with the orcs. Orcs take on characteristics of their environment, and the environment is dictated by your preloaded affinities."

"My affinities?"

A new window hovered to the right of the character selections.

[*Your character attributes can be developed throughout the course of your experiences in* Pantheon. *However, your entry abilities are based on the affinities for skills you had when you arrived. Some abilities can be developed more easily depending on your chosen race.*

For example, your Craftsmanship abilities are naturally a Level 2, with a developmental rating of 15%. While a dwarf will naturally develop at 50%, or a combined rate of 65%, your poor natural affinity will make this skill difficult to level up quickly, resulting in a lower amount of Glory achieved for your patron deity, Nymoria.

Thus, it would not be in your best interest to choose Dwarf.

Et cetera, et cetera, et cetera...]

The prompt vanished.

"That's great," said Jake. "But what are my other affinities?"

It seemed all he'd needed to do all along was voice his desire for this information. A stat sheet appeared in the space before him, and the avatar selections faded into a blur behind it.

Current Attributes for *whoever you are*
◆ Physical Attributes
Affinity Levels

Strength - 5 (+30% Development)
Dexterity - 8 (+45% Development)

Agility - 5 (+30% Development)
Constitution - 5 (+30% Development)
Description: You wouldn't be caught dead in Fight Club, and you're not exactly an Iron Man triathlete. You're reasonably fit, but nothing to write home about. Probably just the fortunate result of decent genes and a high metabolism... you should really work out more!

◆ **Mental Attributes**
Affinity Levels
Charisma - 5 (+30% Development)
Creativity - 2 (+15% Development)
Wisdom - 4 (+25% Development)
Intelligence - 7 (+40% Development)
Description: If there's a creative bone in your body, it's probably the coccyx. You take life way too literally. You're not exactly a meathead, but you never really applied yourself. You could probably learn something, if you didn't waste so much time with these damn VR games.

Jake shook his head. The deprecating style of this game was going to get a little annoying. Some of its conclusions hit just a little too close to home. And the part about wasting time on games took on a whole new light under the circumstances.

But he might as well make the most of it. This game might be the only chance he had for any semblance of a real life. And the information was actually really useful.

"All right, thank you."

The stat page vanished.

"Now, Azmar, show me the orcs."

Jake learned that orc abilities varied by their environment. Woodland orcs were light and agile and skilled hunters. Cave orcs were scavengers and tended to be on the slower side, but they were skilled climbers, possessed uncanny night vision, and had a keen sense of smell. There were similar variations in mountain, desert, and swamp orcs, each fitted with characteristics for greater success in their environment. For example, desert orcs bore a strange carapace that protected them from extreme temperatures, while mountain orcs had thick hides with fur.

There were more variations than in many games, but the ugly creatures all seemed to fit the typical mold. While the idea of becoming some sort of orc raider was intriguing, it did not quite feel right.

Perhaps it had something to do with the girl he'd killed, but even though none of this was real, Jake felt an obligation to choose a more noble creature.

Besides, this game was so realistic, he'd probably smell like sweaty orc ass.

The cherubs could fly, which was really interesting. But their combat skills left much to be desired, and their affinity for study and music was a little off-putting. Jake didn't have anything against a celestial choirboy scholar, but it wasn't exactly how he wanted to spend his free time after what he assumed would be a grueling day's work in Grid Eight.

In the end, he did what most people with Level 2 Creativity skills would do.

[*You have selected the race Human. Do you wish to proceed? Yes/No*]

"Er..." Azmar's gravelly voice interrupted him before he could voice his assent. "You probably shouldn't do that."

Jake glared at the creature. "Why not?"

"I don't really give a damn, and your kind never listen to me anyway, but your affinities are not greatly suited for that race."

"Are you telling me I'm not fit to be human? I *am* human."

Azmar shook his head. "You're currently nothing. And you are fit to be a perfectly average human, but you don't exactly have the affinities to be a Spartan warrior or whatever it is you have in mind. Your intellect is decent. Strength is okay. Charisma is mediocre. Your Dexterity is your only good attribute, and the human developmental rating is only 30% for that. Do whatever you want. It's your funeral."

Jake paused for a moment. The human avatar in Jake's view had begun cycling through a number of nationalities, and all of them looked badass. These natural affinities were not his favorite part of the game, and if anyone from Virtuality ever asked for feedback, he intended to lay into them.

He sighed. "Fine. Give me the damn elf."

[*You have selected the race Elf. Do you wish to proceed? Yes/No*]

"Yes," Jake said. The human avatar blinked and became a tall and much less muscular man. It cycled between the bright dawn elves and the brooding dusk elves. The elves were categorized by clan rather than nationality, and after some inspection, he made his decision.

[*You have selected a dusk elf of Maldan origin. Maldans largely originate from the Isle of Malda in the Arien Sea. They were once a mighty clan, known for orc conquests and explorations. But their organized society reached a sudden end when the Isle of Malda was destroyed in a volcanic eruption. The survivors are a hardy people who wander the realms of* Pantheon *in search of quests, with the hope of one day rebuilding their society.*

Now you must choose: Male/Female]

Jake selected *Male*, and the avatar settled as a tall Maldan man, with tan skin and dark hair that reached slender shoulders. He looked a little stronger than Jake did in his true body. The man wore hide breeches and a dark cloak.

[*Please choose your name. This will be the name you will be called in the realms of* Pantheon.]

"Um, just Jake is fine."

A blaring horn filled his ears.

"What's wrong?" Jake asked, glancing over at Azmar.

"You are not allowed to use your true name, for security purposes."

"Why? Not like I couldn't just tell everyone anyways."

Azmar glared deeply, drumming the talons of his feet on a rock.

"Whatever, all right... how about Thor?" The Maldan history gave him a little bit of a Viking vibe—elf version, anyway.

But the horn blared again.

[*Very original. You're only the bajillionth person to choose that name. Perhaps in your own world, there is a different connotation for the name Thor. But in* Pantheon, *most people with that name end up as mediocre bakers or cow feces.*]

"Fine, how about... um... Gunnar."

The avatar hovered toward him and then flashed. He looked down and saw that at last he had arms and legs. And he could move! He took a few steps and marveled at how natural each movement felt.

A basic character sheet appeared in front of him.

Gunnar Ashwood

Servant of Nymoria

Glory: Level 1

Character Traits

Race: Dusk Elf

Clan: Maldan

Character Stats

Health - 50/50

Stamina - 40/40

Mana - 60/60

[4]

FAST TRAVEL

As his character sheet vanished, so did Azmar's hideous face, and all the world with it. Gunnar's stomach lurched as though he had hit the drop on a rollercoaster.

He was floating.

Drifting.

Through an impenetrable blue haze, which seemed to flash past in a blur.

What the hell happened? he wondered. *Did I…*

"Gods! You haven't died! You haven't even started."

Gunnar nearly leapt out of his skin. "Damn it, Azmar, you're still here?"

He had hoped to be rid of the creature. The way he could practically sense Gunnar's thoughts was a bit unsettling. It was convenient when those thoughts prompted a notification from the game, but with Azmar, it was downright grating.

Gunnar could faintly make out the creature's dark wings beside him.

"I have the *profound* fortune of guiding you through the basic mechanics of this gods-forsaken game," Azmar said sarcastically.

"What is this?"

"We're fast-traveling. *Pantheon* is the most expansive game to ever be developed. Didn't you know?"

Despite the sarcasm, the concept of fast-traveling sent a thrill through him. "You mean I can go anywhere in this world?"

Azmar chuckled darkly. "I can. I am an advanced creature with a vast array of skills. You are a peon with no skills to speak of."

Gunnar gritted his teeth. "Yeah? Well, look who's forced to guide who through the game, oh mighty Advanced Creature."

Though the haze was too thick to make out the features of Azmar's face, Gunnar knew his point had been made. Azmar huffed, then flew on in silence. The only sounds were the soft flapping of Azmar's wings and Gunnar's breaths. He was grateful for the silent journey.

He had often found that some of the worst assholes in the world were people in low-level positions who used their tiny amount of authority to ruin everyone's day.

Perhaps Azmar was just an NPC (non-player character) programmed to be this way, or perhaps he was a fellow prisoner forced to serve in this mentor position. Gunnar didn't know how it all worked.

But either way, he supposed guiding noobs into the game was probably mundane as hell. At any rate, it seemed Gunnar needed to try to stay on the creature's good side for now.

"So..." Gunnar said after some time. "Where are we going?"

"Didn't you read the description of the Maldan clan?"

More like skimmed, but he couldn't give credence to the creature's impression of him. "Of course I did!"

"Right, well, your people—the Maldans you read so much about—were displaced by a volcanic eruption. Maldan entry points are scattered across various port cities in the realms of *Pantheon*. We are traveling to the city of Thailen."

Gunnar wondered where that was exactly, and at his mental prompt, an intricate map appeared in his vision—giant mountain ranges and vast seas, great plains and stark deserts, mysterious cities and nations—the whole thing embellished with icons of gods and beasts.

Quickly, the map zoomed in, focusing on a small bay near the eastern end of a large sea.

[*The city of Thailen lies on the easternmost corner of the Altaean Sea, near the outskirts of the sprawling Reddik Empire. But like most major trade cities in* Pantheon, *it is truly ruled by the Guilds of Luka, the Elysian god of commerce. As the servant of a lesser deity, it would behoove you to tread cautiously.*

Unless, of course, you don't mind becoming a precious sacrificial dove. Hey! You do you!]

The map vanished, and the surrounding haze began to dissipate as they neared their destination. Gunnar could feel the gravitational pressure of his descent tugging at his gut in a jarring manner.

"Damn, how fast are we—"

He nearly threw up as he lurched straight downward.

Azmar didn't answer him.

The shadow of his dark wings was gone.

The blue haze of their fast-travel vanished, and Gunnar landed with a jolt in a new realm of *Pantheon.*

━━━

Gunnar stood at the prow of a small sailing vessel, which slowly drifted through a crowded harbor. It was the dead of night. Tendrils of fog hung over the dark water, but Gunnar could make out the pyramidal shapes of sails a short distance away. The long arms of cranes loomed along the shoreline like a row of gallows.

Gunnar was not alone on the deck of the vessel. Though he doubted it was more than thirty feet in length, dozens of people gathered on deck as they neared the shore. Most of them appeared to be Maldan, like himself. Though they all wore dark hoods, so there was no way to tell for sure.

A young man whispered beside him. "What a sight, isn't it?"

Gunnar paused dumbly before realizing the man was talking to him. He glanced at the city through the fog. A few spires cut through the haze and rose into the night sky in the distance, but the night and the fog and the looming cranes of the loading docks didn't exactly scream: *Welcome to our illustrious city!*

Their ship slowly veered toward an empty dock that looked in dire need of repair. "Er, yeah, sure."

"After so long at sea, I was feeling grateful just to see land again," the young man said. "But this city... makes you think our people might find a future again. I about lost hope after the eruption."

"How long have we been at sea?" Gunnar asked. "I... lost track."

"Nearly a month," the young man said.

The vessel docked, and after tethering it, the crew set up a gangway, and a long stream of refugees disembarked with barely a sound.

For a moment, Gunnar thought the young man was an NPC about to help him orient to the new setting, but he hurried off and did not respond when Gunnar called after him. The man was quickly lost in the crowd of hooded figures.

Gunnar wondered what he should do, hoping his mental prompt would trigger some sort of guidance, but no notifications arrived.

Where's the mind reading now? And where the hell is Azmar?

He scanned the gloomy sky for dark wings, but no such luck. A tall and angry-looking sailor approached. "Less yeh plan ter help us unload our cargo, yeh best piss off."

"Sorry, I was just trying to—"

A pair of sailors hefting a huge crate from belowdecks rumbled past, nearly knocking Gunnar off his feet.

"I don't care what yer trying ter do," the angry sailor said. "We got goods ter unload, wenches ter bed, and a fresh ship-ment ter ferry in the morning. Trust me, yeh don't want ter slow down a crew at the end of a long voyage. We saved yeh from that gods-damned island. Yeh paid yer passage. Now, our busi-ness is done."

"Alright, alright," Gunnar said, hands in the air. "I'm going."

He followed the last refugees off the gangway, drawing his own hood. The Maldans proceeded along the docks and swiftly and silently dispersed into the city. He was about to follow their lead, when a hooded woman approached him.

A handful of people loitered in a small square on the water-front, lit by a few dim lanterns. Most wore hoods like the woman.

"You just come from the island?" she asked, her voice faded with age. Or else a *lot* of smoking.

Gunnar nodded. He couldn't quite see her face in the low light, but she seemed friendly enough. "You?"

"Name's Sheira. Came on another ship a few weeks before you."

Before he could respond, a cry rose up down the docks. Torches lit up the night and Gunnar could make out the distinct form of red-cloaked soldiers. Three of them, about fifty yards away, and they were shoving a pair of hooded refugees forward.

"Maldan swine!" shouted one of the guards. "Show us which ship you came on, or I'll slit your bloody throats right here."

"Shit," Sheira muttered. "We've gotta run."

As she spoke, another pair of Red Cloaks appeared around the corner of a street across the square. And one of them pointed right at Gunnar.

"Ey! There's more over here!"

Red Cloaks dashed across the waterfront.

The old woman grabbed his arm and jerked him toward a narrow alley.

"Come on!"

A notification appeared.

Quest Alert - Safe Arrival

Quest Type: Common

Description: In case you haven't noticed, you have arrived in Thailen illegally. The Guilds aren't a bloody charity, and they have not taken kindly to the arrival of so many of you refugees. It's not their fault about that damn volcano!

Objective: Escape the docks alive.

Reward: You stay alive!

Do you wish to accept? Yes/No

Do I have a choice? Gunnar thought. *YES!*

5

RED CLOAKS

GUNNAR FOLLOWED the hooded woman into the alley, and they sprinted hard. Though Sheira looked to be in her fifties at least, she was impressively quick and agile.

He was a little embarrassed by how hard he had to push himself to keep up. He could almost hear the game reminding him how badly he needed to work out more. His lungs were already burning.

Damn affinities!

The Red Cloaks were close behind him, shouting and cursing and drawing their sabers.

As they turned another corner in the dingy streets, Gunnar noticed an orange bar in the bottom right corner of his vision, and it had dropped significantly.

A notification flashed.

[**Stamina: 55%** — *You couldn't sprint forever back home, and you can't do it here either, Buttercup. Build up the skill Endurance in order to perform strenuous feats for longer durations.*]

Gunnar cursed as they turned another corner and hurried past a row of run-down tenements. Sheira turned to him.

"I can't run like this much longer," he admitted through heaving breaths.

"Of course." She pointed down a dark alley behind one of the three-story tenement buildings, where a ladder led to a flat stone roof.

They sprinted over.

"You first," she said, shoving him toward the bottom rungs.

Back IRL (in real life), Gunnar was a bit nervous about heights, but he couldn't worry about that now. He latched onto the rungs and began his ascent. About halfway up, he heard a shout from the streets below.

"Damn, the Red Cloaks spotted us," Sheira said. "Hurry!"

Gunnar climbed as fast as he could make his limbs go. By the time he reached the top, his Stamina meter had dipped below 40%.

A shout rang out, and Gunnar's heart raced. He looked back over the edge, fearing for the old woman's safety. One of the Red Cloaks had caught up with her on the ladder. She dangled by her hands from a rung just below Gunnar's reach. The Red Cloak grabbed for her.

Then, in one of the more impressive maneuvers he had ever seen, Sheira swung her body to the side with the strength and precision of a gymnast, avoiding the attack, then swung her legs back hard in an arc.

Her boots collided with the Red Cloak's head like a warhammer, and he plummeted to the street below with a sickening thud.

His body did not move.

Sheira swiftly climbed the remaining distance and joined him on the flat roof.

"You let him catch up to you, didn't you?" Gunnar asked.

The old woman grinned, not even winded. She retrieved a pair of daggers from her belt, handing one to him.

Basic Iron Dagger

Item Class: Common, Light Melee or Range
Quality: Average
Base Damage: 10
Weight: 5
Durability: 7
Enhancements: ??
Description: A little worse than a bee sting, but not by much. Is this really all you've got? Gods, man, get to an armory!

Gunnar gripped the small blade tight in his fist, raising it up by his shoulder, ready to stab the first guard to make it to the roof.

Sheira shook her head. "You've got no reach like that. Hold it out in front of you, as though it were an extension of your arm."

He flushed, feeling like a dumbass. But he'd really never fought with a dagger before. He always chose much, much bigger weapons. Apparently, he truly started at zero in this game. Sheira showed him the stance, and he mimicked it, flipping the blade around.

"Don't stab. Slash," she said. "And whatever you do, don't throw it."

He swept it through the air, and the woman nodded.

Unlocked Skill: Slashing Blow

Skill Type: Physical, Combat
Linked Attribute: Strength (+65% Development)
Affinity Level: 5
Requirements: N/A
Cost: 3 Stamina
Effect: Increases Damage of each attack, with further increase based on critical hit points

Description: It won't get you far with that little poker, but it's better than nothing!

New skills already? Gunnar thought. *This is great!* And it meant that he needed to be strategic with the location of his attacks.

"Remember, they've got sabers," Sheira said. "Greater reach, but a slower attack. Red Cloaks are the lowest-level guards, and thankfully, their best and brightest don't patrol the docks in the middle of the night. But don't get too cocky."

Gunnar liked this woman a hell of a lot better than Azmar. He was learning a lot. If this went well, he would probably level up soon.

A surge of excitement shot through him as he anticipated the fight. His Stamina had climbed back to 80% while they'd paused on the roof, but it wouldn't have time to reach full capacity. He could hear the rest of the Red Cloaks at the top of the ladder.

"You attack first," Gunnar said.

Sheira raised an eyebrow.

"You're obviously better with daggers. I've got an idea. Just keep him close to the ladder."

She nodded and prepared herself near the edge of the roof.

Gunnar crouched a few yards back.

The first guard appeared, and a notification provided some less than encouraging information.

Red Cloak Guard

Level: 3
HP: 30/30
MP: 20/20
Description: Not the sharpest tool in the shed, but he's stronger than you!

Level 3 already? So much for a tutorial quest, I guess.

Gunnar wondered briefly whether he'd made a mistake somewhere. But then again, he did have Sheira with him, and she was clearly more advanced in this game.

The Red Cloak stepped onto the roof, but before he could scan his surroundings, Sheira let out a cry and leapt forward. Apparently she'd had another dagger stowed somewhere in that cloak of hers. She dual-wielded the small blades, attacking with a quick succession of blows, driving the man back.

There were two more Red Cloaks on their way up, so he needed to be quick. Sheira stepped back, leaving space right in front of the ladder. The Red Cloak charged, and Gunnar seized his moment.

He leapt into the soldier like a linebacker sacking a quarterback, shoving him hard toward the edge.

Unlocked Skill: Sheer Strength

Skill Type: Physical
Linked Attribute: Strength (+65% Development)
Affinity Level: 5
Requirements: N/A
Cost: 10 Stamina
Effect: Allows you to exert a burst of focused strength
Description: You know, like those moms who can lift cars to save their babies. Except you're just saving your own sorry ass.

The guard's saber clattered on the stone rooftop, and the man plunged over the side right as the second Red Cloak reached the top.

Both guards tumbled to the street below with a sickening thud.

[*Critical Hit! You have dealt +30 Damage to Red Cloak Level 3.*]

[*Critical Hit! You have dealt +30 Damage to Red Cloak Level 3.*]

Gunnar and Sheira leaned over the edge. Neither guard moved, but there was a large pool of blood expanding from their bodies.

A moment passed.

[*Congratulations! You have defeated two bloody Red Cloaks! You have earned 20 XP with a 2x multiplier for your first kill. You're nearly halfway to Level 2. Hey! You might actually be worth something in this place.*]

Gunnar pumped his fist. "Hell yeah!"

Sheira nodded to him. "Nice work! I'm a little sorry to lose those experience points, though."

"Well, I can leave the last one for you."

The last Red Cloak clung to a rung halfway up the side of the building. The man glanced up at them, shook his head, and then quickly descended the ladder and fled the building entirely.

"Whoo!" Gunnar shouted after him. "Run, you pathetic bastard!"

He stood up and his vision blurred for a moment. The run and the fight had taken more out of him than he'd realized. His Stamina meter inched its way back to full strength, but for the first time, he noticed a green Health meter beside it, which had also dropped. Apparently it only showed when you were wounded.

"You're bleeding," Sheira said, pointing to his stomach.

Gunnar cursed. There was a small slash in his shirt, and it was stained with blood. He must have been too caught up in the rush of the moment, but now, it stung fiercely, and his Health meter was not moving at all.

[**Health: 70%** — *What? You really think you can recover*

from a sword wound by just waiting around twiddling your thumbs?]

"Damn it! Health doesn't regenerate?"

"It does," Sheira said. "Just very, very slowly unless you master regenerative spells. Too bad those bodies are on the street. Red Cloaks usually carry healing potions."

The wound definitely stung more than he expected in a game, even if it was full immersion. *Who the hell would design a game where you actually feel pain?*

Gunnar grimaced. "Let's go down, then. This is starting to hurt like hell."

"You're not going anywhere!"

Gunnar turned at the sudden gruff voice, a sinking feeling coursing through his gut.

Six Red Cloaks emerged from a door across the roof. Led by the Red Cloak who'd run off.

That *pathetic bastard* hadn't fled at all.

He'd gone for reinforcements.

6

CAPTAIN OF THE GUARD

THE GUARD from the ladder stepped forward. Just moments ago, Gunnar had thought him a sniveling coward, but he strode forward with confidence now, flanked by five other Red Cloaks. A jagged scar ran along the left side of his face.

Red Cloak Captain
Level: 6
HP: 70/70
MP: 40/40
Description: Well, you had to kick the hornet's nest, didn't you? Pathetic bastard!

The man crossed his arms and smiled as the other five guards stepped forward to face Gunnar and Sheira.

Gunnar snatched up the saber of the guard he'd shoved off the roof, not bothering to assess its stats. It had to be better than his tiny blade. He stowed the iron dagger in his belt and brandished his new weapon.

Sheira met his gaze briefly. No words of wisdom, no last-minute advice.

She charged the nearest Red Cloak, daggers flashing in the moonlight. The woman was brilliant. Though the daggers were weak weapons, with two of them she was able to deflect the guard's blows for long enough to find an opening.

With a slash to the throat, the first Red Cloak crumpled to the ground.

If they fought too close together, Gunnar worried the sheer numbers would be too much for them to handle, but for the moment, the captain hung back and watched his guards work. That left two each.

Can I handle two Level 3s? Only one way to find out.

Gunnar backed away from the group, hoping to draw a couple of the guards away. But only one followed him.

He held his saber out in front of him. He knew some basic maneuvers from previous games, but *Pantheon* was different, more realistic. Though a light class weapon, the saber felt heavy in his grasp. It was meant to be wielded with one, but he gripped it with both hands.

The Red Cloak lunged, and Gunnar barely managed to meet the attack. He swept the blade away, and a thrill of excitement and terror coursed through him.

Unlocked Skill: Parry Blow

Skill Type: Physical, Combat
Linked Attribute: Dexterity (+95% Development)
Affinity Level: 8
Requirements: A melee weapon
Cost: 5 Stamina
Effect: Increases Resistance to enemy attacks
Description: Look at you defending yourself with a real sword. Oh, they grow up so fast!

The guard grimaced and attacked again with a quick succession of blows. Gunnar's body thrummed with adrenaline as he narrowly managed to keep up with the Level 3 guard. Sheira cried out across the roof, and he knew he had to be quick.

With the next attack, his saber clattered across the rooftop, and Gunnar backed away. The Red Cloak grinned and stooped to pick it up.

Just as Gunnar hoped.

He reached to his belt and let his iron dagger fly. He'd played baseball in high school, and for once, his affinities paid off. The blade hit its mark, lodging in the man's neck.

Unlocked Skill: Throwing Blade

Skill Type: Physical, Combat
Linked Attribute: Dexterity (+95% Development)
Affinity Level: 8
Requirements: A throwable weapon
Cost: 2 Stamina
Effect: Increases your Range of attacks
Description: This skill allows you to attack from greater distances. But it also leaves you without a weapon. Not the smartest tactic if you like living.

That was what Sheira had warned him about. *But hey, it worked!*

[*Critical Hit! You have dealt +20 Damage to Red Cloak Level 3.*]

With a graphic display, blood gushed from the deep wound, and the man slumped forward.

Gunnar retrieved his saber and was about to deliver a final blow, when another notification popped up.

[*You have triggered the effect Blood Poison. You have dealt +10 Damage to Red Cloak Level 3.*]

Gunnar was confused for a moment. Then, he remembered

the dagger's description. Some sort of enhancements his HUD hadn't been able to identify.

Blades laced with poison? Well played, Sheira!

[*Congratulations! You have defeated another bloody Red Cloak! You have earned* 10 *XP.*]

His Glory meter shot up to 50%.

With a horrific sucking sound, Gunnar managed to get his poisoned dagger free, and he hurried to help Sheira. She had managed to kill another of the guards.

But now two attacked her at once, and she was struggling. They flashed around the roof in a blur, and Gunnar didn't dare throw the dagger again for fear he would hit the only ally he had in this world.

The two guards were backing Sheira toward a corner. Gunnar shouted, trying to draw them away, but his words were cut off by a concussive blow to his back that sent him sprawling on the ground. His vision blurred, and pain seared his entire body.

His Health meter dropped to a dangerous 30%, and his Stamina hovered at 50%. The Red Cloak Captain stood over him, wielding an enormous warhammer.

Gunnar cursed himself for not paying closer attention to the captain. He had hoped it might be like some games, where you dealt with the lower-level mobs before facing the boss. The man had been hanging back. But no more.

Gunnar swept his saber at the man's boots. The captain easily backed away, but it was enough space for Gunnar to spring back to his feet, and he quickly retreated out of range.

The captain paused for a moment, smiling evilly.

Sheira had reached the corner, but Gunnar realized that spot had all been part of her strategy. A smokestack towered above the rest of the wall, and with another impressive display of agility, the woman launched herself from the wall and over the heads of the guards.

It was his best window of opportunity, and he took it. Gunnar chucked his dagger again. It wasn't as good of a shot as the first, but the blade caught one of the Red Cloaks in the shoulder, hopefully slowing him down enough for Sheira to handle them one at a time.

[*Direct Hit! You have dealt +10 Damage to Red Cloak Level* 3.]

Less damage than the last one, which meant it definitely mattered where he landed his attacks in this game.

Gunnar leapt out of the way of another attack from the captain. The warhammer thundered against the stone rooftop with a spray of sparks and a piercing ring. Gunnar backed away again, unsure how he could face the captain's power with a lousy saber.

He parried the next blow, but that sent jarring tremors shooting up his arms.

In the corner of his eye, he spotted the glint of Sheira's daggers in the moonlight.

He backed further away from the captain. The man paused again, holding his hammer with both hands.

[*You have dealt +10 Damage to Red Cloak Level* 3.]

Gunnar grinned. The poison was still working. The Red Cloak wrenched the blade out of his own shoulder, but it didn't do him any good. He dropped to his knees.

[*You have dealt +10 Damage to Red Cloak Level* 3.]

The man keeled over.

[*Congratulations! You have defeated another bloody Red Cloak! You have earned* 10 *XP.*]

Near the top right of his vision, the red Glory meter was well over halfway full. He just might level up by the end of this damned quest.

The only problem was it meant he had to find a way to kill this captain, and Gunnar was running out of room to maneuver. He was uncomfortably close to the edge of the roof.

Time to mix things up!

Every move he'd made against the captain so far had been defensive. The captain knew he was scared. He knew he was more powerful. But he also wielded a much bigger and heavier weapon, and Gunnar understood now why the captain kept giving him time to back away. The captain needed to regain his Stamina after each attack.

Gunnar parried another blow, but the jarring impact was draining his own Stamina. He was down to 40%, and his Health was worse. If he took another hit, he was pretty sure he'd be done for.

The captain paused again, regaining his Stamina. Gunnar backed up, as though about to retreat again, but this time, he planted his foot hard and leapt forward. The captain barely managed to meet his attack with the unwieldy hammer. They exchanged a quick succession of blows, and Gunnar could tell the man's strength was waning.

Gunnar attacked again. The captain brought his hammer down like an ax chopping wood and pinned Gunnar's saber to the ground. He strained with all his might to wrench it free. He didn't dare lose his only weapon. As he struggled, the captain turned and drove a thunderous kick into Gunnar's stomach.

He staggered back, losing his grip on the saber.

His gut wrenched. He glanced around, but there were no more weapons anywhere near him.

The captain stalked forward, raising his hammer.

Gunnar smiled as the man prepared for his final attack.

The captain laughed. "You've gotten lucky so far, swine. But you and your heathen friend are no match for—"

The captain's words were cut off.

Might have had something to do with the explosion that obliterated his head in a display like emerald fireworks. Blood and bone and brain matter flew everywhere.

The captain's body slumped to the ground, and Sheira grinned, holding a strange weapon vaguely reminiscent of a crossbow, though it had fired no arrow, that was for damn sure.

The thing glowed with a haunting light, and the woman stowed it back in her cloak.

[*Congratulations! You have defeated your foes with a combination of throwing things and dodging the blows of greater warriors. You have reached Level 9 in the skills Throwing Blade and Parry Blow. We all tremble at how powerful you are!*]

[*Congratulations! You made this way harder than it needed to be, and somehow you're still here. You've earned the Skin of My Teeth badge:+1 to Constitution, +1 to Strength, +1 to Dexterity, +1 to Agility.*]

[*Congratulations! You have completed the quest Safe Arrival. Here's 30 XP. Now, collect your loot and get the hell out of here!*]

All of the Red Cloak corpses emitted a brief flash of blue sparks, presumably indicating loot, and Gunnar was excited to see what all these guards had been carrying. Meanwhile, his Glory meter had reached 90%.

Damn, so close.

Sheira spat on the captain's decapitated corpse, then turned to Gunnar. She looked completely spent, though Gunnar was not sure whether that was from the combat or the magic.

She stooped down, looted a blue vial from the captain's body, and downed it. Then, she produced a red one from what Gunnar presumed to be her Inventory, and drank it down in one gulp.

An almost instant change came over her as life and energy returned to her body.

"Thanks," he said. "That was one hell of a first quest."

Sheira shrugged. "Well, it's not exactly supposed to play out like all that. You've got a lot to learn, boy, but you did all right."

"That thing fires magic?"

"Arcane Bolt," Sheira said. "It takes most of my Mana to operate and costs several Soul Gems to keep charged, so I save it for emergencies. But I couldn't let you get any more XP. You might have leveled up before the fight was over."

Gunnar looked up, confused. "What would have been wrong with that?"

He realized the answer a moment too late.

One of Sheira's poison-laced daggers plunged into his gut with a searing pain.

The final 30% of his Health plummeted quickly, and he collapsed on the rooftop.

"Best you learn this lesson right away," Sheira said. "This city is survival of the fittest. Most of all for us Maldans. Tread cautiously."

[*You have been killed by Sheira - Level 14. Damn, betrayal is a real bummer, isn't it?*]

As Gunnar lay upon the roof—dead—there was a brief moment when he seemed to have an out-of-body experience. His vision hovered over his own corpse, and he saw Sheira kneel down and reach a hand over his bloody wound.

Her hand glowed softly, and his Glory meter plummeted.

[*You have been drained by the dark magic spell Vampire's Glory. You have lost 90 XP.*]

Sheira smiled and turned away, then started collecting the loot.

Cold-blooded old bitch, Gunnar thought as he blacked out.

7

TIME TO WORK

A WHIRRING sound filled Jake's ears as he swam up from a thick haze. When he opened his eyes, he was nearly blinded by the white light of his cell back in Grid Eight.

The shadow of a blurry tall figure passed in front of the blaring light, and before his eyes could adjust, he jolted from his seat and crumpled on the floor.

His body ached almost as badly as it had when Sheira's dagger pierced his skin. Everything was a swirling blur, and then, a new pain seared through his entire body.

Fierce, raging pain.

Jake couldn't move.

His body convulsed violently, and he had no ability to resist the source.

There was a flash of blue across his vision, and the pain doubled, tripled. His head jerked back involuntarily, thudding on the hard floor, and he writhed on the ground. It was as though some invisible force were stabbing him with a thousand tiny blades from the inside out.

He nearly lost consciousness.

Jake truly wondered whether he was about to die.

But after some time, the pain slowly began to dissipate. He tensed, waiting for another flash of blue, but it did not come.

His vision began to clear, and Shad the prison guard loomed over him.

"Wh-wha'sss goinggg onnn?" Jake could barely speak. His tongue was a great weight in his throat, and his limbs felt hollow and numb.

"Welcome back to the real world," Shad said, chuckling to himself. "Choked on your first quest. Don't worry, you're hardly the first. The effects will wear off after a few minutes. But I told you the full brunt of that electric shock would hurt like hell."

"Wh-whyyy diddd youuu?" Jake's whole body twitched as Shad's holographic form drew near. "Best get things straight, boy. I didn't do shit to you! The folks upstairs did. You choked. They didn't like it. I get the privilege of explaining it to you. Lucky me."

"I... don't... understand." Jake had regained a little control, but still felt wrung out. His arms and legs tingled. Movement had never felt so difficult. It was as though he had gained a hundred pounds in an instant. He slowly reached for his head. It throbbed worse than any migraine.

"Your life is not your own here, and it is not your own in the game," Shad said. "If you act out of line here, you can expect a good shock. If you act stupid in the game, don't earn Glory for your god like a good little boy, you can expect a good shock. This was a warning. So learn quick. Good news is, nearly everyone ends up just like you on their first time. Assume it doesn't matter. Fool around. A lot of them get duped by some whore preying on the noobs, so I guess it could be worse."

Jake managed to sit up on the floor. He clutched his temples between his fingers, as though that might quell the throbbing.

"So... the people that run this prison... are they in the game too?"

Gunnar was really starting to wonder what the hell he'd gotten himself into.

"Afraid I ain't privy to that sort of information. All I know is you do well in the game, the Suits and Ties do well back here. Something corporate I'm sure."

Shad extended his hand to him. Jake almost reached for it, but remembered the guard was only a hologram.

Shad smiled. "You're learning. Good."

Jake struggled to his feet. His head spun for a moment, as though he were drunk, but it soon cleared. "Now what?"

"Your game time doubles for sleeping and eating, remember? You're rested, even if you feel like hell at the moment. Good thing you didn't heave your food back up. At least not yet."

"Not yet?"

"We'll see how the day goes. Now, it's time to work."

Shad led Jake through the narrow lanes of Grid Eight. The place was filled with holographic guards and prisoners quietly making their way to and from the housing district and the industrial complex on the other end of the dome. Enormous pipes jutted into the ceiling from a massive power plant, and steam rushed all around.

When they reached an entry bay, Shad gestured to a wall lined with hazmat suits.

"What exactly is my job?" Jake asked as he pulled one off a small hook and stepped inside. The material billowed around his body. *Damn, one size fits all.*

Shad smirked. "Nothing too dangerous, don't worry. The folks upstairs want you working down here a good long time. The suit is mostly for the smell."

A giant bay door opened, and the stench nearly knocked him off his feet.

It smelled like ass and rotting eggs.

The room was as large as several football fields strung together, the ceiling at least one hundred feet high. Dozens of little skid steers darted around, scooping up a disgusting yellowish sludge that continuously poured into the room from pipes in the walls. The loaders moved the sludge into several dump trucks parked at the center of the room.

"Don't forget the boots," Shad said, gesturing to a shelf nearby.

The big black overshoe boots, combined with the lessened mobility from the suit, made Jake feel like he was waddling like a duck as he entered the working bay. Even in the suit, the stench was nauseating, and Jake struggled to keep down whatever sustenance he had received while he was in the game.

But the facility was quite impressive.

"Geothermal power," Shad said. "That sludge gets filtered out. Sulfur mostly. You get the joy of hauling that shit out of here."

———

Jake did not get to man one of the skid steers. Along with a dozen others on foot—all newer prisoners, Jake guessed—he got to shovel up the sludge the loaders missed with their buckets. The sludge bay was hot as hell, and it was backbreaking, sweat-inducing, nauseating work. Jake had never done much manual labor, and by the end of his shift, his arms and legs felt like numb noodles, and his entire body ached.

Shad's hologram escorted him back to his cell at the end of the day.

He couldn't stop thinking about those small bits of steak and potatoes he had let go to waste when he'd arrived. He was absolutely starving, but he knew there was no real food to be had. Just those damn food tubes.

"I said you'd be dying to get back to *Pantheon*," Shad said as they arrived back at his cell.

"You weren't kidding," Jake said, collapsing into the monstrous VR chair.

"If you're good, if you shovel that sludge and you take things seriously in the game, you might earn a spot driving one of those loaders. Eventually you might get out of sludge altogether. But that's all on you."

The robotic arm shifted with a whir, and the tubes attached to the metallic disks on Jake's arms.

There was a surge in his neck, and he left the prison behind.

[PART 2]
CITY OF THIEVES

8

RESPAWN

G UNNAR RESPAWNED on the roof where Sheira had shanked him. He had hoped his body would feel better in the game, but his muscles ached.

[*If you think waking up sore after dying is unrealistic, you've clearly never died before.*]

Gunnar rolled his eyes. He rose to his feet and surveyed his surroundings. The bodies of the guards had vanished, along with their loot, and Sheira was long gone.

His Glory meter was back to Level 1 with zero experience gained, but to his surprise, he did find Sheira's dagger on his belt.

Probably rubbing it in!

But he was glad to have anything, should more guards turn up. The fog had thinned and night was fading into the gray of early morning. Gunnar arched his back and stretched.

"Well, you royally screwed that up, didn't you?"

Gunnar spun, not even surprised, just annoyed.

Azmar hovered on the roof behind him, arms crossed over his leathery chest.

"Where were you?" Gunnar demanded.

"My job is to lead you to your entry point," Azmar said, "not hold your hand."

"I wasn't saying—"

"I was waiting for you to clear the docks and get somewhere safe. An extremely simple task, I might add. All you needed to do was use a little Stealth and sneak away into the streets like everyone else on that ship. What part of 'tread cautiously' didn't you understand? Gods! We always get the stupid ones!"

Gunnar gritted his teeth, but he didn't take the bait. In truth, he *may* have taken a bit of a cavalier approach. He hadn't been terribly concerned about how well he did at the opening of the game, and figured he could always respawn if things went poorly. And he had been maybe a little distracted about having just become a damn prisoner in a labor camp.

But *Pantheon* and his life in Grid Eight were intertwined, somehow, and he was determined not to make the same careless mistakes again. At the very least to avoid the shock on the other side of his reality.

"You're right," Gunnar said, raising his hands. "I wasn't careful enough."

"No shit, Sherlock," Azmar said. "This game is populated by killers and cutthroats, and you strode off with the first person you met."

"I mean, she *was* Maldan."

Azmar just glared.

"I'll be smarter this time. Vampire's Glory, is that a common spell?"

Azmar shook his ugly head. "It's a form of blood magic from the dark alignment of sorcery."

"Why drain the noobs? Why not go for someone with some actual XP?"

"Harder to kill, more suspicious," said Azmar. "And once you level up, your Glory is locked. She could only drain your unleveled XP. Noobs gain experience quickly early on, and they're weak and stupid."

Sheira was clever, he had to give her that. Gunnar guessed it would be a while before he could match a Level 14 enemy, but he resolved to make her pay one day.

Azmar sighed. "The good news is you still cleared your first quest, which means you've successfully entered the game. Bad news is you really should have leveled up by now."

"So, I'm already falling behind," Gunnar said. "Where can I grind some skills?"

A holographic map of the city hovered in Gunnar's vision. The majority of it was blank and marked *Undiscovered*, but there was a decent-sized portion in view, mostly near the docks.

A blue dot marked a tavern called the Mermaid's Shells. It was only a few blocks from where he'd run the night before.

"The owner's a man named Sykes," Azmar said.

Quest Alert - Mermaid's Shells

Quest Type: Common
Description: It's about damn time you quit screwing around and get serious about your progress. Sykes can help you meet allies, acquire skills, and go on quests. Just remember, nothing good is ever free.
Objective: Find Sykes.
Reward: You might gain an infinitesimal chance of advancing in this game.

Do you wish to accept? Yes/No

Yes, Gunnar thought, and the window vanished from his vision.

"Sykes is sympathetic to refugees," Azmar said. "He can help you get oriented, but he's got no patience for idiots. So, try not to be yourself. And for god's sake, set a damn respawn point next time. The last thing you need is to get spawn camped in the middle of a bunch of Red Cloaks."

With that, Azmar took flight and disappeared into the foggy morning gloom.

Respawn, Gunner thought. *Just one more thing that would have been great to learn from a tutorial quest.*

As he thought about it, his HUD responded.

[*Would you like to set a respawn point? Yes/No*]

A red dot hovered over his map of the city. He supposed this Mermaid place was as good as any for now. But the map flashed red when he tried to place the marker.

[*Listen, Bonehead, you must have previously visited a location to respawn there.*]

Whatever, I'll do it later. He swept the holographic map out of his vision, and it disappeared.

Gunnar descended the ladder from the rooftop and returned to the streets of Thailen, which were already filling with people. It appeared that a fair amount of time had passed in the game while he had been working back in Grid Eight, though he didn't think the passage of time was the same. He'd spent an entire waking day in that sludgefest. He guessed a few hours had passed, assuming it was only morning. It was hard to tell in the fog. Faint light had hung over the city at night, and now, the light of the day was faint too. But there was certainly a lot more activity on the streets now.

As he walked, Gunnar marveled at the attention to detail in the game. Every person looked so lifelike. At a glance, he could distinguish the finer threads of a merchant's clothes as opposed to the coarse make of a fisherman's, and he caught the earthy scents of sweat and metal from a blacksmith hurrying past him. The salty odor of the harbor and the day's latest catches wafted across the waterfront district of the city. Despite the overcast sky, the world was alive with vibrant colors and the sounds of voices and gulls. It was so realistic, Gunnar wondered if he would start to lose track of reality if he stayed long enough.

That thought brought a slew of other questions. When he'd died in the game, he'd woken back in the prison as though from a night's sleep. Did that mean the only way he could go back to prison was if he died?

And why were the folks upstairs—as Shad liked to call them —so concerned about his performance in the game? Were they here too? What about the prison guards? Could he stumble into Shad somewhere in here? How would he even know?

Azmar hadn't let him use his real name, so they clearly didn't want prisoners making connections between people in the game and the real world. His thoughts broadened to the other grid stations. It could be possible that this place was populated by thousands of prisoners from around the country. An idea that offered him no comfort.

Gunnar pushed the thoughts aside and hurried through the streets, keeping his hood drawn, just to be safe. As he approached intersections in the road, translucent red arrows would hover over the correct turn to reach the navigation marker he'd set.

After ten minutes or so of weaving through busy thoroughfares and side streets, he spotted a sign with a mermaid perched on a rock with a wave crashing over her.

Gunnar pushed open the door.

9

THE MERMAID

The tavern was dimly lit and smoky and relatively full. A few patrons ate porridge and sipped ale at scattered tables, but in the center of the room, there was a small crowd gathered around a large glass tank that stretched from floor to ceiling. The tank was about ten feet wide, and a mermaid slowly twirled through the water.

True to the name of the place, her pale blue skin was dressed only with a pair of creamy white shells covering her breasts, with emerald green fins extending from the waist down. Rough-looking men, and a few women, chattered softly, sipping ale and puffing from pipes, but their eyes never left the mermaid.

She spun slowly, bright green eyes drifting seductively from patron to patron. She glanced in Gunnar's direction and locked eyes with him. His heart fluttered, and for a moment, he thought he saw a shift in her eyes. The brightness faded, and she seemed to stare through him. It reminded him of the vacant look of zoo animals who'd spent their entire lives caged and ogled at.

With a quick flick of her tail, the mermaid shot downward.

A trapdoor in the floor of the tank opened, and she vanished from view.

A chorus of groans filled the tavern at her departure. A pair of serving girls with low-cut blouses darted around the room gathering tips from the gawkers in small leather pouches, letting them know that the "full" show would be in the evening.

When they were finished, one of the girls beelined for Gunnar, who was still standing near the entrance.

"The show en't free, yeh know! Pay up!" The girl was short and curvy, with fair skin and curly brown hair, and she drew very near.

"Oh, er, I'm not here for—"

"I saw yeh watching," the girl said.

"I just got here!"

A strong hand clasped his shoulder from behind, and a tall man sidled up beside him. "Leave the poor boy alone, Jiselle. Clearly, he don't have any coins yet. He's got noob written all over him."

The serving girl scowled, but nodded. "Of course, Sykes, sir."

[*Congratulations! You have completed the quest Mermaid's Shells. Here's 10 XP. You can go from Point A to Point B! Good for you! Now, talk to Sykes about leveling up your sorry keister.*]

Sykes was more intimidating than Gunnar had anticipated. The human bore a thick black beard, and his tan skin was weathered and pockmarked. He stood well over six feet tall, with a huge barrel chest, and even though he wore baggy breeches and a loose-fitting white tunic, there was no doubt that the man bore muscles much larger than Gunnar's, even in his new body in the game.

Gunnar followed Sykes to the bar, where a wiry male dawn elf polished glasses for the serving girls.

"Take a seat," Sykes said as he claimed his own stool.

Gunnar did, and the man ordered a pair of ales.

"Maldan," the man mused. "You'll be needing papers, then."

"Papers?"

"Immigration papers. Work permits. Identification. All that bullshit. You won't last long in this city without them. The Red Cloaks en't crazy about all you Maldans."

Gunnar sighed. "Yeah, I've figured that much out."

"Which god do you serve?"

"Er, Nymoria," Gunnar said.

Sykes grimaced. The elf returned with the ales and handed one to Gunnar. Sykes downed half of his mug in the first gulp.

Gunnar braced himself, anticipating the awful sort of beer that might exist in a sailor's tavern like this. But to his surprise, it was actually pretty good. Like one of those damn craft beers he'd been too cheap to buy.

Back when he could buy real beer.

Back when he'd been starting grad school, and he'd had a future.

He took another long pull from the mug.

Sykes smiled proudly, gesturing to the dawn elf. "En't just the mermaids drawing folks in here. Got me a fine brewmaster. Used to do it back in his old... well, you know what I mean."

"You mean you're a pris—"

"No, no... we don't talk about any of that."

Gunnar had so many questions, but he shoved them down and took another drink. "So, Nymoria... Is she that bad?"

Sykes shrugged. "I'm not about to bad-mouth any gods. But seems like most of you Maldans serve lesser gods like that. She's decent enough. Not very powerful or rich. Or terribly wise, either. Least not in the ways of a city like Thailen. Nature deity and all that. She'll reward you how she can when you earn her enough Glory. Like most places in the empire, the people of

Thailen serve the gods of the Elysian Court. Though Luka is the true king."

It was interesting to learn more about the gods of this world, though he was a little disappointed to hear that he did not serve one of these Elysian gods.

"Do you serve Luka?"

Sykes shook his head. "Taris, god of liquor, parties, and general debauchery. Uncannily fitting, am I right?" He gestured around the room and grinned.

Gunnar just nodded.

"So is Glory based on the god you serve?"

"Nah, it's all class-based," Sykes said. "You can earn Glory doing all kinds of things. You just gotta find the right fit and pass the trials for whatever path you choose."

"Trials?"

"They're a big deal in *Pantheon*. If you prove yourself, you can be set for a hell of a ride, but if you fail, things will be a lot more difficult."

"Sounds high stakes," Gunnar said.

"Only if you dick around and don't come prepared."

"That's where you come in?"

"That's where I come in," Sykes said with a grin. "You'll be needing to develop some skills before your trial. But first, we gotta figure out the right class. Let me see your character sheet."

Gunnar looked up quizzically.

"You got stuck with Azmar, didn't you?"

"How'd you guess?"

"Let's just say you're not the first servant of Nymoria to come in here not knowing shit about this game."

Sykes held his finger up to his temple for a couple seconds. With a flash, a holographic display hovered above the bar top.

"Your HUD, you know, the heads-up display, it shows your Health, Stamina, Mana, and all of that."

"I know what a HUD is," Gunnar said.

"Right, well, there's a lot more you can access like this–Character Stats, Quest Logs, Inventory, the whole nine yards. Give it a try."

Gunnar mimicked the gesture, pressing the tip of his pointer finger to his temple.

Gunnar Ashwood

Glory: Level 1

Servant of Nymoria

Character Traits

Race: Dusk Elf

Clan: Maldan

Class: Undecided... just a naive dumbass for now

Faction: No band of brothers yet

Renown: Complete and Utter Nobody

Character Stats

Health - 55/55

Stamina - 45/45

Mana - 60/60

Physical Attributes

Strength - 6

Dexterity - 8

Agility - 6

Constitution - 6

Mental Attributes

Intelligence - 7

Wisdom - 4

Charisma - 5

Creativity - 2

Physical Skills

Endurance - Level 5 (+15 Stamina Buff)

Throwing Blade - Level 9

Slashing Blow - Level 5
Parry Blow - Level 9
Sheer Strength - Level 5
Mental Skills
Perception - Level 4
Active Items
Basic Dark Cloak (+10% Stealth)
Open Quests
N/A

Sykes perused his stat sheet for a few moments, selecting specific windows where even more detailed information was available, including tables showing the linked attributes for each skill and exhaustive Quest Logs.

Sykes smirked. "Looks like you got into a bit of a scuffle when you entered the game, ey?"

Gunnar nodded. "Red Cloaks."

"Well, you made that a hell of a lot more difficult than it needed to be, but you completed the quest and discovered some combat skills at least. Hmmm, but it doesn't look like you gained any experience at all. That doesn't make much sense."

"Some spell called Vampire's Glory. I don't really want to rehash it."

Sykes nodded with a sly grin as he scrolled to the end of the Quest Log. "Fair enough. Rare spell. Can only learn it from a dark mage, and there's not many in Thailen. Only light magic is technically allowed in Imperial cities."

"Looks like they police it well."

"Don't get too butt-hurt about it. Best leave it in the past and move on."

"You mentioned my Inventory. Can I store anything there?"

Sykes chuckled. "You know how it goes in this game, by now. They like realism, or the illusion of it, anyway. You'd need a Bag of Holding to store anything you can't equip on your person, and there's weight limitations. Wouldn't want anyone getting too OP."

"Yeah, getting powerful sounds awful," Gunnar said dryly. "So, can you help me grind some skills then?"

Sykes nodded. "First, you gotta decide which class you're aiming to pursue."

"Do I have to decide now?"

"No, but unlike in some games, leveling up is a big deal here. It's one of the main ways you'll build up your character. It's a bit easier early on and gets harder as you advance. If you don't know the path you're heading down, you could waste hard-earned attribute points on skills that won't help you later on. Like most things in *Pantheon*, it's best you stick to your strengths. That's the best shot you've got at getting the right connections."

"With who?"

"Depends on your path. But in this city, the most influential powers are the thieves guilds, the servants of Luka himself, the Imperial nobles, and the city watch."

"Like the Red Cloaks?" Gunnar asked. "No way. They can go to hell."

"Wouldn't matter anyway. They en't too keen on you Maldans, in case you haven't noticed."

"Right," Gunnar muttered.

Sykes pulled Gunnar's stat sheet closer, waving his hand across the holographic display. "You've got an interesting set of attributes. Decently strong, but you can't sustain it. Probably won't make a great melee warrior. Dexterous, but not creative, so no crafting. Smart, but not wise. You could probably learn some spells, but I doubt you'd make a top-tier mage... Out of curiosity, what did you do—you know—before you arrived in Thailen?"

Gunnar shrugged. "I was hoping to be a surgeon."

"Bummer," Sykes said. "That would have made for some nice cash flow IRL. Hey, you might make a decent healer. Factions are always looking to recruit them."

Gunnar shook his head. "I was thinking something with a bit more action."

Sykes grinned. "I hoped you'd say that. Besides, you need to earn me some coin."

Gunnar raised a brow skeptically. "Earn you?"

"You owe me for the ale, and the mermaid show. And your identification papers. Oh, and training en't gonna be free either. Let's go. I know just the way to use those nimble surgeon's hands of yours."

Quest Update - Mermaid's Debt

Quest Type: Common

Description: There aren't a lot of honorable professions for your kind in this city, and you can't learn much without money. Follow Sykes and learn a handy new skill. No, not that one!

Objective: Obtain enough coins to pay your debt to Sykes.

Reward: Didn't anyone ever tell you the importance of being debt free?

Do you wish to accept? Yes/No

10

PICKPOCKET

THE STREETS of Thailen were alive with the comings and goings of the day. Sykes led the way along the crowded waterfront, where dozens of ships were being loaded with crates. Gunnar followed along with a thief-in-training from the tavern named Kohli.

Sykes walked ahead of them, greeted by sailors and even a couple Red Cloaks as they made their way from the Mermaid into the city.

Kohli kept his dark green hood up, and Gunnar followed suit. The Red Cloaks were mostly found near the docks, but the last thing he wanted was another race for his life. And another good shock back in the real world. He was determined to be smarter this time around.

He probably needed to increase his Wisdom.

He definitely needed to get those identification papers soon.

But first, he needed to make some coin.

Sykes paused for a moment, near the edge of the waterfront, and Gunnar stopped behind him. The man crossed his arms, as though glancing around, not making eye contact with Gunnar or Kohli. "We're heading to a market just past the trading docks. Practice casting Scan while we go the rest of the way."

Sykes continued walking, and Kohli showed Gunnar how to cast Scan through a concentrated mental command.

As Gunnar triggered it, a slight tingle ran down his fingertips.

Unlocked Spell: Scan

Spell Type: Basic, Celestial
Alignment: Light
Linked Attribute: Wisdom (+65% Development)
Affinity Level: 4
Requirements: N/A
Cost: 2 Mana per second
Description: Use Scan to acquire information about the world around you, just don't get caught creeping.

Both of them hurried to keep up with Sykes, and Gunnar kept casting as he went.

The tingle seemed to be an effect of his Mana at work. *Does that mean it comes from inside me somehow?*

Scan didn't alter Gunnar's vision, but enhanced the information he could see. Little holographic windows hovered over people's heads as he approached them, much like he'd experienced when the Red Cloaks had come close, but this time, he didn't have to be in the middle of combat mode.

[*Sailor - Level 4*]
[*Carpenter - Level 3*]
[*Bard - Level 14*]

And so on. If he let his vision hover over certain buildings, he could determine what shops lay ahead before he could read the signs from the storefront. He Scanned the towering spires of the temple of Luka, located at the edge of the trading docks, and noticed a small blurb around the back that read *Crypt - Level 8.*

That is very interesting.

As they passed the temple and the crowd thickened with traders, the notifications became a little overwhelming to differentiate, and his Mana pool was already down to 60%.

So he quit casting the spell. Thankfully his Mana regenerated more like his Stamina than his Health, and it slowly replenished as they walked.

"What did you notice?" Kohli asked.

"There's a lot of people I can't see information for," Gunnar said. "Why?"

Kohli nodded. "What level's your Wisdom at?"

Gunnar grimaced. "Level 4."

"Well, your Scanning is based on Perception, which is associated with your Wisdom attribute. So your Perception starts at Level 4 too."

"So I can only increase my Perception skill by increasing Wisdom?"

"Yes and no," Kohli said. "Each time you level up, you'll get one attribute point to distribute. Each attribute has several associated skills. Wisdom is tied to Perception. If you level up a Level 4 attribute, you'll get two skill points to distribute. If you were a Level 6, you'd get three."

"So, half."

"Hey, you learned first grade math. Nice work."

Gunnar rolled his eyes. It was a complicated system out of the gate. He was beginning to understand what Sykes had said earlier—he would definitely need to be picky about how he used his points when he leveled up, making his decision about class really important.

Today would make a good trial run for how well he was cut out to be a Rogue.

"So, to get more Scanning info, I'd need to level up my Wisdom."

Kohli nodded. "And distribute to Perception. You can also increase skill points by using the skill. There's training grounds scattered around the city, but what really matters is what you can do in the real world—heh, well, you know what I mean. If you're smart, you might gain some Perception today. But you also want to think about what other people can see about you. Most everyone can use Scan."

"So the people I can see right now are..."

"Probably people with low levels of Stealth or low Resistance to Magic, or just low levels in general."

"I saw a Level 14 - Bard," Gunnar said.

"Bards want you to know who they are. They wear hippie hats and bright-ass colors because they want to draw people's attention. You want to go unnoticed. Your hood increases your Stealth. Enchanted elven cloaks can increase it further, and some mages can render themselves entirely invisible. Seeing as you're already in debt with the big man, you'll need to make do with what you've got today."

They reached the edge of a sprawling market square. Vendors pushed carts of a vast array of wares, and customers haggled enthusiastically. Sykes paused at a cart nearby, beside a large carved image of a mermaid, just like the one outside his tavern. A large keg was set up, and a pair of very attractive women were serving up mugs to eager customers.

The tavern keeper seemed to be a regular entrepreneur in this game. It wasn't the sort of gaming experience Gunnar would personally like, but with the sort of life that the labor camp offered, he could see how someone might want to enjoy more simple pleasures here.

"Should go without saying," Kohli said, "but don't rip off any of the Mermaid's customers. Be careful who you choose, in general. If you can't get any info with Scan, then assume they're too advanced for you to deal with. Watch what I do, and hope for the best. If you get caught, run like hell."

Gunnar's heart raced. He had never so much as shoplifted a candy bar. His parents had been strict, and would have killed him if he'd done something like that. He couldn't imagine their disappointment at what he'd done to that girl back in the real world.

But that wasn't a helpful thought at the moment.

"Don't look too quickly," Kohli said, "but do you see the chick over at the leatherworker's stand? Blue dress."

Gunnar slowly shifted, and after a few moments, he spotted her. She was tall and attractive, though she was clearly not well-off. Her dress was plain and worn, and her dark hair was pulled back in a simple braid that kept it out of her face and let it hang long in the back. Her back was turned, but when she glanced to the side, Gunnar glimpsed her tan skin and pointed ears. A brief Scan confirmed his suspicions.

"She's Maldan," Gunnar said.

Kohli nodded. "Level 5. Maldans tend to be too trusting, in general, and she's new to this city, just like you."

It was silly. This was a game. She was either an NPC or a condemned prisoner. Neither of them had actually been displaced by that volcanic eruption, but Gunnar couldn't help but feel a small sense of kinship with her. She'd probably come on a ship like him in the middle of the night.

Then again, that was probably true of Sheira as well.

And for all he knew, on the other side of reality, both Maldan women were just huge greasy-ass dudes, which helped settle his mind a little.

"She's my mark," Kohli said. "Watch and learn."

With that, the slender man shouldered his way through the crowd. He stopped by the leatherworker's stand and began inquiring about various pieces of work. He flashed smiles at the Maldan girl, and she started messing with her hair in a nervous but flirtatious way. Kohli pointed to a satchel across the table, then reached for it, brushing up against her briefly. Kohli must have had much higher Charisma than Gunnar did. There was no way he could pull that off.

The two flirted a few moments longer, chatting and admiring the leatherwares, and then Kohli moved on to another vendor before returning.

As Kohli strode over to him, Gunnar hit him with Scan, and as he hoped, there was more information to be had than it offered about complete strangers.

Samir Kohli - Level 6
HP: 80/80
MP: 60/60
Race: Human
Clan: Shuri
Disposition: Amiable
Relationship: Just Doing a Damn Job
Description: There's no friends amongst thieves, but Kohli is an ally you want in your corner. Play your cards right, and you might make yourself a comrade. Or keep being utterly feckless, and see how that goes for you.

"So?" Kohli asked.

"You did it when you reached for that satchel," Gunnar said.

"I checked her pockets, then," Kohli said, nodding lack-adaisically. "She had a few coins, but I think she might've been hit before in the markets. Bet she brought only what she needed to get whatever she was here for. Level 5s ought to have more coin than that."

"So, you didn't take anything?"

Kohli grinned. "Got her number instead."

"Her number? Hold on—what?"

"I invited her to a bloody pub, dumbass," Kohli said, rolling his eyes. "You did see her flirting, right? Sometimes you take the coin in front of you. Sometimes you play a longer game. Reckon she's probably got more back at her place. And when the universe offers you an opportunity for booty *and* loot, you take both, mate."

Gunnar shook his head, but couldn't help but envy the man's confidence.

"All right," Kohli said. "Now, it's your turn. Pick your mark and make it count."

Gunnar glanced around the buzzing market, using Scan selectively so he wasn't bombarded with information at once. The majority of people were beyond his affinities for Perception, which helped him narrow down his target. While it might work for Kohli to flirt and snatch, Gunnar knew he would have to rely on his best-rated attribute—Dexterity.

"You got him?" Kohli asked.

Gunnar nodded and stepped into the bustle of the market.

His first mark was a Baker - Level 3, who spoke amiably with several different vendors as he ambled around the market. Gunnar kept close, browsing an assortment of elixirs that were far beyond his price range, which was zero. Gunnar quickly gathered that the baker was looking for a partner to help sell his goods. The man bought a loaf of bread and commented about the subtleties that might make for a firmer bake, and Gunnar noted his small satchel of coins.

The baker was rejected by a couple vendors, but Gunnar kept close and waited until the man had closed a deal with the third. The baker walked away, grinning and bragging about how many more loaves his new partner would sell. The baker glanced back to say one more thing to the food vendor, and Gunnar seized his moment, bumping into him as he turned back.

"Gods!" Gunnar said. "Sorry, friend."

The baker grinned. "No harm done. It's a beautiful day."

"That it is," Gunnar said.

The baker ambled off.

Unlocked Skill: Pickpocket

Skill Type: Physical

Linked Attribute: Dexterity (+95% Development)

Affinity Level: 8

Requirements: Level 5 Dexterity

Cost: N/A

Effect: Acquire money and items at no personal expense

Description: Very handy hands you've got! Use Pickpocket to pilfer things from naive dumbasses like yourself.

[*Congratulations! You have successfully pickpocketed Baker - Level 3, acquiring 14 coins. You have earned 20 XP for ruining his beautiful day.*]

Gunnar's heart pounded as he walked on with the baker's satchel heavy in his pocket. With every step, he anticipated the man would find it missing, but Gunnar had chosen his timing well. He glanced back and spotted the baker leaving the market, smiling and greeting people as he went.

In truth, he felt a small pang of guilt about it. *It's just a game. Get over it.*

GUNNAR SUCCESSFULLY PICKPOCKETED three more people, all Levels 2 or 3. While none of his victims bore a large sum, he quickly gained a total of fifty-three coins, and with the last achievement, he finally regained the XP that Sheira had stolen from him.

Triumphant orchestral music blared in his ears.

[*Congratulations! You can basically steal candy from a baby. You have reached Level 9 in the skill Pickpocket. You have reached Level 6 in the skill Perception. Oh, what nimble fingers and peering eyes you have!*]

[*Congratulations! You have reached Level 2! You have earned Glory for your goddess Nymoria.*]

For a moment, the buzzing market square blurred, and Gunnar realized he was having some sort of vision. Something just for him.

A stunning woman stood before him. She wore a shimmering white gown and a crown that looked like woven branches of gold. Her beautiful brown skin and thick curly hair radiated, as though her body itself emitted light.

The sight of her filled Gunnar with warmth and awe. If this

was a lesser goddess, he shuddered to imagine encountering a greater one. She smiled at him, and he resisted the urge to drop to one knee, settling instead for a slight bow at the waist.

"Well done, faithful servant." Nymoria's voice was melodious as a song. "You have taken the first step on a path to greatness. As a reward, you have earned one attribute point, which can be distributed at any time. But remember that every choice you make will echo into eternity. Choose wisely."

With that, the goddess vanished, and the market continued to buzz around him. No one seemed to have noticed the world pausing like that, nor the breathtaking goddess shining in their midst. They went on as normal, but Gunnar felt a surge of excitement.

He pulled up his HUD. He had initially planned to raise his Wisdom, but his quick successes in the market had him thinking differently. Wisdom was great, but Dexterity had already gotten him to Level 2 in a matter of a couple hours.

Play to your strengths, right? he thought as he quickly applied the attribute point to Dexterity, raising it to Level 9.

[*Dexterity! A fine choice. You will now receive four skill points to distribute how you wish.*]

Gunnar didn't have to think hard. He'd already reached Level 9 in Pickpocketing from his achievements and affinities alone; with Level 13, he could pay Sykes off quickly and move on to some real quests.

After his catastrophic entry quest and his consequences back in prison, things were finally looking up. Gunnar couldn't hold back a grin as he met Kohli at the edge of the market.

"Nice work, mate," the thief said. "How about one more, and we'll get going?"

Gunnar took his time Scanning the crowd before settling on a small Level 4 Milkmaid looking to sell some cheese to a grocer. He drifted amongst the crowd as she visited several stalls and waited until she had made the sale. She slipped the coins into the pocket of her apron. Rather than the bumping maneuver, which had admittedly felt a bit amateurish, Gunnar decided to practice a more subtle tactic. He followed behind as she crossed the market, honing in on that pocket.

The milkmaid glanced up and waved at someone across the way, and Gunnar went for it, slipping his hand swiftly in and closing his fingers gently around the tiny money purse. He turned as he withdrew it and moved slowly away, so as not to appear suspicious.

"Hey!"

A woman's voice.

Gunnar kept walking, heart racing.

A hand seized his own from behind and spun him around.

The milkmaid glared fire at him. To his horror, he realized she was not a milkmaid at all. Just like the previous night when he'd encountered enemies, a notification hovered over her head without requiring Scan.

Red Cloak Guard (Undercover)

Level: 4

HP: 45/45

MP: 20/20

Description: You know they don't all have to wear bright red uniforms, right?

The guard's grip on Gunnar's wrist was like a vice as she dragged him over to the edge of the market.

"I am so sick of you Maldan good-for-nothings tainting this city. You think you can come here, not even bother with honest work. Just rip off good, hardworking folks."

Gunnar realized quickly that the milkmaid had been waving at another guard a moment before, this one actually dressed in his red cloak. The man pressed his way toward them through the crowd.

The milkmaid took Gunnar's dagger from his belt, then reached into his pocket and pulled out her satchel, as well as the one with all the coins he'd gained from his morning of pick-pocketing.

Damn it! Not again!

Her Red Cloak partner was only twenty yards away.

"Like I thought," the woman said. "No papers. Looks like you had a nice haul today, though. Reckon my comrades won't mind a few extra coins to go around."

Gunnar glared. "You don't care about any of these hard-working folks. You make this city this way."

The fierce woman leveled her eyes at him, her hand hovering at the hilt of her saber. "You're done, swine. We got a ship full of undesirables leaving soon, and you're about to join them."

The second guard was only a few yards away. He had to be quick.

"B-but where am I supposed to go?" Gunnar asked.

"I don't give a damn. But you can't stay in—"

Gunnar threw himself at the woman, tackling her to the ground. He seized her sword hand so she couldn't draw her blade, but she landed a good punch to his stomach with her free hand.

The second guard rushed over, but a few feet away, he too went to the ground.

Appearing from nowhere, Kohli tackled him, and the crowd parted as all four of them rolled around on the hard cobblestone street.

Cries rang out across the market. More Red Cloaks, Gunnar was sure.

The woman landed another punch to Gunnar's gut. She

was strong. Her punches didn't do great amounts of damage, but he knew once more guards got there, he and Kohli were screwed.

So, Gunnar did the only reasonable thing he could think of.

He head-butted the woman.

Hard.

Unlocked Skill: Head-Butt

Skill Type: Physical, Combat
Linked Attribute: Strength (+65% Development)
Affinity Level: 6
Requirements: At least 20% Health
Cost: 5 Damage
Effect: Deal damage by literally cracking your skull against someone else's skull
Description: More destructive than your fists, but you might have to sacrifice a few brain cells in the process.

The impact sent a jarring ache shooting through his body, but it was even worse for the woman.

[*You have dealt +20 Damage to Red Cloak Guard (Undercover)!*]

The woman's grip slackened in an instant. She groaned and slumped on the ground, clutching her bleeding nose. Gunnar pulled away, snatching his satchel and dagger back, and scrambled to his feet.

Kohli freed himself from his own assailant.

And together, they ran.

Gunnar's vision was blurry, but he focused on Kohli, who led the way through the crowd, and as they ran, his clarity slowly returned. His Health had dipped to 80%, but not bad, all things considered.

Glancing back, Gunnar spotted the two guards helping the

undercover milkmaid to her feet, and they came racing after them.

Gunnar and Kohli made for the nearest exit, and thankfully, the crowd did not seem to be terribly concerned with who the Red Cloaks were chasing. In fact, judging by the angry cries of the guards, he was pretty sure a few of the people were slowing the Red Cloaks down.

"Come on!" Kohli shouted.

A short distance from the market, they turned into a small alley, but Gunnar could hear the guards in the distance behind them.

And his Stamina was already down to 50%.

They weaved through a pair of narrow side streets and emerged onto a lane filled with craftsmen.

And two more Red Cloaks near the end of the lane.

As soon as Gunnar and Kohli appeared, panting for breath, the guards went on high alert, eyes locking on them.

Kohli didn't even bother to slow down. He led the way as they sprinted through the street, shoving past carpenters and blacksmiths, and the Red Cloaks hollered as they gave chase.

Gunnar's Stamina kept steadily dropping.

Ugh, I need to get into shape! Or else get ahold of some damn potions.

"We gotta get off these streets," Kohli said. He wasn't breathing as hard as Gunnar, but the two of them were better matched than he and Sheira had been. "It's the middle of the day. We'll never lose them out here."

"Better be quick," Gunnar said. "I can't run like this much longer."

Kohli grimaced and nodded.

They couldn't go back to the Mermaid. The waterfront was even more open than these streets. Over the rooftops, Gunnar spotted the towering spires of Luka's temple.

"I've got an idea," he said.

They weaved back toward the market square. But the guards were slowly gaining on them.

In an alley on the back side of the temple, Gunnar found what he was hoping for: a stone doorway across the street from what appeared to be a back servant's entrance to the elaborate temple.

A quick Scan confirmed it.

[Crypt - Level 8]

The street behind them was empty. For the moment.

"We'll hide here, until things die down."

"I don't love this," Kohli said, eyeing the door suspiciously.

Gunnar didn't answer. He shoved the stone door open, just enough so they could slip inside.

There was a small entryway with two corridors branching out into darkness. He just hoped nothing came for them from behind.

Together, they shoved the door back, leaving it open just a crack. Gunnar could hear the guards approaching. The three from the market had joined forces with the two from the craftsman's lane. A couple Red Cloaks shot past the crypt entrance without a second glance.

The other three slowed down. Gunnar guessed that at their levels, they couldn't run much more than he could. Maybe they would give up.

"You're still bleeding pretty bad," said one.

"Give me one of your elixirs," the milkmaid said.

Gunnar wondered if they had some sort of Stamina potions too.

He could hear the undercover milkmaid uncork a bottle and drink.

"Reckon we lost them on the last street."

By the sound of their voices, they were nearly upon them.

Gunnar held his breath.

"Should we double back? Maybe they ducked into a shop or something."

"I'm not so sure," said the milkmaid. Her voice was very, very near. "You don't think..."

"Maybe," said one of the guards with a chuckle. "Thieves are never very bright."

The stone door creaked.

Gunnar gripped his dagger tight and braced himself for a showdown. His Stamina had climbed back to 60%. They couldn't run away. But maybe, just maybe, they could handle these three.

But the door didn't open.

It closed.

Completely.

With a resounding thud, the door fell into place.

Quest Alert - Luka's Crypt

Quest Type: Uncommon

Description: Welp, looks like you got yourself locked in a basic burial chamber. The only way out is in.

Objective: Escape alive. Yeah... good luck with that.

Reward: Your life, and some XP. But we know how this is gonna go, don't we? I guess we'll see you back at your respawn point. I'm sure you set one this time, right? Riiight?

Do you wish to accept? Yes/No

CRYPT

THE QUEST ALERT hovered in front of him, a taunting, flashing reminder of his latest failure.

Kohli tried the door, but it was firmly locked.

Gunnar kicked himself for not remembering to set a respawn before he set out with Sykes and Kohli. He checked his HUD, but it seemed the feature was locked now that they were in the crypt.

Looks like I better not die down here then...

He was getting sick and tired of the game waiting to inform him of things until after he'd made an irreversible mistake. And that wasn't all he was tired of.

The quest notification flashed at him.

[**Do you wish to accept? Yes/No**]

"What's with this game?" Gunnar asked. "Asking yes/no for things we obviously don't have a choice about."

"The developers seem to have an extremely dry sense of humor," Kohli said. "Just accept, will you? So we can get going."

Gunnar grimaced at the thief's shortness. He begrudgingly accepted the quest, and the alert vanished.

The crypt was an engulfing void of darkness. Gunnar felt a

tinge of guilt for getting them into this situation. But then again, how was he supposed to know that Scan could be tampered with to show a milkmaid instead of a damn Red Cloak?

Gunnar's eyes slowly began to adjust to the absence of light. They'd done this IRL, of course, but that had always been with some light, whether from the stars or the lights of the city or whatever. This was different. There was no light in this crypt at all, and though he could not see clearly, he could quickly make out the outline of the entrance hall they stood in. The longer he stood there, the clearer it became.

For once, a helpful notification appeared.

Unlocked Spell: Dark Sight

Spell Type: Race-based, Corporeal
Alignment: Light
Linked Attribute: Constitution (+60% Development)
Affinity Level: 6 (Basic Clarity)
Requirements: Glory Level 2
Cost: 2 Mana per second
Effect: Enhances vision in the dark at a distance up to 20 feet with marginal clarity
Description: Use Dark Sight to navigate the night or delve into the deepest, darkest depths of your soul. Not much to see there, though.

Well, at least one good thing came from this, Gunnar thought.

A racial ability. Maybe Azmar had actually given him good advice about choosing elf over human. This would be a handy skill if he did end up as a Rogue. But not handy for long.

His Mana bar was being steadily depleted.

Gunnar glanced around the small hall, trying to take stock of his surroundings while he could. The stones were crumbling and ancient, with moss and vines poking through from the outside near the entrance.

He could also clearly make out Kohli's scowl as the thief ran his hands along one of the walls as though looking for something. The way he pawed at the stone suggested the human did not possess the same sight Gunnar did.

"What are you looking for?" Gunnar asked.

"Thought I saw some torches when we first came in."

Gunnar spotted a small table near the entrance with several short pieces of wood on top.

"Move a few feet to the right," Gunnar directed. "Then take a couple steps forward."

Kohli did and reached the table. "Right, thanks," he said. "You're an elf, so you've got Dark Sight, I suppose, huh?" He did not sound especially thrilled about it.

"Yeah," Gunnar said. "Maybe it will help us get out of this place."

Kohli nodded silently, grabbing one of the torches.

"You ever see anything like that before?" Gunnar asked, thinking foolishly that more talking might ease the tension. "Undercover guards?"

"Not in *this* world," Kohli said. "But I probably haven't been in *Pantheon* a whole lot longer than you."

Gunnar wondered what circumstances had landed Kohli in this world. Was he a ruthless killer? Or was he more like Gunnar?

But I guess I'm a killer too, aren't I?

That girl's blonde hair and pretty face flashed in his memory. It was strange, but her face had still been distinguishable after the wreck.

He remembered that much.

He pushed the image away.

Kohli produced a small stone from his belt.

"Well, at least we can level up a bit down here, right?" Gunnar said. "Should we form a party or something?"

Kohli sighed. "Look, I took you on to pay a debt to Sykes and try to earn my way into a guild. You and I? We're not friends. We're not members of a party. If me getting out alive means leaving you behind, I'll do it. And I expect you'll do the same. I don't know what's in this crypt, but we should probably keep quiet going forward. Now, let's get this over with."

Kohli struck his flint and lit the torch.

Gunnar dismissed Dark Sight, his Mana already down to 50%. He would probably need to have a much larger Mana pool for it to be a practical skill.

Kohli used his torch to light another and handed that one to Gunnar.

Gunnar nodded his thanks. Kohli might be pissed, but Gunnar wasn't so sure the man was as survival-of-the-fittest as he let on. He could have easily left Gunnar to fend for himself with the Red Cloaks. But he hadn't. He'd jumped in to help.

Maybe it had something to do with his debt to Sykes. Or maybe he was just trying to gain some XP.

Or maybe you really are just a naive dumbass who desperately wants a loyal companion in this world of cutthroats. He could just hear the game telling him what it really thought of him.

But it was what it was. He wanted to believe there was something more to the man.

Torches held before them, they set out from the entrance chamber. Gunnar drew Sheira's dagger, and Kohli drew a dagger as well.

Gonna have to get nice and close to whatever's in here. Great...

They descended a long narrow staircase, which spiraled down and brought them at least thirty or forty feet below the streets. As they turned the first corner, Gunnar barely stifled a scream.

An enormous blob of fur and teeth launched itself at him from a small shelf in the wall with a bloodcurdling screech. Red eyes illuminated the darkness. With a swift stab, Kohli pinned the thing to the ground. A couple more quick stabs and the screeching turned to a whimper and then faded.

Gunnar's heart pounded. He held his torch over the dead creature to find the largest rat thing he'd ever seen. It must have been two feet long, with short barbs jutting out along its spine, claws as long as his fingers, and some very long and menacing incisors.

Spined Sewer Rat
Level: 3
HP: 15/15
Description: Worse than the worst New York could ever muster, these mutant shit eaters aren't terribly hard to kill, but you really don't want those pearly whites piercing your skin.

A couple more shrieks echoed up the chamber.

"Ah great," Gunnar murmured.

Two more of the massive rats came barreling down the chamber.

"Here we go," Kohli said, and Gunnar was pretty sure he detected a small hint of excitement in the thief's voice.

Gunnar readied his blade, blood pumping, adrenaline surging.

He zeroed in his focus.

One of the creatures leapt at him. He dodged to the side and plunged the dagger into the thing's skull.

The monstrosity shuddered as he withdrew the blade, viscous black gunk dripping onto the floor.

[*Critical Hit! You have dealt +15 Damage to Spined Sewer Rat - Level 3.*]

The thing twitched on the ground for a moment.

[*You have defeated a Spined Sewer Rat - Level 3. Here's 5 XP!*]

"Only five?" Gunnar muttered.

Kohli didn't answer. Instead, he knelt down and started cutting out one of the creature's incisors. There was a nauseating wrenching sound as he twisted the tooth free and stowed it in his belt.

"What are you going to use that for?"

Kohli smirked and shrugged. "A trophy. I hear the blood of these things is good for some sort of potion too, but I don't have any vials to store it in, do you?"

Gunnar shook his head. "But from the look of it, these things aren't too rare, so it's probably not a big loss."

"Right," Kohli said dismissively.

The corridor was about ten feet wide, lined with little stone busts of old guild masters or something. The place smelled musty and rotting, but in a really ancient way. Gunnar guessed they didn't still bury people in here. This place looked like it had sat like this for years.

Or it was set up to look that way. It was a leveled crypt, after all.

There were wooden doorways on either end of the corridor, every hundred or so feet—burial chambers, probably—but the main passage kept going and going.

They killed ten more of the Spined Sewer Rats in quick succession. Most of them were Level 3s, with a couple Level 4s mixed in. These were larger and quicker and offered a little more XP. But all in all, the rats were pretty manageable between the two of them. And thankfully, they avoided getting bit, though a couple of the things had come a little too close for comfort.

By the time they were finished, Gunnar was feeling much more confident with his dagger, and found himself hoping for a tougher mob and a larger weapon.

"Don't get cocky," Kohli muttered. "I'm sure these rats are just a warm-up. And you're still only Level 2."

But he was getting close to Level 3 already, and he was eager to get past the early levels of the game and move on to greater challenges.

They descended another staircase, emerging in a wide and very eerie corridor lined with the dead. There were little nooks where coffins could slide into the walls—a few were jutting halfway out of these slots. There were small pedestals where Egyptian-looking sarcophagi stood upright—these were carved with angry human faces on the outside.

Gunnar gripped his dagger tightly. His heart thudded against his rib cage as they walked.

"Use Stealth," Kohli whispered.

"I don't think I've unlocked that one."

"Just, you know, try to creep softly. Like this."

Kohli strode forward, walking on his tiptoes. Gunnar tried to mimic him, imagining the way he'd walked across his parents' wooden floors when he'd come home from a party after curfew. He'd failed that test a couple times, but he'd gotten better over time. He paid close attention to his feet and walked lightly, trying not to step on any loose stones or bump any of the coffins.

After he'd covered about ten feet, a notification appeared.

Unlocked Skill: Stealth

Skill Type: Physical
Linked Attribute: Agility (+80% Development)
Affinity Level: 6

Cost: N/A
Requirements: Level 4 Agility
Effect: Decreases your Audible Detection by nearby mobs
Description: Use Stealth to slither past guards and sneak up on enemies. Stealth will muffle the sound of your footsteps and help you blend into the shadows. Handy skill for assassins and Peeping Toms.

Gunnar tensed as he crept past the first sarcophagus. The face on the outside had once been painted, and there were faint traces of red paint left in its eyes.

They slipped past, and nothing happened. One of the coffins was cracked open, jutting halfway out from its burial nook. Gunnar braced himself as he held his torch toward it.

Neither he nor Kohli dared utter a word.

The corpse within was gray and decayed, but it had clearly been there for years because it was nothing but bone.

They passed a few more sarcophagi, and still nothing.

Gunnar breathed a little easier after they cleared the hall and nothing came chasing after them.

The passage wended around a corner.

But before they turned it, the soft scrape of stone echoed from the chamber ahead.

[13]

COMMON FULCRA

GUNNAR AND KOHLI FROZE. The scraping went on for a few more seconds, echoing from around the corner, and then there was a soft clacking sound.

Footsteps. Very strange footsteps.

And Gunnar was fairly certain they were growing louder. He started to back away.

Kohli's eyes narrowed. "What are you doing?"

"We don't know how many might be up there, but I'm guessing we're probably gonna wake more when we kill whatever it is that's coming. This section seems clear. If we lure it back here, we can pick it off and then handle whatever follows after it. One at a time."

Kohli nodded. "Good thinking."

Gunnar and Kohli set down their torches, which cast haunting shadows around the sarcophagi.

They backed away from the light until the darkness of the crypt enveloped them.

The clacking sound grew louder, and finally, Gunnar spotted the creature at the end of the hall. It was some sort of walking skeleton.

Common Fulcra

Level: 4

HP: 30/30

Description: Fulcra are the reanimated forms of ancient beings. The work of basic necromancy, the common Fulcra are not the sorcerer's finest work. While quite dangerous in groups, if the two of you let one of these kill you by their lonesome, take it as a sign that you're just not cut out for this shit.

The common Fulcra's feet shuffled around as it walked, shifting from side to side, its scrawny arms swaying with the movement. The clack, however, kept a consistent rhythm. Then, it paused and spread out its skeleton hands in a sort of two-handed wave.

"What the hell?" Gunnar muttered.

"I... I think it's dancing," Kohli said.

When it reached the lit area, the Fulcra paused its dance/walk and glanced around. It grunted, though Gunnar was not sure how that was possible for a fleshless undead creature. It was quite a bit larger than your average human, even just with its bones, and Gunnar was fairly certain it had not been human at all. What Gunnar had at first thought was a protruding jawline turned out to be a pair of small tusks.

It peered in their direction. They did not move.

The creature reached up to its own chest, and with a horrific crunch, it cracked off a pair of its ribs.

Then, with a groan, it scurried forward with sudden, manic speed.

Gunnar and Kohli nodded to one another and charged.

They leapt into the light. The Fulcra's ribs were jagged, but awkwardly shaped, and the Fulcra could not fight as quickly as they could. Gunnar ducked an attack and lashed out with his dagger, the iron blade scraping against thick bone.

No damage.

He backed a few steps away, dodging another attack, while Kohli followed up with another of his own.

No damage either.

As Kohli spun away, he cried out. The Fulcra had clipped him in the side with its rib blade. It looked like a glancing blow, but Kohli staggered back.

The Fulcra shifted back and paused, perhaps regaining Stamina.

"You all right?" Gunnar whispered as he and Kohli backed away.

"Just a flesh wound, and all that. Let's finish this bastard."

"How do you think we deal damage to an undead orc thing?"

"Behead it?" Kohli asked.

They leapt forward again and traded blows with the creature. Gunnar tried to get close enough to land a good attack at the thing's neck, but he missed, and his own neck very narrowly missed a swiping blow.

Kohli was also unsuccessful, and they retreated back the way they'd come once more.

"This thing is tougher than that description made it sound," Gunnar muttered.

"The developers, remember?"

"Right. Dry sense of humor. More like dick sense of humor."

Kohli nodded. "It's a Level 4, shouldn't be too hard. We just gotta figure it out."

They stood at the edge of the illuminated area, and the Fulcra shuffled forward, slower now. Gunnar really wished he had something bigger than a dagger to fight with. It seemed to be too light of a weapon against this thing.

But he had an idea.

He backed further away.

"What are you doing?" Kohli asked irritably.

"You lead it back here. I'll take care of the rest."

Gunnar's Mana had recharged since the last time, so he cast Dark Sight. He spotted the looming shadow of one of the standing sarcophagi in the darkness behind them and hurried over to it.

Kohli slowly backed into the darkness, muttering curses under his breath as the Fulcra shuffled after him.

When Kohli passed him, Gunnar whispered, "Okay, stop!"

The Fulcra shifted toward the sound. Gunnar activated Sheer Strength and shoved at the sarcophagus with all his might, using up a surge of Stamina in one moment.

The stone groaned as it shifted, and the Fulcra's mouth went wide.

The coffin toppled, and the skeleton shattered into a hundred shards of bone.

[*You have dealt +30 Damage to a common Fulcra!*]

[*You have defeated a common Fulcra! Not sure how that applies to the undead, but here's 20 XP!*]

Gunnar's chest heaved as his Stamina slowly replenished from the exertion.

"Good thinking," Kohli said. The sarcophagus had cracked and spilled open, exuding a small plume of dust. The thief stooped down and rifled through the interior for loot, quickly pulling out an ancient, dull-looking gladius.

Kohli smiled at the one-handed short sword and stowed his dagger in his belt. "Hope you don't mind."

Gunnar shook his head. "You'll probably deal more damage with it than me, anyway."

Blue sparks hovered over the decimated Fulcra bones, indicating there was some loot to be had.

Gunnar knelt down.

Weak Soul Gem

Item Class: Common, Magic Item
Quality: Average
Weight: 0.3
Description: The inconsequential soul of some ancient dead being. Yeah, we know it's bad luck to speak ill of the dead, but this dude was pretty much worthless living, and ain't good for much now either.

Gunnar smirked, enjoying not having the AI's ire directed at him for once. He held up the gem for Kohli to see.

"Weak one?" the thief asked.

Gunnar nodded.

"Figures. Worth holding on to. If you get enough, you might be able to sell them."

"What do they do? Replenish Mana?"

"Nah. Alchemists and sorcerers use them mostly. They can enchant weapons and that sort of thing."

"Or a Fulcra apparently."

Kohli nodded. "But they're pretty much useless for us."

Gunnar shoved it in his pocket. More blue sparks emitted from the skeleton, so he checked again.

Orc Femur

Item Class: Uncommon, Melee
Quality: Poor
Base Damage: 15
Weight: 11
Durability: 6
Description: The thicc trunk of a dead orc. Makes for a decent club in a bind, and can even serve as a token of friendship amongst certain barbarian clans.

Gunnar shrugged and picked it up. At any rate, it would do more damage than his dagger. The bone was about three feet long and took both hands to wield. He took a couple swings in the air, holding it near the knee, with the hip joint serving as the club head.

Clackety, clack, scraaape!

Gunnar and Kohli both jumped at the sound.

Two more Fulcra appeared around the corner, shuffle-dancing toward them, their movements jerky and awkward as they each dragged a large warhammer behind them.

These were both Level 5, and those hammers left a sinking feeling in Gunnar's gut.

He and Kohli lingered in the darkness. The two undead paused in the torchlit space, glancing around.

Gunnar picked up a small shard of bone and chucked it down the chamber. One of the Fulcra turned toward the sound.

And Gunnar and Kohli leapt into action.

Together, they both attacked the first creature. The femur took a lot more Stamina to wield, but his first attack dealt +15 Damage and managed to dislocate the Fulcra's right forearm. It dangled uselessly from its elbow by one tendon. Kohli landed a blow to the creature's shoulder. The gladius sheared through the collarbone, but the Fulcra jerked back, and the blade lodged in the bone.

The ground thundered as the second creature brought its warhammer crashing down only inches from Gunnar's feet.

He backed away, hoping to regain a little Stamina before landing another femur blow, but the first Fulcra grabbed onto his cloak with its only good hand. Gunnar tried to spin away, but it was latched on good. The creature bit into his shoulder, and Gunnar screamed.

His Health dropped to 60%.

Gunnar stomped on the creature's foot. With a loud crunch,

the Fulcra jerked back. Gunnar spun and swung the femur hard into its skull.

[*You have dealt +20 Damage to a common Fulcra!*]

A crack formed along its face, and the skull fell away in several pieces.

[*You have defeated a common Fulcra with an assist from Samir Kohli! Here's 10 XP!*]

Kohli was currently dancing to avoid an attack from the second Fulcra's warhammer. The creature had to pause for a moment before it could raise its enormous weapon again. Having lost his own weapon, the thief seized one of the torches and shoved it into the Fulcra's rib cage.

Sparks flew, but the flames didn't do much damage.

Gunnar leapt in to help and brought the femur down hard against the creature's spine.

[*You have dealt +15 Damage to a common Fulcra!*]

Unfortunately, that was the last attack the femur could handle, and it splintered in Gunnar's hands.

The Fulcra spun around, sweeping its hammer at his feet.

Gunnar leapt out of the way and somersaulted. The Fulcra came shuffling toward him.

The Fulcra raised its warhammer above its shoulders to attack. But it was enough distraction for Kohli to snatch up the other Fulcra's weapon. With a sweeping blow from behind, the thief obliterated the last creature's neck. Its skull toppled onto the ground and shattered on the stone.

[*You have defeated a common Fulcra with an assist from Samir Kohli! Here's 10 XP!*]

14

LEVEL 3

"Thanks," Gunnar said, chest heaving.

Kohli nodded to him, leaning on his new large weapon.

"How much farther you figure we've got in this place?"

Kohli shrugged. "This crypt is built for grinding, if I had to guess. And it's in the middle of the city. So it can't be too much longer. Anyway, we ought to have it a bit easier going forward with these warhammers."

Gunnar stooped to pick the other one up.

Iron Warhammer

Item Class: Common, Melee

Quality: Average

Base Damage: 20

Weight: 14

Durability: 12

Requirements: This monstrosity requires at least Level 7 Strength

Description: Looks like you're too much of a weakling there, Sport!

Gunnar cursed under his breath. *Of course.*

"Looks like I'll have to settle for another damn femur," he muttered, glancing around. The burnt Fulcra still had an intact thigh, but the durability was terrible. The other one had a solid leg bone, which Gunnar wrenched free.

"You sure you don't want the gladius?" Kohli asked, hefting his warhammer on his shoulder.

Gunnar shook his head, patting his trusty new orc femur. "Nah, I think the bone clubs work better on these things, anyway."

He retrieved both Weak Soul Gems, offering one to Kohli and keeping the other for himself.

"How the hell do you think those skeletons wield hammers like that?"

Kohli shrugged. "Part of the enchantment I guess. What's less logical? That a skeleton can attack you at all? Or that it can also wield a heavy-class weapon?"

He had a point.

"You usually grind in these sorts of places?" Gunnar asked.

Kohli smirked. It was the first good humor he'd shown since they'd arrived in the crypt. "Usually I prefer a different sort of grinding in dark, secluded places."

Gunnar just shook his head.

"Sykes has got a training course I don't mind using every now and then," Kohli said. "But nah, nothing like this."

Interesting. It seemed Sykes had quite the system for profiting off the noobs being directed his way.

"You good?" Kohli asked.

Gunnar nodded. His Stamina had replenished, though his Health was pretty much frozen around 60%.

"Let's carry on, then," Kohli said. "I've still got a date with that Maldan chick from the market."

At that, he actually smiled.

Down the next corridor, they faced another pair of Fulcra, though these were much smaller, probably human in their last life, and only Level 3s. With the femur and the warhammer, Gunnar and Kohli dispatched them both with little trouble.

Gunnar worried about the way their torches announced their arrival. The creatures had no eyes or ears—they were skeletons after all—but the Fulcra definitely seemed to detect them before they turned the corner.

They were using Stealth, so he doubted the creatures heard them. Which had to mean the flames were alerting them somehow. That was fine when there were only two to fight, but if they encountered more...

He kept thinking about what the original Fulcra notification had said about their dangers in larger groups.

They descended a staircase and reached a fork in their path. Two identical dark passages loomed before them.

"What do you say I scout ahead?" Gunnar asked.

"And what? I just wait around like a douche and let you get all the loot?"

Gunnar crossed his arms. "Do you have Dark Sight?" It was labeled a race-based spell, so Gunnar assumed the human didn't have it.

Kohli shook his head. "But unless you've got a Mana pool the size of my mum's arse, you won't be making it far without a torch."

"Exactly," Gunnar said, annoyed. "How much loot you think I'm gonna run off with? How much have we even found down here? These Fulcra aren't carrying anything. Look, I know we're all hardened criminals or whatever. But we're not going to last long in this city without allies. I'm the one who wanted to form a party, remember? I offered to split everything down here, so of the two of us, I'm the one who can be trusted."

"All right, all right," Kohli said, crossing his arms. "Point taken. You ever heard of beating a dead horse?"

Gunnar let a smile slip. "I don't know how these things see, but I'm pretty sure that torch is attracting the Fulcra to us. And I'm guessing this crypt is about to get a lot harder. I'll just check things out, make sure we're not about to walk into a herd of them or something, and come right back."

Kohli shrugged. "Fine. Go."

Gunnar gripped the man's shoulder. "It's my fault we're down here. And the only reason I didn't lose all my coins and end up in chains with the Red Cloaks is because you helped me. I'm not going to leave you here."

Gunnar chose the chamber on the left first. Something about the air that direction felt lighter. Like maybe ventilation was coming from somewhere. At least he hoped so.

The torchlight flickered behind him, lighting his path for about thirty yards or so. Until he nearly tripped over a displaced stone jutting up about an inch from the floor. He activated Dark Sight, and his vision grew... hazy, but better.

As he walked, it cleared, and he was pretty sure it had something to do with the light of Kohli's torch diminishing behind him. The darker the corridor got, the clearer his vision became.

He turned a corner and found a lone Level 4 Fulcra shuffle-dancing down the hall. Away from him for once. He activated Stealth, lightening his footfalls, and crept forward.

Gunnar really wanted to know what was up with these creatures. Was some necromancer just goofing around when he designed these things, or was it an accident? Or maybe it wasn't a dance at all, and the magic was just that terrible.

The Fulcra paused and fanned its arms out, and Gunnar was almost positive it was the undead version of jazz hands.

Gunnar remained still, and the creature soon carried on down the corridor. If the Fulcra was made of more than bone, he would have stabbed it from behind, but he would have to settle for clubbing it.

He crept forward, holding his breath as he neared it. When the creature paused its movement for its jazz hand wave, Gunnar brought the orc femur down on its skull.

Unlocked Skill: Stealth Attack

Skill Type: Physical, Combat
Linked Attribute: Agility (+80% Development)
Affinity Level: 6
Cost: N/A
Requirements: Level 4 Agility
Effect: Allows you to deal damage before your opponent is engaged in combat
Description: Nothing like killing a defenseless man, right?

[*You have dealt +15 Damage to a common Fulcra!*]
The Fulcra swayed dangerously for a moment, dazed, and then turned.

Heart pounding, Gunnar gathered all his strength into the next attack. He swung the femur at its head like a baseball bat, a surge of energy rushing from him, draining a significant portion of his Stamina.

Unlocked Skill: Enhanced Blow

Skill Type: Physical, Combat
Linked Attribute: Strength (+65% Development)
Affinity Level: 6
Cost: 15 Stamina
Requirements: At least 20 Stamina
Effect: Increases the damage of your attacks

Description: Probably not the blow you're used to back home, but it's the same general idea. You go nuts for a while, then crash. Or die.

The Fulcra's skull exploded in shards of bone.

And so did Gunnar's femur club.

The Fulcra's remaining bones crumpled to the ground, and a flurry of notifications came Gunnar's way.

[*You have defeated another common Fulcra! Here's 20 XP!*]

[*You've unlocked two new combat skills in one kill. Here's a 20 XP bonus for not being a total waste of imaginary flesh!*]

[*Congratulations! You're actually learning how to not run from a fight. You have reached Level 6 in the skill Slashing Blow. You have reached Level 10 in the skill Parry Blow! You have reached Level 6 in the skill Sheer Strength! You have reached Level 7 in the spell Dark Sight! Yippee ki yay!*]

[*Congratulations! You have reached Level 3! You have earned Glory for your goddess Nymoria.*]

The flurry of notifications vanished, and the breathtaking goddess stood before him, wearing her same luminescent white gown. She held out her hand to him. Something glowed in her palm and drifted over to him, and he glowed too for a moment, his entire body enveloped in warmth.

"Well done, faithful servant," Nymoria said. "You have taken another step on the path to greatness. As a reward, you have earned one attribute point, which can be distributed at any time. But remember that every choice you make will echo into eternity. Choose wisely."

Nymoria disappeared, and the chamber returned to darkness.

When he'd attacked, his Mana bar had been close to 40%. Both his Stamina and Health had been depleted too. He hadn't noticed it the first time he leveled up, since he had only been pickpocketing, and hadn't lost anything. But now, Nymoria had replenished all three bars, and he could have sworn the bars were slightly larger too.

He deactivated his Dark Sight and examined his stats.

Gunnar Ashwood

Glory: Level 3

Servant of Nymoria

Coins: 68

Character Traits

Race: Dusk Elf

Clan: Maldan

Class: Undecided... just a naive dumbass for now

Faction: No band of brothers yet

Renown: Complete and Utter Nobody

Character Stats

Health - 65/65

Stamina - 55/55

Mana - 70/70

Physical Attributes

Strength - 6

Dexterity - 9

Agility - 6

Constitution - 6

Mental Attributes

Intelligence - 7

Wisdom - 4

Charisma - 5

Creativity - 2

Physical Skills

Endurance - Level 5 (+15 Stamina Buff)

Throwing Blade - Level 9

Slashing Blow - Level 6

Parry Blow - Level 10
Head-Butt - Level 6
Enhanced Blow - Level 6
Sheer Strength - Level 6
Pickpocketing - Level 13
Stealth - Level 6
Stealth Attack - Level 6
Mental Skills
Perception - Level 6
Active Items
Basic Dark Cloak (+10% Stealth)
Inactive Items
Weak Soul Gem (2)
Spells
Scan - Level 6
Dark Sight - Level 7
Open Quests
Mermaid's Debt
Luka's Crypt

Just as he had thought. His Health, Stamina, and Mana had all increased by five points each time he'd leveled up.

That would certainly come in handy going forward, and really made this entire crypt fiasco worth it for that alone. Assuming he made it out alive.

He pondered what to do with his attribute point. His Stamina could use some work, and that was tied to Constitution. But he had also already put off increasing his Wisdom.

In the end, he decided to wait. His first goal was to escape this crypt, and he didn't know what lay ahead. He could apply the point once he knew what would be most important for their escape. Assuming he would have the time to make the decision in the moment.

He dismissed the stat sheet from his vision.

Blue sparks hovered over the skeleton. He found another soul gem, of course. Since his Orc Femur had been decimated in the killing attack, Gunnar harvested another bone from the new creature's remains as well. This one, unfortunately, was a reanimated human, and its bones were even less durable than the already shatter-prone orc leg.

He pressed on down the corridor, only using Dark Sight sporadically, in order to preserve his Mana. He would switch it on and get a feel for the next stretch of the corridor, then switch it off and walk in the darkness whenever the way was clear enough.

This hall contained no coffins. There were a few empty chests and some displaced stones that seemed to have dropped out of the walls.

He encountered a couple more of the Spined Rats, and since he had a selection of weapons now, he decided to practice his Throwing Blade attack. He hit the first rat in the back and had to finish it off with the femur.

But he hit the second rat straight between the eyes.

[*You have killed a Spined Sewer Rat - Level 3. Here's 5 XP with a 10 XP bonus for a Perfect Kill Shot!*]

The hall ended and opened up into the widest room Gunnar had seen yet in this place.

A massive burial chamber at least thirty feet high and as long as a football field. The high ceiling was supported by pillars the size of tree trunks, and the walls were lined floor to ceiling with burial nooks. There were hundreds of them. Maybe thousands.

And it was a dead end.

There was no hallway at the other end. No doors. Just burial nooks. Dozens of stone coffins littered the ground. And across the room, Gunnar glimpsed something hanging from the ceiling. And it was moving.

His heart raced, and he ducked back into the corridor he'd come from.

To hell with that, there must be dozens of Fulcra in there.

He quickly made his way back to where he'd left Kohli.

15

LOOT

THE THIEF SAT on an empty chest at the base of a small dais, scowling as Gunnar returned.

"So?" Kohli asked.

Gunnar told him about the massive burial chamber. "Good thing we didn't take a torch that way. We would have probably brought a herd of those Fulcra on us."

Kohli got up and grabbed his torch. "Well, we've only got one more option then."

They set off down the corridor, Kohli leading the way this time. The thief seemed to have grown more agitated being left alone.

Two more Spined Rats jumped out, and Kohli made quick work of them with his hammer. Gunnar let him take the XP. But then, a third leapt out, teeth bared, right behind Kohli.

Gunnar let his dagger fly, and the creature dropped dead.

[*You have killed a Spined Sewer Rat - Level 3. Here's 5 XP with a 5 XP bonus for a Perfect Kill Shot!*]

The bonus had already diminished since he'd leveled up.

Kohli turned and nodded. "You're all right with those

blades." He reached to his belt and handed Gunnar his own dagger. "Reckon this'll do you more good than me."

They descended another staircase, and Gunnar began to wonder if they'd missed a turn further back somewhere. This place seemed to keep going and going.

Did they really still want to be descending? How big was this crypt?

At the end of the corridor, there was an open doorway, guarded by a lone Fulcra wielding a gladius.

"Alright, that must be the way out," Kohli said eagerly. "This one's mine."

Kohli sprinted forward, swinging his warhammer. The Fulcra crumpled into pieces, and Kohli knelt to examine the remains. Gunnar was about to shout a congratulations when a dark shadow loomed in the doorway.

Gunnar didn't have time to warn him. A warhammer struck the thief from behind. Kohli barely made a sound; he just slumped over the remains of the creature he'd killed. His hammer clattered on the ground, and his dropped torch sent shadows dancing across the chamber walls.

Gunnar froze as the corridor filled with the swift clacking of bone. Several Fulcra poured from the room beyond.

Gunnar activated Stealth and slunk back against the corridor walls, cursing Kohli's impulsiveness. There were way too many of the creatures for Gunnar to handle. He had hardly realized that he'd left his torch back at the fork in the corridor. It was sheer luck, but it was the only reason the creatures weren't coming for him too.

The skeletons gathered around Kohli.

Gunnar knew it was a slight risk, but he had the feeling that these creatures were not advanced enough to sense magic. He hit Kohli with Scan, his body tingling as the Mana coursed through him.

The thief's health bar hovered at 25%, but to Gunnar's surprise, the Fulcra did not finish him off.

Kohli lay dazed and weaponless. One of the Fulcra leaned forward and grunted, as though speaking in some primitive language, and a pair of Fulcra grabbed Kohli by the legs and dragged him into the next room.

⸻

"Well, shit," Gunnar muttered, now alone in the corridor.

He thought of what Kohli had said when they first entered the crypt. If it were reversed, would Kohli leave him to the Fulcra like he'd said he would?

Gunnar didn't know. But Kohli had helped him escape the Red Cloaks, and he knew it was his own fault they'd wound up in this mess in the first place.

He knew what he had to do.

With Stealth still activated, he crept toward the open doorway. Torches flickered softly from within, casting a wavering glow from the room beyond. Much clacking and grunting echoed from the chamber after the Fulcra dragged Kohli inside.

From outside, it was hard to tell whether the beasts were just shuffling around or if they were actually talking. The clacking seemed to come in flurries. Gunnar supposed it was possible the things could communicate, considering they were the work of necromancy.

They dance, for god's sake.

Within, Kohli cried out in protest, but a swift blow followed, and he fell silent. There was more clacking, and then, to Gunnar's surprise, he heard a human male voice.

"Good work, my children," the man said airily. "You've found another. Excellent. Now, let's prepare the ceremony."

Another?

Gunnar cursed under his breath and sunk back into the shadows. But no Fulcra came back for him. Which meant the man must have been referring to another prisoner, and the way the man called the skeletal creatures children did not make Gunnar feel any better about the ceremony he had in mind for them.

Soon, the flames began to fade, and then, the clacking was gone altogether.

Nothing but utter silence filled the corridor.

Gunnar waited for a full minute to be sure no Fulcra were waiting for him. Then, he crept forward, casting Dark Sight in the complete darkness.

He retrieved a femur from the Fulcra that Kohli had killed, then poked his head through the doorway. The group of Fulcra had left, along with Kohli. Only a single guard remained, standing outside yet another door at the end of the chamber, this one closed.

Gunnar held his breath as he crossed the room, stepping lightly in the dark. He activated Enhanced Blow and swung the femur as hard as he could into the creature's face, and the Fulcra crumpled to the ground.

[*You have defeated another common Fulcra! Here's 20 XP plus a 10 XP bonus for a Perfect Kill Shot!*]

No bonus for Stealth Attack this time. *Must have been a first-time achievement bonus or something.*

But he was quite pleased with the kill shot. His melee attacks were really getting effective, and his Glory meter was already at 70%. It was in no small part due to the Enhanced Blow skill, though he knew it was not going to be much use to him if he faced more than one mob at a time.

Almost to Level 4.

And Gunnar had a feeling he was definitely going to need

it. He braced for the arrival of more Fulcra from the other side of the door, but none emerged.

Beyond, there was a dull thudding sound, like huge hammers pounding in the distance.

He looted another soul gem, then decided to let his Mana and Stamina replenish before facing whatever lay ahead. After lighting a torch, Gunnar took a look around.

He was pleased to discover that the chamber was filled with loot.

Kohli's warhammer and gladius were propped against a nearby table. But that wasn't all.

There were dozens of items scattered haphazardly around the space: shields, random pieces of low-grade armor, some stale-looking slices of flatbread, a heap of tunics and pants and boots, and three potions—a red Potion of Minor Stamina and two green Potions of Minor Healing.

The sight triggered a random memory.

When he was first arrested after the accident, he'd been stripped naked, giving up all his personal effects: key fob, smart watch, ID, and so on. He'd been given a gray jumper, and an officer took his things to a room filled with personal items in little containers.

This room seemed to be filled with the personal effects of adventurers past, but without the plastic containers of the precinct.

Gunnar shuddered to think of the number of people who must have been captured in this crypt, but they might be his and Kohli's salvation now.

The potions both had a 30% increase effect. Those would definitely be useful. He found a small leather bag tossed on the floor and nearly shouted with excitement as the notification appeared.

Basic Bag of Holding

Item Class: Uncommon, Enchanted
Quality: Average
Weight: 3
Durability: 14
Capacity: As much as you both can bear
Description: A Bag of Holding is an Enchanted item that allows you to store items in your Inventory rather than on your person. It's not a purse, it's a satchel!

Gunnar threw the strap over his neck and shoulder with glee, and was even more pleased to discover that he did not actually have to wear it at all. As he equipped it, the bag glowed softly, and then, vanished.

[*You have unlocked the HUD feature, Inventory. You may now store a limited number of items without equipping them.*]

Hell yeah! Gunnar thought. *Now, to fill it up!*

Many of the weapons were relatively useless for Gunnar. There were several more gladius swords, which were not effective against the Fulcra, and more warhammers, which were still too heavy for him to wield. However, there was one melee weapon that interested him.

Oaken Club

Item Class: Common, Melee
Quality: Average
Base Damage: 15
Weight: 8
Durability: 10
Description: A length of wood fashioned for bludgeoning. What more do you need to know?

It was more durable than the fracture-prone femurs, so

Gunnar added the club to his new Inventory and began examining the random assortment of armor. Basic iron plate provided a nice Resistance to Damage, but reduced his already slow speed. The heavy wooden shields offered a similar downside.

Though he hadn't selected a class yet, if his affinities lent themselves toward a Rogue, he figured he ought to play to his strengths. So, he chose what pieces of leathern armor were available.

Leather Vambraces

Item Class: Common, Armor
Quality: Average
Weight: 2
Durability: 11
Effect: Increases your Resistance to Damage by 10%
Description: Protects your forearms from enemy attacks.

Leather Greaves

Item Class: Common, Armor
Quality: Average
Weight: 2
Durability: 11
Effect: Increases your Resistance to Damage by 10%
Description: Protects your shins from enemy attacks. Now, you just need elbow pads, and you're ready to roller derby!

Gunnar stowed a couple pieces of iron armor in his Inventory, thinking he might be able to sell them later.

There was a small chest with thirty-one coins in the corner of the room, and beside it, another prize—a set of four steel throwing knives. A leather sheath fixed to his shoulder, and would allow him to draw quickly and let them fly. He also took two more basic iron daggers and fixed those to his belt.

He fetched Kohli's pants and tunic and an extra cloak for their mysterious second prisoner and stowed them in his Inventory. He guessed that the Fulcra had not given them any gray jumpers to wear.

But with those final items, a warning message flashed.

[*You have reached the Carrying Capacity limit for your Bag of Holding!*]

Gunnar cursed and examined his HUD. Even with a magical item, the developers continued to strive for a grating sense of realism. The bag only allowed a weight of 20 kg for non-equipped items.

After some deliberation, he decided to ditch his trusty orc femur and all the extra iron armor. Though he did take a gladius, since he figured it might be useful outside this damn crypt.

Beyond the door, the drumming had increased in intensity, and he knew he needed to hurry.

Gunnar pushed back his nerves. He extinguished the torch, activated Dark Sight, and opened the door to the chamber beyond.

16

THE CEREMONY

A LONG CORRIDOR extended toward a broad archway. The thunderous booming was much louder beyond the holding cell and grew more and more cacophonous as Gunnar crept down the passage. A raucous chant—a groaning sort of cry from the Fulcra—accompanied the pounding: *Ah ah uh ah, ah uh ah ah!*

As he moved closer, Gunnar could make out another cry timed to a drumbeat. The Fulcra were shouting something unintelligible, along with their guttural chant.

Dun dah!
Ah ah uh ah, ah uh ah ah!
Dun dah!
Ah ah uh ah, ah uh ah ah!

Gunnar reached the end of the corridor and gazed out at one of the most bizarre things he'd ever seen. The vast chamber beyond the archway was filled with dozens of Fulcra, all facing a raised platform.

No, it was more like a stage, and Gunnar was looking out from the backstage area.

A pair of enormous tribal-looking drums were set on either side of the stone platform, played by two very large skeletons, likely orcs, or maybe something larger. With each drumbeat, a pair of cauldrons erupted with a plume of flames. The flashing light forced Gunnar to turn off his Dark Sight.

The Fulcra were gathered around the front of the stage, and as they shouted, they pumped their bony fists. Gunnar was pretty sure they were shouting the word *thunder* with some sort of undead speech impediment.

Dun dah!

Ah ah uh ah, ah uh ah ah!

Dun dah!

Ah ah uh ah, ah uh ah ah!

There was a final drumbeat, a pause, and then...

A human man appeared from behind a tall stage curtain to Gunnar's left. The Fulcra roared with clacks and groans. The man was pale and scrawny, and he wore a ridiculous attempt at a schoolboy outfit, with cut-off black pants, an untucked white shirt, a black jacket, and a loose-hanging black tie.

What the hell? Gunnar thought.

As he fixed his vision on the man, a notification appeared.

Angus the Necromancer/Bard

Level: 12

HP: 110/110

MP: 230/230

Description: This bad dude may seem kooky. Maybe even a little insane. Kinda like all the best rock stars. And that disconnection from reality is what makes him truly dangerous.

Good god! This dude was recreating some sort of old-school rock concert fantasy. Except there was no music, really. Just those drums and the hellish chant of the Fulcra.

The drumbeat shifted to something steadier.

Dun dun dun dun, dun dun dun dun.

Dun dun dun dun, dun dun dun dun.

And the Fulcra started shouting and pumping their fists again.

Oy! Oy! Oy! Oy!

Angus dashed around the stage madly for a while, then approached the edge, where the Fulcra were gathered.

And the necromancer/bard began to sing—screech was more like it. Gunnar was pretty sure he'd heard this song somewhere, but it sure as hell wasn't like this.

The Fulcra grunted, *Oy! Oy! Oy!*

And that was it, over and over and over for a full minute.

The drums grew more and more cacophonous, to the point that the beat was nearly lost.

Angus dropped into the splits, raised a finger to the sky, and screamed atonally.

There was a massive eruption of flame from the stage as the song ended, and a pair of figures were lowered down from the ceiling with ropes.

Kohli and a young woman with fiery red hair.

Their hands were bound, they were naked but for the rudimentary attempts at underwear in this world, and their bodies were covered with splotchy-looking writing in red paint.

The stage was painted too, Gunnar realized. A crude pentagram etched in white. A few of the Fulcra began to haul up some long wooden crates from the sides of the stage. The skeletal creatures pried open the tops of the crates to reveal five new skeletons.

Shit, I think this is how he makes these Fulcra creatures.

Gunnar's grandma had once told him that when she and his grandpa were kids, some wackos believed that rock and roll was secretly connected to Satanic rituals or something.

Wonder what they'd make of this!

The drumbeat grew soft but steady as the five coffins were

set at each point of the pentagram. Angus moved to the center, where Kohli and the redhead dangled about three feet above the ground.

Angus reached into his cloak and produced several glowing blue soul gems. He smiled and raised his hands into the air.

The Fulcra quieted.

"Children, we've come to welcome five new members to our little family. But all creation requires sacrifice, and you have brought just what we require."

A stream of crimson dripped from the redhead's arm, and the necromancer let it run through his fingers.

That is definitely not paint...

Gunnar felt sick to his stomach. This felt way too real.

One of the smaller Fulcra came forward with a scythe and handed it to Angus.

The redhead glared with icy fury. "When I am strong enough, I am going to come back and burn this crypt to the ground!"

The necromancer smiled. "Ah, you see, that is the beauty of a leveled crypt. Noobs come in to gain experience. By the time they're strong enough to pose any real threat, they've leveled too far, and must move on to grind somewhere else. Most take the easy exit through the burial hall, but there's always a few that wander too deep. Just enough to keep this operation running. It's nothing personal. But I'm afraid I *will* have to slit your throats."

The drumbeat picked up, and the Fulcra began chanting, "Oy! Oy! Oy!"

Gunnar had slipped into the shadows of the staging area, but the drums were accompanied by more flames from the stage.

In the flashing light, he spotted two Level 5 Fulcra coming his direction. Gunnar leaned back against the stone wall, but there was another eruption of flames from the stage, and the Fulcra shot forward, warhammers raised.

Gunnar leapt to the side just as the first Fulcra brought its hammer down with a thundering crash. He was really close to leveling up, and this was probably his only chance.

He activated Enhanced Blow and swung the oaken club as hard as he could, sending the first Fulcra's skull flying like a softball.

[*You have dealt +30 Damage to a common Fulcra!*]

The remainder of the skeleton crumpled to the ground.

[*You have defeated another common Fulcra! Here's 10 XP with a 5 XP bonus for a Perfect Kill Shot!*]

Gunnar's Stamina dropped close to 60% at the exertion. The second Fulcra swung its hammer at his head. He ducked, rolled, and activated the skill again. His club connected with the back of the creature's spine.

[*You have dealt +30 Damage to a common Fulcra!*]

The Fulcra exploded in shards of bone, and Gunnar leaned over, panting as the notifications came in.

[*You have defeated another common Fulcra! Here's 10 XP with a 5 XP bonus for a Perfect Kill Shot!*]

[*Congratulations! You actually used some strategy and brute force in the same attack. You have reached Level 7 in the skill Enhanced Blow. Kapow!*]

[*Congratulations! You have reached Level 4! You have earned Glory for your goddess Nymoria.*]

The bizarre rock concert paused, the drumbeat quieted, and the world lit up, and not from the flames. Nymoria reached out her hand to him, and Gunnar glowed as he leveled up.

"Well done, faithful servant. You have taken another step on the path to greatness. You now have two attribute points, which can be distributed at any time. But remember that every choice you make will echo into eternity. Choose wisely."

With everything paused, Gunnar knew he had to act quick. His kill had drawn the attention of two more Fulcra, and the necromancer had his scythe raised at the redhead's throat. The ropes were rigged in the rafters of the stage, but he didn't have time to get there. And the necromancer had said the true exit was back in that massive burial hall, which meant they had a lot of ground to cover to get out of this damn place.

But he had an idea of how to do it.

He applied one point to Constitution, increasing his Stamina and Health by another five points, with an additional five each from leveling up. He added the three accompanying skill points to Endurance, which added a 20 point Stamina buff.

Next, he raised his Dexterity to Level 10 and dumped all five skill points into his Throwing Blade skill. He could only hope his Level 14 attack would be enough for what he had in mind.

The world unfroze, and everything happened in an adrenaline-induced blur.

As Angus swung the scythe at the redhead's porcelain neck, Gunnar let one of his throwing blades fly. Gunnar shouted in triumph as the blade severed the rope, and the young woman dropped to the ground, missing the necromancer's attack by mere inches. The redhead landed in a crouch, whipping the remains of the rope around. Her hands were still bound, but the rope was thick, and when it struck Angus in the face, he staggered back.

But Gunnar didn't see the rest.

The two attacking Fulcra reached him, and he leapt into action.

17

THUNDERSTRUCK

GUNNAR DODGED A WARHAMMER ATTACK, leaping to his left. He swung the oaken club at the creature's face, but the Level 6 Fulcra raised its arm in defense, and the club lopped it off at the elbow.

[*You have dealt +10 Damage to a common Fulcra!*]

The second creature—a Level 5—bore a gladius, and Gunnar narrowly raised his club in time. The blade lodged in the wood and was wrenched from the creature's grasp as Gunnar swept his club away. The Fulcra grimaced, and Gunnar activated Enhanced Blow and drove the club into the creature's skull.

[*You have dealt +30 Damage to a common Fulcra!*]

The Fulcra's skull shattered.

[*You have defeated another common Fulcra! Here's 5 XP with a 5 XP bonus for a Perfect Kill Shot!*]

Gunnar cursed. Though he was pleased that Enhanced Blow had cost him less this time, he was getting less experience for killing these Fulcra now that he'd reached Level 4.

With only one arm, the other Fulcra could no longer lift its heavy weapon, so it attacked with one of its own ribs, but

Gunnar made quick work of the creature, earning another 5 XP. He wrenched the gladius out of his club, leaving a large gash in the wood, and tossed it aside.

"A little bloody help here!" Kohli shrieked.

With enchanted drummers pounding, the majority of the Fulcra were still facing the stage from the floor below, pumping their fists, and shouting, "Oy! Oy! Oy!"

Their master was rolling on the ground, trying to break free from the redhead, who had managed to wrap her length of rope around the man's neck.

Meanwhile, a pair of Fulcra clawed at Kohli, who still dangled from the stage rafters. He had impressively managed to pull himself higher up the rope, just out of their skeletal reach. One swung a warhammer, and Kohli barely managed to swing himself out of the way.

It wasn't much better down below, but at least, then, the thief could help fight.

Focusing his vision and calming his breath, Gunnar let another throwing blade fly.

Kohli dropped a couple inches as the rope frayed. But it was not a direct hit, and about half of the rope remained intact. Gunnar chucked two more knives, but missed both times. As Kohli shifted around, the rope slowly began to unravel, bearing him closer and closer to the Fulcra below.

The chanting and drumming continued.

A loud cry pulled his attention from Kohli. The necromancer had freed himself of the redhead's rope and now had her pinned down, bare bony knees pressed into her neck.

Gunnar gritted his teeth and sprinted across the stage.

Angus looked up just as Gunnar tackled him to the ground. The two of them rolled across the stage, arms and legs thrashing. For such a wiry man, Angus was tough to pin. Or maybe

Gunnar was still just that weak. Gunnar let the man squirm away. He reached for a throwing blade, but came up empty.

Damn!

He settled for a dagger from his belt.

Just as he was about to throw it, a skeletal hand latched onto his boot from behind. His vision blurred and his feet were wrenched out from under him. One of the Fulcra from below the stage had managed to reach him from the floor. Gunnar kicked but the Fulcra was clamped on like a vice. Sharp, bony fingers dug into his ankle.

Angus grinned a short distance away as he formed long tendril-like fingers into a spell sign. Visible blue magic emanated from his fingers, and the other creatures from the floor ceased their chanting and began to claw toward Gunnar, a wall of skeleton limbs reaching for him.

Gunnar kicked and tried to roll away with all his might, but several creatures latched onto his feet and his clothes, dragging him toward the edge of the stage. Bony appendages tore at his skin, and his Health began to drop as one of them drove a shard of bone into his leg.

Gunnar's heart raced. He was about to fail again. About to wake up to a mind-numbing shock. About to work his ass off back in prison only to respawn back in this damn crypt.

But just as Gunnar reached the edge, the creatures' grips slackened. Gunnar jerked his body forward and flung himself out of reach. The Fulcra backed away from the edge of the stage and quickly started shuffling toward the sets of stairs on either end of the platform.

When Gunnar turned back, he realized why.

Angus was on fire.

Flames shot all across his schoolboy suit jacket and down his arms and back. The redhead was grinning maniacally as the necromancer/bard writhed and thrashed around the stage, apparently having never been taught to stop, drop, and roll.

Fulcra began to stagger up the stage steps. The two massive creatures who had been manning the drums had quit their pounding and gathered around a screaming Angus.

"Water! Get some fucking water!" Angus's dying voice sounded even worse than his singing.

Gunnar reached the redhead and freed her from her bindings. He was impressed she'd managed to light Angus on fire while still bound.

"Thanks," she said.

"All right, my turn to be rescued!" Kohli shouted.

Exasperated, Kohli still dangled above the stage, though no Fulcra were trying to reach him any longer. All of them were gathering around their master, trying feebly to assist. Several of them got too close and ignited themselves.

With a flick of his wrist, Gunnar launched a dagger, and Kohli dropped. Straight into the redhead's arms. The sight of them both in their archaic skivvies made Gunnar chuckle despite the horrific circumstances.

"Put me down! Put me down! I don't need you to bloody catch me!" Kohli glared at the redhead, and she dropped him instantly. Too instantly. He nearly toppled as his bare feet hit the ground.

"Nice of you to leave me hanging there," Kohli said, huffing as he turned to Gunnar.

"Sorry, there's only one of me and a whole lot more of them."

"It's all well and good when you're not the one dangling like meat over a lion's den. I only have 10% Health left! She's got... well, plenty more than that!"

There was a giant splash as the Fulcra drummers dumped

huge jugs of water over Angus's head, followed by a loud hiss and a plume of smoke as the fire went out.

There was no more time to argue.

Angus turned toward them, a furious mess of singed clothes and charred flesh.

But he managed to form his fingers into a spell sign, and his Fulcra charged.

Gunnar tossed Kohli one of the Health potions he'd found earlier and led the way back to the room full of loot as Angus and his Fulcra chased after them. The three of them pulled the door closed, and Kohli rammed the shaft of a spear through the handle.

The thud of skeletons crashing against the door made clear it would not hold for long. The spear clattered against the crude iron handle, and Gunnar wasn't sure whether the spear or the door handle would break first.

The redhead ignited a torch while the groans of Fulcra beyond the door echoed. It sounded as though they were breaking their own bones against the stone.

Torchlight flashing across her face, the young woman grinned as she turned to Gunnar. Despite the spells written in her own blood, he couldn't help but notice how attractive she was. He guessed she was in her early twenties. Her flushed skin was specked with light freckles, and green eyes sparked with confidence as she lit a second torch with the flames from her own and handed it to Gunnar.

"Good thinking lighting him on fire," Gunnar said.

She shrugged. "Figured it would keep them all distracted long enough."

"Barely," Kohli said, eyeing the door.

"You a fire mage, then?" Gunnar asked.

She smirked. "Right, cuz of the hair? You don't have a lot of creativity, do you?"

Her voice was also remarkably attractive considering she was making fun of him. She had a lilting accent, but he couldn't quite place it. He thought it might have actually been unique to the game, but he didn't really have the international experience to know for sure.

Gunnar shrugged. "Take that as a no, then?"

The redhead held up the flint she'd used to light the first torch. "I tackled him into one of those cauldrons from his show."

"Look, can we save the bloody pleasantries for later?" Kohli asked, still wearing nothing but his skivvies. "That spear is about to break."

"Your friend's a bit bent out of shape, isn't he?" The redhead smirked at Gunnar again.

"It's been a hell of a day," Gunnar murmured. "But he's right. We should go. I know the way to the other exit. Kohli, grab another spear, and we can wedge the other door to this room shut on our way out."

Without a word of acknowledgement, the redhead retreated to the backstage door they'd come through.

"What the hell are you doing?" Kohli demanded.

She stooped down in front of the rattling door. There were some roots or something sticking out of the crumbling walls, and she pressed her hands against one of them. There was a soft luminescence around her fingers, and the roots began to expand in an instant, sending tendrils of new shoots spreading all across the doorway, twisting around the handle and then climbing up into cracks in the stone on the other side of the door.

It still rattled, but far less now. The Fulcra groaned from the room beyond, and Gunnar heard Angus hollering an unintelligible order.

"That ought to buy us some time," she said, sauntering past

them and glancing around the room. "I think my clothes are somewhere in here."

Gunnar laughed. "Oh, that reminds me..." He pulled Kohli's clothes from his Inventory and handed them over.

Kohli quickly slipped into his pants and pulled his shirt and cloak over his head. Though still irritable, he managed a slight nod. "Uh, thanks."

"I would have grabbed yours too," Gunnar said, turning back to the redhead, who was sifting through some shabby clothes on one of the tables nearby, "but I didn't know which ones they were. I brought a cloak, though." He pulled that out of his Inventory too.

The redhead took it and smiled, but she promptly set it down. "Appreciate the thought, but I think I know where they put mine." She moved to the far corner of the room.

The girl had the build of a track athlete, tall and lean and impressively muscular. Gunnar glanced away, feeling a little awkward now that she was the only one without clothes. He began sifting through some of the items, searching for more throwing blades.

"So, er, what's your name anyway? I'm Gunnar, and this is Kohli."

"Em," she said.

"Short for what? Emily? Emilia?"

"Just Em."

"And you gave me crap for creativity?" Gunnar quipped. He spotted a couple daggers and stowed them on his belt.

Em turned back and smiled again. She'd found her clothes and quickly slipped them on. She returned, wearing what looked like a black ninja getup with the hood pulled down.

"Alright, boys, let's go."

They crossed the room and returned to the main corridor of

the crypt. Gunnar was about to close the second door behind them when Kohli grabbed his arm.

"Why's it so quiet?"

Gunnar hadn't realized that the Fulcra had quit rattling against the backstage door until Kohli called his attention to it.

It was deathly silent. They turned to Em, who was glancing into the looming darkness of the chamber.

"Uh, don't bother barricading that door," Em said, grimacing.

She pointed further down the corridor. Gunnar had been so distracted when they'd reached this place—what with Kohli getting captured—he hadn't paid attention to the fact that the corridor continued on into the depths of the crypt.

A faint light glowed from around a corner far down the corridor. And then, Gunnar heard the distant clatter of bones against stone. *There must have been another way out of that ceremonial chamber.*

Em, Kohli, and Gunnar all glanced at each other.

Em grinned.

Gunnar nodded.

And Kohli groaned. "I am so sick of this place."

Without another word, they ran.

18

CRYPT KEEPER

THEY DIDN'T BOTHER with any degree of Stealth. Torches held high, they hurried as fast as they could through the winding corridors of the crypt, back the way Gunnar and Kohli had come earlier.

By the time they reached the chamber where Gunnar had left Kohli while he scouted ahead, Gunnar was panting for breath and his Stamina was below 50%. He was glad he'd leveled up his Endurance, or he really would have been screwed.

But none of them were in good enough condition to keep this up for much longer, and Gunnar did not want to have to face a horde of Fulcra while low on Stamina.

The stone echoed loudly with the approaching undead, bones clacking hollowly as they loomed somewhere in the winding caverns behind them.

"I don't think those bastards are shuffling anymore," Kohli said, breathing heavily.

"Not much farther," Gunnar said, panting hard. "We've fought those things. They've got Stamina just like we do. They can't run forever either."

"Unless that asshole is using a more powerful spell," Kohli said.

Gunnar shook his head, more out of hope than certainty. "It's gotta be taking all he's got to keep that horde moving."

Em grimaced. "I hope you're right."

Something wasn't adding up. Even if the man's Health had no impact on his ability to form spells, there had to be something more going on than just his Mana pool. Gunnar just didn't know what.

The corridor that led to the massive burial hall was narrow and run-down, with large chunks of stone that had crumbled into the walkway, forcing them to slow their pace to a fast walk.

Gunnar was fairly certain the clacking was getting louder behind them, though every time he turned back, all he saw was that glow coming from beyond whatever corner they'd just turned. He tried to focus on calming his heavy breathing, syncing it with his pace.

He'd dated a track girl in college who had really wanted to get him to like running.

Just focus on a steady rhythm, she had told him as he panted desperately and tried and failed to keep up with her.

It hadn't worked for shit, but anything was worth a shot now. His lungs were screaming from the fight and escape, but as he focused, the pain seemed to fade a little.

An unexpected notification appeared.

Unlocked Skill: Mindful Breathing

Skill Type: Mental, Race-based
Linked Attribute: Constitution (+60% Development)
Level: 6
Cost: N/A
Requirements: Breath
Effect: Increases Stamina restoration rate by 20%

Description: Look at you, Zen Master! You can control your own body if you pay attention to it. Level this skill high enough and you might even shut off that damn voice in your head telling you you're not good enough. But it won't stop us from telling you!

Sonofabitch! Mindfulness? Come on! Are elves some sort of damn hippies in this game?

But he had to admit, the effect was noticeable.

It was not astronomically faster, but his Stamina climbed as he walked, his breathing steadied, his head cleared, and by the time they reached the burial hall, he was back up to 80%.

The clatter reached a roar behind them. They hurried across the length of the chamber, crossing several hundred yards, giant pillars of stone towering around them like a forest.

At the edge of the chamber, there was a distinct wooden doorway, but when Kohli tried the handle, it didn't budge.

"I'm afraid you'll be needing the key."

The sudden voice made Gunnar spin around, but there was no one there. Though the glow was growing increasingly bright in the halls they'd come from.

"Up above you, dimwits!"

Gunnar glanced up. Three cages hung from the ceiling. They were semi-cylindrical with pointed tops, like gigantic bird-cages. Two of them contained corpses well into the decomposition process, but the middle one held an elderly woman with long white hair and very pale skin. She looked a bit like an old Jaime Lee Curtis.

"Where can we get the key?" Gunnar shouted up to her.

Jaime Lee scowled. "From me, numbnuts! But I'll be needing some help from you first."

Kohli groaned. "We don't have time for a damn side quest, lady. We've got an undead army on our tails."

The clatter of the Fulcra was making it hard to talk.

"You'll make time," Jaime Lee said in a stern matronly tone, "if you want to escape. Get me down from here, and I'll open the door."

Quest Update - The Crypt Keeper

Description: Talk about bad timing for a side quest! The Crypt Keeper used to rule this place, until that little rock star wannabe took over. Now, she's trapped. Let her down nice and careful, and you just might make it out of here.

Objective: Free the Crypt Keeper.

Reward: Get the keys to your freedom before that horde of Fulcra rip you apart like shredded beef. To think you came into this very room and could have made it out easy-peasy. But let's be honest, this is way more interesting.

Do you wish to accept? Yes/No

Gunnar begrudgingly accepted.

"Angus just happened to give this old Crypt Keeper the keys?" Kohli asked exasperatedly.

Gunnar grunted. "It's obviously just part of the script for this place."

"So, how do you think we—"

But Kohli didn't finish.

They both turned to find Em leaping up the nearest wall like a woodland creature, jumping from the top of a coffin up to a stone ledge about eight feet up, and then, she leapt again, up to one of the burial nooks that lined the entire room. She nearly slipped as she leapt from one nook to the next, and Gunnar could have sworn he heard a scraping sound, like claws, as she latched onto the wall to steady herself before continuing her way up.

Gunnar wondered whether his animal impression was actually founded in reality. When he had freed her back on the stage, she had landed with impressive grace for someone bound by the hands. Now, she leapt with ease and landed soft and easy between nooks, moving too fast for him to confirm whether the claws he'd heard were real or not.

He hit her with Scan.

Em (Just Em)

Level: 7
HP: 80/80
MP: 100/100
Race: Chimera
Clan: Gray Fox
Disposition: Friendly
Relationship: You Scratch My Back, I'll Scratch Yours
Description: Part human, part fox. Like all low-level chimera, she's still mostly human. But watch out for those claws!

Em climbed until she was about thirty feet up before pausing at a ledge, facing a nearby pillar.

"You've got this!" Gunnar shouted, suddenly filled with hope that she might make it in time.

Em took a breath, then jumped.

Her claws scraped against the side of the pillar, but she managed to latch onto a ridge of decorative stone encircling it.

The clacking of bones had reached a fever pitch, and Gunnar and Kohli turned their eyes away from their chimera companion to see dozens of creatures pouring through the chamber entrance.

19

THE HORDE

THE FULCRA BORE torches and an array of weapons—swords and warhammers, spears and clubs. Their master had unleashed his entire arsenal, though even in attack mode, they did not move terribly quickly. Probably due to Stamina limitations, as Gunnar had suspected. Few were over Level 5, but it didn't matter a damn thing.

There were far too many for them to handle.

And there was nowhere to escape.

Em would not be able to free the Crypt Keeper before it was too late. They had struggled to fight even a few at a time. Gunnar cringed as he imagined the agony of the shock he would receive back in Grid Eight.

Behind the small horde, Angus hobbled after them, bearing a staff with a glowing emerald stone embedded at the top. His robes were tattered, his hair was charred, and he looked angry as hell. His Health hovered around 20% and his Stamina was low too, but with the horde of Fulcra between them, they weren't going to get anywhere near him.

"Come on!"

Gunnar turned to find Kohli climbing up on the same coffin

that Em had leapt up from moments ago. Gunnar steeled himself and hurried over, latching onto Kohli's wrist as the man helped him up. They both surveyed the wall of burial nooks, searching for a handhold. A small ledge jutted out above them, just far enough that Gunnar wasn't confident he could make the leap.

"You first," Kohli said.

"Me?"

"You're an elf! You swing in trees and shit, now go!"

Gunnar backed up a step and took a long breath, then ran across the coffin and leapt at the wall.

His body thudded against the stone, but his fingers latched onto the ledge.

Unlocked Skill: Wall Climbing

Skill Type: Physical

Linked Attributes: Dexterity and Strength (+80% Development)

Affinity Level: 7

Cost: 1 Stamina per second

Requirements: Level 5 Strength and Level 7 Dexterity

Description: Another fine skill for assassins and Peeping Toms. Walls were built to keep guys like you out, but that won't stop you. Unless, of course, you plummet to your death. No conveniently placed bales of hay will save you here.

Gunnar's high Dexterity had paid off again. He swiftly pulled himself up. Kohli nodded to him and backed up to the rear edge of the coffin. The Fulcra were only twenty yards away and closing in quickly.

Kohli leapt and groaned as he reached for the ledge. His fingers slipped, but Gunnar latched onto his arms and pulled the thief up to join him. They were only about eight feet above the chamber floor, and Gunnar did not feel any more comfort. Some of the orc-originating Fulcra were nearly that tall.

"Hoist me up," Gunnar said, pointing to a burial nook further above them.

With Kohli's help, Gunnar scrambled up two rows of burial nooks, and the two of them squeezed into a space exactly large enough for a stone coffin. About fifteen feet below them, the Fulcra clawed at the walls, longing to reach them.

A scream filled the chamber, and Gunnar and Kohli looked up.

The Crypt Keeper sat scowling from the middle giant bird-cage, swaying some thirty feet above the chamber. Em dangled precariously from the bars of the first cage, the metal container swinging violently back and forth.

But that was not why Em screamed.

Gunnar's gut churned. From the ceiling a dozen more Fulcra appeared, lowering chains from small openings throughout the room. Looking like undead Navy SEALS, the creatures lowered themselves down until they reached the same height as the cages and began swinging toward Em's cage.

She scrambled inside the cage just as one of the creatures latched onto the bars. She crushed the creature's fingers with some sort of mallet-type weapon, and the Fulcra plummeted to the ground.

A spear glanced off the stone near Gunnar's face, and he ducked back in with Kohli.

"What do we do?" Gunnar asked.

Kohli's eyes stared out in horror. "Uh, stay right here."

"Em's gonna die out there."

"That necromancer's Mana is nearly spent. He's using everything he's got to keep up this chase. Our best shot is to wait him out and hope she can last. And us too."

Another creature plummeted from the cage as Em swung

open the cage door and unleashed a kick at its chest as it tried to enter. Two more Fulcra swung at her, reaching out scrawny skeletal arms.

Gunnar glanced at Angus, who stood back behind his horde, supporting himself against his staff. He reached into his charred cloak and produced a Mana potion. His Mana immediately increased by 50%, but quickly began depleting again. Thirty seconds later, he down another potion. And then another.

He seemed to have an Inventory full of the damn things.

Kohli was wrong. Angus's magic was not going to be dying out anytime soon.

Below them, the Fulcra had begun forming a very shaky Fulcra pyramid, stacking on top of one another in an attempt to reach their burial nook. Another spear glanced off the wall, and Kohli cursed.

"We gotta get higher, mate."

But Gunnar had a different idea.

"I need you to go down and distract them."

"What?" Kohli demanded.

"I need you to distract the Fulcra."

"You want me to distract fifty undead? How the hell am I supposed to do that?"

Gunnar grabbed Kohli's shoulder. "Angus is throwing down Mana potions like Jell-O shots at a frat party. Those Fulcra are going to figure out a way to reach us, and if we climb, we'll be sitting targets for one of those spears."

"And how is going down better?"

"Look at him! His Stamina and Health are still really low. He's banking entirely on magic. If you can draw the Fulcra away, I think I can take him out."

Gunnar held up one of his throwing blades. "I just need to get a little closer."

Kohli groaned. "If I die, mate, I will come back and kill you."

Gunnar reached into his Inventory, withdrew the remaining potions he'd looted earlier, and handed them to Kohli. "You don't need to last long. Just long enough."

Kohli downed them, then reached out and took Gunnar's hand. "Good luck, mate."

Above them, Em sent another Fulcra flying. She began shifting her weight in the cage, sending it swaying even more sharply toward the middle cage.

Below, the Fulcra pyramid had nearly reached them, and the top few creatures reached up, bony fingers scraping against the walls below.

Kohli drew a small wooden shield from his Inventory, something he must have looted back in Angus's holding chamber. He let out a battle cry and leapt from the burial nook, landing right on one of the topmost skeletons. The sudden impact sent the whole tower of creatures swaying treacherously, and Kohli and the top Fulcra tumbled down the side of the pyramid to the chamber floor below.

Kohli managed to cushion his fall with the shield and the creature he took with him. The Fulcra shattered on the stone floor, but Kohli rolled away, ditching the splintered shield.

"Come on, you bony bastards!"

And with that, he ran.

The pyramid became a teetering, chaotic mess as some of the top and bottom creatures attempted to pursue Kohli at once.

The Fulcra tower fell apart like a rockslide, bony limbs cascading from the chamber walls. Several of the lower-level creatures were crushed in the process, and though he had several Fulcra hot on his tail, Kohli shouted with glee as he leveled up from the kills. His low Health and Stamina bars shot up to full, and he ran even faster.

The majority of the undead hurried in pursuit. Several had lost limbs in the collapse, but they staggered on. A few of the more damaged creatures shifted unsteadily around the ground below, gazing back up the wall as Gunnar peered out.

He didn't have any more time.

Above, Em leapt from her cage and latched onto one of the chains the Fulcra had used to drop down and attack her. She swung back and forth and then leapt again, latching onto another chain and slowly making her way to the Crypt Keeper's cage.

Angus stood near the center of the room, leaning heavily on his staff, and attempted to bring order back to his horde.

Gunnar scrambled down the side of the wall, grateful again he'd leveled his Dexterity as high as he had. A Level 5 Fulcra with a shattered shoulder waited at the bottom. Gunnar drew his Oaken Club, and with two strikes, it was over.

[*You have defeated another common Fulcra! Here's 5 XP!*]

A few injured Fulcra staggered around nearby, but the rest of the pyramid collapse survivors were chasing after Kohli, who moved impressively fast. Though Gunnar worried how long his Stamina would hold out.

Gunnar had to be quick.

Another Fulcra came into range, and Gunnar swung the club at the creature's legs, crippling it, but he didn't bother finishing the kill.

He strode across the room, right at Angus. The cages loomed above in the space between them. Em had reached the Crypt Keeper's cage and was scrambling up the bars to reach the top.

A few injured Fulcra hobbled after Gunnar, but he was confident he could handle them if they got too close.

He turned to face the necromancer.

20

REGIME CHANGE

Angus's eyes lit with rage at the sight of Gunnar approaching.

He had a couple Fulcra who had stuck close to him, but the majority were damaged or chasing Kohli, who was beginning to lose his speed. Gunnar just hoped he could pull this off in time.

Angus shouted for backup, but the Fulcra were in a battle frenzy, and none turned as Kohli dashed around the vast chamber. He raised his glowing staff.

Gunnar let a blade fly.

Angus ducked, and the dagger went clattering across the chamber floor.

The sorcerer glowered and took a step forward. Em pulled herself up to the top of the cage directly above where Gunnar was standing. A pair of Fulcra dropped down from an opening in the ceiling and began swinging toward her.

Come on, Em. Come on.

Gunnar let another blade fly. This one grazed the necromancer's shoulder, and he shouted with pain, though it did virtually no damage.

"I'm not going to let my children kill you," Angus said through gritted teeth. "I'll do it myself. Nice and slow."

"I hear fire is good and agonizing," Gunnar quipped.

That really got the necromancer worked up. His eyes went wide, and even from ten yards away, Gunnar could see the veins in the man's neck bulging. Angus began walking forward, and Gunnar took a couple steps back.

He chucked another blade right at the man's head. Angus reacted quickly. His staff glowed brightly as he released a spell that disintegrated the blade in midair.

It was impressive, but Gunnar also noted the effect on the Fulcra, who all slowed as their master focused his magic elsewhere.

Em made quick work of one of the Fulcra above, and a goblin skeleton crashed to the ground between Gunnar and Angus.

Just a little bit further, Gunnar thought.

He took three more steps back. A pair of Fulcra were slowly closing in behind him.

Angus grinned as he neared. "What do you think you're going to do? I've got an army." He downed another Mana potion. "I've got all the magic I could possibly need."

Gunnar took another step back. He was out of daggers and throwing blades, so he drew his Oaken Club once more.

"I'm going to free the Crypt Keeper you've kept prisoner," Gunnar said calmly. "I'm going to replace you, and then, I'm going to get the hell out of this damn pit."

Angus laughed. His staff glowed brightly, and he released a surge of magic that struck Gunnar full in the chest, knocking him on his back. His Health dropped to 20%.

Angus stepped forward one last time, his staff glowing. A Fulcra latched onto Gunnar from behind.

Gunnar shouted, "Now, Em!"

There was a shriek of metal against metal, and a loud groan.

Angus looked up.

Just in time to see the Crypt Keeper's cage come down on his head.

———

The Crypt Keeper staggered from the cage, looking dazed but incredibly pleased as she left her confines. Angus was nothing but a splattering of blood and bone on the stone beneath her feet.

Directly above, Em hung on to the chain that had once held the Crypt Keeper's cage. Several Fulcra plummeted to the ground, suddenly gone utterly still.

The Fulcra's grip had gone limp on Gunnar's arm, and he scrambled to his feet, wrenching the bony fingers away. All around the burial chamber, the Fulcra collapsed where they stood, the spell animating them vanishing the moment the necromancer died.

Just as Gunnar had hoped it would. The place erupted in tiny plumes of blue sparks, and he relished the thought of what he might buy once he found somewhere to trade all these soul gems.

Em made her way carefully back down to the chamber floor, swinging her way from multiple chains back to the wall, then climbing down the burial nooks. Gunnar couldn't help but envy how easy she made it look.

Kohli hobbled over to Gunnar and helped him to his feet. They both were panting heavily, Stamina slowly regenerating.

"Did you know Em would do that?" he asked.

Gunnar shook his head. "I just hoped she'd catch on to what I was setting her up for."

Kohli was happier than Gunnar had seen him since they'd met. A wide grin stretched over his face as he surveyed all the damage they'd done. He was winded, but triumphant. Kohli gripped Gunnar's hand. "I'll admit, I was pretty sour about getting stuck down here. But you're all right, Gunnar. I gained two levels from collapsing that Fulcra tower alone. And two more the rest of the time."

Gunnar smiled. He hadn't gained anything new since freeing Em and Kohli during the ceremony. Since Em had released the cage, he guessed she had gotten the XP for defeating the necromancer.

But Gunnar was just glad they were getting out of this place.

On stable ground again, Em strode over to them, smiling.

"Nice work, boys." She clapped Gunnar on the shoulder. "Good idea drawing him under the cage like that."

A surge of warmth shot through him. "Glad we were on the same wavelength. You did more than either of us."

Em winked. "As long as you know it."

Together, the three of them turned to face the Crypt Keeper, who was standing just outside her cage with arms crossed.

As they neared, a bombardment of notifications appeared.

[*Congratulations! You didn't fail! Seriously, we were betting against you. You have reached Level 7 in the skill Endurance. You have reached Level 8 in the skill Wall Climbing! You have reached Level 7 in the skill Perception! Neat-o, gang!*]

[*Congratulations! You ran for your life and let others make the big kills. In your case, that was truly the right plan of action. You've earned the Resourceful Wuss badge: +1 to Constitution, +1 to Creativity, +1 to Wisdom.*]

[*Congratulations! You have completed the quest Luka's Crypt. Reward? You escaped with your head and limbs intact. Don't be greedy. Oh, all right, fine. I guess we're all a bunch of bleeding hearts around here. Here's 120 XP!*]

[*Congratulations! You have completed the secret quest*

Regime Change. *You have returned the realms of the dead to their rightful ruler. Pray to the gods we never have to see another Fulcra forced to dance or sing again. Here's another 80 XP!*]

Gunnar's Glory meter shot up to 100%, not once, but two times, taking him to Level 6, with a little more Glory left over.

The world froze around him. And Nymoria reached out her luminescent hand to him.

"Well done, faithful servant. You have taken another step on the path to greatness. You now have two attribute points, which can be distributed at any time. But remember that every choice you make will echo into eternity. Choose wisely."

As she vanished, Gunnar let out a *whoop*, which Kohli and Em both echoed as they examined their own achievements.

The Crypt Keeper stooped down and wrenched Angus's staff from his dead hand. She frowned as she surveyed the carnage in the room.

"I've been in that cage for months now. It was torture to watch that asshole use the dead to fulfill his own pathetic fantasies."

Gunnar was confused. "I thought you got out if we did. Surely we're not the first ones to come down here?"

The old woman shook her head. "That was a cruel trick. All part of the enchantments set in place. Just Angus rubbing it in. Time and time again, I was released from my cage by some new adventurer, and time and time again, they would go free. But as soon as they left, I was magicked back to my cage to wait for the next person to come down here so it could play out all over again."

Kohli grimaced. "Yeah, he seemed like a real prick."

The Crypt Keeper nodded. "It was all made worse by the fact he was my apprentice. I could only truly go free if he died. And you three gave him what he deserved. So, as I said, I am in your debt."

"Well, there's plenty of loot," Kohli said.

"I'm afraid I can't let you take any of the soul gems. They belong to the spirits I've been entrusted to safeguard. I must ask that you let me restore them to their proper place."

Kohli scowled, then glanced at Gunnar.

He dug his own out of his Inventory. "You said they aren't worth much to us anyway."

Kohli grumbled, but all three of them handed over the gems they'd previously looted.

The Crypt Keeper bowed her head in thanks. "I'm afraid I have no coins or enchanted weapons to offer in gratitude, but I can offer you each a spell. These are only good once, so please reserve them for a time when you are truly in need."

Kohli cocked an eyebrow, and Gunnar grinned. This might end up better anyway.

The Crypt Keeper strode over to Em first.

"For the Fox Girl who cut me loose, I offer you *Temporary Full Transformation*. You have the lithe feet and fierce grip of your animal kin, but you have much advancing to do before you are able to transform at will. But this spell will grant you a temporary taste of your future chimera capabilities."

Em smiled and bowed her head. "Thank you, mistress."

The woman turned to Kohli. "For the Scoundrel who created the distraction that allowed others to enact my escape, you played your part well, as I expect you usually do. I offer you *Fatal Attraction*, which will make you nearly impossible to dislike for a short period of time. Word to the wise, I would not recommend using it for the sake of carnal pleasure. If the effect lasts too long, it may get you into trouble. Save it for a moment of truly desperate need."

Kohli nodded his thanks. "Reckon I'm glad we found time to help you out, after all."

Lastly, the Crypt Keeper fixed her gaze on Gunnar. "For the

Rogue who played that rock star like a fiddle, you may not have gained the experience of your comrades, but if not for you, I might still be imprisoned by his spell. To you, I offer *Cloaked Dagger*. If ever you need to sneak a blade out in the open, this spell will have your back. Use it well."

Cloaked Dagger
Spell Type: Rare, Illusory
Alignment: Dark
Restrictions: One-time use (30 second maximum duration)
Requirements: Sufficient Mana
Cost: 2 Mana per second
Description: Render your weapon invisible for a short period of time.

"Thank you," Gunnar said, after analyzing the spell. He expected it would come in very handy in a den of thieves like Thailen. And the fact that it was a dark magic spell especially excited him.

The Crypt Keeper made her way across the room and unlocked the wooden door to the outside world. As soon as the key turned, the door swung open, letting glorious sunlight cascade into the chamber.

The woman straightened herself and bowed her head to them. "I have much work to do. This was once an honored place for the dead, and it has been a fun house for far too long. May your gods keep you, and may you stay clear of the wiles of Luka the Trickster. Farewell."

[PART 3]
ROGUE IN TRAINING

21

DARK SOUL OF THE NIGHT

BACK AT THE MERMAID, Sykes let out a barrel-chested guffaw as they recounted their story over pints of ale and a plate of roasted pork and potatoes. Sykes especially appreciated the moment when Em set the rock star sorcerer on fire.

"God, I would have paid to see that!"

Gunnar smiled and downed his plate of food. By the time they reached the inn, his Stamina had flatlined around 60%, and the food offered some much needed rejuvenation.

[*Buffs Added - A Decent Meal* — *You have decreased your Stamina usage rate by 15% over the next four hours. Build up your Constitution for an even greater effect.*]

As Kohli continued their tale about the crypt, Gunnar leaned back and took long sips from his ale and ordered a second helping of pork. While Gunnar had been less than impressed with many aspects of the realism offered in the game so far, the delicious seasoning of the Mermaid's food was incredible.

Things might have got off to a rocky start, but he was feeling significantly better about his prospects. And it wasn't just because of the achievements.

Kohli might have focused a bit excessively on his own distraction efforts as he recounted their victory, but neither Gunnar or Em cared.

The chimera sat beside him, and Gunnar found himself very much enjoying her company.

Sykes downed his ale and pounded the empty on the table. "You two've turned out all right," he said, turning to Gunnar and Kohli. They smiled. Then, the large man glanced at Em. "And you, I hope to see more of you around here. I've got a couple good guilds I think might be interested in offering you a trial, assuming you keep up the good work. If you three train well, you just might find a home in this gods-forsaken city."

Sykes gathered up the empties and handed them to one of the serving girls rushing around. "That first round was on me. But you'll have to pay for more. Which reminds me, Gunnar, did you scrounge up enough coins today?"

Gunnar nodded and grinned. A trading window appeared, and Gunnar sent over fifty coins.

[*Congratulations! You've proven yourself capable to a mentor of thieves. You've earned the Promising Young Buck badge. Sykes is intrigued by your potential. This will lead to greater possibilities on the path of a Rogue: +1 to Dexterity, +1 to Charisma.*]

[*Congratulations! You have completed the quest* Mermaid's Debt. *You robbed the poor to pay back the big man. Here's 40 XP!*]

Sykes grinned and stowed the coins in his Inventory. "Kid, you got a place to stay? If you got more where that came from, I can hook you up while you prepare for your trial."

"That'd be great actually."

Gunnar paid thirty coins to cover a week's worth of lodging, and Sykes gave him a key to a nearby tenement.

"Stick around," the barkeep said. "The night's show is about to begin."

He winked and then ambled off, still chuckling to himself about the rock star and his ceremony.

Loud murmurings filled the room as one of the serving girls announced that the mermaid show would begin in two minutes.

Em rose from her seat. "Think I'll pass."

Gunnar nodded quickly and stood to join her. "Better be quick. Those serving girls will charge you if you so much as blink in that direction, once the show starts."

"Got a lot of experience with that, do you?" Em teased.

Gunnar stammered. "Er, well—"

Em grinned mischievously.

Kohli glanced over at them, then at the currently empty mermaid tank, then rose to join them. "Well, I got no problems with a good show, but I reckon I should go too. I've got a date with a Maldan maiden I don't want to miss. I'll walk you both out."

The three of them made it out of the tavern not a moment too soon.

As Em opened the door, the crowd began to cheer, and Jiselle the serving girl came hurrying to guard the door, giving Gunnar a sharp look.

They laughed as they reached the street. Darkness had fallen on Thailen, and the city was alive with nightlife. Humans and elves, dwarves and orcs strode through the narrow lanes, several pouring through the Mermaid's door.

Em turned to Gunnar and Kohli. "You boys are all right," she said. "I expect I'll see you around, though hopefully under better circumstances."

Gunnar grinned. "Sykes has some good facilities. Kohli and I will be training around tomorrow, if you want to join us."

Em didn't smile immediately, and Gunnar wasn't sure why. Her thin lips twitched, as though she were considering saying something and thinking better of it, then she forced a thankful smile. "Appreciate the offer. I like to make my own way, but maybe I will sometime. I know where to find you."

She looked up at the sign of the Mermaid, then turned and ventured out into the night.

Kohli shook his head. "Be careful, mate."

"What do you mean?" Gunnar asked.

"I think you know exactly what I mean. She seems cool, but we know nothing about her. She en't connected with Sykes, which means she's connected with someone else. Other guilds. Other masters."

"God, can we trust no one in this place? I don't know you either."

"And do you trust me?" Kohli asked.

Gunnar paused a minute, then scowled. When they'd first met, Scan had told him that their relationship was *Just Doing a Damn Job*. When he checked it after they left the crypt, it had changed to *Ally for Mutual Benefit*.

Was this the most reliable metric for determining who he could trust?

Gunnar wasn't so sure. He wanted to trust his gut, but he also knew his gut had a bit of a naive dumbass tendency.

"You're a scoundrel," Gunnar said. "But we can help each other. Just like in the crypt."

Kohli nodded. "Good. And the girl?"

"She needed our help to get out of that crypt, but up here, I don't know."

"You're getting smarter." Kohli winked. "Or less stupid."

"Thanks."

Kohli shook his hand. "Just remember things aren't always what they appear."

"What do you mean?"

"We got in that mess because of the Red Cloaks. And she just happened to be down there."

"She was ahead of us. You said she was there when you got captured."

Kohli shrugged. "Does that mean she was ahead of us?"

"What? Do you think she's with the Red Cloaks or something?"

"I don't know... Just be careful."

Gunnar chuckled. "I just think that precious ego of yours is hurt because she was more into me than you."

Kohli grinned slyly. "Never said I'm not a petty man. But the logic of it is what gets me. My Charisma is way better than yours."

"You were a grouchy asshole down in that crypt. I doubt that won you any points."

At that, Kohli laughed. "Speaking of Charisma, I'm off to meet that Maldan maid."

"Good luck with that. I'll see you tomorrow."

The thief strode off and out of sight.

Gunnar watched him for a minute, still wondering who he could trust. Then, he made his way down the block to a small tenement at the end.

All the buildings on that street were pressed up right against one another, and Gunnar had a feeling Sykes owned the whole block, maybe more.

Sykes had given him a key to a room on the third floor, and Gunnar found it easily enough. It reminded him a bit of his old dorm room. The only furniture was a framed wooden bed, a nightstand with an oil lamp on it, a small chest that he assumed was for clothes, and a small chair and little round table in the corner.

There was a shared privy and washroom down the hall, which he was not keen on using, based on the smell as he walked past.

Minus the roommate, exactly like the dorms.

Then again, he hadn't actually had to piss since he'd arrived in Thailen. He could see why the developers would remove that particular detail. Come to think of it, that was the first obvious thing in the game that reminded him this was not a real place. He'd been so engrossed in the events of the day, he hadn't thought about the real world at all in hours.

Not that he wanted to remember.

His real world was shit for the foreseeable future, maybe forever. For all intents and purposes, this game was his life now. This realization hit him like a wave, and he suddenly hated that he was alone.

He stripped out of his cloak and pants and lay in bed, trying not to think about the depressing nature of his situation.

He'd had an incredible day. Despite the setbacks, he'd leveled up and found allies, and with a little luck, he might get connected with a guild soon.

But what does it matter? None of this is real.

"The hell are you moping around for?"

If Gunnar *could* piss, he was pretty sure he would have pissed himself. He leapt from his bed, grabbing for the dagger at his bedside.

But it was only Azmar.

The disgusting creature hovered outside his window, which was not really a window at all, just a barred opening with a curtain flapping in the breeze. It faced a narrow abandoned alley.

Gunnar set the dagger down and glared at the creature. "What do you want?" he demanded.

Azmar latched onto the windowsill. "Just here to remind you that jumping off a bridge won't do you any good here. You'll come back."

"Thanks for the advice. If you don't mind, I'd like to be alone."

"Well, the brooding type do well around here, I suppose. Just thought you might like to know that you've caught the eye of Nymoria."

"What do you mean?"

Azmar grinned and leaned up close to the bars of the window. "I mean you did good today. She likes you."

"She's just a damn program, and so are you."

"Considering your Wisdom is still abysmally low, I don't think we'll be trusting your insight."

"Whoopdeedoo, my goddess likes me! I'm still just a damn prisoner doing time."

"You're a Maldan dusk elf and a servant of Nymoria, and she is pleased with your work today. If you keep this up, you might actually make something of yourself in this game. What the hell is wrong with you?"

Gunnar shrugged. "Nothing."

"Well, snap out of nothing then. I said your goddess is pleased with you. She has hundreds of wards, and she sent me to you, by name, to tell you she is pleased with your performance today. That is the entire purpose of your existence, and it could lead to much better things for you—and me! I don't care what triggered this little dark soul of the night—"

"That's not what it's called."

"I don't care what your kind calls it. If you keep this up, I'll move on, and so will Nymoria. And you'll be cow feces like the rest of the good-for-nothings we always end up with."

It wasn't the first time that Azmar had said something like this, and it piqued his interest. Gunnar assumed that Nymoria was connected to the Suits and Ties back in the prison, maybe Azmar too, though he was not entirely sure how. But clearly, there was some inherent inequality going on here. And it affected more than just noobs like Gunnar.

A revelation came to him.

If I'm important to Nymoria, that must mean I'm important to someone IRL.

He turned to Azmar. "Sorry, it's just been a long day. How can I serve Nymoria?"

22

PING

"For starters," Azmar began, still looming in the alley outside his window, "we need to talk about your plans for advancement."

"I'm training with Kohli tomorrow in one of Sykes' facilities," Gunnar said.

"Good. Sykes was impressed too, then. That's good."

"You said that already."

"That's because it's important," Azmar quipped. "Sykes is your best shot at getting into a guild, and that's where your real opportunities lie. If you keep showing yourself capable, Sykes will be good to you."

"And if I screw up?"

"Sykes is an opportunist. He'll get bored quick if he doesn't think you're worth his time and effort. Suffice it to say, for all future references, and for all time, don't screw up. Ever."

"Right," Gunnar said.

"But also, you need to take risks."

"Helpful advice. Don't screw up, but be risky. Sure."

Azmar's yellow eyes glowered in the darkness of the alley. "You need to prove yourself, just like you did today. You were resourceful, you played to the strengths of yourself and your allies, and you didn't screw up."

"Barely. There were about a million ways things could have gone wrong."

"There always will be."

Gunnar sighed. But he had to admit, though things had taken some strange and dark turns, he had truly had a blast down in that crypt. His accomplishments in life had not made a terribly long list, but he was the reason they had escaped. He'd rescued Em and Kohli, and he had led that necromancer to the perfect spot so Em could crush him. He felt a rush of pride.

"So Nymoria could see all that? Everything in the crypt?"

Azmar nodded his ugly head. "You may not see her, but your goddess is paying attention. For now."

The thought did not really bring Gunnar much comfort.

"Speaking of Nymoria," Gunnar said. "Does that same script have to play every time I level up?"

Azmar nodded. "Nymoria hates that recording too. It's really nothing like her at all, but she didn't have any choice in the matter. Go ahead and change it."

"Change it?"

"Check your HUD. You can customize all kinds of things. And you can always revert back to the default settings if you change your mind."

Gunnar pulled up his display and began scanning through tabs he'd not yet had time to peruse.

"Select that little gear wheel in the corner," Azmar said.

Gunnar held his finger over the holographic image, and a whole list of settings appeared. He unchecked the box for the Deity Interaction during Level Ups. He debated whether to continue with the play-by-play notifications during combat, but ultimately decided he liked knowing the exact amounts of damage he was dealing. It would help him strategize weapon choice and the locations of his attacks in the future.

If he wanted, he found he could make a lot more things appear continuously in his vision. But he didn't really need to see his status bars unless they were depleting, and most of the other options were superfluous things like a Money Bag icon or a Hunger meter. He preferred the simplicity of the default setup.

There was, however, an option that intrigued him: Character Scan - Threat Level. If he turned it on, he could differentiate between hostile characters, and it would also appear on his map. Unfortunately, it was a locked feature.

His finger hovered over the check box on the holographic window.

[*Threat Level Scan requires at least Level 10 Perception.*]

Damn, that would be nice. He still had some stat points to use after reaching Level 6 at the end of the crypt quest. Maybe he would have to apply them there.

Azmar cleared his throat, and Gunnar looked up.

"Sorry, any other advice?" Gunnar asked.

"Why would I bother? You don't listen to my advice, anyway."

"What are you talking about? I'm a damn elf because of you."

"Have you set a respawn point?" Azmar glared at him through the window bars.

Gunnar paused. "Er, no... I was going to, but I needed to set it somewhere I had been before. So, I waited. And then, I forgot."

"And then, you forgot..." Azmar let his demonic gaze linger on him.

"Quit it, you're creeping me out."

"You—still—haven't—set—it!" Azmar ground the words out,

as though he were chewing on them and spitting them at Gunnar.

"Alright."

Gunnar pulled up his game map.

He pointed to the location of his own tenement building. "Here seems like a good enough place."

"Does it?" Azmar said, more like an insult than a question.

"No, then?"

"Let's say, hypothetically, somewhere in this world of fiends, you make—I don't know—an enemy. Let's imagine that said enemy finds out where you sleep. They break in. They shank you good and hard. And you come back. Over and over again."

Gunnar grimaced. "Someplace more public? I was thinking about setting it to the Mermaid before."

"Better, but public means someone watching closely could figure it out. Especially considering your association with Sykes."

"Not here, not the Mermaid. So, somewhere secluded."

"Somewhere no one would guess. Somewhere we've been."

"We?" Gunnar scowled. "You want me to mark that damn rooftop from my failed entry quest?"

Azmar nodded. "It's secluded, but close to everywhere you'll need to go. Multiple exit points."

"God, I could have set that this morning."

"I told you to do just that."

Gunnar gritted his teeth, but he shifted the map to reveal that rooftop, and he let his finger hover over the location.

[*Would you like to set a respawn point? Yes/No*]

Gunnar voiced his assent.

Azmar's face settled into something like a smile. "Make the next few days count. You want to make Sykes and Nymoria want to come back for more."

"You make this sound like a date."

"Probably the most important date of your life. And the most exciting I'm sure."

Gunnar laughed. "You're not entirely wrong there."

Azmar seemed a little annoyed that Gunnar had found humor in the jab. He glowered as his long clawed feet released the barred window.

He hovered in the alley, flapping his wings hard. "Getting into a guild is the next step, and the only way to lock in your Rogue class. If you don't prove yourself quickly, people like Sykes will move on to other new recruits with more potential, and Nymoria too."

"And then what?"

"You end up like that leech who stole your XP during your first quest."

Gunnar was surprised by that. "But she was strong."

"In comparison to a noob, sure. If you don't get into a guild, you don't get any of the good and lucrative quests. There are plenty of urchins wandering around like her, forced to prey on whatever they can find, while the real players have the real fun. You don't have to end up like that."

"No pressure, then," Gunnar muttered.

Azmar smirked. "Be smart about how you use those stat points. You can't fix every problem by throwing a knife at it."

With that, the creature flew away.

Gunnar actually felt a little better about his situation, surprisingly. Since he already had his HUD pulled up, he began perusing his character sheet. He still wasn't sure what sort of character he needed to be in this game. A more rounded one? Or more specialized? If he was trying to work his way into a thieves' guild, he needed to know more about them. What were they looking for in new recruits?

His Dexterity had really gotten him out of some binds today, but he expected that Azmar was right. He was embarrassingly weak in a lot of areas. He couldn't run worth a damn, and he really needed to build up Endurance, which was linked to his Constitution. He had already planned and failed to increase his Wisdom. This meant his Perception remained low, and probably limited any spell-crafting he might develop.

More Strength would be helpful in combat. He could handle a couple Fulcra, but things were only going to be getting more challenging, and he wasn't even strong enough to handle heavy-class weapons. Better Charisma couldn't hurt either, especially when he needed to impress guild leaders soon.

He cursed to himself as he scrolled through skill trees with varying degrees of requirements for advancement, all linked to different attributes that needed work.

But what he really needed was to level up, and do it often. And that meant good quests. Between the experience and the bonuses from his achievement badges, that seemed to be by far the best way to progress.

He had nearly settled on a decision when there was a soft ping, announcing a new type of notification.

[*You have received a DM request from Em (Just Em). Do you wish to read it? Yes/No*]

Gunnar paused, thinking of what Kohli had said earlier. It was true, he did not know this woman. But she was also more advanced in the game than he was, and for all he knew, she might be a key ally. Or she could be setting him up somehow.

How was he supposed to know?

Finally, Gunnar did what he should have done the first time he leveled up. He applied both his attribute points to Wisdom, increasing it to Level 7, and he applied his skill points to Perception, raising it to Level 13.

Then, he accepted the message.

23

WISDOM AND ENDURANCE

Em: *Took me a while to find you. There's more Gunnars in this game than you might think. Guess I was right about your creativity, eh?*

Gunnar read the message a couple times, shaking his head and chuckling at the jab. He had enjoyed her company today. But what did she want exactly? He thought for a while about what to write.

Getting to know anyone in this world seemed to be a risk. But he couldn't really think of a reason to be more suspicious of Em than anyone else he'd encountered.

Kohli was using him to gain experience and work his way into a guild. Azmar was using him to look good for Nymoria, who had *her* own agenda. Sykes surely didn't have pure motives.

And if he was honest, neither did he.

This world was already rubbing off on him. He was attracted to Em, but he was mostly thinking about how she could help him.

And the only way he could really assess whether she was a threat or a potential ally was by engaging.

Gunnar: *Whatever you say, Em-Short-for-Nothing.*

There was a pause, and then a flashing ellipsis indicating that Em was forming a new message.

Em: *Sorry I took all the XP with Angus. You did half the work, just got none of the damage.*

Gunnar: *The curse of being the set-up guy who can't sprint up walls and leap from cages, I guess.*

Em: *You did good today.*

Gunnar: *You too. What were you doing down there anyway?*

Em: *I just got in with the Nighthawks...I was looking for a place to grind skills, and wound up down there at the suggestion of another guild member. I bet she knew something about that psycho down there.*

A Nighthawk, Gunnar thought. *So she is with one of the guilds.*

This piqued his interest, but he tried not to let on about it. He didn't want her to think that was what he cared about, so he didn't mention it.

Gunnar: *Well, it's probably messed up, but I'm glad you got stuck down there with us.*

Em: *Me too... hey, um, that Sykes guy, is he all right?*

Gunnar: *He's a con man, a crook, and a sleaze. Seems to be perfectly content profiting off of noobs. But yeah, I think he's all right. As much as anyone is in this place, right?*

Em: *I suppose, but I don't think I trust him... not sure why, just a feeling.*

Gunnar: *Okay...*

Em: *Just be careful.*

Gunnar: *Well, I should probably go to sleep. Big day training tomorrow. See you around.*

Gunnar didn't wait for a reply. He dismissed his Chat window and closed down his HUD. Everyone distrusted everyone in this place, and he was beginning to grow tired of it. He had a feeling that Wisdom was going to be a very important attribute going forward.

He lay down on his decently comfortable bed, and a prompt appeared.

[*Would you like to exit the game while your character rests? Yes/No*]

Gunnar thought, *No.*

But nevertheless, his thoughts drifted to the real world. Particularly, his parents.

The sedation had dulled his memories back when he arrived in Grid Eight, but now, their faces haunted him from his very brief court appearance. His mother had cried. His father had held her, stoic as always.

He tried to push away the guilty feelings and focus instead on good memories from his life before, but nothing specific seemed to settle.

For some reason, he was reminded of when he'd first received a VR headset as a birthday gift when he was twelve. His dad had given the gift, and his mom had said he would waste all his time and it would never amount to anything useful. She had said that a lot in middle school when his grades dropped.

He was beginning to feel as though all those gaming sessions had been preparing him for this.

But he knew that was just his mind trying to make more meaning out of his situation than there was.

His destiny ended the day he killed that girl.

That was reality.

This was just doing time. No matter how many times he reasoned himself into that logical conclusion, he couldn't shake the feeling that there was something more.

He just didn't know what.

[*Buffs Added - A Good Night's Rest — You have increased your Stamina restoration rate by 20% over the next four hours. Build up your Constitution for an even greater effect.*]

———

"Morning, sunshine!"

Gunnar leapt out of his bed in the darkness to find Kohli stooped over him.

He let out a string of curses and the thief laughed, igniting a small lantern. It was still dark outside Gunnar's window. Pitch-black kind of dark.

"What the hell are you doing in my room?" Gunnar demanded, his heart racing.

Kohli grinned, holding up a set of lockpicks. "Time to start training."

Gunnar was the sort of dead stiff he hadn't felt since two-a-day football practices freshman year of high school, which had quickly prompted him to stick to baseball.

He groaned. "It's still dark out. This is a damn game. Wake me up when there's—I don't know—even a hint of light."

"Not if you want to get into a guild. You gotta hustle. Look at me, I was out till 2 AM wooing sexy young maidens. Had some fun. Caught a quick snooze, and now, I'm back to another type of grinding."

Gunnar grunted and turned away from the lantern light.

Kohli ripped off his blanket, leaving Gunnar naked on the mattress.

"Ah, what the hell! You sleep in the nude?"

Gunnar was freezing, and clearly Kohli wasn't letting up, so he stood and got out of bed.

"How I sleep is my damn business," Gunnar said. "Don't wanna see it? Don't wake me up at the butt-crack of dawn."

Kohli laughed. "Good one. Well, quit waving that thing around and get ready."

Gunnar stooped to retrieve his clothes from the floor. "We heading to one of Sykes' training gyms?"

Kohli shook his head with a smirk. "Nah, mate, we're going for a run."

"A run?" Gunnar stopped with his pants halfway up his legs. First the mindfulness skill, and now this? It was his ex all over again. "You gotta be kidding."

"Only if your pathetic Endurance was an act yesterday."

Gunnar grimaced. "I hate this game."

They ran. And ran. And ran. They ran through the streets and along the docks, over bridges and through the empty shells of the markets. They ran all the way to the southern edge of the city, and then, they ran back.

Gunnar's lungs burned after only a few minutes, and his heart felt like it might explode out of his chest. His Stamina kept running down to dangerously low levels. When he told Kohli this, the thief said that was the entire point. They would slow down their pace just enough that Gunnar wouldn't collapse in the streets, and then, they kept running.

Gunnar had to use that damn Mindful Breathing skill to increase his Stamina restoration. But he had to admit, it helped. He even leveled the skill up to 7.

The one and only good thing about running was that it vastly expanded his knowledge of the city. His map had been largely blurred out before, except in the area around the Mermaid. Now, he could see a large portion of the southern part of the city.

Finally, he spotted the glorious sign of the Mermaid. Kohli

slowed his pace and then stopped in the square outside. Gunnar stooped over, hands on his knees, his entire body heaving with desperate breaths.

"Stay standing," Kohli said. "You'll breathe better that way."

Gunnar sucked in a huge breath and said, "Go to hell."

Kohli was grinning. The thief was breathing heavily too, but it didn't take a rocket scientist to tell he had some better physical attributes to work with. The man had made it look way too easy. But then again, Kohli had leveled up a lot in the crypt.

"H-how far... did we... go?" Gunnar asked between labored breaths.

Kohli shrugged. "About two miles."

"That's all?"

Something twisted in Gunnar's gut. He turned and retched next to a lamppost. His stomach had managed to dredge up what little was left of his food from the night before, along with everything liquid he'd had since. Gunnar wiped his mouth with his sleeve and turned to face a laughing Kohli.

[*Congratulations! You pushed yourself so hard you reached the brink of vomiting and leapt right over that precipice. Here's 30 XP!*]

Gunnar shook his head, grateful the streets were still relatively empty. The developers continued to have a sick sense of humor. Achievements for puking? One of them must have been a damn football coach or something.

"Breakfast?" Kohli asked, gesturing toward the Mermaid. "You look like you might need to replenish."

"You're a dick," Gunnar muttered as he followed him inside.

24

THE MISTRESS

THE PLACE WAS dead quiet at this hour. No mermaid shows. No seductive waitresses bustling around. Just the dawn elf who'd served him the first time he'd come.

Gunnar and Kohli sat at the bar.

"What can I get for you, boys?" the elf asked.

"You got any chicken-fried steak?" Gunnar asked hopefully. His head had cleared and his breathing had calmed for the most part. Now, he just felt weak.

The elf shook his head.

"Omelets? Biscuits and gravy? Belgian waffles?"

The elf offered only a quizzical expression in return, and Gunnar had a feeling the man was just an NPC with a limited degree of knowledge outside the actual Mermaid menu.

Gunnar looked at Kohli and the thief said, "We'll take a couple hot breakfasts, Theodore."

The elf nodded and retreated to the back kitchen.

"What's a hot breakfast?"

Kohli shrugged. "Better than the cold one. But don't get your hopes up for one of your fatty American brunches, mate."

The comment was subtle and probably unintentional.

Maybe nothing. Gunnar had assumed Kohli's accent had something to do with his character in the game. But what if it was something more? Gunnar had assumed the man was a fellow prisoner. An American prisoner. But was it something bigger than that?

Theodore the elf returned.

"No coffee either, I suppose?" Gunnar asked hopefully.

Theodore nodded, seeming pleased to have something Gunnar wanted.

But Kohli grabbed his arm and shook his head. "Not the way you're used to. It's black and thick and gross. I've always preferred tea, and that's not terrible here."

"Two teas then," Theodore said and left to fetch them.

"Morning, boys!" Sykes emerged from a back room, grinning far too wide considering it was barely dawn. "What's the schedule today?"

"I'll be hitting the markets this morning," Kohli said. "Then, training gyms this afternoon. I think I'm about ready for one of the guild trials, if you think there's one that might be interested."

Sykes stroked his beard, thinking. "You're close. You reached Level 10 yesterday, which is a fine pace considering you entered the game, what? Three days ago?"

Kohli nodded.

"Give it another day or two. You never know what a guild is going to throw at you. Have you done any break-ins yet?"

Kohli shook his head. "Nothing more than slipping into a few apartments and lifting some coins."

"Pull a job on a minor noble. Not the Golden Hills, and sure as hell not in the High City. But something more than common folk. A merchant lord of the Heights would be good. Now, I'm talking guards and everything. Even better if they have a family. But don't go too crazy. If you fail, it'll set you back. I think I've got one in mind."

A holographic window popped up in front of Kohli, and the thief perused his new quest.

"What about me?" Gunnar asked.

"You proved yourself resourceful and capable yesterday," Sykes said. "Which is good. I was about to give up on you after you fell for that undercover milkmaid."

"I'm working on my Wisdom."

"Good." Sykes crossed his arms. "You showed you're worth my time, Gunnar. For now, at least. Your first goal today is to get your papers sorted out. That will help you avoid a few run-ins with the Red Cloaks. The guilds won't take on recruits who could get deported at a moment's notice. Next step is preparing for the trials. Bad news is you've got a time cap to get ready. You have to successfully complete a trial within your first week in the game."

"Only one attempt?" Gunnar asked.

"Most guilds aren't interested in failures. But some of the lesser ones have been known to take Rogues on a second trial. Rarely a third. Never more. If you fail the trials, you'll be out on your own, no guild, and it is much harder to advance without one. If you die and have to go back to the real world, you lose game time, as you've already experienced. So be careful. You need all the time you can get. But if you prove yourself, you just might turn out all right. But first, the papers."

Quest Update - The Forger

Quest Type: Common

Description: Ugh! A paper-gathering quest? Who cares about all this political mumbo jumbo? You do, if you want to get anywhere in this game. And you don't exactly have a great track record without these stupid papers. Love 'em or hate 'em, boring administrative quests aren't going anywhere. Least, not for you.

Objective: Meet the Forger and get your papers sorted.

Reward: A little less harassment from the fuzz.

Do you wish to accept? Yes/No

━━━

Gunnar had discovered a feature called MiniNav during his perusing the previous night, and it allowed him to keep a small version of his map of Thailen pulled up in the corner of his vision. If he was more advanced, he could use the map to see mobs coming before they reached him. But right now, the streets on the map were empty.

It was the exact opposite on the streets themselves. The city was brimming with people. Gunnar swore it was busier today than the day before. People pressed up real close all around him.

He couldn't help but practice his skills as he made his way through the city. He didn't expect to spend too much time pick-pocketing, unless, of course, he failed to earn his way into a guild. But it made for some non-combat XP, and he figured it would only help his Dexterity, which, thus far, had been his best and most productive attribute.

Might as well make this gathering quest worth something.

He stuck to people around Levels 5–7 and tried to make sure he knew where they stowed their money before he made his move. He also tried to avoid people who could kick his ass if they caught him, which included basically every orc and anyone carrying a sword.

Merchants tended to act suspicious whenever he came near, maybe because he was Maldan, so he tried to focus on customers. Preferably common-looking folk.

In the crowded square in front of the Temple of Luka, there were vendors selling doves and other small animals for offerings, and there were a number of minstrels and other performers, which offered fine distractions for unsuspecting targets.

Gunnar robbed four people in all, gaining sixty-three coins and 20 XP, the largest amount coming from a Level-8 Bard who left his hat out for tips while he played. Gunnar acted as though he were giving money, but instead, stole a handful of coins. It was right as the man finished his song and many in the crowd were applauding. The man was too fixated on the attention of the crowd.

Gunnar increased his Perception skill as well, but he decided to stop after that. Something about stealing from normal folks made him feel uneasy, and he just couldn't shake it.

If they were nobles, like whoever's estate Kohli was hitting tonight, he didn't think he would feel the same way. But preying on other low-level people seemed too much like what Sheira had done to him.

He thought back to what Azmar had said last night. He had to prey on low-levels to prepare for the trials. Sheira preyed on low-levels because she'd failed the trials. Something about it felt too intentional. Maybe it was different for those in the guilds. But even they weren't the ones running this city.

That was made clear when Gunnar was shoved out of the way near the edge of the temple square by a pair of Red Cloaks.

He was about to make a run for it, when he realized that they were shoving everyone out of the way, not just him, not just the Maldans. They were clearing the way for an elegant black carriage pulled by a pair of shining ebony horses, which slowly ambled through the streets. Some of the people in the crowd shouted complaints, and the Red Cloaks beat the shit out of one man who became too vocal.

Gunnar kept still, watching as the man tried to get back to his feet.

His face was covered in blood from a blow from the butt of a sword, but the man kept protesting. "I pay my bloody taxes. I pay for these streets, and I damn well—"

A ruthless guard drew a bludgeon and cracked it over the protestor's back, dropping him prostrate on the stone.

"Damn it," Gunnar muttered.

He knew this was just some NPC, but he couldn't help himself. He hurried over and stooped beside the beaten man. Blood streamed from his mouth, and he could barely lift himself up to his knees.

"All right, you've made your point," Gunnar said, holding up his hand pleadingly over the man.

The Red Cloak had the bludgeon raised for another strike.

"He's done resisting," Gunnar said.

"I en't..." the protestor spluttered.

"Shut up!" Gunnar said through clenched teeth.

The guard smiled, as though dying for another chance to use the club.

But at that moment, the shiny black door of the carriage opened, and a woman in a white gown with a scarf of white furs emerged. Her skin was pale as the moon, her hair as dark as night, and her eyes even darker. She leveled a cold gaze on the crowd as she stepped out.

"Bow before Mistress Leilani!" one of the guards announced.

The others in the crowd dropped to one knee immediately and bowed their heads. Gunnar followed suit, but the damn idiot beside him somehow managed to pull himself up to his feet, head held high.

"Bow," the Red Cloak said angrily.

"For god's sake," Gunnar whispered, "know when to jump through a damn hoop."

The man spat blood before he spoke. "The nobles won't

take another thing from me," he said, looking straight at the Red Cloak. "All of 'em can go to—"

The Red Cloak bludgeoned him again, right in the face. Blood flew everywhere, and this time the man didn't get up.

Blood poured from his cratered face, but he didn't move.

Gunnar doubted there was any hope for him, but he hastily checked the man's pulse.

He was definitely dead.

Gunnar's heart pounded in his chest. He was worried he might be next, but no one seemed to care about him. Or the dead man for that matter.

The mistress made no expression. Gunnar wasn't even sure she had noticed what was going on.

Blue sparks hovered over the man's body.

[*Would you like to loot Glenn the Courier? Yes/No*]

Gunnar had no intention of doing any such thing. But before he could respond, the Red Cloak who'd killed him stooped and took all the man's items, including his cloak.

The blue sparks vanished, and the Red Cloak turned away.

The crowd parted, and a stream of Red Cloaks spread out, clearing a path all the way to the inner gates of the temple. More carriages approached behind her, and more nobles emerged.

It was only then Gunnar realized that not all people were allowed inside. That's why it was so crowded on the streets. This square was as close as the common people could come to the temple.

Gunnar watched Mistress Leilani make her way to the Temple of Luka, fear and rage coursing through him.

That was the sort of person he wanted to rob.

As soon as the noblewoman reached the inner temple gates, the crowd returned to what it was doing, and Gunnar hurried away from the square.

25

HEL'S OASIS

The crowds thinned as Gunnar moved beyond the temple area, past the market where he'd pickpocketed the day before, and into an "undiscovered" zone on his map, where he was forced to work off of general compass directions. Slowly, he made his way to the western edge of the city.

Here, the buildings were mostly one or two stories, and Gunnar could see treetops and the crests of rolling hills beyond the city walls. In the distance, a massive peak cut into the horizon. Its brilliant glacial snowcap reminded him of the way Mt. Rainier had dominated the landscape back home. Even from this distance, he could tell it was massive, maybe even a volcano too.

A large market surrounded the western city gates, and there were a number of permanent shops in the area as well. It was nowhere near as crowded as the markets near the wharf. Gunnar understood enough about the city to know that shipping dominated commerce around here.

According to his greater map of the realms of *Pantheon*, there were no major cities or nations to the west of the city until you crossed the mountains and reached a kingdom called

Bahkar. But Gunnar's fate seemed to be tied to Thailen for the foreseeable future, so he was not too concerned with what lay beyond at the moment.

Finally, Gunnar located the trader's shop he was looking for. It was situated between a barber and a butcher, and the sign said "Hel's Oasis."

Inside, a corner of the place looked about how Gunnar imagined a general store might have looked in the Old West. There were several large barrels and sacks of goods, most labeled for what they were: flour, sugar, and so on. But the rest of the store looked like one of those old consignment shops his grandmother had liked. Shelves were lined with completely random items—an assortment of weapons, alchemy supplies, tools, scrolls, in no particular order. There were leather-bound books on the same shelf as a pair of blacksmith hammers and some hand-carved wooden children's toys.

There was a counter at the end of the room, and an enormous person stood behind it. Or rather, an enormous creature. A desert orc, judging by the strange horny carapace that encased its back. The creature was tall and gray-skinned and ugly, dressed in a plain brown skirt, so he assumed it was female. Her graying long black hair was pulled back in a messy, matted braid. The orc did not smile. Or scowl. Or offer any expression at all.

"You the owner?" Gunnar asked.

The woman pursed her thick gray lips. "Who wants ter know?" Her voice was somehow gravelly and whiny at the same time.

"A friend of Sykes. I'm here for—"

"I know what yeh're here for." The woman pushed open a door behind the counter and gestured for him to come with her.

Gunnar glanced around, but there was no one else in the place. He followed the orc into a back room stacked with crates and barrels and lined with messy shelves filled with everything from potions to food to weapons.

"Hel's Oasis," Gunnar said. "That's some nice irony."

"What yeh talking 'bout?" she asked irritably.

"You know... Hell... Oasis?"

"Hel's short for Helgerazandgra. The sign en't big enough, so I shortened it."

"Oh."

There was a small table in the back of the storeroom spread with papers. At a glance, it looked like receipts and ledgers, and like everything else in the store, it was not especially organized.

There were two chairs at the table. Hel took a seat and motioned for Gunnar to join her.

The disorganization clearly posed no problems for her. She reached beneath a sheaf of paper and pulled out an official-looking scroll of parchment.

It had Gunnar's name, a sketch that looked remarkably accurate, and some BS information about his origins.

"How'd you draw me so well?" Gunnar asked, impressed by the attention to detail in the sketch, though it did throw him for a moment remembering that this was his new face. It had been a while since he'd seen his reflection, in this world, or the real one. "You've never met me. It's really good."

Hel laughed. "Heh, yeh think I can draw with these paws?" She held up her big thick hands for him to examine. "I got an artist. Sykes gives him a description, and he makes the sketch. Elves en't the easiest ter forge papers for, least not in a city built for humans. But there's another clan of dusk elves at the base of the mountains—the Arkan. Humans still don't love 'em, but they done business with the Arkan for decades, and there's more than enough round the city ter cover up yer Maldan-ness."

Gunnar felt a twinge of resentment about that. "Cover up? Why can't I just be a legal Maldan?"

Hel huffed. "Maldans have a reputation for laziness in this city. Island elves and all that."

"Sounds a bit racist."

"Welcome ter Thailen. That's why yeh're bloody here, getting yer damn papers forged."

Gunnar took the papers from her.

"So, I'm Arkan. Been in the city for three years. Hold on, it says here I immigrated to get away from the... barbarism of the elven clans?"

Hel smirked. "Red Cloaks love that sort of shit. Yeh want them ter harass you? Or yeh want them ter let yeh go 'bout yer business?"

Gunnar shrugged, but knew it wasn't worth arguing over. There was more information about a work permit. Apparently he'd been a street sweeper for the past year. And at the bottom was a fancy insignia, the kind that required pressing a specific ring into melted wax.

"The ring's what makes forging these tricksy. And expensive. They change the rings every few months, and when there's backdates involved... Most Red Cloaks might not know which ring was used during the winter three years ago... but all it takes is one, and yeh're on a ship filled with scum, set to be dumped off on some island somewhere."

So that's what they do with the "undesirables."

Hel opened up a trading window showing his purchase. Gunnar sent her forty coins, and she handed the forged papers over to him. Gunnar stowed them in his Inventory.

Hel crossed her thick arms over her chest and scowled. "Anything else yeh're looking for?"

"What've you got for a Rogue class?"

Back in the main part of the store, Hel sifted through layers of junk to locate some items of interest. Several were beyond Gunnar's price range, including a dark elven cloak, a set of polished steel daggers in a black leather case, a pair of enchanted glasses that enhanced Dark Sight, an array of potions and spells, and so on.

Unfortunately, Gunnar did not have much money left. Suddenly, he felt foolish for feeling guilty about pickpocketing. But he also knew that cutting purses was hardly the way to gain the sort of items he would need if he managed to gain the favor of a guild. He needed some real money, which meant a real job. Soon.

In the end, he replenished his sheath of throwing knives and promised himself that he would be back soon for better items.

"Do you trade?" he asked after he'd paid her.

Hel grunted. "Stolen items, yeh're asking about?"

Gunnar shrugged.

"Look around," Hel said with a laugh. "What yeh think all this stuff is?"

Gunnar smiled. The gruff orc woman was growing on him.

"Yeh bring me something good, I'll always take a look. But be mindful who yeh steal from. Someone too high interest, and they come looking. And it should go without saying, but never from the Red Cloaks."

"Never?" Gunnar asked.

"Never. There's an agreement. A peace, yeh might say. Yeh're a good Arkan boy now and a citizen of Thailen. Yeh been in this city for a good long time, and yeh're supposed ter know the way of things. Never touch the Red Cloaks. Never touch the priests of Luka. Never touch the nobles of the High City. And yeh just might make yerself something. Now, if our business is concluded, I'll ask yeh to kindly carry on. I don't like anyone lingering around too long."

"You worried about Red Cloaks?"

"Yeh've still got plenty to learn, boy. But yeh might do all right. Good luck too yeh in the trials. Yeh keep coin coming my way, and we'll get along just fine."

With that, Hel turned away and returned to her back room, leaving Gunnar alone.

For the briefest moment, he considered all the unattended items before him. But something told him Hel had thought through those sorts of basic risks. He couldn't imagine there was surveillance, but maybe enchantments or something.

It wasn't the sort of job he was looking for, anyway.

26

GRINDING

An hour later, Gunnar and Kohli met outside one of Sykes' tenement buildings. A door led down to a basement area, and Kohli led the way. Out of curiosity, Gunnar had hit the place with Scan as he approached, but it offered no information. On the outside, it appeared to be an utterly irrelevant part of the game world.

They wound down two flights of stairs and reached a short, dimly lit hallway. At the end, a large bouncer stood with arms crossed before an iron door. Sykes had given Gunnar a wooden coin with a mermaid stamped on it, and when he showed it to the bouncer, the man nodded and opened the door for them.

The room beyond was open and vast and contained elaborate training equipment. There were some strength training stations that were fairly typical of a real-world gym, if more primitive—rudimentary weights made of hunks of iron linked together with chains, pulleys anchored to the wall that lifted large crates from various angles to work different muscles. And, just as in the real world, there were large men in skintight shirts working through sets, grunting and groaning as though they were making love to their precious weights.

There was an entire chamber filled with automatons wearing cloaks arrayed in a complicated cutpurse's course. The training dummies were set on tracks that moved around as though they were people walking through a market square. Impressively, they could shift, stop, turn around, and even lash out. A teenage boy worked his way through the maze of trainers, but when he reached for a pocket in one of the cloaks, the dummy spun and punched him in the stomach with a mechanical arm. Gunnar watched the boy try and fail multiple times, and each time red lights flashed while a dummy clocked him good in the stomach.

"Are they all mechanical?" Gunnar asked. "Or are there enchantments involved too?"

"Both, I expect," said Kohli. "Whatever would require electricity to run IRL, I reckon it runs off magic here."

There were other sections focused on combat, including melee, distance, and stealth attacks. Some trainees fought dummies, while others sparred with partners.

But the part of the training gym that intrigued Gunnar the most was the climbing walls at the far end. He'd been on a few rock climbing walls in his life, mostly just fooling around with some friends, but this was tailored for breaking and entering. As they approached, a tall, lanky thief scaled a wall of stone, hanging on by nothing but his fingers, clinging to small ridges and cracks until he reached small platforms and eventually a windowsill at least twenty feet up. It was impressive how fast the man moved. He practically leapt from hold to hold, despite the fact he wore no safety rope.

"You should see him in the parkour room," Kohli said.

Gunnar just shook his head, enamored. The man leapt up from the window, and with a pair of lightning-fast moves, he reached the top, thirty feet above them.

"I've got a second-story job tonight," Kohli said. "This is

where I'll be grinding. But you're free to do what you like. The cutpurse course would be a good one for you."

Gunnar shook his head, eyeing the climber, who rappelled back down with a rope from the top of the wall.

"I'm not going to pass any trials pickpocketing," Gunnar said.

━━

Needless to say, Gunnar did not start out on the thirty-foot wall. In the corner, there was a ten-foot beginner's wall, the sort he imagined lined the gardens of noble estates. Even on the short wall, Kohli insisted he wear a rope tied around his waist, which one of the gym workers tended to while Gunnar attempted his first ascent.

The cracks between stones were minuscule, and Gunnar marveled at how easy the man on the big wall had made it look. Gunnar tried pulling himself up with weak handholds, but then found a better foothold a little further down the wall. He stepped up with one foot still on the ground, and looked up. On the side of one stone, the crack was deeper than the others. Gunnar slid his left hand up and wedged his fingers between the stones, activating the Wall Climbing skill he'd unlocked during their mad flight from the horde in the crypt.

Gunnar quickly discovered there were holds all over the wall, if he looked closely enough. One stone jutted out slightly more than the others, and he reached with his right hand, lifting both feet off the ground. Then, he located a groove between stones for his left. And so it went for several more moves.

Until his foot slipped.

The rope cinched tight around his gut, cutting into his skin, but he didn't hit the ground. He hung there, swinging violently for a moment. Glancing down, he realized he had only made it three feet off the ground.

The rope attendant lowered him down, and Kohli smirked. He had removed his boots, Gunnar realized.

"Those leather boots don't have great traction," the thief said. "Find the right merchant, and you might be able to buy some better ones for this sort of thing. I've heard there's some custom-made ones that ninjas wear with grippy soles. Pretty sure that Em chick had some. There's enchanted ones too that are even better. But for now, I prefer to climb with bare feet."

Gunnar took the rope off and rubbed at his stomach. That thing was going to saw right through him by the end of the day if he kept falling.

"You couldn't have told me that before I fell?" Gunnar asked.

Kohli shrugged. "Better to learn from mistakes, right?"

That sounded annoyingly like Azmar.

Kohli took his place at the base of the wall. "My turn."

The thief didn't bother with the safety rope on the short wall, and he made it look way too easy. With a series of quick intentional movements, Kohli pulled himself to the top and grinned back down at Gunnar.

It took Gunnar four attempts, but he scaled the beginner wall, earning a paltry 5 XP. Kohli said that while you could level skills quickly in places like this, the game made it much harder to advance in Glory just from training scenarios. It pushed players toward taking on dangerous quests.

There were other spots along the short wall that were more difficult, and by the end of the afternoon, Gunnar had conquered a section of the twenty-foot wall. His Strength and Dexterity both leveled up from the experience, and Wall Climbing reached Level 9 by the time they were done. Gunnar was determined to keep going as long as Kohli, but when the thief finally said he was done, Gunnar was nearly spent. His forearms were pumped and his fingers were stiff and aching.

"I've got to go get ready for my job tonight," Kohli said as they exited the training gym. "I'll see you tomorrow."

"Good luck," Gunnar said, trying to mask his jealousy. He'd hoped the thief would invite him along. But he knew that was a stupid thing to get sore about. He didn't even know if that was allowed with a job like that.

Once he was alone, he deliberated what to do. Despite the fact that he had accomplished much today, he couldn't shake the feeling that he was falling behind. He thought about pinging Em—perhaps she could help him make more contacts with the Nighthawks—but decided against it. He didn't want to seem like he needed her, or her guild.

He went to the Mermaid to catch a meal before things got crazy during the evening shows. Sykes was nowhere to be seen, and Theodore, the dawn elf man who tended the bar, was not particularly chatty or knowledgeable. When Gunnar asked him about getting some quests, the man suggested mingling around the bar, like a good NPC would.

Gunnar downed an ale, glanced around the room full of rough-looking men and women, and shook his head. The likeliest quest coming out of a place like this probably involved drunks or prostitutes, and he was not particularly eager to deal with either.

He couldn't stop thinking of the man who'd been clubbed to death right before his eyes. He knew none of this was real, and yet, he found himself thinking of the prison less and less. In a matter of days, this place had begun to feel more like his actual reality. And something about that thought scared him.

Gunnar was half tempted to exit *Pantheon* on his own tonight, while he slept in-game, just to see his actual face, his actual body again.

But no. What he really needed was to make some legitimate progress.

Yesterday, the crypt had been a big risk with a good payoff. He'd gained several levels and caught the notice of Nymoria. Today had been interesting enough, and he'd accomplished some necessary mundanities, but he wanted more excitement. Kohli was out on a quest, and here he was moping.

Better to take a risk and fail than sit around, right?

Maybe it was time to put his new Wall Climbing skills to use. Gunnar paid his tab and made to leave the Mermaid. But as he crossed the room, he noticed a very angry-looking dwarf staring at him with cold dark eyes. As Gunnar reached the door, the dwarf left his seat. Gunnar hurried outside. The last thing he needed today was to deal with some piss-drunk little craftsman.

Outside, the night was cool and damp. The breeze cut straight through his cloak and shirt. He shivered, wishing he had some thicker clothes. Maybe next time he went to Hel's Oasis.

Gunnar was in the middle of the square outside the Mermaid when he heard the rapid patter of small boots on the stone. He turned.

"'Ey!" the dwarf shouted. The little guy's red beard flapped in the breeze, and he pointed right at Gunnar and shouted again. "Yeah, I'm talkin' ter yeh, yeh daft bastard! We need ter talk!"

27

WHEN NOT TO PUNT A DWARF

Gunnar grimaced as the impressively quick dwarf approached. Now that he wasn't in the middle of a pub, where anyone else might join the brawl, he felt more confident. There was a reason he hadn't chosen the dwarf race when he entered the game. Dwarves were not warriors in this world, and he felt confident he could take him if it came to it.

Never punted a dwarf before...

He braced himself, ready to draw a dagger at a moment's notice.

Dimble the Dwarf

Level: 9
HP: 100/100
MP: 60/60
Threat Level: White
Description: Dwarves can be feisty little buggers, and you really don't want to get on their bad side.

A new Scan feature had unlocked when he'd leveled up his

Perception last night, but based on the dwarf's expression, its accuracy seemed highly questionable.

"The hell do you want?" Gunnar demanded.

The dwarf slowed his pace, still looking angry. "I saw yeh at the temple today."

Gunnar didn't like where this was going. "Don't know what you're talking about. So, you can kindly piss off. I've got things to do."

Dimble let out a low growl. "Gods, all yeh elves are the bloody same! Heads up yer own asses. As though the tall folk o' this city have treated yer kind any better than they have us. They don't even care about their own kind!"

Gunnar paused. He was no longer sure this dwarf was drunk. Or about to attack him.

"What're you talking about?" he asked.

"That human yeh tried ter help at the temple. Don't try an' deny it. I know what I saw. He was being stupid, an' yeh tried ter help him. Right in front of the bloody Red Cloaks."

Gunnar felt uneasy. Was this some sort of bounty hunter or something? Had the guards come looking for him?

But he pushed the thought aside. He was a Thailen citizen now, and he needed to act like it.

"I tried to stop him from doing anything stupid," Gunnar said. "Like mouthing off to a damn noble. But it didn't matter. He got himself killed."

The dwarf lowered his voice. "Yeh put your neck on the line for someone yeh didn't know."

"How do you know I didn't know him?"

"Because yeh didn't mourn for him. Yeh did what yeh could to try an' help him, and when it didn't work, yeh carried on."

"Did..." Gunnar was not sure what to make of this dwarf. "Did you know him?"

Dimble shook his head. "I'm part of an acting troupe. We

perform in the square every Altar Day. That's how I saw yeh with that man who was killed."

"And what? You followed me?"

The dwarf chuckled. "The grace of Barduum, I s'pose. I was walking home and saw yeh go ter the Mermaid, so I followed yeh in. I need help, and I thought yeh might be able ter..."

The dwarf's voice broke off, whether intentionally or not, Gunnar was not sure. A single tear streaked down his face.

"It's me brother, yeh see. He's been abducted by one o' them bloody nobles."

Gunnar scowled. But then again, he had been wanting a quest.

"What would a noble want with your brother?"

"The high folk like ter use us for entertainment. They do... terrible things ter us at their damn parties."

Gunnar felt uneasy. "You don't mean they..."

Dimble nodded. "Yeah... dwarf tossing."

Needless to say, that was not what Gunnar was expecting, and the disgust with which the dwarf said it made it sound even more absurd. Gunnar fought to remain composed, but for god's sake, they had watched a man get beaten to death in the streets earlier today, and this dude was worried about some party game?

Dimble gritted his teeth with righteous anger. "Nimble's a good man. A true craftsman. He's served Mistress Periden for years, fashioning weapons for her guard, even things for her own escapades. Yeh know, battle corsets."

Battle corsets? This sounded like an interesting noblewoman.

"I'm not sure I'm following the... direness of the situation here," Gunnar said.

Dimble's face grew red. Gunnar worried the small man

might try and tackle him or something, but he merely stamped his thick boot on the cobblestone.

"Not following? What do yeh think happens ter a man after hours o' being tossed around on the stone ground? What do yeh think happens if the damn nobles decide ter make dwarves duel with smithy hammers an' hot pokers? I had a friend who couldn't walk for a month after being *summoned* for a party. An' his fingers were so abused, he couldn't craft for a year. Some never craft again. An' some never come home at all. If that happens ter Nimble, all he's worked for... his children... please, I need yer help."

Quest Alert - Dimble's Nimble

Description: Dimble's brother Nimble is being held captive at the estate of a middle nobleman named Count Dravingdel. This place may not be a fortress, but it is surrounded by a fifteen-foot wall and guarded by plenty of Red Cloaks.
Objective: Save the dwarf, save the world.
Reward: You get to get off your ass and do something today!

Do you wish to accept? Yes/No

Gunnar mentally accepted the quest, and the alert vanished.

Dimble gave him directions to the estate, and Gunnar placed a marker on his MiniNav. The party was in two days, so he at least had some time for reconnaissance before he dove all in with this quest. The estate was in the northern part of the city, in an undiscovered zone, so it would take a while just to get there.

He set out, drawing his cloak tight around him against the cool coastal air. He followed the waterfront, passing rows of ships loading and unloading crates of goods from who knew where. It reminded him of the night he arrived, and he wondered how many more Maldans would be arriving later tonight, and whether Sheira was out here somewhere waiting for her next target.

Gunnar continued past the massive Temple of Luka and crossed the heart of the city, slowly making his way toward the hillsides beyond, which were lined with the spires of noble estates like the spines of a ferocious beast.

It impressed him, not just the level of detail in this world, but the originality. Thailen did not seem to imitate any real world city that he could think of. The architecture was similar enough to depictions of ancient Earth cities that it didn't throw him. But the sharp jutting towers and harsh angles of the stone felt otherworldly. Almost Gothic, but different, though he didn't have the architectural knowledge to quite put his finger on it. Even the geography beyond the city felt alien, as though he were visiting a newly discovered corner of the world.

Or maybe I just never got out much, Gunnar thought with a chuckle.

As he walked further, a message notification flashed, and he pulled it up.

Em: *What you up to tonight?*

Gunnar dismissed the message for now. He was getting close to the Golden Hills of Thailen.

Two small rivers cut their way through the city. They winded down from mountains, threading between the city's hillsides and eventually pouring into the bay. Beyond the second river, the city swiftly transformed, streets widening and buildings spreading farther apart. Trees towered above him like in the parks back home.

There were iron gates across the road ahead and an outpost of Red Cloaks. Gunnar realized he had already reached a wealthy, unwelcoming part of the city a moment too late. A pair of guards came alert and strode toward him.

Red Cloak Guard

Level: 5
HP: 65/65
MP: 30/30
Threat Level: White

With its accuracy no longer in question, Gunnar loved the new information. Not only could he detect the level of threat by these mobs, there was also a white dot on his MiniNav corresponding to each guard. That could prove really useful, especially with this new mission.

As the guards neared, Gunnar produced his identification papers, crossing his fingers that Hel had done her job. One of the guards glanced briefly at them, then waved them away.

"What business do you have in the Golden Hills?" he asked.

"We've got no need for any new street sweepers or the like," the other said.

Gunnar shrugged. "Heard rumors of a big party in a couple days. Thought there might be need for temporary work. For the cleanup."

The guards frowned. "At this hour?"

Gunnar didn't skip a beat. "These are a sweeper's waking hours. Thought I'd check before I begin work for the night."

Both their faces softened, seemingly satisfied at the answer.

"You'll be wanting to talk to a man named Turk from Dravingdel's staff. Afraid he's not available at this hour."

"We'll pass the message along," said the other guard.

Gunnar smiled. "I'd appreciate it."

The guards took down his message, and Gunnar bid them good night. He walked back the way he'd come, waiting until the moment that the guards' dots disappeared on his MiniNav. Before he reached the bridge across the river, he ducked into the trees, activated Dark Sight, and sprinted into the darkness.

Gunnar came to a thick stone wall at the edge of the wooded park. The trees had been intentionally trimmed back so as not to provide an easy means of summiting, and the wall itself was formed so that it leaned back. To climb it, he would have to hang at an angle.

He cursed, ducked back into the cover of the trees, and followed the park's edge for a half mile, but it was the same everywhere. And beyond the park, there were more gates guarded by Red Cloaks. But he was not about to give up that easily.

Gunnar investigated the wall more closely. It was a solid twenty feet tall. There were small iron outlets fixed into the stone intermittently along the length of the wall, likely for draining the streets above when it rained. These were set at different heights in a diagonal pattern up and down the wall. But between them, the stone was cut so smooth, there was hardly a grip in the space between them.

With a couple brief attempts, he confirmed that he was not going to be able to climb it. Not with his current skills.

He pulled up the chat feature in his HUD and decided to respond to Em's message.

Gunnar: *Doing some recon for a new quest. Interested? I think I could use your skill set.*

28

RECON

GUNNAR WATCHED the ellipsis flash as Em formed her response. He instantly wondered if he was making a mistake. Truthfully, he'd been excited to hear from her, but he also kept thinking about what Kohli had said the previous night.

Em: *Uh, you THINK you could use my skill set?*

Gunnar: *All right. I could most DEFINITELY use your help. I'm at the edge of the Golden Hills, trying to figure out how to scale their walls.*

Em: *Get creative!*

The ellipsis hovered for a full minute before she completed her response. He began to wonder whether she thought this quest was a bad idea.

Em: *On my way. Send me your exact location.*

It took him a couple minutes to figure out how to share his location from his MiniNav, but Gunnar was glad he didn't have to ask her for help with that too. Em found his spot in the forest about a half hour later, and together, they surveyed the wall.

"I was thinking maybe those drain holes," Gunnar said, pointing, "but I don't know if I can jump between them."

Em just shook her head, grinning. "Yeah, you could try that, I suppose, if you're trying to make this recon as hard as possible..." She reached into her Inventory and produced a length of rope with a four-pronged grappling hook attached at one end. "Or you could use something like this."

Grappling Hook
Item Class: Uncommon, Dwarf-crafted
Quality: Above Average
Weight: 3
Durability: 14
Description: A length of rope attached to a metal hook. You toss it around and hope it sticks. I'm sure there's an insult lying around in there somewhere.

The hook was dark gray and made of a lightweight metal, like aluminum or something, though it seemed far sturdier.

"Or maybe something like this," Gunnar said with a nod.

"You need more gear," Em jabbed.

"I need more money first. Hence, why I'm here."

"Fair enough. What sort of bonehead quest brings you to the Golden Hills, anyway?"

Gunnar shrugged. He told her about his quest, and the trouble it was already throwing at him.

Em chuckled. "I could have told you a Golden Hills quest might be more work than it's worth."

"That's very helpful now."

"Hey, don't complain too much." With that, Em heaved the

hook up. It disappeared in the dark night above, but when Em gave the rope a tug, it held. "You first."

Gunnar took the rope in his hands and began to pull himself up, but as soon as he did, something shifted. The rope came tumbling back, and Gunnar fell on his ass.

The hook clanked on the ground between them.

"Damn, it slipped out," Gunnar murmured as he got back to his feet.

"Don't beat yourself up, some just aren't very good their first time."

[There's the insult we were looking for!]

Em smirked, picked up the hook, and gave it another heave. Gunnar pulled hard on the rope before climbing this time, and it held fast. Then, he tested it with a little weight.

"Get it in there good?"

Gunnar just shook his head. "You're the worst."

Hand over hand, he began ascending the rope. The first couple moves were not too difficult, but his arms quickly began to tire, and his feet did not offer great grip. The rope swayed more and more as he went.

He was glad he'd worked on his climbing skills so much. He felt stronger and more comfortable than he had even earlier today. Once he was about halfway up, he realized if he wrapped the rope once around his leg, his feet could find better purchase. He quickly made it to the top of the wall and pulled himself over.

On the other side, the wall was only a few feet tall, with a narrow road built into the hillside. He checked the hook, which had wrapped around the trunk of a small tree. When Gunnar was satisfied it would continue to hold, he looked back over, just in time to see Em's face pop up and over the wall.

She had made the climb a whole lot quicker than he had.

Her chimera claws probably didn't hurt. Em wrapped the rope up and stowed it and the hook back in her Inventory.

There were several roads branching up the sides of the hills, leading to large estates. Gunnar could make out the soft glow of lanterns across the hillsides, and at least a few guard towers along the roads. He expected these streets were patrolled by plenty of Red Cloaks, in addition to whatever guarded the estates themselves.

After checking his MiniNav, he led the way up the road. They kept quiet as they went, hoods up, Stealth activated, and carefully avoided the rings of light around each lamppost. The line between the lit area and the darkness seemed to Gunnar as though it were a near-physical barrier, and if they were to cross it, he feared they would instantly be detected by one of the distant guard towers. It was one of the few times when it was clear that this world was fabricated. Light behaved differently IRL, not drastically so, but it was noticeable.

Gunnar wondered if he would always notice things like that. If he spent multiple days here each time he slept in the real world, would the prison start to feel like the odd place?

Em grabbed his shoulder and pulled him back toward the shadowy hillside. A pair of soft voices echoed from around the corner. Gunnar and Em crouched behind a small bush as two Red Cloaks came into view. One man, one woman, both Level 8s. The man held a lantern out in front of them, a circle of light radiating from it. He turned, and the light came treacherously close to where they were hiding.

The guards whispered to one another, complaining about the cool weather and the coming winter.

Em pressed her palm to the base of the bush, and it began to softly expand and thicken. The branches rustled a little.

"What was that?" The man turned around and shone the

lantern in their direction again, but they were shielded by the thicker branches of the bush.

"Squirrel or something," the female Red Cloak said.

Gunnar and Em held their breath and kept absolutely still.

Finally, the light passed, and the guards continued on their way, remaining white dots on his MiniNav until they passed out of sight. But he and Em waited a full minute before moving.

"That was close," Gunnar murmured.

"Guards are on high alert in the Golden Hills. Higher-level Red Cloaks than you've probably run into in the rest of the city. But hey, that's what you get for accepting this quest."

＝

Dravingdel's estate was another quarter mile up the road, and they reached the outskirts without event. The entire place was surrounded by a fifteen-foot wall. The area around the road was especially well lit, and there was a guardhouse outside the wrought-iron entrance gate to the sprawling manor. Gunnar and Em ducked off the road and followed the wall along the steep hillside. The thick grass made him a little nervous about snakes, though he truly didn't know anything about the wildlife in this realm of *Pantheon*.

On the back side of the estate, Gunnar and Em ascended the wall and peered at the sprawling extravagance within. Several acres of gardens and fruit trees surrounded the massive home. A great circle drive led up to two gigantic doors that reminded him of a cathedral entrance. There was a barn, a carriage house, and a greenhouse, as well as a path lined with trellises and a large paved patio with a fountain. Gunnar tried using Scan, but much as he expected, the place offered him no information.

"This is a middle nobleman?" Gunnar murmured.

204 / S.A. KLOPFENSTEIN

"You should see the High City," Em said.

Guards bearing lanterns patrolled the interior of the estate with large black dogs. Gunnar counted eight stationed around the grounds, plus three more around the perimeter of the house. The manor itself bore three towers, with guards posted on the roof of each one.

"Damn," Em said softly. "You know how to pick 'em."

"Guessing Dravingdel doesn't keep prisoners in the barn, eh?"

"Not likely. You're not thinking of trying anything tonight, are you?"

"Tomorrow. The party is the next day. So I guess it has to be tomorrow. With a house like that, he must have some sort of holding cell in the basement."

"Maybe," Em said. "I don't like it, though." She slipped back down the wall.

Gunnar took one last look at the estate, then dropped down to join her. "What do you mean?"

"Bad luck to hit a noble like this. Too much can go wrong."

"Well, I don't have much choice now."

"You could quit the quest. You'd pay a penalty, but there's worse things. If I've learned anything in this place, it's that messing with nobles is not a great idea."

Gunnar shook his head. "I need to at least try. What's the worst that could happen? If I fail, I'll drop the quest."

"If you fail, you could end up in exile. Or marked for life by the Red Cloaks. I can tell you, the guilds don't take on new recruits like that. If you fail, things could become a lot harder for you going forward."

Gunnar gritted his teeth. "I'm not ready to bail just yet."

Em nodded. "Then you're going to need better intel."

[29]

NIGHTHAWKS

EM SAID NO MORE, she just walked off into the night. Gunnar hesitated. He wanted to observe more about the guards' patrol patterns.

But in the end, he hurried after her.

The chimera girl walked briskly through the brush, straight down the hillside, rather than returning to the road. Gunnar struggled to keep up with her, and nearly tumbled down the hill at one point.

But they reached the outer wall of the Golden Hills after only a few minutes. Silently, Em set up her rope, this time without the hook. She tied a careful knot around the tree. "Whatever you do, don't let the rope go slack."

And then, she began rappelling. Gunnar held on to the rope, keeping the pressure on once she'd reached the bottom. He followed after. When he reached the base of the wall, Em took the rope from him. She let it go slack, then gave it a sharp tug, and the rope cascaded down.

"I'll be in touch," she said, gathering up the rope in a loop over her shoulder.

"Wait, better intel. Do you have any ideas?"

"I told you, I'll be in touch." Em stowed the rope in her Inventory, and it vanished from Gunnar's sight.

"You mind being slightly less cagey?"

"Yes."

Gunnar shook his head. "Give me something here."

Em pulled him closer and spoke softly. "I want you to talk to someone from my guild. But I need to see if she's even interested. So, I'll be in touch."

With that, Em strode off into the darkness, leaving Gunnar alone at the base of the wall.

———

He didn't feel like waiting around for answers, so he returned to his apartment and slept. Not for terribly long, as Kohli turned up very early for their morning run. Gunnar felt less winded this time, so he supposed that meant he was improving.

But he still hadn't leveled up Endurance since the crypt, a harsh reminder that his development ratings were a big deal. He seemed to level up Dexterity-based skills every time he practiced. But he definitely needed to be a better runner, so he pushed himself hard the entire time and tried to focus his Mindful Breathing, syncing with the cadence of his footfalls. He was able to find a rhythm for a while, but by the time they finished their loop, his lungs were an inferno in his chest.

It paid off though.

[*Congratulations! You've self-flagellated enough to reach Level 9 in Endurance! We would like to see more puking though.*]

When they returned to the Mermaid afterward, Sykes was nowhere to be found, and Kohli was especially silent.

"Everything go all right last night?" Gunnar asked, after the quiet grew too awkward for him. He'd always hated long silences.

"What?" Kohli shot to attention as though Gunnar had woken him from a stupor. "Er, yeah, it was fine. Really fine. I got my summons for a trial actually."

"Really? When? Which guild?"

"Tonight. The Marauders. They're not one of the major ones, but they're pretty decent. I'd be lucky if they took me on."

Gunnar felt a pang of jealousy, though he was truly glad for the thief. Kohli had one job to prove himself. If it went well, he would be set with the Marauders. He'd have consistent quests and lodging and legitimate allies. All the things Gunnar needed as well. It struck him that he and Kohli could end up in rival guilds.

But he didn't say any of that. He congratulated him.

"Say," Gunnar said, "you heard much about the Nighthawks?"

Kohli's eyes went wide at the name. He glanced around, though the place was nearly empty. "I'd be careful about mentioning them around here."

Gunnar lowered his voice. "What do you know?"

"Not much. Look, Sykes don't take sides in guild wars. He's a hustler who deals with the highest bidder. The Mermaid is neutral territory. All I know is when Nighthawks come around, Sykes gets nervous. They're big time, and he don't seem to like them."

Gunnar thought of what Em had said the other day. She didn't seem to like Sykes much either. He wondered if the man had known who she belonged to.

"Where'd you hear about them anyway?" Kohli asked.

Gunnar thought better than to say that it was Em, and he definitely didn't say that they might be helping him with a quest.

He shrugged. "Around the city. Noticed people mentioning their name in whispers, and it piqued my interest."

Kohli eyed him for a moment, then nodded. "Well, I should go. See you at the gym this afternoon?"

Gunnar nodded, and Kohli ran off to prepare for his task that night.

The conversation left Gunnar feeling uneasy. He didn't much care whether Sykes liked the Nighthawks. Once he was in a guild, he didn't expect it would matter anyway. But something about the way Kohli reacted left a gnawing feeling in his gut. Kohli feared the Nighthawks.

And that unnerved him.

But that wasn't all that was making him nervous. Hard as he had tried the past few days, he couldn't seem to figure out what the connection was between the prison and Thailen. At first, he had assumed it had to do with the gods, but he felt less sure about that now. The gods seemed little more than a mechanism for experience in the game thus far. As best he could tell, they didn't seem to have any actual sway in this city. The guilds seemed more likely.

He knew he needed to go back to the prison soon and try to learn more.

Gunnar made his way out of the Mermaid as more customers began to arrive. Outside, the square was filled with people and vendor carts and more than a few types of livestock, but what instantly drew his attention was what sat parked near the center.

A black carriage drawn by two black horses.

It was enclosed, with a large door on either side, elegantly carved, and though Gunnar knew nothing about woodworking, he could tell it must belong to someone very rich or very powerful. In addition to the black-clad driver, there were two cloaked figures standing guard outside. And they were staring right at Gunnar.

He glanced behind him, but there was no one else they could be looking at. Gunnar met the gaze of one of the men, and he gestured for Gunnar to approach.

A lump formed in his throat. He couldn't imagine this was good.

The guard gestured to him again.

Gunnar tried to reassure himself that he had papers now. He was a proper citizen of Thailen, and he needed to act like he had done nothing wrong. Which was actually true for once.

He tried to act casual, ambling his way over.

"What can I do for you, fellas?" Gunnar asked, trying awkwardly to sound casual.

"Our mistress wishes to speak with you," said one guard.

"Y-your—"

The door popped open from within, and Em glared out at him. "Just get in, will you?"

Gunnar was flummoxed. "This is your..."

Em just glowered at him, and Gunnar quickly entered the carriage. The inside was dark. He tried to use Dark Sight, but it didn't activate.

Shit, this carriage must have some sort of protection against magic.

As he took a seat, he realized Em was not alone.

A woman sat in the dark on the bench opposite him. She wore a black gown with a dark hood drawn up over her head. A long slit traced midway up her right thigh, her long porcelain legs the only part of her immediately visible.

Gunnar looked up into the dark expanse of her hood, but could not quite make out her face in the low light. She had a presence that felt somehow immediately imposing and inviting at the same time. Which unnerved him.

Em sat down beside him, and both of them faced her. For the first time, Em's company offered him no comfort. The door closed and the carriage started moving. Wheels clacked on the stone, and the whole thing swayed back and forth.

"This is the young man you spoke of," the woman said in a quiet but firm voice.

Em nodded. "He's the one from the crypt. Currently under the tutelage of Billy Sykes."

The woman offered no reaction to this information.

"I've seen you before," she said, leaning forward in her seat.

"I doubt that," Gunnar said. "I've not been around any nobles."

The woman scowled and drew back her hood. "Weigh your words, boy. Those who don't appear only as fools."

The woman's skin was porcelain-white, her hair as dark as her eyes. Her black clothes gave her a very different look than the first time he'd seen her. Gunnar's senses went on high alert as recognition dawned.

"You're Mistress Leilani," Gunnar said. It came out more of a whisper than he had hoped.

"You do know her?" Em demanded.

"There was an... incident in the streets," Leilani said. "Outside the temple."

Gunnar bristled at her casual tone. "Incident? A man was murdered."

Leilani nodded. "Indeed. You cared about that man, did you?"

"I didn't know him. But no one deserves what your men did to him."

Leilani smiled enduringly. "My men? What did I tell you about weighing your words?"

Gunnar glowered. "Are you saying those guards were not there clearing the way for you to go to the temple?"

"Of course they were. As they do for all high nobles. But that does not mean that I ordered that man's death."

Gunnar tensed, and Em gripped Gunnar's shoulder.

"What are you saying?" Gunnar demanded.

"This city is not all that it appears," Leilani said. "There are systems set in place far beyond my control. Those guards obey the orders of the magistrates of the city, dictated by the High Priest of Luka and the great trading masters of the Altaean Alliance. I did not kill that man in the temple square. I was a bystander the same as you. You would be wise to reserve judgment until you understand the way this city works."

"Well, this city is... fucked up," Gunnar said after a moment.

"And you're observant," Leilani said.

Gunnar glared over at Em, suddenly doubting that anything she'd said had been true. She was no Nighthawk. She served the damn nobles.

Em remained expressionless.

"Look, I don't know what's going on here, but—"

"Weigh—your—words—Gunnar—Ashwood."

As she spoke, Leilani drew up her sleeves, revealing long, slender arms. For a moment, Gunnar had no idea what she was doing. But then, something flickered and came into focus on her pale skin. An intricate tattoo of a black hawk diving for invisible prey.

Gunnar shook his head. She was such a powerful noble, he could hardly believe it.

"You're a Nighthawk?"

30

PARTY INVITATION

THE CARRIAGE RATTLED SOFTLY as it winded its way through the streets of Thailen. The noblewoman grinned slyly.

Em just nodded. "I told you, you needed more intel."

Gunnar sat still, not entirely sure what this meant. *A noble is part of a thieves guild?*

Whatever he had expected coming into this carriage, he had not expected that the mistress from the temple square was a leader of the Nighthawks.

"Em tells me you show promise," Mistress Leilani said. "It is my understanding that you helped her when she got into a bind. She tells me you are not a typical scoundrel. Is that true?"

Something about the woman's question seemed to hint at something beyond. As though she wanted to delve into the heart of his character in a way that went beyond his actions in the game.

Gunnar shrugged. "Depends on the incentives."

"You don't know what type of person you want to be. That's all well and cute. But you will need to choose soon."

"That's why I'm here, I assume."

Leilani leaned forward in her seat. "This city is ruled by

manipulative bastards. And the scoundrels of this city, and their little guilds, have long played right into their hands."

"What do you mean?"

"Your friend Sykes is a prototypical example," Leilani said. "He's very comfortable in his position, isn't he?"

"Sure," Gunnar said. "Are you saying he's one of these manipulative bastards?"

Leilani let out a soft chuckle. "More like a *manipulated* bastard. He helps thieves find their guilds, takes their coin, and he gets more and more comfortable in his little mermaid strip club. The Red Cloaks don't bother him, the guilds don't bother him. He's just another cog in this despicable machine."

"And the guilds? More cogs?"

"Guilds are allowed to rule their corners of this city, but only because it is just so. They have no true sway, much as they might like to think they do."

"And the Nighthawks?" Gunnar asked.

"The Nighthawks are not a typical guild. You may have heard murmurings about us in the underbelly of this city. Your quest at the Dravingdel estate interests me."

"Got a lot of love for the dwarves, do you?"

"Your sarcasm will not get you far," Leilani said coldly. "Let me guess, you have been instructed by some scoundrel in this city to leave the nobles and the Red Cloaks alone."

"And the priests," Gunnar added. "Don't forget about them."

"Yes, and why do you think they are to be left alone?"

"Well, we're a bunch of thieves. Makes sense not to rock the boat too much if you don't want to get caught."

"A convenient system, isn't it?" Leilani asked. "For the nobles and the priests."

"Doesn't seem too bad for the guilds either, or for Sykes."

"You are right about one thing," Leilani said. "It is all about incentives. You understand this, hence your hesitance to accept you are different."

"I'm a damn criminal."

Leilani paused for a moment, and Gunnar worried he had acknowledged something he shouldn't have.

"You have made specific actions, Gunnar Ashwood. You might say, your choices have the power to echo into eternity in this world. This city is built for self-serving bastards. But you have shown yourself to be cut from a different cloth. So, what happens? A dwarf turns up with a quest you are meant to fail."

"You're saying that dwarf is working for this system too?"

"No, I'm saying you are meant to fail that quest. But that does not mean it is impossible."

"And that's where the Nighthawks come in," Gunnar said.

Leilani shifted in her seat and nodded. "Something like that. Em tells me you plan to attempt a jailbreak tonight."

"Yeah..."

"I would like to propose another way." Leilani reached into her ornate leather purse and produced a scroll of parchment.

Work Order

This hereby states that Gunnar Ashwood, a dusk elf of the Arkan clan, is cleared to enter the Golden Hills. He shall report for service at Dravingdel Estate on the eighth evening of the month of Curran, as an attendant at Lord Dravingdel's party. Per the orders of,

Turk Landis

Captain of the Guard

Gunnar read over the work order multiple times. "This won't work. The entire point is to rescue the dwarf before the party begins."

Em had been silent for some time, but she gripped his arm

now. "These types of sideshows never come out right away. They begin with more standard fare."

Leilani nodded. "The nobles like to put on the appearance of propriety. But once they're good and drunk... their baser inclinations emerge. I expect there are worse things than dwarf cockfights prepared. Dravingdel is not a high lord, but his security is strong enough that you will not make it far if you attempt to break in before the event. We can get you in on the night of the party. The rest is up to you."

"So, what? I'm just supposed to sneak into his dungeons in the middle of a party full of nobles?"

"There will be a lot going on," Leilani said. "Plenty of distractions. This is not a castle, and it will have no dungeon. Dravingdel likely only has a few holding cells down in his cellar. A few tossable dwarves will hardly be the focus of his security that night, and as a servant you will be expected to go in and out of the house throughout the night. Em will be there to help you. It should be straightforward enough."

Gunnar thought for a moment. Em smiled at him. But something felt a little too good to be true about all this.

"And for your help?" Gunnar asked. "What do you want from me?"

Leilani leaned back in her seat and smiled. "Em told me your Wisdom was not terribly high, but I'm not sure I believe her."

"I'm working on it," Gunnar said, gritting his teeth despite himself.

"Very good," Leilani said. "There is a man named Admiral Benton who is expected to be in attendance at this particular party. He has been away for some time, rounding up pirates across the Altaean Sea. He's a well-known man in the city. Bombastic and loud and easy to spot in a crowd. He'll be conversing with plenty of people over the course of the evening, but one of them will be delivering a secret letter. I need you to intercept this letter and replace it with one I have drawn up."

"What's in the letter?"

Leilani hesitated.

"You want me to trust you?" Gunnar asked. "You gotta give me something."

Leilani grimaced, then spoke in a soft voice. "The letter contains the whereabouts of a notorious privateer named Black Heart."

The name meant nothing to Gunnar, but he chuckled at how clichéd it sounded.

"Saving cutthroats doesn't sound terribly noble."

"Nobility is always a facade," Leilani said. "And I never said the Nighthawks were concerned with piety."

"This sounds quite a bit more important than a dwarf," Gunnar said. "I'm not sure this is really a fair trade."

"Fair trade?" Em said, appalled. "Don't you get it? You're being offered a guild trial."

Gunnar had not picked up on that. "Oh."

Well, that is very interesting...

Leilani smiled and leaned forward, her fingers brushing his knee. Her eyes flashed in the dim light.

"I can assure you, Gunnar, if you succeed, you will be well compensated. The scoundrels under my care want for nothing. But first, you must prove yourself."

Quest Alert - The Purloined Letter

Quest Type: Rare

Description: Admiral Benton carries a letter of grave importance to the Nighthawks. If you want to know more, looks like you better show yourself useful to the mistress.

Objective: Steal and replace Benton's letter with one from Mistress Leilani.

Reward: You complete your Guild Trial for the Nighthawks.

Do you wish to accept? Yes/No

Gunnar mentally assented.

Immediately, Leilani sat back in her seat, and Gunnar felt a rush through his body, a part of him longing for her touch again.

The carriage came to a halt, and the door opened. Leilani gestured for him to exit.

"I must ask that you tell no one of this trial," the mistress said.

Gunnar did not ask why, he merely nodded.

"You'll be needing some nicer clothes as well. This is a high-brow event, even for the staff."

"Yes, ma'am."

Leilani's lips drew into a pursed smile.

"I like you, Gunnar Ashwood. Don't prove my intuition wrong."

With that, she closed the door.

Gunnar stood on a strange street in the heart of the city, watching as the horses ferried Leilani and Em away. It was not until the carriage vanished from sight that a sudden chill came over him.

He did not fully understand what had happened. But he was fairly certain that the mistress had cast some sort of charm on him, and only now had it worn off enough for him to notice its absence.

Her absence...

Whatever her true reason, Leilani had wanted to be damn sure that Gunnar would accept her quest.

Gunnar set out into the city at a brisk pace, wondering what exactly he was getting himself into.

31

OLD FRIEND

Gunnar found a haberdasher's shop near the temple market, but quickly found he did not have enough coin for any decent black tie getup.

So, it was back to the streets.

There might not be anything glamorous about swiping coins from unsuspecting victims, but Gunnar did find a certain satisfaction at his successes. He pushed himself into situations that he suspected would be more like his upcoming transaction at the party. He even tried his hand at swapping out coin purses with purses filled with pebbles, so they wouldn't realize anything was missing. It was harder than it sounded to swipe and drop in the same movement. The first couple attempts, he was sure he would give himself away, and he was ready to sprint away. But he continued to rack up successes and a little non-combat XP along with them.

Outside the temple, he struck up a conversation with a dawn elf, critiquing the quality of a certain merchant's sacrificial doves. The end result was a bargain for the dawn elf and a fifth successful snatch for Gunnar.

He walked away, and a notification appeared.

[*Congratulations! You've got a knack for purses there, Coach! You have reached Level 14 in the skill Pickpocketing. You have reached Level 15 in the skill Perception.*]

[*Congratulations! You have reached Level 7! You have earned Glory for your goddess Nymoria. You have received one attribute point, which can be distributed at any time. But remember that every choice you make will echo into eternity. Choose wisely.*]

Gunnar shook his head. It was pretty much the same spiel, with or without Nymoria's recorded appearance. The little jingle was annoyingly repetitive, but he actually found he missed seeing his patron goddess. Something about the impersonality of the new message left him feeling more alone in this world than he already had been. As though the AI were now his only ally in this game, which was not a comforting thought in the least. He pulled up his HUD and reconfigured his settings for Nymoria's script.

He opted to delay placing his attribute point for the time being. With enough coin in his own purse now, he returned to the haberdasher and left with a decent suit with a frilly white shirt and collar that felt very Revolutionary War era. He just needed a good powdered wig. And maybe some Ben Franklin–style shoes.

Gunnar had tallied up a good haul—over a hundred coins, even after purchasing his suit. It was getting too easy, and it began to show in the results, as he achieved lower XP and fewer coins with each snatch, especially after passing Level 7.

He was going to have to find some better ways to earn money in this world soon. Though hopefully his trial would solve that problem.

Gunnar lost track of time as he made his way across the city. When he reached the training gym, Kohli had already left for the day.

Gunnar spent some time in the pickpocketing course,

maneuvering amongst the mechanical figures. It was good enough practice, but he felt it was not quite a match for the real thing. He spent some time on the climbing walls until his forearms got too tired, and then he finished out his grinding session with throwing knives. He probably should have reversed the order. His forearms were pretty pumped from climbing, and his aim was not as great as it had been in the crypt. But with focus and time, he managed to adjust for the discomfort.

He advanced his Throwing Blade skill and improved his ambidextrous throws. He wasn't sure how necessary the skill would be for his party-crashing quest, but it had come in handy before.

When he left the training center, night had fallen. He was growing tired of the routine of eating all his meals at the Mermaid, and besides, it was late enough that the shows were probably about to start.

So, he ventured into the city.

The streets were largely empty, though the taverns were rocking with shouts and cheers and maniacal laughter. Gunnar strolled along the wharf, taking in the scents of the sea. Fishermen unloaded the day's catch, heaving enormous swordfish into wheelbarrows that then were rolled over to a cleaning station strewn with blood and entrails. There were metal cages filled with lobsters and barrels of shellfish lining the docks. It was not all that different from the fish markets back home, just with older and ricketier gear.

There were few other pedestrians at this time of night, just fishermen and sailors going about their business, so when Gunnar spotted an older woman talking hurriedly to a young orc, it caught his attention. The woman gesticulated as she talked, and when she pointed back down the wharf, he caught sight of her Maldan face in the lantern light.

Oh, you've got to be fucking kidding me.

He hit her with Scan, and sure enough...

Sheira - Level 15

HP: 120/120
MP: 130/130
Race: Dusk Elf
Clan: Maldan
Disposition: ??
Relationship: Single and Ready to Mess You Up Again
Description: She might share your heritage, but she's not exactly sentimental about it. Steer clear if you know what's good for you.

His entire body tensed at the sight of her, and he quickly resolved what to do.

Gunnar kept his hood up. Neither she nor the orc seemed to notice as he neared.

Sheira grasped the orc's arm, as though about to hurry off, and Gunnar couldn't help himself.

"I wouldn't go with her, man!"

They both glanced up. Gunnar was only about ten yards away. Sheira glared as he approached.

"What're yeh talking about?" the orc grunted.

"Look, I don't give a damn," Gunnar said. "You do you. But whatever she just told you, she lied."

"Don't listen to this street rat," Sheira said. Her eyes leveled on Gunnar, recognition dawning. They weren't filled with the rage he expected, but rather, resigned defeat.

The orc glanced from Sheira to Gunnar and back again, then shook his head.

"She'll shank you good and hard the first chance she gets," Gunnar said. "Just sneak off into the city. Get someplace safe. But this ain't it."

Sheira did not seem to know what to say. She shrugged, trying to act like she had no idea what he was talking about.

"I'm outta here," the orc said, and hurried off.

Gunnar gripped the hilt of one of his daggers as the elf turned to him, suddenly remembering that she was the one who had given this particular blade to him in the first place. And after she betrayed him, she'd left it. And somehow, that realization stole the satisfaction of this little piece of revenge.

"That's for Vampire's Glory," he said, lacking the angry resolve he'd imagined only moments ago.

Sheira gritted her teeth, hand at her own blade. Then, she shook her head. "Well, you've wisened up, at least, I'll give you that."

She turned to walk away.

"That's it?" Gunnar asked.

Sheira turned back. "If you wanted a duel, you'd have attacked by now. We're even, as far as I'm concerned. I've got things to do, unless you're planning on following me and scaring off every noob I target."

When Gunnar hit her with Scan after first spotting her, to his amazement, he had found that she had only leveled up once since their last encounter. He'd advanced six times in that time. And he now realized that Azmar hadn't been lying about people like her.

Gunnar guessed she'd done most of her leveling before her trials and was now just scraping away an existence in this world. Hell, even her progress bars seemed low for her level.

The AI had warned him about approaching her to begin with, but somehow, that only steeled his resolve.

"How long has it been?" he asked.

"What're you talking about?"

"Since your trials?"

"What trials?"

"You failed your guild trials, right?"

Sheira glared. "How could you know that?"

"Intuition, I guess."

Something changed in her, then. Her body relaxed. She released the dagger at her belt. Her face was expressionless, but there was something in her eyes.

"I didn't fail... I was set up. Basically screwed over my chances in this place. That orc was the closest I've come to another good mark since I got you."

"My trial's tomorrow," Gunnar said.

Sheira shrugged. "Good for you."

"Which guild did you try out for?" Gunnar asked.

"Doesn't matter. They're all the same. Chew you up and spit you out as soon as it suits them. Look, I've got work to do."

"Let me buy you a drink," Gunnar said.

Sheira looked at him suspiciously. "What do you want?"

Gunnar reached to his belt and produced the dagger she had left him back on the rooftop. "Why'd you leave this?"

Sheira grimaced and then nodded. "All right, I'll have a drink with you, but not at a pub."

Gunnar looked up quizzically. "Where else would we get a drink?"

"Someplace neither of us has to pay."

32

DRINKS ON THE HOUSE

SHEIRA LED Gunnar into the western portion of the city. Not far off from Hel's Oasis, the city walls and most of the buildings in the area were shorter. There were small inns with rowdy crowds, but the streets themselves were largely empty. They passed a row of nicer townhomes, set back against the walls, each secured by several personal guards. The black-cloaked sentries glowered at them from doorsteps as Gunnar and Sheira walked by.

When they passed the row and moved into a quiet business district, Sheira turned to him. "Those houses belong to some of the lesser merchants. Merchants in this district conduct most of their business themselves. They aren't backed by the bigger trading companies like the sea merchants are."

"Not sure I follow."

"Merchants like that leave for days, sometimes weeks at a time. Most have families, but there's a few that stand empty, except for a few guards outside."

"But how do you get in?"

Sheira motioned for him to continue following. They passed

through a winding market and soon reached the square where Hel's place was located.

The western gates towered above all else in this corner of the city. Even from the streets, Gunnar could see the imposing crimson cloaks of several members of the city watch posted upon the battlements on either side. Large torches cut through the night like fiery blades high above.

The gates themselves were twenty-foot-tall slabs of thick wood, and they were barred shut with large metal locks all the way up the sides of both doors.

Sheira pointed at the gates.

"You taking me out to the woods?"

Sheira smiled. "We're breaking into Xander Fero's house."

"From the woods?"

"From the unguarded back side."

Now, Gunnar smiled back. He'd instantly liked the elf woman, that is, until she shanked him, and now, he remembered why. That same spark was showing again, and he had to remind himself that she could still be a threat. He knew this might be a stupid idea, but his gut told him this was important.

Sheira was important somehow. The AI had tried to turn him away from her, and he was beginning to wonder if there had been a reason.

There was a smaller door cut into the gate to monitor travel into the city. A pair of guards stood watch, but as they approached, the two stepped aside and let them go without a word.

"The Thailen government don't care about who's leaving," Sheira said, "just who's coming in."

A trader's road winded off into the night, but Sheira led the way off the road and into the woods. After twenty minutes of trekking through bramble, they emerged along the western wall in a small clearing. The spot was midway between two towers, about one hundred yards in either direction. As usual, the night was cloudy over Thailen and offered sufficient darkness for them to sprint across the clearing undetected.

Sheira removed her shoes and stowed them in her Inventory, then gestured for Gunnar to do the same. Without another word, the elf woman began climbing. In less than a minute, she had reached the top. The wall was a good thirty feet high, taller than anything he'd climbed yet. He was about to begin his ascent when a rope smacked him in the face from above.

Gunnar had kind of wanted to test his abilities, but a thirty-foot fall would not exactly be good for him. He took hold of the rope and began to climb. The stone was freezing on his feet, and the rough-hewn rope left his hands feeling raw, but he reached the top with no trouble. Sheira was crouched behind the crenellations along the wall-walk, gathering up her rope. She glanced over the other side, then moved a short distance down. Below, the wall was lined with rooftops about ten feet down.

Sheira slipped over the parapets and quickly climbed down the short distance.

Gunnar glanced up and down the wall, but there was no movement from either of the towers.

Just Red Cloaks gathered around torches.

The wall was formed of rectangular stones about two feet in length and one foot in height, and the mortaring between them left just enough space for Gunnar to wedge his fingers and toes. The cold sent aches shooting up his bones.

Gunnar reached the roof, which was flat and covered with bird shit and crumbled pieces of stone. He quickly put his shoes back on and blew warm breath on his hands. Sheira led the way to a locked door, which she swiftly picked.

Inside, the townhome was silent but for the creak of their footsteps on the floorboards. It was nice enough, Gunnar supposed, though the walls were decorated with rather generic tapestries.

Even he could tell that this place was owned by someone who wanted to be like the rich, but wasn't one of them. The wood paneling on the walls was painted white, but was cut at plain, sharp angles, with no decorative engraving.

The entire top floor seemed to be an office. There was a plain-looking and very untidy desk at the far end of the room, some shelves lined haphazardly with scrolls and ledgers, and a table with a pair of chairs.

Sheira scanned the room, then made for a cabinet by the table. She produced a pair of glasses and poured from a decanter of yellowish liquor.

"Nothing fancy," she said, handing it to him.

"You break into a lot of these places?" Gunnar asked.

Sheira shrugged. "When I feel like it. Merchants like these are just wealthy enough to have a liquor cabinet to try to impress business partners, but they're also just wealthy enough to keep their real valuables in banks, so it's not good for much. Unless you like thrift store tapestries."

Gunnar glanced at one of the decorations, which boringly depicted a caravan traipsing along a road in a meadow. The colors were muted and everything was very linear and uninteresting to look at.

There were a couple small cushioned chairs at the back of the room, and they took their drinks and sat. For a while, they just sipped what Gunnar thought was probably gin in silence. It stung his throat but warmed him up quite a bit.

"Drinks on the house," Sheira murmured, downing her glass with the second swig. She filled it again. "It's the simple pleasures, am I right?"

Gunnar nodded and much more slowly sipped his own liquor.

"You had a spark," Sheira said after a pause. "That's why I left that dagger behind. Most noobs in this game are cutthroats from the moment they get here. But you were different. And a bit helpless. Figured you'd need it."

She might not have said it, but the dagger was as close to an apology as he figured this woman ever got.

"Looks like I may have underestimated you, though," she added. "A trial, eh? Who with?"

Gunnar hesitated. "I'm not really supposed to say."

"Nighthawks, then?"

"You heard of them?"

"Enough to know they're powerful, and other guilds envy them. Could be good fortune for you."

"Could be?"

Sheira sighed. "You need guilds to advance. But it doesn't mean they need you."

"What happened?" Gunnar asked. "How did someone like you fail their trial?"

Sheira downed another drink and sat silently for a moment, weighing her words. "I was betrayed by my guild, and a player I'd grown close to. Gave me up to the Red Cloaks. Nearly got deported from Thailen. Barely escaped. I've just been scraping by ever since. This isn't a fair game, Gunnar. I was the most promising recruit in my guild. I did everything right. And I still got screwed."

"Why would they betray you?"

"Don't know. Maybe I was too ambitious. Maybe they didn't want me to get too far."

With that, Sheira stood. She returned the decanter of gin to its rightful place, but she set her empty glass in the middle of the desk.

She wants Fero to know someone was here.

Gunnar shook his head with a smile and did the same.

"We should go," Sheira said. "We can drop on this side of the city with my rope. Then, split up."

Gunnar nodded. "Thanks for the drink."

Sheira turned to him from the doorway. "Don't forget who runs this show, Gunnar."

[PART 4]
GUILD TRIAL

HE SWAM BACK INTO CONSCIOUSNESS. Real actual consciousness. Not because he died. This time, he chose to return.

After successfully descending from the rooftops in-game, he'd returned to his apartment back in Sykes' tenements and gone to sleep, but before he had, he'd selected the option to exit the game while his character rested.

My character...

Because Gunnar was not his actual name. He was Jake Darrow, the convicted felon.

The machine whirred as tubes retracted from his body and the needle withdrew from the receptor in his spine. He sat up, feeling dizzy as his mind adjusted to his actual body.

"Wanted to feel what the old bones are like again, did ya?"

It was Shad. The prison guard loomed over him, looking uncannily iridescent in the harsh light of the room, a reminder that he was only a hologram. Jake blinked hard, and the image returned to normal.

"Something like that," Jake said. He carefully stepped out of the chair. His legs felt shaky for a moment, and his head spun.

He held on to the chair's edge, and the vertigo faded away, though there was a mild ache in the back of his head.

Jake massaged his neck for a moment, his fingers repeatedly brushing against the disk of metal attached there.

"The headache will go away shortly," Shad said.

"How long was I in there?"

Shad shrugged. "Same amount of time as the last time. It's the morning of your second day in Grid Eight."

Jake shook his head. It was what he'd expected, but it was no less disorienting. He'd spent three full days in-game, and as far as a sense of time went, they'd felt like very long, full days.

And it could have been much longer.

He'd chosen to come back.

"Most prisoners come back of their own will early on," Shad said. "You'll get over it after a couple times. Eventually, you'll wish you could stay there forever."

"Can't they just pull us out?"

"No need to. It's the same time here either way. You come out after a good night's rest. Time's relative and all that shit, right?"

It was hard to get his head around.

"Does it work that way for you too?" Jake asked.

Shad smiled, but didn't answer.

"Reckon it's time to go to work. That sludge ain't gonna shovel itself."

It didn't take long shoveling sulfurous gunk before Jake regretted coming back. It was monotonous, backbreaking labor. He worked alongside two other dudes, who were assigned to a specific skid steer. The only breaks they got were while it unloaded its bucket into a larger truck.

The other guys kept quiet for the most part, except to complain about the stench, which was persistent despite the hazmat suits. But it was the worst when they had a water break in between loads and had to pull back their hoods.

Around midday, they took a longer break in a small nook of a room outside the main bay of the power plant, where the stench was slightly more bearable. Their skid steer driver went off on his own, leaving the three lowly inmates alone, slumped on a bench, chugging cups of water.

Right before their break, there'd been an incident with one of the neighboring crews. A huge dude had flipped out on another inmate, yelling and throwing a few punches. It ended quickly, when an electric shock hit him like a wave and left him twitching on the ground with his tongue hanging out.

"What a dumbass," said Isaac, a bald black dude on Jake's crew.

Jake nodded.

"Probably earned himself a week stuck IRL," said Kyler, a pale blond guy with a Mohawk.

"Hell, he mighta pissed the bed on the game entirely."

"Can... can that actually happen?" Jake asked.

All three looked hard at him.

"Sorry, new guy," Jake said.

"Right," Isaac said.

"Course you can," Kyler said.

"But isn't that how we eat and everything? While we're hooked up."

"Oh, you get hooked up still," Isaac said. "You just don't play. You lay there and try to sleep with a needle up your neck and tubes everywhere else. That's what I heard, anyway."

"That dumbass has been in trouble before," Kyler said. "Some dudes never learn."

A flashing timer over the door indicated they had three

minutes left of their break. They sipped their water in silence for a bit.

Finally, Jake just decided to ask. "You guys know what the deal is with this game?"

Isaac and Kyler glanced at one another, then glanced up, as though someone were watching overhead, which might well have been true.

Kyler shrugged. "I signed up to test a game and cut my time. That's all I need to know."

The driver of their skid steer returned from wherever he'd gone, and they followed him back out and finished their shift. Both the others were even more quiet while they worked. Gunnar couldn't tell if they knew more and weren't saying, or just didn't know.

When his shift was done, Jake shed his hazmat suit, showered, and donned his jumpsuit once more. Shad was waiting for him outside the facility and escorted him back through the prison camp in silence.

Shad opened the door to his room, and Jake nearly leapt out of his skin. There was a woman in there, dressed in a navy pantsuit, standing beside his Virtuality Core console. She had straight blonde hair and dark brown eyes, and her gaze seemed to cut through him.

She nodded to Shad. "You may leave us, Officer."

Jake glanced over at the man, but his hologram had already vanished. The door to his cell closed with a clank as metal mechanisms locked him in.

The woman approached. She was several inches taller than him, probably well over six feet.

"You've been asking questions, Jake Darrow."

"Is that a crime? You guys don't give many answers around this place."

She nodded. "And you think you deserve answers, do you?"

"Guess I want to know what I'm living for."

"So says the killer. How quaint." The woman's eyes leveled on him with cool indignation. "You're living because rather than let the world waste scum like you, my bosses decided to invest in you instead. Your life belongs to Virtuality now."

Jake scowled. "I just want to know how this all connects. The game and the real world. How am I supposed to perform well if I don't know my audience?"

The woman smiled. "That's why I'm here." She stuck out her hand, offering a handshake, but Jake just shook his head at the holograph trick.

"Very good," she said. "I'm Vera Silver, one of many Virtuality associates monitoring the beta on *Pantheon*. You're hardly the first to ask for more details. My superiors like to see your pure reactions to the immersion experience. But I suppose you have been there a few days now."

"Why are you so concerned with how we perform in the game?"

"It is imperative that you continue down a proper path. The problem with a virtual lifelike environment is that players have a tendency to... lose focus. This seems especially true in the case of prisoners like you, at least early on. When most prisoners enter, they tend to wander. They tend to spend way too much time drinking and screwing."

"Seems like that would keep people hooked on the game when it launches."

Vera smiled. "We don't exactly want to be the whorehouse game. But we also want an open world."

"But not too open."

"All games have parameters, and incentives. Early advancement is important."

"So your solution will be to—what?—shock players if they don't advance?"

"You're the guinea pigs. We're working out the bugs on you as we speak. The key is to leave everything as a tantalizing taste to be chased. We want you to want to play over and over and over. And that starts at the very beginning."

"What does that do for the people upstairs?"

"The greatest incentive of all—money."

Jake nodded and moved past her to sit in his console seat.

"Thanks for clearing things up, then," he said.

"You see, you already want to go back," Vera said sweetly. "Very well."

She moved over to the control panel and triggered a few buttons on the screen.

The arms of the machine shifted, and tubes began to attach themselves to Jake's body.

Vera leaned over him. "Play well."

Jake closed his eyes as the console whirred, but her face remained in his vision for a moment.

And in an instant, she was gone.

34

FIT FOR A GODDESS

To HIS SURPRISE, Gunnar awoke in his room alone. Kohli had not come to wake him for their morning run. The thief had been out on his trial the previous night—perhaps it was still going on. So, Gunnar lay still for a moment and enjoyed the quiet of the early morning.

The first thing he noticed upon returning to *Pantheon* was how vivid the details were, even in the dim morning light. The wood had a hint of redness to it, and the grains were dark circular mazes tracing along the boards. His blankets were a forest green with darker threading that etched a wavelike pattern around the edges. His sheets were the faded cream of too many rough washings.

The details were a stark contrast to the washed-out bright lights, smooth surfaces, and plain white boringness of everything back in Grid Eight. He brushed his fingers over the fabric of his blankets. And then felt at his elven face. There were traces of stubble and tiny—*blemishes* wasn't the right word, but there was texture to his skin—bumps and creases. It was astoundingly real. Almost too real.

His taut muscles pressed against his skin, as though he were constantly flexing. Though perhaps not the elite melee warrior he had first envisioned, he was certainly more impressive in this form than back in Grid Eight. He stood up from his bed and glanced in the mirror.

Nope, don't mind that at all.

Gunnar had to remind himself that his enhanced physique was one of many things intended to keep him hooked. To keep him subservient. To make him want to come back again and again.

And damn it, it's probably working.

"Get some clothes on, will you?"

Gunnar leapt at the gravelly voice. He turned to find Azmar hovering outside his window in the pre-dawn gloom.

"You know, you could knock. Or clear your throat. Or announce yourself in all kinds of ways other than scaring the piss out of me."

"Sounds less fun. But seriously, enough of the peep show."

Gunnar stooped and pulled on his clothes, feeling a little embarrassed. "Just, you know, appreciating the details in this game."

"Way more information than I need to know."

Gunnar ignored the quip. "How's Nymoria?"

Azmar scowled. "She's a minor deity whose most promising ward is currently a dusk elf obsessed with staring at his own ass."

"That's not what I was—whatever—so, I'm truly her most promising ward?"

"I know, shoot me now."

"That's a good thing."

"For you, perhaps."

Gunnar grinned. "So she's still pleased with my performance, then?"

"Until about a minute ago."

"I wasn't asking if *you* were pleased."

Azmar huffed, which elicited a sort of screech from his strange reptilian/avian body.

Gunnar was pretty sure he'd just made Azmar laugh.

"This quest in the Golden Hills, it was a good move?"

"You're in over your head, as usual," Azmar said. "But after your performance so far, Nymoria has confidence you will pull it off."

"That's probably the nicest thing you've ever said."

"She said it."

Gunnar smirked. "Fair enough."

"The Nighthawks might be controversial amongst the guilds themselves, but they're becoming a powerful force in this city, which means they offer much Glory to be earned. There's far more riding on you not being a dumbass than I would prefer. I trust Nymoria feels the same, because she has asked me to deliver something."

Azmar hovered close to the window and latched onto the bars. He was holding a small satchel in his mouth like a stork delivering a baby.

Gunnar took it.

"A gift from your goddess," Azmar said.

Gunnar untied the satchel and quickly opened it up to find two items.

Lockpicks

Item Class: Common
Quality: Average
Weight: 1
Durability: 7
Quantity: 12
Description: Thin iron rods. Work them right, and the lock just might spread its mechanisms for you.

Stealth Boots

Item Class: Uncommon, Elven-crafted
Quality: Above Average
Weight: 4
Durability: 18
Effect: +10% Stealth
Description: Black boots made of supple leather, crafted to soften the sound of your footsteps on hard surfaces.

Gunnar hated the word *supple*, but he loved the gifts. They would certainly come in handy during his trials.

The boots gleamed a little in the lantern light, clearly brand-new.

"Can gods give gifts anytime?" Gunnar asked.

"Of course not. Only at the final sequence of a stage. Your trial will be the last step in your Initiation stage. It locks in your Rogue class and basically determines whether you'll be of any use at all to Nymoria."

"Can anyone get gifts?"

"Sure, but they're costly."

"How so?"

Azmar shrugged. "I'm powerful, but I don't know the ways of gods. But usually only the most promising players get gifts."

"Look at you dishing out the compliments."

Azmar rolled his eyes. "You'll be needing to tread carefully tonight. I hope Nymoria is right about you."

"Now, that is truly the nicest thing you've said."

"Don't get teary on me. I've got plenty of insults reserved for next time."

Gunnar smiled. "I'd expect nothing less."

Azmar leaned close, and his expression softened. Gunnar was not entirely sure what to make of it, but he had the impression that there was something riding on this quest he didn't understand.

"Hopefully, next time we meet, it will be a celebration of a successful guild trial."

"Have you had anyone pass the trials?" Gunnar asked.

Azmar sighed. "Not in a long time."

"Well, it's about time then."

"Trust no one, Gunnar. Only yourself."

With that, Azmar disappeared into the darkness.

Gunnar decided against the run today, with no overeager Kohli to force him. Instead he went to Sykes' training facility first thing and worked on his strength training. He hadn't done a ton of lifting since high school, and the quality of these hunks of iron were lacking, but his old routine came back to him. He cycled through sets with free weights—curls, chest press, shoulder press, and so on—starting with shorter sets and increasing with each new set, then decreasing them back to zero.

Despite his lean elven muscles, he tired quickly, but not before advancing his Sheer Strength skill to Level 7.

Once his upper body felt good and exhausted, he headed to a previously overlooked lockpicking station and tested out his new gift.

There were several chests set up in a corner, with locks of varying size and difficulty. Gunnar chose a lock, slid the metal rods inside, and shifted them around, testing the pressure as he attempted to turn. The lock gave.

Unlocked Skill: Lockpicking

Skill Type: Physical, Stealth
Linked Attribute: Dexterity (+95% Development)
Affinity Level: 11
Requirements: Level 8 Dexterity

Cost: N/A
Description: Your handy hands prove useful once again!

Gunnar grinned as he opened the chest, but found it empty. He moved on to the second. With the third, he received 5 XP.

But with the fourth lock, he started breaking picks. After losing three, he decided to save the rest for his quest.

⸺

When he returned to the Mermaid, Kohli was already there, slumped over the counter. Gunnar patted him on the back, and the thief jerked up, as though startled from sleep. Or perhaps just a daze. The man looked like he hadn't slept all night.

"Missed you on our run," Gunnar said.

"Mmhmm." Kohli's breath reeked and his eyes were bloodshot.

"You been here all night?"

Kohli shrugged. "Not all... had my trial."

Gunnar had a feeling he knew the answer to his next question. "What happened?"

"Screwed it up," Kohli murmured. "Din't pass."

"What went wrong?"

"It's bullshit... alluvit is bullshit. This whole place. Alluvit."

"What are you talking about?"

Kohli shook his head back and forth, cursing softly to himself.

Gunnar couldn't help but think of what Sheira had said about her own trial. How someone had betrayed her. How she was set up, somehow. And it struck him that Azmar too had hinted at a similar rigged system. Always receiving mediocre recruits, no one passing the trials.

Don't forget who runs this show, Sheira had said.

Something was starting to click, but Gunnar just didn't understand the reason. Why would players be set up to fail? Was it some part of the test or something?

Sykes emerged from the back room, looking jovial until he took a sour glance at Kohli, who had once again slumped over on the bar top.

"My god!" Sykes said. "So you screwed the pooch. You've got another couple days to try to get another shot. But you sure as hell won't get it like this."

Kohli just shook his head. "Izallbullshit."

Sykes turned to Theodore the bartender and ordered him to get some food to sober the thief up. As the elf hurried off, Sykes muttered about the idiocy of letting the man get this drunk.

"Well, you're having a better morning at least," Sykes said, turning to Gunnar.

His entire body tensed. Did Sykes know about his trial with the Nighthawks?

"I... I am?" Gunnar asked.

Sykes grinned and held out a parchment.

Gunnar eyed it suspiciously. "What is it?"

"Your friend is messing with you. It's a summons from the House of Daggers."

Kohli sat up at the name.

"They're a damn good guild," Sykes went on. "And one of their leaders wants to meet with you. You know what that means, right?"

"A... guild trial?"

Another one? What am I supposed to do with that?

35

AIN'T NO MURDERHOBO

Gunnar ought to have been thrilled. And he would have been if he didn't already have a secret trial he wasn't supposed to talk about from a guild that Sykes and Kohli didn't trust. But he couldn't let on about any of that.

"Er, that's great," Gunnar managed, though he sounded more dazed than excited.

"Damn right it's great," Sykes said. "What's wrong with you?"

"Sorry, just surprised. And, you know, nervous, I guess."

"Don't let Kohli mess with your head, kid. This is a good opportunity. Pull up your map, and I'll show you where you're heading."

Gunnar wasn't sure whether he would actually go to this meeting, but for now, he needed to at least act interested. He pulled up his map and let Sykes scroll around toward the center of the city.

The barkeep pointed, and Gunnar placed a marker over a tavern called the Hellhound.

"There's where you're having dinner this evening."

Gunnar simply nodded. "Okay, sounds good."

"Six o'clock. Don't be late. Just take a seat at a booth, and Karl will find you and give you the details of your trial."

Gunnar's map zoomed out away from the tavern, briefly showing the whole city, or at least the areas Gunnar had visited. The rest was grayed out and marked *Undiscovered*.

"Say," Sykes muttered as Gunnar's display shut down, "what've you been doing over in the Golden Hills, of all places?"

Gunnar tried not to physically react, but cursed himself for not closing the map quicker. He shrugged. "Just exploring. I've been wandering at night when I haven't had a quest or anything. Getting oriented."

Sykes' fingers brushed his bearded chin. "I'd steer clear of that place. Nothing good happens to noobs in a place like that. The Red Cloaks watch it close, and the nobles there are the worst kinds."

"I thought they were the middling lords. Not very powerful."

Sykes nodded. "That's what makes them the worst. The middling lords don't have much sway over the city, but they try hard as hell to feel powerful. A great lord wouldn't bat an eye at a lowly elf like yourself, but a Golden Hills lord, you never can tell. Just be careful where you roam, kid."

Gunnar nodded. "Thanks for the tip."

Sykes crossed his arms over his barrel-chest and smiled. "That's what I'm here for."

He turned to Kohli, who had been silently devouring a plate of hot breakfast. "Look, if your friend ain't too much of a soak this morning, I've got some work needs done for a new investment of mine. If you don't mind a little combat training, that is."

Gunnar nodded. He needed something bigger than the gym to keep his mind off the task before him that night. "Sure, I've been itching for some real action."

"Good," Sykes said. "Reckon you could use some more combat if you're taking a House of Daggers trial."

"What do you say?" Gunnar asked, turning to the thief.

Kohli barely looked up from his food, a little bit of porridge dribbling down his chin, but Gunnar could tell he was excited.

———

Twenty minutes later, they stood near the wharf outside a massive complex that stretched half a block. It looked like it had once been some sort of warehouse. A very long time ago. The outside of the building was formed of old wood and sheets of rusty tin haphazardly thrown together. Gunnar wasn't sure if the sheets were part of the original design or some sort of shoddy patch work.

It was set back from the waterfront, just enough that they couldn't see the crowds of sailors and dockworkers, but they could hear the rattle of carts, the groan of cranes, and the bellows of foremen barking orders. The stench of fish and something burning hung over the place.

"Looks like a shit investment," Kohli muttered.

Sykes frowned. "The bones are good, and that's all I care about. I got a good deal on this place. It could make a good housing project or another training facility. But I need it cleared out."

"Cleared out of what?" Gunnar asked.

"Squatters."

Gunnar and Kohli glanced at one another as a notification appeared in front of them.

Quest Alert: Ain't No Murderhobo

Description: This dump once belonged to the West Arran Trading Company. But after the notorious pirate Black Heart plundered a series of valuable shipments, the company went under, and this place fell into... disrepair. Lately, it's become a favorite landing pad for the hobos of Thailen.

Objective: Clear the warehouse of undesirables.

Restrictions: We don't want squatters in this city, but we're not completely heartless. Use of lethal force will result in negative XP, unless used in self-defense.

Reward: What? Helping out an old friend ain't enough for ya? Fine, we'll make it worth your while.

Do you wish to accept? Yes/No

Gunnar accepted.

He was intrigued by the mention of Black Heart again. Had the Nighthawks been involved in the demise of that trading company somehow? It was an interesting coincidence—assuming it was one.

"Well, how're we supposed to get them out of there if we can't kill 'em?" Kohli complained.

"That's why I'm hiring you," Sykes said with a grin.

"I thought it was combat," Kohli said.

"Best kind. It requires strategy. And control."

Kohli cursed, but made his way toward the giant wood doors at the front.

"What happens to the hobos when we're done?" Gunnar asked.

Sykes shrugged. "They figure their shit out, or they get deported. Not my problem."

Gunnar felt a twinge of guilt about the quest, much as he had about pickpocketing low-levels. *It's just a game...*

Sykes walked off with a wave. "Good luck."

Gunnar followed after Kohli, who drew a gladius as they reached the door.

"What're you doing?"

Kohli shrugged. "Didn't say we couldn't maim them. If we give 'em a good scare, maybe that'll set them running. Worth a shot, right?"

Gunnar nodded, but he had an uneasy feeling about this. He drew a pair of daggers, and Kohli threw open the doors.

Right by the entrance, a large metal barrel proved to be the source of the burning stench permeating the air outside. Heaps of trash were scattered all around, and wisps of browned paper floated into the air as the fire crackled.

Gunnar didn't want to know what that paper had been used for. The pungent stench rushed out the open doors and nearly stopped him in his tracks.

A pair of ragged-looking older dwarves hovered around the barrel, holding pokers over the flames.

"What're yeh lookin' at?" demanded a dwarf with long white hair.

Several more faces emerged from the dark expanse of the warehouse beyond the fire, bright eyes flashing in the light pouring in through the large doors. The hobos looked dazed at the intrusion.

"This property has been repossessed," Gunnar shouted.

The white-haired dwarf laughed. "We're but lowly urchins here. Afraid we don't take yer meaning."

"He means the party's over, asshole," Kohli said, raising his gladius. "Time to get the hell out of here!"

The white-haired dwarf laughed, a deep-bellied guffaw that echoed from the reeking warehouse and triggered laughter from the others.

More of the hobos moved toward the entrance.

The white-haired dwarf raised a very shoddy-looking dagger in the air.

Cork the Dwarf Miner

Level: 8
HP: 90/90
MP: 60/60
Threat Level: Orange

Gunnar hadn't seen an orange level threat before, but judging by the fact that the dwarf wasn't leaping out to attack them, he guessed there was still hope to prevent this from escalating.

Gunnar surveyed the room as best he could in the dim light. There were at least a dozen hobos, most wearing baggy and raggedy clothes. A couple of naked blurs flashed from a loft, where there were piles of blankets that must have served as beds. The blurs looked greenish, and Gunnar was pretty sure they were goblins of some fashion. A scrawny mother emerged from a corner, clutching a crying babe, and she looked like she would happily kill the person who woke it.

None of the hobos looked like formidable threats in combat, but there were quite a lot of them.

And the old dwarf miner seemed to know it. "Yeh won't be killing any of us. Not unless we take the first shot, and as far as I'm concerned, we en't gonna be fighting no one." The dwarf tossed his weapon to the ground with a clatter.

He turned away and returned to tending to his poker in the garbage fire. He pulled out a skinned rat, inspected it for a moment, and set it back over the blaze.

The others did not look quite as at ease. They watched their leader carefully.

Gunnar didn't like this. It wasn't as though he hadn't played the villain in any video games before. He'd hijacked enough virtual cars and killed enough strippers for it to have been a part-time job back in high school. But *Pantheon* felt different than any of those old games. More real.

It's just the immersion. You're taking this too seriously.

And yet, he found himself glad that Black Heart had ruined the trading company that owned this place. It had probably been owned by some cruel noble. And he didn't really think Sykes needed another base to take advantage of noobs from, either.

"Look, maybe this isn't worth it," Gunnar muttered.

"What the hell are you talking about?" Kohli asked.

"They know we can't attack them."

"Screw that," Kohli muttered, stalking forward.

"Kohli!"

But the thief ignored him. Kohli tossed his blade aside, grabbed the dwarf miner by the back of the neck, and threw him to the ground.

36

SELF-DEFENSE

THE HOBOS DIDN'T MOVE. All eyes were on Kohli and the dwarf, who slowly raised himself up on hands and knees. Kohli gave the old miner a swift kick to the ribs, and he crumpled back to the ground.

Kohli stalked around the dwarf, eyes alight. Gunnar understood now why Sykes had chosen Kohli for this task, at this exact moment.

Sykes didn't give a damn about their gaining or losing experience. He knew Kohli was crazy and desperate enough after his failed mission to do whatever it took to get these squatters out. He was so bent on completing the quest, he might not even care if he killed one of these people. He might not care about losing all his XP either. He was in a drunken rage.

The dwarf miner groaned on the ground, clutching his chest, and Gunnar didn't know what to do. Another dwarf snatched up a stick—probably something used to stir trash in the garbage fire—and ran at Kohli. But the thief was ready.

He leapt back, drawing a dagger, and plunged it into the dwarf's back. The fire stick clacked on the ground at Gunnar's feet.

The dwarf didn't move, and Gunnar's stomach twisted.

"Self-defense!" Kohli shouted, looking up at the horrified group of hobos with his hands raised, daring anyone else to make a move.

That elicited angry murmurs from the warehouse, and more of the hobos staggered forward. More dwarves, some scrawny humans and elves, and the goblin couple who were still naked. The baby shrieked.

None of these people were experienced fighters. Gunnar could tell that at a glance.

The dwarf miner stooped over his friend and let out a groan.

Kohli raised his gladius threateningly at the encroaching squatters.

"Anyone else?"

Gunnar had seen enough. He knew where this was going. Maybe it would work, or maybe not. But he didn't care.

Kohli glanced at him. "Come on, mate, don't make me take the whole quest on my own."

Gunnar stooped down and picked up the dwarf's fire stick. Kohli turned and brandished his weapon at a scrawny drunk-looking man who staggered out of the darkness, a dagger raised.

Gunnar leapt forward, activating Enhanced Blow, and brought the fire stick down on Kohli's head. The wood shattered on impact, and Kohli crumpled to the ground, his gladius clattering on the stone.

[*You have dealt +15 Damage to an ally. Here's -20 XP!*]

[*Your well-placed blow has triggered the effect Concussive Stupor!*]

Kohli did not stir. The drunk man kept coming, and Gunnar turned to him, raising one of his daggers.

"Stay back!" Gunnar shouted.

The man stopped, confused. "B-but you attacked him."

"To stop him from doing anything else stupid."

"He killed Furin!" the white-haired dwarf miner growled. "We oughta gut him right here!"

"Yeah," said the drunk man. "Let me finish him off!"

Several of the others nodded.

"And what will that do for you?" Gunnar asked.

"Self-defense," the dwarf miner said, spitting on the ground at Kohli's feet. The thief's eyes were open, but he didn't stir, as though in some sort of paralyzed daze.

"If you try to kill him, you're gonna have to go through me," Gunnar said, trying to steel his courage. "And that won't be self-defense because I never attacked you in the first place."

Unlocked Skill: Art of Diplomacy

Skill Type: Mental
Linked Attribute: Charisma (+70% Development)
Affinity Level: 6
Cost: N/A
Description: This ability allows you to influence and persuade others, but effectiveness can be blurred by the user's own audacity or stupidity. Sound familiar?

Murmurs filled the warehouse. More faces emerged from the darkness, and Gunnar was pretty sure there were actually around twenty hobos in the building.

He cursed himself.

This could easily backfire, and he knew that he had little chance against this many of them, no matter how inexperienced they were.

But Gunnar still had an unused attribute point. He had hoped to save it for the party, but there was no way he was getting out of this without it. He leveled up his Charisma, applied all three skill points to his new Diplomacy skill, and hoped that it would be enough.

"So? You're giving up then?" the white-haired dwarf demanded, rising to his feet.

Gunnar shook his head. "No."

"If you try to force us out, you can be damn sure we'll fight you."

"I'm not going to fight you."

"So, you *are* giving up," the dwarf said.

"If it's not me, it'll be someone else," Gunnar said. "This warehouse is going to be taken over one way or another. It has a new owner, and Sykes has a lot of connections, and a lot more grunts like my friend. They're desperate enough to prove themselves that they'll do what it takes to get you out of here."

"Then this warehouse'll be our last bloody stand," the dwarf miner said.

"Give me liberty or give me death," said an elf maiden with dreadlocks tied back with a faded green bandana.

Gunnar grimaced, her patriotic quote confirming his suspicions. Some of these hobos weren't NPCs. They were down and out players just like Sheira.

"That's the dumbest thing I ever heard," Gunnar said. "You all want to die rather than leave?"

"Where do yeh think we're s'posed to go?" the drunk man asked.

The elf maiden nodded. "This place is all we got."

The entire group of hobos had surrounded him now.

Here goes nothing...

"Look, I don't know what you all have been through," Gunnar said. "And I won't pretend to. This city is a cruel place. I know that much. Sykes *will* come back here, and I know it won't do anyone any good if you all fight to the death. But there might be another way."

The group looked at him in silence, eyes wide with what he hoped was a trace of hope.

"What way?" asked the dwarf miner.

"I know a place where you could stay, at least for a while, until you can find someplace new."

It was a gamble. He didn't actually know if this was something the sorceress would allow, but she *had* said that she was in his debt.

"I cleared out an old crypt," Gunnar explained. "It was used as a training ground for a while, but now, it's just sitting in the middle of the city. There'd be plenty of room until you could find a new warehouse or someplace else to live. I'll need to deal with Sykes, but I can tell you where to meet me later, and I'll get you in."

The dwarf miner stroked his beard. "An intriguing proposition, but how can we know this en't just some machination to get us to evacuate the premises?"

"I'm only a humble thief," Gunnar said. "Afraid I don't take your meaning."

There was a pause. Then, the dwarf howled with laughter. The others joined in, and the roar echoed from all around the warehouse.

"I like yeh," the dwarf said, stepping forward and extending his hand. Though small, he gripped Gunnar's fingers with remarkable strength. "Me name's Cork."

"Gunnar."

"Look, it's lost on none of us that there's no saints in this city, and we'll not be blaming yeh for the circumstances of our meeting. But we'll also not be soon forgetting the fact that yer friend here killed one of our own."

Gunnar nodded. He didn't notice Kohli stirring from his Concussive Stupor until Cork jerked his head up from the ground and the thief yelped in pain.

"Bloody hell!"

"Quiet!" Cork bellowed, jerking his hair harder, and some

of the other hobos pinned Kohli down. "Or I'll lop yer tongue off meself."

That threat shut Kohli right up.

"Don't make me fight you," Gunnar said, hands hovering at the hilts of his daggers.

"I've no intention of fighting," Cork said. "Like I was saying before we were so rudely interrupted, your friend killed a friend of mine." The dwarf lowered his voice for a moment. "Lucky for the both of yeh, Furin will respawn. But we all know that don't come without a cost."

Before Gunnar could react, the dwarf raised his voice again.

"A killing like that tells me something of a man's character. I don't know how it's done where yeh're from, but amongst the dwarves, we make no deals without assurances. Yeh say there's a crypt, and I wanna believe that's true. But the only way I'm taking my people there is with a guarantee."

"What do you want?" Gunnar asked.

"While you deal with this Sykes fellow, we'll be taking yer friend along with us."

37

MAN OF THE MERMAID

Kohli squirmed violently at the proposition, but the movement only forced more pain from the dwarf's tight grip on his hair. He howled, but quit resisting.

"Don't be stupid, mate," the thief muttered.

But Gunnar shook his head. "You were already stupid enough for the both of us."

"You're just going to leave me with them?"

"You put me in this spot," Gunnar said. "Lucky for you, I'm the one with the history of keeping his word." Gunnar turned to Cork and extended his hand. "Alright, Kohli goes with you."

Quest Alert: Hobo Abode
Description: Prefer the humane approach, do you? Well, then, you'll have to take on the additional task of relocating these urchins. If you fail, it won't end well for Kohli. Or you.
Objective: Find a new home for Cork and his people.
Reward: Build trust with a new faction.

Gunnar pulled up his map and showed the dwarf where to meet him, near where the Crypt Keeper had helped them exit back into the city. He noted that neither the entrance or exit revealed any information about the place now that Angus was no longer running it as a training ground. It was just a nondescript burial chamber again. He just hoped they could still get inside.

"I'll meet you there at dusk. But make sure you don't all arrive at once and bring the Red Cloaks down on the place."

Cork nodded. "We'll be there, lad. Come on, folks, pack it up."

The hobos moved through the warehouse gathering their things, but packing it up did not amount to much more than fetching a few blankets and ragged packs of clothes. Or for the goblins, simply putting clothes on. Two or three at a time, the hobos began dispersing into the waterfront crowds.

Cork and a pair of mountain orcs took Kohli, but not before taking all his weapons.

The thief's head hung at his shoulders, and Gunnar was not sure if he was still dazed from the concussion or whether his failures in this world were starting to weigh on him. But he offered no further protests.

Cork was the last to exit the building, and as he did Gunnar was hit with several notifications.

[*Congratulations! You have successfully talked your way out of a bind while knocking out your comrade in one blow. You have reached Level 10 in the skill Art of Diplomacy. You have reached Level 7 in Enhanced Blow.*]

[*Congratulations! You have completed the quest* Ain't No Murderhobo. *You have successfully removed all squatters from Sykes' new investment property. Here's 120 XP!*]

[*Congratulations! You have completed this quest in an unusual fashion, without the use of violence, threat, or intimidation, earning the Thoroughly Modern Gandhi badge: +1 to Charisma, +1 to Creativity, +1 to Intelligence.*]

Gunnar's Glory meter shot up as he surpassed Level 8 and then some.

Nymoria's glowing form appeared, her beauty and elegance a stark contrast to the grit and grime of the warehouse.

"Well done, faithful servant. You have taken another step on the path to greatness. You have earned one attribute point, which can be distributed at any time. But remember that every choice you make will echo into eternity. Choose wisely."

Nymoria disappeared, and Gunnar was left alone in the decrepit building.

___

"You did good, kid," Sykes said a short while later as he walked around and took stock of his latest investment. "I know it's not much to look at, but it'll be a whole new place when my crews are finished."

Sykes handed Gunnar a silver coin with the sign of the Mermaid engraved on it.

Man of the Mermaid coin

Item Class: Rare, Non-currency
Weight: 0.1
Description: This coin is a sign of goodwill from Sykes. It will grant admittance into the Mermaid without cover charge, as well as any of Sykes' training facilities.

"I don't hand these out to many of my wards. Just the ones I think have a promising future. You've done well since you got here. If you keep this up, you'll get in good with the House of Daggers, no problem. You'll get set up nicely with a guild like that, but feel free to keep training in my facilities, and if you feel like stopping by for a show, or just to say hi to an old friend, you're welcome at the Mermaid anytime."

The large man stuck out his hand, and Gunnar shook it vigorously.

"Thanks a lot," Gunnar said.

"Don't mention it. Say, where's Kohli? Expected he'd be here too."

Gunnar had rehearsed his answer to this before Sykes arrived. "Went to have another drink. He didn't feel like waiting around."

Sykes shook his head. "Even more impressive you completed the quest with an ally like him."

"He did alright," Gunnar lied.

"You're loyal," Sykes said. "It'll do you good in your guild. But that thief is digging his own grave. Be careful not to let him drag you down with him."

Gunnar nodded.

"Well, I've got a big project to get started," Sykes said. "And you've got a trial to gear up for. Good luck tonight."

Gunnar smiled and nodded, and with that, Sykes wandered off, whistling softly to himself.

It was midafternoon, and Gunnar had a little time to kill, so he grabbed some food from a vendor. It was something between a street taco and a gyro, with slimy strips of meat and grilled veggies folded up in a piece of flatbread and lathered in brown sauce. But like most things in *Pantheon*, it didn't taste too bad.

[*Buffs Added - A Decent Meal* — *You have decreased your Stamina usage rate by* 15% *over the next four hours. Build up your Constitution for an even greater effect.*]

The note about Constitution reminded him that he still had an attribute point to distribute.

He took a look at his character sheet and considered what to do.

Gunnar Ashwood

Glory: Level 8

Servant of Nymoria

Coins: 106

Character Traits

Race: Dusk Elf

Clan: Maldan

Class: Leaning toward Rogue... Ah, it's cute you think you're so tough!

Faction: Look at you, Mr. Noncommittal! Got two guilds on the hook. You know we're all sick of love triangles, right?

Renown: Known Nobody

Character Stats

Health - 95/95

Stamina - 85/85

Mana - 110/110

Physical Attributes

Strength - 6

Dexterity - 11

Agility - 6

Constitution - 8

Mental Attributes

Intelligence - 8

Wisdom - 7

Charisma - 8

Creativity - 4

Physical Skills

Endurance - Level 9 (+25 Stamina Buff)

Throwing Blade - Level 15

Slashing Blow - Level 6

Parry Blow - Level 10

Head-Butt - Level 6

Enhanced Blow - Level 7

Sheer Strength - Level 7
Wall Climbing - Level 10
Lockpicking - Level 11
Pickpocketing - Level 14
Stealth - Level 6
Stealth Attack - Level 6
Mental Skills
Perception - Level 15
Mindful Breathing - Level 7
Art of Diplomacy - Level 10
Active Items
Basic Dark Cloak (+10% Stealth)
Stealth Boots (+10% Stealth)
Leather Vambraces (+10% Resistance to Damage)
Leather Greaves (+10% Resistance to Damage)
Inactive Items
Parchment (Work Order)
Lockpicks (9)
Coin (Man of the Mermaid)
Spells
Scan - Level 15
Dark Sight - Level 7
Cloaked Dagger (one time use)
Open Quests
Dimble's Nimble
The Purloined Letter
Hobo Abode

Gunnar felt a momentary sense of accomplishment at all he'd done the past few days, but it was quickly overpowered by the awareness of all his remaining inadequacies.

He'd played games where the early levels were passed in a few hours, and he could advance quickly through skills, but

Pantheon was designed differently. Each of his levels were hard-earned, and his attributes and skills required a lot of work to advance. He had managed to advance a few skills through running and training, but this seemed to largely help his already higher attributes.

Early on, he had thought that it might make sense to pour points into his stronger attributes and skills. But he was beginning to think the points could actually make up for some of his deficiencies. He was able to level up skills tied to Dexterity quickly, hence how he had improved his pickpocketing and climbing abilities so easily with a bit of practice.

But *Pantheon* had really been forcing him into situations where he needed to round out his abilities, and he expected the party to be no different. He would most certainly need Charisma amongst the nobles at the party if he was going to get near Admiral Benton.

He applied the attribute point and added four more skill points to Art of Diplomacy, bringing it to Level 14.

By then, the sun was beginning to descend behind the Temple of Luka, casting Thailen into the long shadows of dusk.

As Gunnar set out for the crypt, he tried not to think about how much depended on this night.

38

ART OF DIPLOMACY

"What do you think this is? A soup kitchen?"

The Crypt Keeper crossed her arms over her chest and scowled furiously.

They stood in the center of the massive burial chamber where Gunnar, Em, and Kohli had freed the sorceress only days ago.

The room was still a mess of skeletons and rusty weapons, and there was a foul smell that Gunnar was pretty sure belonged to Angus's decaying corpse, still crushed beneath one of the cages.

Gunnar had brought Cork alone to negotiate with the sorceress, to ensure that all was in order before the others arrived. The dwarf stood to the side, a deep furrow in his brow.

"You said you were in my debt," Gunnar said. "They'll only stay until they can find somewhere else."

The Crypt Keeper shook her head. "This place is enough of a mess from the last person who was let in here."

"Don't look like the dead need all this space," Cork said, scanning the vast chamber.

"You have no idea what the dead require, fool."

"Yeh see?" Cork muttered. "Even the dead don't want to deal with no homeless."

Gunnar shook his head. "If it weren't for me, that idiot rock star would still be ruling these dead."

The Crypt Keeper nodded dismissively. "For which we are all grateful. It's not that I don't sympathize with this charity situation."

"Charity?" Cork muttered.

"But you must understand that matters of the dead are sacred, and I won't have a bunch of lazy tramps mucking up the place even worse than it already is."

Cork huffed, turning visibly red in the torchlight. "Lazy tramps? Yeh don't know a damn thing about my people!"

"And you don't know a damn thing about matters of the dead!"

"Dead are dead!" Cork said, gesticulating at the massive chamber surrounding them. "This is a waste of space."

The Crypt Keeper's eyes lit with anger. "You prove my point entirely, uneducated swine!"

Cork growled and turned to Gunnar. "Kid, I should have known better than to fall for this bullshit charade. I won't sit here and be insulted. This is clearly not going—"

Gunnar gripped his shoulder gently. "Let me handle the negotiations."

"What's there to handle?" Cork asked.

"I must agree with the dwarf there," the Crypt Keeper said.

"Can we all take a moment to breathe?" Gunnar asked. He looked from Cork to the Crypt Keeper. Both grimaced but nodded.

"Alright," the Crypt Keeper said.

"Fine," said Cork, crossing his arms over his chest.

"You're both so busy insulting one another that you seem to be missing the opportunity before you." Gunnar turned to the

Crypt Keeper. "This place doesn't look much different than when I left a couple days ago. Why's it still such a mess?"

"I'm one woman," the sorceress said. "And my first priority is putting the dead to proper rest."

"Couldn't you reanimate some of these dead and put them to work?"

As Gunnar expected, the Crypt Keeper's mouth gaped in disgust.

"Fulcra are an abomination. An extraordinary disrespect to the great people who rest here. I have been entrusted with their care and would never dishonor them in such a way. Angus did enough for many lifetimes."

Gunnar nodded. "And your hobos," he said, turning to Cork, "are they a bunch of useless bums?"

Cork gritted his teeth at the term, but shook his head. "Course not. We hit some bad luck in this city, but we've all got useful skills of one kind or another."

"I'm not asking for charity," Gunnar said. "I'm offering an opportunity for mutual gain for all of us. These folks need a place to stay for the foreseeable future, and this crypt needs a lot of work. This place extends much farther than this chamber, and I'd guess there's even more that I didn't see when I was here. Surely there are a couple chambers that could be converted to house twenty people. In exchange, they could help clean this place up, make it a proper resting place for the dead."

The Crypt Keeper thought for a minute, offering one last glare at Cork, but she nodded her assent. "That could be an agreeable arrangement."

Cork still crossed his arms, but he also agreed. "My people have no reticence toward labor if need be. Seems this place could become a decent home with some work. A lot of work."

The two eyed each other for a moment, but finally, the Crypt Keeper extended her hand to the dwarf.

[*Congratulations! You've reached Level 15 in Art of Diplomacy! Don't let this go to that thick head of yours! You've got plenty of other relationships on thin ice.*]

[*Congratulations! You have completed the quest* Hobo Abode. *You have found a new home for Cork and his people. Here's 70 XP!*]

[*You have fostered negotiations between two suspicious parties. You have increased trust between yourself and both parties. You've earned the Cordial Business Partner badge. Not quite allies, but every great partnership has to start somewhere: +1 to Creativity, +1 to Charisma.*]

The experience was just enough to reach Level 9. The world paused as Nymoria congratulated him and awarded him one more attribute point, which was going to be real important tonight.

The burial chamber soon filled with hobos, and the Crypt Keeper led them back into the maze of corridors, with a plan to convert Angus's concert hall into a sort of dormitory.

Kohli was brought in last. He glared at everyone, including Gunnar. But he was visibly relieved when the mountain orc hobos released him, and he stood close to Gunnar.

The dwarf Kohli had killed stood by Cork's side, having respawned and rejoined his crew at some point during the day. The dark-haired dwarf did not pay Gunnar any mind, but his eyes never left Kohli.

Cork clapped Gunnar on the back and cackled. "I'll be honest. I din't expect yeh'd come through."

"Why'd you go along with it?" Gunnar asked.

"Like you said, if it wasn't the two of yeh, it'd be someone else. Least this way, we had a chance. This place might turn out alright. I'd like yeh to meet Furin, my brother from another mother, as they say."

Gunnar stuck out his hand and the dwarf shook it.

"Sorry about what happened back at the warehouse," Gunnar said.

"Aye," said Furin, glaring at Kohli. "Yer mate is lucky I don't repay the favor. But I reckon this place holds promise."

"It's temporary, remember," Gunnar said. "Once this place is cleaned up, you'll need to move on. But maybe this will give you a start."

Cork and Furin both furrowed their brows at this, as though they'd expected him to say something else. "Right, a start."

"The Crypt Keeper can give you small quests, help you earn some XP. But once this place is finished up, you'll need to find someplace more permanent."

The dwarves nodded. "Well, we'd best be seeing to our people."

Gunnar nodded, and the dwarves shuffled after the rest of their party.

Kohli shook his head. "You best hope this don't come back to haunt us."

"Us?" Gunnar said mockingly. "I think I'll take my own advice from here on out."

Gunnar began to walk away, but Kohli gripped his arm.

"Look, I know I was a little out of line."

"You were a damn idiot."

"I was drunk and angry, and you're right, I was an idiot. It's this stupid game."

"What happened during your trial?" Gunnar asked.

Kohli sighed. "I don't know. It was going great. We were running a job against the leader of another guild. All of a sudden some mystery person showed up and hijacked the quest."

"What do you mean by *hijacked*?"

"I mean I wasn't the only person sent to rob this dude. Maybe it was someone from another guild. I don't know. But it all went to shit. They got the loot, and I died trying to get away."

Gunnar gripped his shoulder. "I'm sorry. This place is rotten, and I don't think it's an accident."

"What do you mean?"

"I think you're right. It's all bullshit. I think this game is... weighted against us."

"Like it's rigged?"

"I don't know. Maybe... or maybe it's just... I don't know, a twisted system."

"Twisted how?"

"I don't know," Gunnar said. He started walking toward the crypt exit, and Kohli kept pace beside him. "To turn us against each other. It's been that way since my opening quest. Look at the trials and the guilds. All the incentives are for looking after yourself, even if it means turning on a potential ally or plundering and pillaging all the low-level characters in the game. And what's the result? We all steal small gains from other low-levels."

"So what do we do?"

"Look, I should have left you behind in the crypt. I think the game wanted me to. You should have left me when that under-cover Red Cloak turned up. We definitely should be at odds now."

"You did beat me over the head with a fire stick."

Gunnar chuckled. "You see? We shouldn't be friends."

"Are we friends?"

"I guess that's up to you. But for my part, if I can help you get another trial, I will."

They exited the crypt and emerged in the narrow nook of an alley in the heart of the city. The cloudy sky was lit up with brilliant colors. Which meant Gunnar needed to hurry to get to the Golden Hills in time for Dravingdel's party.

"You think that's actually possible?" Kohli asked. "Another trial?"

"Maybe... but if I can help, I will. So long as you don't get piss drunk like that again."

Kohli clapped his shoulder. "You're a good man, Gunnar."

"You too." Gunnar shook the thief's hand. "Look, I should be going. But I'll see you tomorrow for training?"

"We run at dawn."

Gunnar smiled and headed north as they separated at the first major intersection.

"Hey," Kohli shouted after him. "Thought you were having dinner with someone from the House of Daggers."

"Er, yeah," Gunnar said.

"You're heading the wrong way," Kohli said.

He cursed himself for not thinking about that. "Er, right, thanks, forgot to check my MiniNav."

Kohli pointed at his temple. "Good thing you got someone looking out for ya."

With that, the thief turned and headed south.

Considering everything Gunnar was dealing with—Sykes and Kohli, Em and the Nighthawks, and now the Crypt Keeper and the hobos—he decided that he definitely needed more Wisdom. He applied the attribute point and distributed all his skill points to Perception, bringing it to Level 19. His HUD teased him with a new Scan ability at Level 20, which would allow him to alter his own Scan information.

The possibilities of that excited him, but for now, he would have to settle for his fake papers and work orders.

Gunnar set out, veering west for a couple of streets. Then, he hurried back north, toward the glittering lights of the Golden Hills.

39

SERVANT

GUNNAR WAS nervous when the guards at the entrance to the Golden Hills asked for his work order. It didn't help that he had no weapons equipped, having stowed everything in his Inventory when he changed into his party attire. Should they see through his facade, he was screwed.

But when he showed them the parchment Leilani had given him, they swiftly waved him through the gates.

The roads leading up the hills toward Dravingdel's estate were lit up with far more lanterns than the other night. A short way from the entrance, a minstrel serenaded from an overlook while nobles dressed to the nines made their way to the party. Gunnar felt a bit like a buffoon in his Ben Franklin suit, but he fit right in alongside the nobles.

But for one unavoidable feature, which was made all too apparent when he stopped alongside a group of young nobles watching a troupe of ax jugglers.

"Don't doddle, Tree Humper!" The young man spat as he spoke, eyes wide with disgust. "There's privies to be cleaned at the estate, I'm sure."

It took Gunnar a moment—the moment another young man

made an obscene gesture that involved rubbing off a pair of invisible horns on the sides of his head while grunting and making lewd expressions—before he realized why the hell they were even talking to him.

Gunnar instinctively felt at his long ears, then shook his head and chuckled. "Right, Tree Humper. Cuz my people live in trees and shit. Real original."

The young women accompanying them let out soft gasps.

"Watch your tongue," said Spit Talker. "Or I'll—"

"What?" Gunnar asked. "Cut it off? You might have to get your hands on it to do that, and you don't want to know where this bad boy's been."

He glanced at the blonde woman who was clearly with the man.

"You dare suggest that my girl would ever—"

But Gunnar was already trotting off. The other couple chuckled, arousing an angry outburst from Spit Talker.

When Gunnar reached the top of a hill, he glanced back, and the group was once more fixated on the performance.

All talk, Gunnar thought. *Typical.*

Dravingdel's estate was lit up like a department store during the holidays. The castle glowed against the night from far off, and it was bright as day at the gates.

Nobles were ushered inside while servants parked their carriages. Gunnar was swiftly ferried around the back of the carriage house, after he showed another guard his work order.

He had to hand it to Leilani. It was almost too easy.

A surly woman handed him a black apron. "You should have been here fifteen minutes ago."

"Apologies, madam."

"Don't waste time, get to work." She pointed him toward a massive table filled with several trays of wineglasses.

Gunnar immediately took up a white cloth and began

polishing them. It was tedious, mindless work. Glass after glass after glass. There must have been hundreds.

He was joined by a dawn elf maiden and a young human woman.

"You're slow," said the human after he finished his first tray. She had bright green eyes and plump freckled cheeks and began filling the glasses from a crystal decanter, impressively spilling no wine as she swiftly went from glass to glass.

The elf maiden shook her head. "Both of you are slow." She gestured to two trays waiting to be filled.

"Why don't you take these out to the patio?" the human said as she finished a tray.

Gunnar glanced briefly around the room of servants, but caught no sight of Em. He'd expected she'd be here already.

He nodded to the human and the elf and carefully eased one of the trays of full glasses off the table. It was wide and awkward to hold. He placed his right hand at the center of the base, palm up, with his other hand steadying the tray along the side.

Servants bustled all around him, carrying drinks and hors d'oeuvres, and Gunnar held his tray as high as he could to avoid spilling.

Dexterity's a good fit for a bartender too, who knew?

Well, more like bar delivery boy, but it was no matter.

The circular patio contained a large fountain with a sculpture of a pair of pegasus—*pegasi?* Water gushed from their mouths into a pool about thirty feet across, which flashed in colors of purple and yellow and orange. The patio itself was probably twenty yards across and enclosed by trellises bedecked with vines and flowers. Glowing orbs of light hung from the beams, casting everything in a soft glow.

Nobles began to fill the patio, pouring out of the great hall of Dravingdel's manor and leisurely making their way down a wide set of steps from the balcony. A large half-moon bar was set at the edge of the patio, and Gunnar set the tray on a small table beside it.

The bartenders were busy preparing an array of drinks, and serving girls ferried them quickly out to the nobles. The servers carried smaller trays, but Gunnar was impressed at how deftly they maneuvered with precariously balanced glasses. Each of the girls was dressed in the same short black skirt and low-cut maroon blouse. Like the girls at the Mermaid, they were as much a part of the show as any actual performer.

"I'll take one of those if you don't mind."

Gunnar spun at the voice, and he had to make a conscious effort not to let his mouth gape.

Em flashed a bright lipsticked smile. She was dressed in a sapphire gown that rivaled that of any noblewoman in the entire garden party. Her red hair was pinned back with golden brooches specked with tiny jewels that made her green eyes shine. The gown itself was strapless, with a plume of fabric that billowed out from her waist in frills and trailed behind her.

She looked stunning, and not at all how Gunnar had expected. She was *attending* this party.

"I, er, sure, madam," he said, fetching a glass from the tray. There was no one too close, so he added in a whisper, "I thought you would be here, you know, looking like me."

Em leaned back and chuckled a little harder than seemed appropriate in response. She leaned close and took the glass of red wine from his hand. As she took it, he felt something drop into the front of his apron.

With a wave of her hand, Em spun away and hurried over to chat with a small troupe of young noblewomen.

Gunnar shook his head, perplexed.

She carried herself with such confidence and grace, it was hard to picture her as the same girl with whom he'd fought

Fulcra and climbed walls. It seemed the Nighthawk connections ran deep. She pulled off the noble so well, he almost wondered whether she actually descended from some type of wealth or nobility.

Unlikely, but then again, he did not know with any certainty that prisoners were the only source of players in this world.

Gunnar quickly glanced down into his apron and found a tightly sealed envelope.

Benton's Letter

Item Class: Rare, Quest-based
Weight: 0.1
Description: This letter is identical in form and seal to a second letter, which Admiral Benton is expecting to receive from another party. You must replace that letter before he has a chance to read it.

"Hurry up," hollered one of the bartenders behind him. "Those wineglasses won't fetch themselves."

Gunnar hurried back to the serving station and hauled several more trays out to the party.

By the time he was done, it was time to deliver food. The silver platters contained all kinds of delicacies—ornately glazed meats, steaming loaves of bread, brightly colored vegetables and fruits, caviar, lobsters and crab legs, and oysters. The smells made his stomach grumble, and these platters were much heavier than the glasses. His arms ached a little by the end, and he was glad for a brief pause while Dravingdel addressed his guests.

The nobles had moved to tables at a second patio at the edge of the gardens, and the nobleman stood upon a small dais and raised a toast.

Gunnar leaned against a pillar at the edge of the dining space while Dravingdel humble-bragged about the recent business successes that had brought him to the Golden Hills and allowed him to throw this party.

No more than twenty seconds into the address, a message appeared.

Em: *You look good in a suit. For a servant.*

Gunnar: *A gracious compliment from someone so high class.*

Em: *Should have told you I'd be attending, not working. But your face was priceless, so I regret nothing.*

Gunnar: *Of course you don't.*

Em: *You spot Benton yet?*

Gunnar: *I've been a bit busy.*

Em: *Things should slow down once the meal's over. Look for the feathery captain's hat, the table closest to the water.*

Gunnar scanned the seated guests. There were a few hats in the crowd, though most were worn by women, so Benton was not too hard to spot.

He was tall and bore the slight paunch of a middle-aged man who had once been incredibly built. Even seated, he towered over the other guests at the table and dominated the space.

Though few seemed to care about what Dravingdel had to say, most still gave the appearance of listening. Admiral Benton, on the other hand, remained with his back toward Dravingdel, gesticulating wildly as he spoke to an enraptured table of guests.

One of whom was Em. The chimera leaned forward on her elbows and smiled and nodded and giggled as the charismatic man spoke.

Em: *A douche, isn't he?*

Gunnar: *Dravingdel keeps glaring over at him. It's kinda funny.*

Em: *I'll be keeping an eye out for the arrival of the first letter. I don't expect anything to happen during dinner. Too many people around to see something. Just make sure you're ready when the time comes.*

40

THE DROP

Finally, Dravingdel finished his address to the crowd, and dinner was served. The garden came alive with music as servants pulled silver lids off the platters and nobles dug into their delicacies. Gunnar wanted to keep an eye on Admiral Benton, but he soon was hissed at by one of the lead servants to grab empty plates the moment the nobles were finished.

This kept him rushing the entire meal, as most of the nobles wanted new plates for literally every dish they tried. Gunnar found himself darting back and forth across the dining area, thanking the gods he'd never taken a job as a waiter IRL.

It was constant. If it wasn't a new plate, it was an empty glass, or cleaning up something that had fallen on the ground. The nobles did not even acknowledge his existence as Gunnar hurried around, attempting to meet every need while being as invisible as possible.

This was more than could be said for the experience of the cocktail waitresses. More than a few old men pulled the girls close by the waist to tell them some joke, and they were forced to offer obligatory giggles and smiles. The nobles stared unabashedly at their asses as they walked away, more than once after an unsolicited squeeze or slap.

It was not as though this was unique behavior to these nobles—every bar or party Gunnar had ever been to had contained plenty of assholes like that. But this was different. Everything at this party was for the nobles' personal disposal.

Gunnar's first impression of the party was that it was wondrous, but his sense of wonder quickly turned to contempt as he watched the real nature of the nobles on display. It was the waitresses. The man who'd been slaughtered in the streets. The dwarves he knew were locked up somewhere in this estate. As Gunnar scurried around, he took plate upon plate of wasted lobster and caviar and steak that only had a bite or two taken out of it before the noble decided to move on to another delicacy.

He could not help but picture the rat the hobos had been eating only a few hours ago.

The way everyone carried on in this city as though this behavior were just to be expected made Gunnar angrier than anything. This was supposed to be a game, and yet it was just like all the worst parts of the real world.

Soon, Dravingdel announced the end of the main course, and the nobles moved from the garden back to the fountain area for more cocktails.

Two twenty-foot poles had been rigged over the large pool of water, with small platforms on each. A pair of dusk elves began a routine of acrobatic stunts, hopping and spinning and flipping back and forth between the platforms. The man swung down and hung from the sides of the poles. The woman leapt and the man caught her, and together, they twirled around the pole. Then, with an impressive swing, the man flipped the woman back up to the opposing platform.

The elves were remarkably talented, but most of the nobles in attendance offered little more than a golf clap as the acrobats finished their routine. Seeming to read the room, the couple upped the ante. The woman shouted something in a foreign language.

From beneath the surface of the fountain pool, large spikes emerged directly below the platforms. A flurry of murmurs filled the place.

The pair began a new routine, with the man standing on his hands while the woman stood upon his feet. He transferred her to only one foot, and with an arc of her back, she flipped, landing on one hand supported by only one of the man's feet.

Now, the nobles were paying attention. The male acrobat cocked his leg and launched the woman over to the other platform.

But he overshot.

The woman flew over the platform, the edge slipping from her grasp.

Gasps filled the garden as she plunged toward the spikes below.

Gunnar's stomach knotted as he feared her grisly end.

Impossibly quick, the man dove after her, leaping from his own platform in a swan dive. In the same movement, he caught her by the arms while his legs latched onto the pole supporting the platform. The two twirled down and down, stopping mere inches from the threatening spikes.

The crowd erupted in cheers.

The spikes vanished into the base of the pool, and the couple dropped into the water to even louder cheers.

Gunnar shook his head, wondering how anyone could choreograph a moment like that.

All eyes were on the pair when Gunnar received a message.

Em: *Benton has the letter! Right coat pocket.*

Gunnar: *Where is he?*

Em: *By the bar. Don't let him get alone with that letter, or this is over.*

Gunnar caught sight of the large sailor at the edge of the patio and inched his way closer as a new act began—this time an opera singer. Gunnar recalled what Em and Leilani had said about how the nobles of the Golden Hills liked to put on an air of sophistication. But their tastes would devolve as the night went on. He'd already seen hints of that with the acrobats. Several had seemed a little disappointed that the act had ended so successfully.

And sure enough, as a woman in a billowing silver dress belted out her melody, most of the nobles returned to their drinks and their conversations.

Benton was no different. In one hand, he raised a highball of some dark liquor to the crowd around him. His other hand was wrapped around the waist of one of the waitresses. Several nobles were gathered as he recounted some tale of hunting pirates in a booming voice that carried over the patio and clashed with the singing.

No one around him seemed to mind.

Gunnar hurried over to the bar.

Gunnar: *What's he drinking?*

Em: *No idea. He calls it Kraken Piss.*

Gunnar: *Is that a real drink?*

Em: *I dunno, it's really dark.*

He turned to one of the bartenders. "You don't happen to know a drink called Kraken Piss, do you?"

The woman's scowl answered the question. He cursed to himself, but decided he would just have to go with his gut.

"Sorry, one of Benton's jokes. I need a, er... black rum."

Gunnar snatched up the drink, but as he approached, the admiral excused himself from his group of nobles and began to wade through the crowd, heading straight for Dravingdel's manor.

He hurried after the man as quick as he could, spilling the drink a little over the sides of the glass. He hurried up the stairs to the balcony, where several tall doors were spread open so nobles could come and go from a vast hall.

"Hey, servant!"

A hand grabbed him by the shoulder and spun him around. His breath caught.

It was Dravingdel.

"Y-yes, my lord," Gunnar said softly, offering a quick bow.

The nobleman wrapped his arm around his shoulder and pointed out to the crowd, few of whom were paying attention to the singer's performance.

"Look at them! Most of them are already half drunk."

"It's a great party."

"And they're fucking bored!"

"No one's bored, my lord. The party is still young."

Dravingdel shook his head, and Gunnar realized the man was half drunk himself. "Nah! They want blood. You could see it on their faces with those damn spikes in the fountain. Tell Turk I want a bloody show. And quick!"

"My lord, they've not yet had dessert."

"Sweets? I said they want blood. It's time for the nightlife to begin."

"Yes, my lord."

Gunnar cursed to himself and turned. Benton had just gone inside when Dravingdel grabbed him. His heart pounded as he scanned the crowd of nobles in the great hall. Benton had already disappeared from sight. There were two narrow halls that branched out at the ends of the room, and another broad corridor that Gunnar guessed would lead back to the entrance.

Considering Benton was looking for privacy, he chose the nearest narrow hall.

He turned the corner and scanned the open rooms. His heart raced when he caught sight of the man's voluminous hat.

Benton stood in a small library, chatting with a man in an old and rather faded suit. The strange man had his back to Gunnar, but something he'd said sent Benton into a fit of laughter.

"You mean to tell me you sailed with Old Blueballs?" Benton howled.

"Never let us go to the gods-damned shore!" the man said. "The crew nearly went mad!"

Benton keeled forward, hands on his gut as he roared. "He was always a bloody prick."

This was not the private moment that Gunnar had hoped for, but it was all he had. He hurried into the library, holding out the drink.

As he entered, he froze. The man Benton was talking with was Kohli.

[41]

LIARS

THE THIEF's suit was drab and out of place amongst the finery in Dravingdel's estate. His curly hair was a mess. And yet he was here.

Why the hell is he here? How did he even know where I was?

Kohli merely flashed a smile at him.

Gunnar managed to recover from the surprise, and stepped forward into the library.

"What do you want?" Benton asked as Gunnar neared.

"My lord, another drink for you. Courtesy of Lord Dravingdel himself."

Benton's eyes widened. "A drink, hm? What drink?"

"Kraken Piss, I believe."

Benton leaned forward to investigate, giving the drink a literal sniff. It was just enough for Gunnar to do what he'd come for.

The grab and drop was easier than he'd expected. Or perhaps he had just gotten that good at pickpocketing over the past few days. As the admiral bent over, Gunnar held the drink out with his right hand, and with his left, he swiftly replaced the letter in Benton's pocket with his own.

"Ah, black rum, it is," Benton said. "Dravingdel's not as daft as I thought. And you can tell him that. But I've got to go dump my own piss, first. Where the hell do I do that?"

"The corner would serve just fine," Kohli said.

"Fire in the hole!" Benton shouted.

The two men laughed.

But Gunnar shook his head. "Check down the hall near the kitchen, my lord."

"Hold my drink till I get back."

Admiral Benton staggered off down the hall, leaving them alone.

Gunnar turned on Kohli. "How the hell did you get in here dressed like that?"

Kohli smirked and shrugged. "Enough Charisma can get you in anywhere."

"You used the Crypt Keeper's spell? Why are you here?"

"This don't look like a dinner with the House of Daggers, does it?" Kohli leaned in close, a finger pressed against Gunnar's chest in accusation.

"I lied," Gunner said irritably. "I'm sorry. I wasn't supposed to talk about it. I'm still not. I had a quest tonight. I couldn't make it to that meeting."

"A quest so bloody important you'd pass on a chance at a trial with the House of Daggers? Come on, mate. I may be dumb, but I en't stupid. I know you've been making other connections. I know you've been running around with that chimera chick ever since the crypt. I warned you she was bad news."

"Just trying to make my way in this damn city."

"It's all right," Kohli said softly, leaning close. "You're not the only liar."

"What are you talking about?" Gunnar felt sick to his stomach, but he didn't understand what was going on. "Why did you follow me? Why were you talking to Benton?"

"Just following orders."

"Whose orders?"

"Who do you think? Sykes had his suspicions, so he tracked you here, and sent me after. Looks like he was right."

"Tracked me?" And then, Gunnar understood. He reached into his Inventory and pulled out the Man of the Mermaid coin.

Kohli smiled. "Sykes knew there was something off about you. He didn't trust you from day one. That's why we were paired. That's why I followed you into that crypt. Why I played along when you stabbed me in the back in that warehouse."

"I don't know what you're talking about."

"You're a damn traitor!" Kohli hissed, shoving him back into the bookshelf.

Gunnar's mind was whirling. "I'm here for the same reason as you. Just trying to get into a guild."

"Oh, I doubt that," Kohli said spitefully.

"Look, I've got to go before Benton gets back."

"Yeah, he'll be looking for what you took, won't he?"

Gunnar's gut churned as the thief withdrew a letter from his cloak. Gunnar scrambled to check the inside pocket of his coat. The letter he'd stolen was still there.

Kohli had stolen the one he'd planted moments after he'd made his drop.

Gunnar cursed himself for ever trusting a thief like him. "You're making a big mistake."

Kohli glowered. "I told you Sykes don't like the Nighthawks. I warned you to stay away from them."

"When Benton realizes it's gone, he's going to be furious."

"With you, sure. But me, I'll be swooping in at the perfect moment. Saving the day. That'll get me in good with Sykes and the rest of the higher-ups in this city."

The thief shoved him again, and the back of Gunnar's head cracked against the thick wood of the shelf. Kohli stepped back and drew a dagger. "It's no hard feelings, mate. I need a break, and Sykes can get me another trial. Now, I'm gonna need that original letter too."

Gunnar shook his head and drew his own blade. "No."

"Don't be a fool. We both know I'm the better fighter. Give it to me peacefully, and I swear to god, I'll let you go. I doubt you'll make it far once Benton realizes what you were doing. But I'm a nice guy, so we'll give you a shot."

"And if I refuse? You're just going to shank me?"

"You were the one who took me out from behind."

"Afraid it won't be the last time!"

The new voice pulled Kohli away.

He turned.

There was a loud thud, and Kohli slumped over and collapsed on the floor.

Em stood over him, bearing a large bronze candlestick. She set it back on a small table by the entrance and grinned. Strands of red hair stuck out in a disheveled, but very attractive manner. Em straightened her dress and glanced around the room, then closed the library door behind her.

"Told you I didn't trust this dog. Or his master."

"Thanks, er, you're not gonna..."

"Kill him? He'd just respawn anyway. Besides, we don't want to rile anyone up before we're done here."

Kohli twitched on the ground, but he was very unconscious.

"Move him over by the shelf."

Gunnar picked the thief up under the armpits and pulled him back so he was sitting slumped against the bookcase. Em snatched the highball of Kraken Piss, which had spilled on the floor during the confrontation, and set the nearly empty glass by his limp hand.

"What the hell is going on here?" Admiral Benton's voice boomed from the doorway.

Em spun and offered a wide smile. "Afraid this fellow's had a bit too much already, Admiral."

Benton crossed his arms and surveyed the room, then shook his head. "Typical. No one can hold real liquor anymore."

"My lord," Gunnar said, hurrying over. "This must have slipped out of your pocket when you left." He handed the Nighthawks' letter to the sailor. Benton turned it over with clear relief as his fingers swiftly brushed over the seal.

"Much obliged." Benton stowed it in his pocket and turned to leave.

"Er, my lord," Gunnar said. "I'm afraid this gentleman took your drink after you left. But I'd be happy to fetch you another."

"My drink?" the admiral asked. He glanced at Kohli, then Gunnar. He was clearly preoccupied with the letter, and Gunnar had a feeling the man was pretty liquored up as well. "Oh, right. Think I'll switch to water. Put out the fire for a while."

With that, he left, closing the library door behind him.

Gunnar took the first letter out of his apron and handed it to Em. She inspected the seal, which was thankfully unbroken, then walked over to the hearth and tossed the letter in the flames.

[*Congratulations! You have completed the quest* The Purloined Letter! *You have successfully swapped Admiral Benton's letter with one from the Nighthawks. Here's* 150 XP!]

[*Congratulations! You have completed a guild trial. You have passed the entry stage for a class. You are now an Initiate-level Rogue. You have built trust with the Nighthawks and have the opportunity to join their guild:* +2 *to Dexterity,* +1 *to Intelligence,* +1 *to Wisdom.*]

[*Congratulations! You have reached Level* 10 *in Glory!*]

The flames froze, and Gunnar turned to find Nymoria standing before him. She reached out her hand, and her warm fingers gripped his own. His entire body felt warm and light at her touch.

"Well done, faithful servant. You have reached a new level of achievement. Not all my servants reach such heights. As a bonus reward for reaching Level 10, you have earned double attribute points. Both points can be distributed at any time. But remember that every choice you make will echo into eternity. Choose wisely."

Nymoria vanished, and the room flickered with the lapping flames as the last curled bits of paper disintegrated in the fire.

Gunnar was filled with relief, and he leaned against the shelf for a moment. His heart was still pounding. He'd thought for sure that Benton would figure out what was going on. But he'd done it.

"Congratulations," Em said with a grin. "Your trial is complete. Leilani will meet you outside the Golden Hills once all this is over."

Gunnar nodded, but he didn't feel the satisfaction he ought to. Only now was he able to fully take in all that had just happened.

Kohli had betrayed him. And Sykes had been tracking him. Still was tracking him.

He took out the Man of the Mermaid coin and stuck it in Kohli's breast pocket.

Standing, he turned to Em, who said, "I should be getting back to the party, and you should be getting to that dwarf. The nobles' darker fare is going to be starting soon."

But Gunnar shook his head. "Why would someone like Kohli want to interfere with that quest? He wanted to help a noble. On Sykes' orders."

Em nodded. "Because most of the guilds are in the pockets

of the nobles. That's the way this city works. That's why you can't bother the Red Cloaks or the priests or the high nobles. That's why the Nighthawks are—"

But Em didn't finish.

There was a commotion at the door.

42

WINE AND CHOCOLATE

SOMEONE FUMBLED with the handle of the library door, giggling loudly. Em and Gunnar glanced at each other. A drunk passed out on the floor was one thing, but there was no reason for a servant like Gunnar to be in here. His heart pounded as the handle turned.

Then, Em did something he was not at all prepared for.

She shoved Gunnar up against the bookcase, hands grasping the sides of his head, and pressed her lips against his. Gunnar's entire body instantly went from icy terror to fire. The chimera tasted like strawberry wine and chocolate, and the rosy scent of her perfume enveloped him.

The door was thrown open, but Em just kept kissing him, nipping at his lip, her tongue flirting at the edge of his mouth, brushing fleetingly with his own. Her claws protracted from the tips of her fingers, brushing against his skull, sending shivers coursing through him.

"Ah, looks like this one's already taken," a woman behind them said with a cackle.

But neither Em nor Gunnar acknowledged them. The door clicked closed again, and Em pulled her lips gently away and paused, listening. Her eyes were bright and wide, and for the first time, Gunnar noticed a curious ring of gold around her irises that made them radiate in the fiery light of the room. Her breaths were warm and rapid.

Em sighed with relief as she glanced at the closed door, then slowly eased her body off of him.

Her fingers slipped away from his elven ears, her face flushed as she met his gaze. "Sorry, I couldn't think of anything else."

Gunnar glanced from Em to the floor, then back. "No, it's, er, fine. I didn't mind. I mean, well, it's no problem. It worked, right?"

Gunnar was pretty sure he'd never been so embarrassed and turned on at the same time. Unfortunately, this elicited an unconscious laugh, which was precisely *not* the reaction he wanted.

Em glanced away, and then she laughed too, her hand touching her mouth. She pulled away, and she moved for the door.

"Your friend won't stay in that stupor much longer. We should go. There's a guarded door near the kitchens. Pretty sure it leads down to Dravingdel's wine cellar. I bet that's where you'll find your dwarf."

Em slipped out the door, leaving Gunnar alone. His mind whirled at what had just happened. But he didn't have time to dwell on it. He opened the door and glanced out into the hall. A roar erupted from the courtyard beyond.

It had been maybe fifteen minutes since his run-in with Dravingdel, and Gunnar guessed the noble had found some-body else to get his *bloody show* started. Which meant Gunnar really didn't have much time.

A Red Cloak came hurrying down the hall, heading toward

the great hall, and Gunnar waved at the man as he neared. The guard grimaced.

"There's a problem in here," Gunnar said, pointing back into the library.

The guard's brow furrowed. "That so?"

"Someone's out cold," Gunnar said. "I... I'm worried he's dead."

The guard shook his head. "Well, that would be my damn luck tonight, wouldn't it? I'll have a look."

Gunnar pointed to Kohli, who was still slumped against the shelf.

The Red Cloak grimaced. "Probably just piss drunk, but better check."

The guard stooped down and felt at Kohli's neck for a pulse.

Gunnar seized the moment. He grabbed the bronze candlestick off the end table, activated Enhanced Blow, and swung with all his might at the back of his head.

[*You have dealt +15 Damage to Red Cloak Level 12.*]

The Red Cloak turned, eyes whirling with shock and rage, and Gunnar clocked him again. The second blow knocked him to the ground. He didn't move, though a thin line of blood leaked from his nose.

[*Your well-placed blow has triggered the effect Concussive Stupor. Here's 5 XP!*]

Gunnar swiftly closed the library door again, then wrestled the man out of his cloak.

Crimson Cloak

Item Class: Common, Stolen
Quality: Average
Weight: 2.5
Description: These cloaks are only issued to conscripted members of the Thailen city watch. If you are caught wearing it

without the proper conscription papers, it will be assumed you have stolen it. Penalty usually results in execution. Execution usually results in death.

Beneath his cloak, the guard wore a fancy shirt and tailored pants much like all the other servants at this party, and a standard issue saber and thick black belt, which Gunnar also took. A stream of blue sparks indicated there was still loot to be taken, and upon quick inspection, he found twenty-four coins and a Potion of Minor Healing.

Once Gunnar propped the man against the shelf and wiped the blood from his nose, he and Kohli looked like they'd passed out together. The guard was of a thicker build than Gunnar, so the cloak wasn't a perfect fit. But it was close enough.

It didn't solve everything about his disguise, however. All it would take was for another guard to hit him with Scan, and they would instantly realize Gunnar was not a true Red Cloak. But from studying his progress earlier that day, he knew just what might help.

He applied one of his attribute points to Wisdom, bringing it to Level 10, and applied all five skill points to Perception.

[*Congratulations! You have made progress along your path. You have unlocked a new feature for the spell Scan. You may now adjust the information that others can perceive when they hit you with Scan. Understand that this only works against characters with a lower level of Perception than you possess.*]

His Scan had already been adjusted once, thanks to his forged papers from Hel. But now, he was able to select the information and enter what he wanted. He hastily changed his information to reflect a Red Cloak.

Considering it had taken him two attacks to successfully knock out the latest Red Cloak, he decided to assign the last point to Strength. He applied two skill points to Enhanced Blow and the last one to Sheer Strength.

Gunnar set the bludgeon/candlestick back on the small table at the entrance and hurried out of the room, closing the door behind him. He pulled his hood up, hopefully masking his elven ears.

There was a lot of noise coming from the courtyard, gasps and shouts and raucous cheering, and Gunnar hoped he wasn't too late. Winding down a couple more narrow hallways, he found a door where another Red Cloak stood watch.

Here goes nothing, he thought.

The man stood at attention, crossing his right hand over his chest. Gunnar returned the salute.

"Ready for more already, are they?"

Gunnar nodded. "You know how these parties go. Lord Dravingdel wants the dwarves next."

The man chuckled. "Ah, I wish I could watch that one. Always love watching those dumb buggers get tossed around. The way they squeal, ya know?"

Gunnar forced himself to laugh. "Oh, I know! I'll be sure to give you the play-by-play when I come back for the next round."

"Aha, good man." The Red Cloak opened the cellar door. "You just get assigned here for the party?"

Gunnar's heart rate quickened, but he nodded.

"I figured as much. Look, Dravingdel don't like having those buggers so much as passing through his home. Make sure you take them out the back entrance."

Gunnar nodded. "Of course. Turk mentioned that too."

"Turk," the man muttered.

"The worst, isn't he?"

"Twats like him always are. You'd think he worked for one of the high lords. Give a small dude a little taste of power... am I right?"

Gunnar grinned and nodded. "I'll be sure to tell him you send your regards."

That got the man laughing. "You need any help with those dwarves?"

"Only two, and they're chained up. I'll be good."

"Good man. It's a shame the rest of the shipment didn't come in time, ey?"

"Shipment?" Gunnar asked.

"From the Isles. You know, proper slaves. The shipment got delayed apparently. Dravingdel had all sorts of plans for this party, but had to settle for whatever he could dredge up from the gutters. I've a buddy who does dock duty. Hear it's coming in tonight. A shame. Dravingdel was only a few hours away from a real good time. Anyway, have fun down there."

The guard handed him a torch from the wall just inside the entrance, then closed the door behind him.

Once alone, Gunnar swiftly returned the torch to its hold and equipped two daggers from his Inventory, stowing them on his belt. Then, he descended a winding staircase into the bowels of Dravingdel's estate.

The light quickly faded behind him, and Gunnar cast Dark Sight.

[PART 5]
THE REAL GAME

43

PRISON BREAK

THE STAIRS MUST HAVE DESCENDED forty feet or more beneath the surface of Dravingdel's estate. Clearly this place had been designed with the intent of storing much more than wine. At the base of the stairs, Gunnar could see glints of light at the end of a long corridor lined with thick doors. He contemplated checking each one, but considering the fact that Dravingdel had an exterior exit from this place, he suspected the first rooms were the ones used for food or liquor storage. A quick glance behind the first door confirmed it.

Barrels upon barrels of food.

Gunnar continued on to the end of the hall. Between activating Stealth and the new boots Nymoria had gifted him, his steps were nearly inaudible. He crept down the dark corridor and slowed his pace as he neared the corner. A single lantern was fixed to the wall. Gunnar suddenly wished he'd had time to learn some magic. Fire or air magic could easily extinguish the flames, he expected. If he survived this quest with his future intact, he'd make sure to explore his magic options further.

One of his throwing blades might be able to dislodge it from the wall, but that would make noise. If there were any guards nearby, broken glass was sure to set them on alert.

It's a shame I haven't leveled Perception higher, then I could know for sure.

Currently, once he had physically spotted a mob, they would appear as a dot in his MiniNav, along with a color corresponding to their level of threat. Once he reached Level 30, he would unlock more informative features that would allow him to see mobs on his map before they reached him. But for now, until he turned that corner, there was simply no way to know what lay ahead.

He deactivated Dark Sight as he neared. His hand hovered at the hilt of his blade as he stepped into the light and turned the corner.

Another long corridor extended straight ahead, lined with more doors. At the end was another corner lit by a lone lantern. Gunnar walked carefully forward once more in the dark, listening for any signs that these doors contained any of Dravingdel's prisoners.

He could hear a distant clamor ahead, but this hall was silent as well. Gunnar poked his head through one door, but found only shelves of cloths and linens. He hurried to the next corner and stepped once more into the light.

One of the doors creaked and voices echoed up the hall.

Gunnar dashed forward into the darkness of the next corridor and dropped to one knee.

Near the end of the hall, a pair of Red Cloaks emerged from one of the doorways, chattering and laughing as they dragged a goblin from the room. Dressed in nothing but a loincloth, the creature hobbled on a bum leg as the guards jerked him forward.

They headed down the hall, away from where Gunnar hid. He followed after, boots treading softly on the hard stone.

The end of the hall opened into a wide room the size of a

gymnasium filled with crates and cages. Gunnar remained back in the shadows and watched.

There were two more Red Cloaks that Gunnar could see, who took the goblin from the other guards and headed toward a staircase at the far end of the expansive chamber. There was a series of loud growls coming from the cages that set Gunnar's teeth on edge.

Two more Red Cloaks came into view, holding a pair of lunging dogs. They were massive, probably one hundred pounds and all muscle. Even with leather muzzles, the dogs made an incredible amount of noise.

The guards and the dogs set off after the Red Cloaks with the goblin, and Gunnar shuddered at the thought of what sort of show might be about to occur in the party aboveground. Two Red Cloaks remained in the large room. They chatted for a while, and Gunnar tried to decide what to do.

Clearly some of the rooms in the hall behind him contained prisoners. But the crates and cages here contained some as well. The chamber was filled with the pawing and growling of beasts and the muffled cries of presumably gagged prisoners.

Gunnar had hoped to find a way to do this stealthily, but time was not on his side. Hood drawn tightly, he strode into the room with as much confidence as he could manage.

The two Red Cloaks spun, hands hovering at the hilts of their swords, but at the sight of his cloak, they relaxed.

Gunnar offered a salute and they returned it, then he walked over to greet them.

"Gods! You gave me a start," one of them said.

"What're you doing walking in the dark?" asked the other.

"Sorry, my torch winked out. Must have caught a draft a ways back."

The Red Cloaks nodded, as though they had encountered this before.

"Here for dwarves," Gunnar said. "Can you point me in the right direction?"

The taller of the guards glanced at his companion, then nodded. "Aye, they're back down the hall you came from."

"We'll show you," said the other.

The two Red Cloaks led the way back down the hall, the taller of them lighting the way with a lantern. There were stirrings from beyond the doors as they walked past. Whatever was within began hollering beneath gags and rattling chains.

"Exciting night," Gunnar said as he followed the taller Red Cloak. The shorter one followed behind them.

The tall one grunted softly in answer.

"It's been a long week," the short one said. "And since that shipment was delayed, it put Dravingdel into a piss-poor mood about this party, had several of us out all last night hunting more lowlifes for this bloody show."

"Only two dwarves," said the tall one, pointing at a door halfway down the hall. "Too bad they'll be used up in five minutes by the nobles."

"The nobles look nice and tidy for such a bloodthirsty bunch, don't they?" the short one asked with a laugh.

Gunnar nodded. The door was made of thick, solid wood, and Gunnar heard no noise coming from the other side.

"There were all kinds of things coming in on that ship," said the tall one, fiddling with a big ring of keys and finally inserting one into the lock.

"Goblins from the Rancid Forests," said the other. "Merfolk from the Dark Lagoon, elves from that bloody volcano."

"What're they called again?" asked the tall one.

"Maldan." The door opened as the man spoke the name of Gunnar's true clan, and just as Gunnar realized that the cell was empty, he felt a shove from behind.

He stumbled into the small room. Bracing himself against

the back wall, he turned to face the guards. Both had already drawn their weapons.

Heart racing, Gunnar reached for the sword he had taken from the Red Cloak.

"Don't think about it," the tall guard said, aiming a crossbow at his head.

Gunnar froze.

"You know the punishment for impersonating a member of the city watch?" said the shorter of the two men as he stepped into the room. He pointed his sword at Gunnar's chest and gestured to a pair of shackles hanging from the ceiling. "Hold up your hands."

Gunnar obeyed.

The short man threw back Gunnar's hood. "Maldan sw—"

But the man never finished. The moment Gunnar realized what was happening, he had drawn his Cloaked Dagger. The reach for his sword had only been a feint to distract them while he accessed his Inventory and activated the spell from the Crypt Keeper.

Gunnar plunged the invisible blade up through the man's throat and into his skull.

[*Critical Hit! You have dealt +50 Damage to Red Cloak Level 8.*]

The short man slumped forward and Gunnar caught him, blood gushing all over. The taller guard instinctively let his bolt fly, but his companion shielded Gunnar from the shot. The bolt shuddered in the man's back, and he dropped to the ground.

[*You have defeated Red Cloak Level 8 with an assist from an enemy! Here's 10 XP!*]

As the tall guard frantically worked to load a second bolt, Gunnar let a throwing blade fly. It struck the man in the thigh, and he staggered back, dropping the crossbow onto the ground.

[*You have dealt +20 Damage to Red Cloak Level 8.*]

[*You have triggered the effect Mortal Bleeding on Red Cloak Level 8!*]

Now, Gunnar drew his sword and stepped over the dead guard. The remaining Red Cloak scrambled to get away. Unable to lift off the ground, he dragged himself, shrieking as blood poured from the wound and trailed behind him.

"You're only going to make it worse, doing that," Gunnar said.

The man kept pulling himself along.

"Damn it, man, don't make me kill you."

The Red Cloak's chest was heaving, though he'd only made it a few yards down the hall.

"Stop!" Gunnar commanded.

And finally, the guard did. He was whimpering pitifully, though for once, Gunnar didn't feel bad about what he'd done.

[*You have dealt +10 Damage to Red Cloak Level 8.*]

"That blade hit your femoral artery," Gunnar said. "You'll bleed out if you keep that up."

"Just kill me and be done with it! Gods damn you!"

"I'm not going to kill you," Gunnar said. "You're going to drag your ass back to that cell. You're going to tie a tourniquet around your leg, and you're going to sit there with your dead buddy, applying pressure to that wound and thanking the gods that you're still alive. You hear?"

The Red Cloak nodded.

"But first, you're going to tell me where I can find my dwarves."

44

PANDEMONIUM

AFTER LOOTING the Red Cloaks for a pair of daggers, some coins, and two more Potions of Minor Healing, Gunnar returned to the open chamber of the cellar. In the distance, he could hear a low roar from the world above. He cringed imagining the sort of game that poor goblin had endured with those dogs.

The noise set him on edge. More Red Cloaks would be coming soon to collect the next show. Cages and crates rattled and rumbled as he walked past them. A wild boar charged the door to its cage when Gunnar walked a little too close, and he was pretty sure there was a tiger or a lion in one of the others.

Em: *What's taking so long?*

Gunnar: *Ran into a delay with a couple Red Cloaks. Took care of it.*

Em: *Things are getting wild up here. Hurry up, before they come for your dwarves.*

Gunnar: *Working on it.*

Em: *Your buddy Kohli is awake. Saw him running around the house. Looking for you, I'd guess.*

Gunnar: *I'll be up in a few minutes. Hopefully.*

Em: *Ah, shit. I gotta go.*

Gunnar: *What? What's going on? Em?*

But there was no reply. The noise from aboveground suddenly grew louder.

Gunnar just had to hope that Kohli didn't figure out that Em had been the one to knock him out.

At the far end of the room, Gunnar found the cage he was looking for. A pair of dwarves sat in the center of the small space.

"Come to do the dirty?" a redheaded dwarf said. He looked strikingly similar to his brother Dimble.

Gunnar threw back his hood. "I'll do you one better."

"Nimble, what's going on?" the other dwarf asked.

"Your brother sent me," Gunnar said.

Nimble glared at Gunnar, then shook his head at his companion. "This must be some sort of sick Red Cloak joke, Nort. It's time to face our fate. Let's just hope they give us a chance at glory before the end. I en't much of a fighter, but I'll go out in a blaze if I must. Gods know, I won't go home a broken man."

Gunnar fumbled with the keys for a moment until he found the one the Red Cloak had pointed out to him. Thankfully, it worked. The cage door opened.

"You won't be dying tonight," Gunnar said. "Not if I can help it."

He stooped through the low entrance and stepped into the cage. As he did, his hood fell back.

"A bloody elf?" Nimble demanded.

Nort's eyes went wide. "Never seen an elven Red Cloak before."

"Only thing worse than an elf," Nimble began, "is can elf who bends over for the Red Cloaks."

"Easy, easy," Gunnar said. "Hasn't the elf versus dwarf thing pretty much run its course, anyway? These humans have dumped on you same as me."

"Ugh! You sound like my damn brother."

Gunnar grunted with frustration. "That's what I'm trying to say. Your brother was in a performing troupe, and saw me try to help some idiot who refused to bow before the nobles."

"Good for him," Nimble said. "I don't believe a word you've said. You elves have always sided against us when it suits you."

Gunnar dropped to a knee and began fiddling with Nort's shackles first. "Dimble said you've got a family. That if you were to lose the use of your hands, they'd be in a bad place. So he offered me a quest."

None of the keys on the ring seemed to be small enough for the shackles.

Nimble sighed. "Me brother always was a bleeding heart. Reckon he mighta been desperate enough to offer an impossible quest around the city. And you must be desperate too, if you're the best he found. But you en't no Red Cloak, I can tell that for damn sure."

"Yeah?" Gunnar grunted, sifting through more keys.

"They got a separate key for the shackles, boy. Only the guards upstairs have it."

"Shit," Gunnar muttered, tossing the key ring aside.

He pulled out his lockpicks. The thin rods of metal slipped into the mechanism, and Gunnar carefully shifted them. Tension built as the rods ever so slightly brushed against the metal inside. He could feel something start to give, but just as it did, Nort shifted slightly, and both picks snapped.

"Leave it to my brother to send a professional," Nimble muttered.

"Gods, hold still," he commanded Nort. Shooting Nimble a glare, he added. "And you, stuff it."

He slipped a new set of rods in and turned one over the other. The mechanism shifted, and he gave one of the rods a turn.

Snap!

There was a thunderous roar from the world above. But this was different. It didn't sound like the climax of a show, bloody or not. This was the din of complete pandemonium. Shouts and screams and the thunder of frantic feet.

Gunnar: *What the hell's going on up there?*

No response.

Gunnar's nerves made it even harder to keep his fingers steady, and these tiny mechanisms were much more sensitive than the locks he'd tried at the training facility.

He snapped a third set of lockpicks the moment he turned them.

"Here, give me those."

The sudden voice made him leap and grab for a dagger. Both of the dwarves yelped in surprise.

There was no laughter in Em's voice. She stood there, still in full regal attire, though she looked a bit disheveled now. Without explanation, she grabbed the lockpicks from his hands and set to work on Nort's shackles.

"Who's she?" Nimble demanded.

"A friend," Gunnar said.

"A bloody noble?" Nort asked.

"Shut up!" Em commanded the dwarves.

"What the hell are you doing down here? What's going on topside?" Gunnar asked.

"You too! I'm trying to concentrate."

Gunnar grimaced at the rebuke, but said no more.

Em gritted her teeth and maneuvered the picks carefully, twisting them slightly over one another, and with a soft click, Nort's shackles fell away.

"Why didn't you bring *her* down in the first place?" Nimble asked.

"What's going on?" Gunnar demanded again.

"No time," Em said. "You next." She grabbed Nimble's shackles and set to work. Twenty seconds later, both dwarves were free, and Em led the way out of the cage.

"As soon as you two get to the surface, run as fast as you can for the south wall. It'll take you farthest away from the mayhem." Em handed the dwarves her grappling hook and rope from her Inventory. "How high can you toss this?"

"Far enough," Nimble said.

"We'll lead the way," Em said. "If there's trouble, run for the wall and get yourself out."

"I like her," Nort said.

"Very capable," Nimble said, shooting a pointed look at Gunnar.

Gunnar grabbed Em's wrist. "What is going on up there?"

"Benton is dead."

"What?" Gunnar demanded, but the moment he said it, he understood. "This wasn't just some damn letter swap."

Em shook her head. "The entire courtyard is going nuts. Dravingdel is trying to maintain order, but the nobles are freaking out."

"That's why Kohli was trying to stop me. To prevent an assassination."

"We don't have time for this, Gunnar. Your friend was talking to the Red Cloaks when I snuck away. They know we're behind this. We've got to go. Now!"

The four of them hurried through the maze of captured creatures. Gunnar wished there was something he could do for the others imprisoned in this place, but he knew there was no time.

A clamor arose down the hall. A pounding sound, followed

312 / S.A. KLOPFENSTEIN

by voices. Gunnar glimpsed the glow of a torch and crimson cloaks down the hall of cells he'd come from.

Gunnar, Em, and the dwarves ducked behind a large crate and peeked around the side. The crate rumbled, sending shivers shooting up Gunnar's spine. Something massive was inside that crate. Whatever it was let out a low growl.

They were close to the exit leading up to the gardens. But to reach that staircase, they would have to go out in the open.

The guards were not coming to the main chamber though. They stopped halfway down the hall. Right where Gunnar had left that Red Cloak bleeding out.

"We better just go for it," Gunnar said, a wrenching dread in the pit of his stomach.

Angry voices chattered as they opened the door to the cell. Gunnar couldn't tell for sure, but he guessed there were four or five Red Cloaks down there. More would come soon, and there were surely more at the surface. Though perhaps this business with Benton would keep most of them preoccupied up above.

"You lead the dwarves out," Em said.

"What're you going to do?"

Em smiled deviously. "Create a diversion."

She began fiddling with the lock at the end of the crate they were hiding behind. She pulled out Gunnar's lockpicks.

"These will probably work better," Gunnar said, holding out the guard's key ring.

"Nice," Em said, trading him for his picks.

Gunnar equipped his throwing blades, then motioned for the dwarves to follow, and they stepped out into the open chamber, hurrying for the staircase.

As soon as they reached the stairs, there was a shout from the hall.

Gunnar glanced back to find several Red Cloaks hurrying toward them.

"Go!" Em shouted.

Gunnar led the way up the stairs, but he glanced back one last time to see Em open up the crate. Gunnar had never seen a wolf outside of a zoo, but this particular one was larger than any he'd ever seen, with a huge metal ring around its neck.

Gunnar had forgotten about the Crypt Keeper's gift for Em, but she now stood on all fours in the full form of a fox.

The wolf sniffed her, then reared its head and charged toward the Red Cloaks.

45

CALL OF THE WILD

Em dashed over to another cage, and set to work on its lock. The guards cried out and drew their swords as the dire wolf barreled toward them. But Gunnar didn't see the rest. He hurried up the steps with the dwarves in tow. Just as they neared the top, the metal door at the surface opened.

At a glimpse of crimson, Gunnar let two throwing blades fly. One struck the guard in the shoulder but the other hit his neck.

[*Critical Hit! You have dealt +40 Damage to Red Cloak Level 9!*]

[*You have triggered the effect Mortal Bleeding on Red Cloak Level 9!*]

Impressively, the guard did not collapse. He hollered out into the gardens, then reached to his belt and produced a green vial.

Gunnar leapt up the last few stairs, drawing his sword as he went. Before the man could down the healing potion, Gunnar plunged his blade through the man's chest.

[*You have defeated Red Cloak Level 9! Here's 20 XP!*]

The potion tumbled down the staircase with a clatter, but one of the dwarves deftly snatched it from the air and stowed it away. Gunnar grabbed his throwing blades, wiped the blood off on his cloak, and returned them to their sheaths.

Screams and growls echoed up from the cellar below as they emerged near a greenhouse at the edge of the party.

Dravingdel's gardens were utter mayhem. Red Cloaks rushed around the fountain. Servants tried to calm frantic nobles. The Red Cloaks ordered people away from the dining area, where several bodies littered the ground in the midst of upturned tables. All the victims were regally dressed, but Gunnar could spot Benton's huge feathery admiral's hat lying on top of a table, even from a distance.

It wasn't just Benton who died.

Gunnar quickly shed his crimson cloak and tossed it into the bushes. There was still a little blood that had leaked onto his servant's uniform beneath, but considering what was going on below, he doubted it mattered.

He glanced back down the stairs. A Red Cloak appeared at the base, only to be mauled by a beast that Gunnar was pretty sure was a giant crustacean. A massive claw snatched the guard, and a gigantic blur charged past the door and out of sight.

Gunnar's heart pounded, but he couldn't help but marvel at what Em had orchestrated. There was no sign of her, in human or fox form.

Gunnar: *We're clear up here. Get out of there!*

No response.

Cursing to himself, he pointed beyond the greenhouse, where the wall of the estate loomed in the darkness.

"You two, get going," he ordered.

"What about you?" Nimble asked.

"I'm not leaving Em. We'll find you on the other side."

Nort and Nimble nodded, and the two dwarves trotted into the bushes and out of sight.

Gunnar hurried back down the staircase, body tensing as

loud growls echoed from below. But he never reached the bottom.

In fox form, Em turned the corner at the base of the stairs and came dashing past him. A Red Cloak raced after, and Gunnar let a throwing blade fly.

[*You have dealt +20 Damage to Red Cloak Level 7!*]

It wasn't a good shot, hitting him in the side, rather than anywhere critical. But the man paused and clutched the wound, and as Gunnar turned away, a dire wolf leapt upon the guard and dug massive fangs into his throat.

[*You have defeated Red Cloak Level 7 with an assist from Dire Wolf Level 10. Here's 5 XP!*]

The wolf looked up at him, and Gunnar could have sworn it nodded its thick muzzle. Then, it bounded after another Red Cloak with a snarl.

Unlocked Spell: Call of the Wild

Spell Type: Race-based, Celestial

Alignment: Light

Linked Attribute: Wisdom (+65% Development)

Bonded Creature: Dire Wolf

Bond Level: Basic

Description: You have shared a kill with a wild beast. As a dusk elf, this act has formed a basic spiritual bond with the creature. This tender moment of slaughter will not be forgotten.

Em: *Come on!*

She had nearly reached the surface. Gunnar turned away from the bedlam below and raced back up the stairs, closing the steel door behind him. When he reached the surface, there was no sign of the fox.

A couple of Red Cloaks came rushing over and clamped

thick locking beams over the door behind him, and Gunnar was especially glad he'd removed his cloak earlier.

"What the hell is going on down there, elf?" one of the them asked, securing one of several locks holding the beams in place.

Gunnar shook his head. "I was down fetching more wine, when I heard screams. Some of the beasts got out. It's a bloodbath."

"Gods!" the Red Cloak muttered.

The door rattled and there was a vicious growl beyond the door, but the beams held in place.

"What about the door in the house?" Gunnar thought aloud.

The two guards looked at each other in horror and hurried off.

There was still no sign of Em, so Gunnar dashed into the bushes and made for the wall.

Loud shrieks and snarls behind him suggested that the two Red Cloaks did not manage to secure the cellar door in time. Gunnar couldn't see the mayhem, but between dead nobles and loose beasts, he hoped it would be enough for them to get safely away.

The trees and shrubbery were cleared around the edges of the wall. Gunnar reached the space, but did not find Em or the dwarves.

Kohli stood in the clearing, dagger in his hand. The man looked haggard and beaten, and he was panting as he raised his blade.

Gunnar drew his sword. "Couldn't get any Red Cloaks to help you?"

Kohli glared. "They're a little busy, thanks to you."

"It's done, Kohli. You failed."

"Admiral Benton is dead. You've no idea what you've done."

Gunnar rolled his eyes. "What do you care?"

"Sykes cares, and I need Sykes if I'm going to survive in this world, so there you have it."

"Looks like you chose the wrong side," Gunnar said.

"There is an order to the underworld of this city, and you broke that order. There will be consequences."

"Maybe. But they won't be coming from you. As soon as Sykes realizes you failed, he'll cast you aside, just like all the others."

Kohli's eyes went wild with rage. "Then I guess I might as well go down with a bit of glory, eh?"

The thief leapt forward, but he never reached Gunnar.

Out of the darkness, a massive beastly blur leapt in front of Gunnar and collided with Kohli, tackling him to the ground with a loud snarl.

Kohli screamed like a child as the dire wolf's fangs buried into his side.

A grappling hook dropped from above, nearly smoking Gunnar in the head.

Back in human form, Em grinned from the wall above. "Let's get the hell out of here!"

Gunnar grabbed the rope and quickly ascended the wall as the hook retracted.

Kohli shrieked as he tried to resist the wolf, but he'd lost his dagger and was no match for such a powerful, vicious creature.

"Hey!" Gunnar shouted from the top of the wall.

At his commanding voice, the wolf lifted its head and backed away from Kohli. The thief groaned.

"We're safe now," Gunnar said. "Now, get out of there and save yourself."

The wolf glanced at Kohli, whose ragged suit was now drenched in blood. The wolf let out a low growl, then looked back up at Gunnar and nodded its thick head.

The creature bounded into the darkness. It had saved his

life. Gunnar just hoped it made it out of Dravingdel's estate safely.

"I'm gonna... ruin you," Kohli murmured from the ground below. His words were barely distinguishable, uttered between groans of agonizing pain.

Gunnar just shook his head. He'd been a fool to think the thief would learn. "Bring it on, asshole."

With that, Gunnar and Em quickly climbed down the other side and joined the dwarves at the base of the wall.

"That was bloody brilliant," Nimble said, shaking his head with a wicked grin.

"No time for celebration till we're out of the Golden Hills," Em said, leading the way down the hillside.

Clouds shrouded them in darkness, and Gunnar activated Dark Sight, letting him quickly and silently traipse through the tall grass and bushes. At one point, Gunnar could have sworn he heard Kohli hollering after them. But he guessed it was just some cry from Dravingdel's estate. The thief might be able to scale Dravingdel's wall, after taking a Health potion or something, but Gunnar knew Kohli didn't possess Dark Sight.

And besides, the man was a damn coward.

It only took them a few minutes to reach the walls of the Golden Hills. After rappelling the outer barrier, they slowed their pace, making their way carefully and silently through the small forest that led to the inner parts of the city.

When they neared the edge of the woods and could just see the glow of streetlamps beyond, Em held up her hand and they paused.

There was a rustle in the forest behind them.

46

ASSASSIN

A PAIR of glowing eyes shone from the darkness. The lights from the nearby streets addled Gunnar's vision, and he disabled Dark Sight. But that still didn't help him much.

There was a soft crunching of feet on the forest floor, and a dark shadow took shape at the edge of the forest.

"What the bloody hell is that?" Nimble murmured.

"Stay back," Em said softly. She transformed in an instant back into her fox form. She stepped into the shadows toward the glowing eyes.

Gunnar made to follow, but the fox turned and shook its head.

Em: *Leave this to me.*

But Gunnar ignored her. The dire wolf stepped out to meet them.

Gunnar's heart pounded in his chest, but he thought he knew why it had followed.

Stooping down to a knee, Gunnar held out his hand, keeping his eyes on the ground. He remembered hearing something about how eye contact was a sort of challenge for dogs, and he thought perhaps that was true with wolves as well. The dire wolf let out a low growl and sauntered forward.

Gunnar hadn't truly appreciated how large and powerful a creature it was back in the cellar. The wolf's shoulders were nearly as high as his own, while standing upright.

It sniffed him and then licked his fingers.

The wolf turned to Em's fox form and let out a series of low growls. Em did not move, offering only some soft growls of her own in return, keeping her eyes down.

Em: *She's thanking us. On behalf of all the creatures that were imprisoned down there.*

Gunnar responded out loud. "You're the one who freed them."

Em: *She seems to like you. You bonded with her. How?*

"Seems to be a racial ability. She finished off one of those Red Cloaks after I got him with a dagger."

Em: *Dravingdel ripped her away from her pack. The bond of the hunt is the strongest bond there is for her kind. You're not interested in a familiar, are you?*

Gunnar shook his head. "A dire wolf in a city like Thailen? I wish."

Em: *I'll let you break the news to her. I think she understands you when you speak.*

Em backed away from the wolf and trotted over to join the dwarves, who were shaking their heads, lingering grimaces of fear on their faces as they watched.

Gunnar reached out his hand once more to the wolf, and she brushed it with her nose. He let his fingers glide under her muzzle and scratched her neck. She let out a soft groan.

"Em may have set you free," Gunnar said, "but none of us would have gotten out of that hellhole without you. I wish you could stay with us, but there's nowhere for you to stay in this city."

The wolf glanced behind her, and somehow, Gunnar understood what she meant.

"These woods are too small for a big girl like you," Gunnar said. "You belong in the wild."

The dire wolf growled softly.

"You'll find a new pack. I'm sure of it. You saved my life back there. If we meet again, I hope I can return the favor."

The wolf nuzzled his hand with her nose and grunted.

[*Your bond with Dire Wolf Level 10 has increased to Novice. It's too bad you don't bond like this with women.*]

Gunnar cursed to himself, wishing he had a greater opportunity to develop the bond. If he were to ever leave this city, he could use an ally like her.

"Get out of Thailen. The Golden Hills lead to the mountains eventually, if you keep climbing beyond all the noble estates. Be careful."

The dire wolf let out one last growl, then turned and trotted into the darkness.

———

They soon returned to more familiar parts of the city.

Nort decided to part ways before they passed the busier trading districts. "Thought my life was over after I ended up on one o' them slavers. I'm most grateful."

He offered Gunnar and Em both a firm handshake.

"I only wish the others might've made it in time from that ship tonight," the dwarf said. "Maybe they would've got free too."

"Others?" Gunnar asked.

Em: *We don't have time for this...*

Gunnar offered her a glare but didn't respond.

"Sure," Nort said. "We all got rounded up together in Mavenport. Don't suppose there's anything you could do, is there?"

Quest Alert - Chainbreaker

Description: Nort and Nimble aren't the only slaves in Thailen. They come in by the shipload from cities all across the Altaean Sea.

Objective: Feeling cute. Might kick some ass and piss off some nobles.

Reward: Freeeedoommmm!

Do you wish to accept? Yes/No

Em: *Gunnar! We need to go.*

Gunnar sighed and clapped the dwarf on the shoulder. "Sorry, Nort. Don't think we can pull off another heist in one night." He figured it would expire on its own anyway, so he simply dismissed the prompt from his sight.

"You got a place to stay?" Gunnar asked.

Nort snorted with bemusement. "Not unless you include the clink. Afraid all I've seen of Thailen is the inside of a cage. But I'll figure something out."

"I might know somewhere you can go if you don't find a place."

"You've done too much already."

"I'll DM you the location. The rest is up to you."

Nort smiled. "Much obliged. Not met many good elves, Gunnar."

"You still en't met one," Nimble said with a chortle.

The two dwarves shared a very grunty embrace, and then

Gunnar, Em, and Nimble headed toward the spires of Luka's temple.

⎯⎯

Dimble the dwarf met them at the edge of the temple square. He and his brother clasped one another on the shoulder, then Dimble turned to Gunnar. The dwarf's family was there too. A bearded woman and a crew of four tiny dwarven kids smothered Nimble in embraces.

Gunnar felt warm inside as he watched the reunion. Though Nimble tried to maintain his gruff composure, he couldn't help letting a smile or two slip as he greeted his family.

Dimble grinned at Gunnar's side and slapped him on the back.

[*Congratulations! You have completed the quest* Dimble's Nimble. *You have returned Dimble's brother to his family safe and unspoiled. Here's 160 XP!*]

[*Congratulations! You have completed this quest while rescuing another innocent prisoner. You've earned the Two for One badge: +1 to Constitution, +1 to Strength, +1 to Agility, +1 to Dexterity.*]

[*Congratulations! You have made progress along your path. You have reached Level 16 in the skill Throwing Blade. You have reached Level 7 in Stealth. You have reached Level 8 in Dark Sight. You have reached Level 10 in Endurance.*]

[*Congratulations! You have reached Level 11 in Glory!*]

Nymoria appeared in the temple square and reached out her hand to him.

"Well done, faithful servant. "You have taken another step on the path to greatness. As a reward, you have earned one attribute point, which can be distributed at any time. But remember that every choice you make will echo into eternity. Choose wisely."

The goddess vanished, and Dimble shook Gunnar's hand vigorously.

"I'm forever grateful," Dimble said. "I wish there was more I could do."

Nimble grunted. "Quit groveling. The boy'll be amply rewarded for my rescue."

Gunnar raised a brow at the dwarf. "Is that so?"

"Have your foxy friend bring you by my shop sometime. I'll set you up well."

The dwarves left them alone in the square. There were a few pedestrians passing through, and a few drunks gathered close to the temple, but there was no one near.

Gunnar turned to Em. "You knew Nimble before all this?"

Em shrugged. "Maybe."

Now that the adrenaline of escaping the estate had faded, Gunnar's frustration with the way things had played out began to set in.

"None of this was a coincidence," Gunnar said. "The rescue quest. Our recon. Leilani."

"Nimble is a member of the Nighthawks. Our weapons master. The party provided multiple opportunities if you were ready for it. Turns out, you were."

There was a soft clanking sound that echoed up the streets. A sleek black carriage pulled up to the edge of the square and parked in the shadows. Waiting for him.

"You knew what would happen with that letter, didn't you?"

Em smiled coyly. "You're an assassin now."

"I took that quest to deliver a letter. To save a dwarf."

"You did save a dwarf, and with Benton dead, many other good people who would have been killed are saved too."

"Benton wasn't the only one who died," Gunnar said, picturing the bodies in the gardens. People he was pretty sure *he* had killed. Suddenly, the image of that blonde girl flashed through his mind. Car swirling. A scream and a thud. Her body covered in blood.

"I am not a killer!"

Em sighed. "You are though, Gunnar. That's what this is all about, and you know it. Benton's letter contained a poison, released into the air when he opened the letter. I can assure you that everyone who died deserved it, one way or another. You saw what kind of people were at that party."

This did little to quell the ache in his gut. "You played me."

Em gripped his shoulder. "You passed your trial with flying colors, Gunnar. I played you because I saw potential when we met in that crypt. And you proved what you're made of. So, quit whining like a little kid, and let's go celebrate with Leilani. She is going to be very pleased." Em tugged his arm toward the waiting carriage, but Gunnar shrugged her off.

"I can't celebrate yet," he said.

"What are you talking about?"

"You said this was about doing good? Well, there's a ship coming in tonight. More slaves for Dravingdel. Probably for other nobles as well. I couldn't free everyone back at that party. But maybe I can stop more from ending up there."

"Gunnar, you're a Nighthawk now. You can't just run off on whatever quest suits your fancy."

"I thought you Nighthawks were all about resisting the corruption of the nobles in this city."

Em glowered. "We are. But there is a process. You need approval from the guild masters, and—I don't know—a fucking plan?"

"That ship comes in any moment. If I talk to Leilani and join the Nighthawks, you think she'll let me go?"

"No, she won't. We've caused a lot of uproar tonight, and we've had no time to stake out this job. It's too risky. We have to be calculated. You can't save everyone in this city."

Gunnar began to walk away. "Well, maybe I'm not a good fit for the Nighthawks."

"Gunnar, don't be an idiot. This guild is your future in this world."

He didn't respond. He turned, making his way toward a nearby alley.

"What am I supposed to tell Leilani?" Em shouted.

"I'm sure you can think of a good lie."

Gunnar left Em behind and hurried into the city. As he ran, he sent a message.

Gunnar: *I've got a crazy quest for you. Interested?*

He had nearly reached the docks when he received the reply.

Sheira: *I like crazy.*

47

THE LEAP

GUNNAR AND SHEIRA met on the roof of a warehouse near the shipyards, not too far from the one Gunnar had emptied for Sykes.

After he finished telling the Maldan woman about the ship, Sheira just shook her head. "You want to rip off the cargo of an entire slaver?"

Gunnar nodded. "Or, you know, as many as we can pull off. But yeah, preferably all of them."

"Assuming it hasn't already come in."

"You track these sorts of ships, don't you?"

"You think I know about every ship in this city?"

Gunnar smirked. "Well, you sure had my ship's number when I first got here."

Sheira nodded. "You bet I did."

"So, do you know anything about the ship I'm talking about?"

"I might."

"Did it come in?"

"You're talking about the delayed slaver from Mavenport.

Had a shipment for Dravingdel. Kierkoven. Glavinstone. And Sykes."

Sykes? Gunnar thought. Then, he remembered one of the Red Cloaks saying something about merfolk on the ship's manifest. *So, that's where he gets his showgirls.* After what Sykes had pulled with Kohli and the tracking coin, Gunnar savored the thought of hurting his business.

"That's the one," Gunnar said.

"It was supposed to come in last night," Sheira said, "but there was a delay. Rumors of pirates."

Gunnar wondered if it was Black Heart. And whether the Nighthawks had had anything to do with it. "And tonight?"

Sheira grinned, seeming to enjoy dragging this out. "Those sorts of ships come in late. I mean really late."

"Dravingdel wasn't too shy about bringing his slaves out for the show."

"At a party of nobles," Sheira said. "You said you went for a dwarf who'd been abducted. He wasn't taken out in the open. The nobles don't hide it amongst themselves, but strictly speaking, slavery is illegal. Doesn't mean it don't happen, but it's in the dark as far as the lower classes are concerned."

"What about Sykes' mermaids?"

Sheira raised an eyebrow at this. "Got in with that snake, did you?"

"Well, you didn't take me under your wing, so someone had to, right?"

"Judging by your reaction when I listed off his name with the others, I'm guessing you had no idea he dealt with slaves until just now. Or that he was up to his ass in the nobles' coin purses either."

"Well, I already caught on to the nobles' purses bit when he tried to sabotage my guild trial, but yeah, I wouldn't have known before that."

"I'm guessing few do," Sheira said. "Those mermaids are probably under some spell. Or else he threatens them, or people close to them. That's how these people work. Sounds like your trial turned out better than my own."

Gunnar shrugged. "Marginally. I still got stabbed in the back."

"Figuratively."

Gunnar nodded. "But I completed the trial."

"So you're a Nighthawk now."

"I haven't accepted anything yet."

"Hmm," Sheira said. "That ship will arrive soon. We should go."

She didn't wait for an answer. The elf dashed across the rooftop and practically slid down the ladder to the ground below, and Gunnar tried to keep up.

Sheira might not have leveled up much since they'd met, but she was still stronger and faster than him. She raced through the shadows of the wharf, ducking under loading beams and weaving amongst the hundreds of crates that littered the area, waiting to be loaded and carted off around the city.

Several of the warehouses had guards posted, and a few Red Cloaks patrolled the main roads, but Sheira seemed to know exactly when to pause, or sink deeper into the shadows. They alerted no one, and soon stood near the edge of the shipyards at the base of a massive crane, whose arm jutted out over the water.

"Up you go, noob," Sheira said with a chuckle.

She pointed up the length of the crane. Gunnar paused, taking stock of the task before him. The arm was composed of beams of wood, set in a pyramidal pattern for support. But to even reach the arm, they had to climb the base, which stood thirty or forty feet high.

Gunnar gripped the coarse wood in his hands.

Sheira pointed out into the gloom of the harbor. White sails emerged from the fog. "Not much time."

He hoisted himself along the first massive support beam. Like the arm of the crane, the base was constructed with angled beams, making it difficult to ascend. He had to climb at an angle until he was high enough to reach the first crossbeam. The shift was awkward, but once his fingers latched onto the even grip of the beam, the next move was much smoother. Soon, he was twenty feet up, and Sheira began to follow, making it all look stupidly easy.

But Gunnar's climbing abilities had been improving, and though there were far fewer holds than on a wall of brick or stone, the coarse beams provided better grip. Once he found his rhythm, his speed increased. He soon pulled himself to the top. Sheira followed only moments behind him, and together, they walked out to the end of the crane's arm.

The wind was stronger up there, and Gunnar took each step with care. At his current Health levels, he doubted he would survive a fall from this height, and with the delay in his respawns, his chance to complete this quest would be over.

Sheira stooped to a knee at the end of the crane, peering into the fog as the ship drew nearer. Despite its size, the arm barely reached over the pier below.

"The ship won't come close enough," Gunnar muttered.

Sheira grinned. "We'll have to jump."

"Of course."

"The upper rigging of the mainsail will be our best bet."

The ship was only about twenty yards away.

"That still looks like a hell of a jump," Gunnar said.

"It is." Sheira chuckled. "There'll be someone in the crow's nest. Leave him to me. In fact, leave all the crew up top to me. You'll need to get down to the hold and free those prisoners as quick as possible. When you feel the ship coming to a stop, it's time to go. I don't care if you've got twenty, one, or none. You leave, got it?"

Gunnar nodded.

The ship crept slowly through the harbor, the only comfort he had for the jump ahead of him.

"A ship this small still has at least a dozen crew, maybe more. The fewer bodies, the less noise, the more likelihood we pull this stunt off. I'll keep an eye on the outside, try to keep anyone from surprising you. This close to port, they should all be at their stations. Keep in mind, this ship en't full to the brim of slaves. There's probably a handful of cages down below—the rest is likely actual trade goods."

The ship's bow passed below them, well out into the water.

Sheira began to back down the crane's arm, and Gunnar followed her.

He still had one unused attribute point, and he quickly applied it to Agility, throwing all four skill points into Stealth.

The jutting arm of the mainsail began to pass below them. Still at least fifteen feet away.

The elf grinned. "Jump far."

Sheira sprinted across the arm and leapt. Gunnar followed a second behind her, waiting until the last possible moment to fling himself from the edge.

Unlocked Skill: Leap of Faith

Skill Type: Physical
Linked Attribute: Agility (+80% Development)
Affinity Level: 8
Cost: 30 Stamina
Requirements: Level 7 Agility
Description: Go out on a limb. Take a real huge leap. This still won't do you any good if you fall.

Mists swirled below him. The wind rushed through his long hair as he flew out over the open water.

Sheira gripped the edge of the boom, and in the same motion, managed to swing herself up. Gunnar's landing was not so graceful.

As Sheira swung out of his way and onto the boom, he latched his fingers on to the end of the wooden beam. He tried to swing himself up, but one hand slipped, and he barely managed to keep himself from plunging into the water. His heart thundered as he tried to regain his grip, but he missed, and dangled precariously by one hand. His fingers burned, but he fought through it and reached up with all his might.

Sheira grabbed his free hand and swiftly pulled him up to join her. His chest heaved. He nodded his thanks to her and caught his breath.

Sheira: *Smooth.*

Gunnar: *We can't all be acrobats.*

Sheira: *Just so we're clear who's the greater badass here.*

Gunnar: *Who failed their trial again?*

Sheira: *That's a low blow.*

Gunnar shrugged and grinned.

Sheira pointed down to the deck, then without another word, she disappeared, swinging from beams and rigging up toward the crow's nest.

Gunnar made his way carefully along the beam, until he was no longer hanging out over the water. Then, he paused to take stock of the situation.

He could make out the silhouettes of two sailors at the helm. A couple more were at the bow of the ship, three were readying ropes and planks across the mast deck, and several stood near the open loading hatch leading belowdecks. The crew all seemed preoccupied with preparations for docking. Considering the fact they were ferrying illegal cargo, Gunnar guessed they would have to unload it fast.

Which did not leave him much time.

The area around the hatch was too crowded, but Gunnar spotted an open doorway below the quarterdeck, illuminated by a dim lantern.

If possible, he thought it best to get below without any casualties, which meant he had to be quick. Activating Stealth, he dropped his hands to the boom and then swung down to the deck, ducking behind a large barrel near the rail.

He paused, waiting for any reaction from the sailors across the deck.

A lone sailor, possibly the captain, stood a short distance from the door with his back to Gunnar. There was a ruckus over by the hatch, and the captain hurried forward, shouting at the sailors readying the ropes.

Gunnar seized the moment, hurrying the short distance to the doorway and down the stairs to the deck below.

BREAK THE CHAINS

GUNNAR CREPT DOWN A NARROW STAIRCASE, pausing to douse the lantern on the landing of the middle deck, where a cluster of barrels were stored. The staircase continued down to a third deck, which was entirely dark. Up here, he could make out the outline of sailors in the main chamber, hollering up through the hatch at the crew above.

There was a creak behind him, and Gunnar spun.

"Hey, a little help here, will ya?"

A young man was attempting to shift one of the barrels. Gunnar hadn't even seen him when he came down.

"What happened to the bloody light?" the boy complained, grunting as he shoved futilely against the barrel. His voice was scratchy, as though still in the height of puberty.

"Er, oil must've run out. Look, tip it over." He moved beside the boy and helped him heave against the side of the barrel, and it clattered over.

"Thanks," the boy said, glancing up at him in the dim light leaking in from the main chamber. "Wait, who the hell are—"

Gunnar didn't let the boy finish. He clasped one hand over

the boy's mouth to stifle any screams, and clocked him over the head with the hilt of his dagger. The boy went limp in his arms.

[*KO! You have triggered the effect Concussive Stupor. You knocked Cabin Boy Level 3 out cold. Not exactly a feat. Here's 1 XP!*]

One? Gunnar thought. *Might have been less insulting to get zero.*

He dragged the boy back into the depths of the cabin. He wanted to find some ropes and something he could use for a gag, but he feared there was no time. The boy had nothing handy to loot, like a ring of keys. Only a thick brush caked in grime. So Gunnar left the unconscious boy lying in the depths of the ship and hurried away.

Activating Dark Sight, Gunnar descended the staircase into the belly of the ship.

The lowest deck was barely tall enough to stand in, and he had to stoop underneath each support beam. Both sides of the deck were lined with barrels, and there were a few small crates at the center. At the far end of the deck, lengths of white cloth, maybe for repairing sails, were draped over what looked to be large crates.

Gunnar hurried across the deck and pulled the thick canvas aside to reveal a cage filled with several slaves, packed in tight.

"Who the hell are you?" demanded a goblin at the front of the cage.

"I'm here to spring you out of here," Gunnar whispered.

This stirred a flurry of murmurs amongst the prisoners.

Gunnar found a padlock and began fiddling with it, preparing his lockpicks. He only had three left. And all the prisoners appeared to be shackled as well.

He gently slipped the rods inside and began to turn them, carefully sensing the pressure of the mechanisms.

Snap!

He grimaced as he pulled them free. Thankfully only one broke.

But he could not afford another mistake. *Ah, I wish I'd had more time to practice with these damn things.*

He focused hard, closed his eyes, and drew a long breath to calm himself. Suddenly, he felt a warm sensation travel down his arm, along his fingers, and into the slender pieces of metal, as though something were guiding his movements.

Unlocked Spell: Mindful Moment

Spell Type: Race-based, Celestial
Alignment: Light
Linked Attribute: Wisdom (+65% Development)
Affinity Level: 10
Cost: 5 Mana per second
Description: The Zen Master strikes again! For a brief period, you can focus your superior mind beyond the ability of the unenlightened peons. Use this ability to guide your body into the present and become the best version of you!

He opened his eyes. The lock clicked, and the slaves could barely contain their excitement. There was a soft ringing of chains. In the same moment, a light shone down from the stairs at the other end of the deck.

"Don't move," Gunnar commanded. He swiftly drew the covering back over the slaves and ducked behind the row of barrels leading to the cages.

A sailor thudded his way down the steps as someone above hollered that they were getting close to the dock. His footsteps thundered as he crossed the deck, and Gunnar gulped as he took in the sight of the massive man.

He was well over six feet tall, with a blade at his hip and a huge sack in his hand. He stooped as he plodded across the low deck.

"All right, you sewer rats, time's up!" the sailor said, banging against the side of the cage.

Gunnar activated Stealth and crept up behind the man. The sailor drew back the cloth.

And the goblin did precisely what Gunnar had told him not to do.

The creature threw open the gate and leapt out, still shackled, tackling the sailor to the ground. The man cried out, and Gunnar had no options. As the two struggled on the ground, he drove his dagger at the man's skull. But at the last second, the man shifted. The blade grazed his ear and plunged into his shoulder.

[*You have dealt* +20 *Damage to Sailor Level* 10*!*]

The man roared. The goblin pressed the chain binding his shackles down upon the man's thick neck, holding him relatively in place, minus his flailing arms and legs. And Gunnar drove his blade again and again into the man's skull, dealing more damage with each attack.

[*You have defeated Sailor Level* 10*! Here's* 20 *XP!*]

"Hey, Bannon! What's going on down there?"

The voice echoed from the deck above, and the thudding of footsteps set Gunnar's heart racing.

"Good work," Gunnar muttered. "Now, we'll have them all down here."

The goblin wrenched Gunnar's dagger from the sailor's skull with a sick squelching sound. "Bring it on. I relish the thought of watching the life drain from each of their eyes."

"Bannon!" shouted another sailor.

"Y-yeah! All good down here!" Gunnar shouted, giving his best impression of the man's gravelly voice.

He fumbled in the dead sailor's pockets and found a ring of

keys. The rest of the slaves emerged from the cage—another goblin, a kobold, and an elf woman—all shackled at the hands and feet, with an additional chain connecting the two sets together.

Gunnar tried the keys on the goblin's shackles, but none of them would fit.

"These only work on the cages, huh?" Gunnar said.

The goblin nodded. "They never send one guy down with both. Probably for this reason."

"You dumb little shits!" The voice came from the staircase. Two sailors emerged at the end of the deck. Both men drew large scimitars.

"They got the other keys," the goblin muttered.

Gunnar shook his head and drew the saber he'd stolen from the Red Cloak back at Dravingdel's party. "Empty the rest of the cages, now!"

One of the men carried a lantern that cast violent shadows around the room.

Gunnar launched one of his throwing blades. The lantern shattered, and the sailor cursed as he dropped it on the ground. The room plunged into darkness.

And Gunnar attacked.

With Dark Sight to guide him, he threw another blade. It struck the first sailor in the shoulder.

[*You have dealt +20 Damage to Sailor Level 10!*]

Gunnar raced across the deck and barreled into the second man. The impact sent the sailor staggering back. Gunnar clashed with his saber, but incredibly the man managed to deflect it. There was still some faint light pouring down through the slats in the loading deck above, messing with his Dark Sight. He attacked again, but the sailor deflected the blow.

And all at once, his vision blurred. Pain rushed up his left arm. The first sailor had wrenched the throwing blade out of his own shoulder and offered Gunnar a taste of his own medicine.

The blade jutted out of his biceps, sending shooting pangs through his bones. Gunnar staggered back, barely managing to deflect an attack from the second sailor. The sailor was much stronger than he was, and combined with the pain, Gunnar lost his grip on his saber. The blade clattered on the deck.

"Look out!" shouted a woman's voice behind him. He was struck by the odd feeling that he recognized that voice.

Gunnar glanced back, then leapt to the side of the room, just in time, as a huge barrel rolled past, sending the two sailors scrambling. Two more barrels followed, the second taking one of the sailors off his feet. Gunnar launched another throwing blade, nailing the other sailor in the throat.

[*Critical Hit! You have dealt +40 Damage to Sailor Level 10!*]

The man dropped to his knees, hands at his neck. He withdrew the blade, and blood gushed from the wound.

[*You have triggered the effect Mortal Bleeding on Sailor Level 10!*]

The other sailor scrambled back to his feet, swinging his blade in the dark with maniacal attacks. Gunnar backed away, dodging a massive stroke that stuck in the floorboards. The man wrenched his scimitar free with a crack.

The whole ship shuddered violently, sending more barrels rolling, and the sailor fell back.

"Now!" shouted the woman behind him.

The slaves were still shackled, but they managed to move remarkably quick.

The ship groaned and swayed. But it had come to a stop, and Gunnar realized Sheira must have crashed it somewhere in the harbor.

[*You have dealt +20 Damage to Sailor Level 10!*]

Blood poured from the throat wound, and Scan told him the man's Health would be finished in moments.

The slaves charged past Gunnar, tackling the other sailor to the ground. The goblin drove his dagger into the man's huge chest.

The remaining bleeding sailor was now prostrate on the ground, and the kobold dug its ferocious teeth into the man's throat, ending his life in a spray of blood.

[*You have defeated Sailor Level 10 with an assist from Hank the Kobold! Here's 10 XP!*]

There was a mad scramble as the goblin looted the keys and began unlocking shackles. The ship was still swaying. Shouts echoed from above, but Gunnar guessed whatever had happened was keeping the remaining sailors plenty preoccupied.

Gunnar's arm was still shooting with pain. He gripped the throwing blade, but that only sent more pangs coursing through him. He cried out.

"Let me help you with that," said a woman behind him.

Gunnar turned. A dawn elf, with wavy blonde hair and piercing blue eyes, brushed his uninjured shoulder and smiled.

His breath caught and his head pounded.

He... recognized that face.

49

REWARD

GUNNAR DRIFTED between astonishment and utter confusion. Was this some sort of sick joke?

If not for the sharp, slender elven ears, she looked exactly like Alex Keynes, the young woman he had killed back in the real world.

Even her in-game name confirmed his fear.

Lex - Level 12

HP: 90/90
MP: 140/140
Race: Dawn Elf
Clan: Luminari
Disposition: Friendly
Relationship: Glad to not be in that cage
Description: Dawn elves are known more for scholarship and the celestial arts than combat. An alliance might help make up for the Wisdom you lack. Assuming you don't royally screw this up.

His mind whirled. But the fact that her disposition was

friendly suggested this must be some demented game developer messing with him.

But still it was unsettling as hell.

Gunnar's eyes met hers for the first time, and for a moment, he wondered whether she recognized him too.

"Do I—"

The elf gripped his wrist, and he cried out, pain shooting up his arm from the dagger still buried in his biceps.

"Hold still," Lex said, softly yet forcefully.

Even her voice sounded familiar, which made no sense. To the best of his memory, she had been dying when he reached her.

Or maybe he had suppressed the true memory.

At this point, he had no idea what to think. But for the time being, he seemed to be the only one freaking out.

Lex patted his shoulder gently. "Relax."

Come on, get it together, he thought. *They're trying to throw you off your game.*

He took a deep breath, and she withdrew the throwing blade from his arm in one swift motion. He groaned, but held back a scream.

"Thanks," he said, clasping his fingers over the wound.

"You freed us. It's the least I can do."

Well, she's definitely an ally at any rate.

He sure as hell wasn't going to let some punk computer nerd ruin this quest.

"One of those whole-asses had a green juice," said Hank the Kobold, scurrying over to them.

"Think you mean assholes," Gunnar said.

The reptilian creature shrugged and held out a Potion of Minor Healing, and Gunnar quickly downed its contents. There was a momentary tension in his arm and one last sharp pang, and then the blood quit flowing and the pain dissipated for the most part. His Health shot back up to 80%.

The goblin had managed to free all the others from their shackles, and the slaves gathered around Gunnar, awaiting instructions.

There were ten total, all non-human creatures of one sort or another, including a merman, who was being carried by a large gray-skinned mountain orc.

"Anyone else hurt?" Gunnar asked, remembering he still had three healing potions himself.

The goblin and the mountain orc had both gotten pretty torn up in the scuffle, and they eagerly finished off Gunnar's potions as well as two more of the kobold's.

"Don't have any more, do you?" he asked Hank. It would be nice to get back to full Health before they faced the rest of the crew.

But the kobold shook his head.

Ah, well...

Gunnar turned to the others. "We should get outta here. As soon as you get off the ship, split up, and get as far as you can from the harbor."

"Where're we supposed to go?" asked the mountain orc in a gruff voice.

"I know a place," Gunnar said, pulling up his display and showing them the location of the crypt on his map of Thailen.

Lex smiled at him and patted his shoulder. "Thank you, Gunnar."

He filled with warmth at her touch, but then tensed, wondering what the hell was going on.

But there was no time to inquire now. A strange greenish glow sifted between the slats from the deck above.

Sailors were shouting and scrambling around the ship above.

"Get off as fast as you can," Gunnar commanded. "Don't engage unless you have to."

The creatures nodded and took off up the stairs with Gunnar taking up the rear. The middle deck was deserted and lit only by the violent flashing emerald light coming from above.

The main deck was madness. Sailors were desperately trying to salvage the foremast, which was hanging precariously off the side of the ship, the base engulfed in green flames.

The moment he saw it, Gunnar knew Sheira had saved her Arcane Bolt for the opportune moment. The chaos had been enough to distract the rest of the crew from anything going on belowdecks.

At the sight of the escaping prisoners, several sailors began shouting frantically. One let go of his rope, and the foremast nearly plunged into the sea at the shift in support.

A wiry sailor drew his sword, but the prisoners barreled over him and leapt off the side of the ship for freedom. Lapping flames cast wild shadows all over.

Gunnar was filled with pride and satisfaction as the slaves made their escape.

But it was cut off by a blazing pain in his spine.

He turned.

The cabin boy withdrew a dagger from Gunnar's back, drenched in his blood. Gunnar drew his sword, but before he could attack, the boy's blade plunged into his chest.

His Health dropped to 50%.

[*The effect Mortal Bleeding has been triggered. You will suffer +2 Damage per second until healed or until you succumb to death. Ah, the rewards of being a merciful assassin.*]

Rage filled him. He had spared the damn kid, and this was what he got?

His vision blurred from the pain, but Gunnar managed to

parry the boy's next attack, and with a sweep of his saber, the boy lost his dagger and his right hand with it.

[*You have dealt +10 Damage to Cabin Boy Level 3!*]

The kid cried out, and against all odds, he tried to attack again, reaching for a second dagger at his belt. Gunnar gritted his teeth and drove his saber into the boy's skull. Finally, he went still and silent.

[*You have defeated Cabin Boy Level 3. Look at you kicking ass and taking names. You've earned 0 XP!*]

Gunnar changed his mind. One XP did *not* feel worse than zero.

The foremast groaned, and there was a sharp crack of wood as mast and sails teetered over the edge of the ship. The slaves had fled in all directions, and Gunnar was the last to escape the ship.

His vision spun. He raised his saber, thinking one of the sailors was closing in, but then, they vanished from his sight. Sorcerous flames began to shoot up the main mast in a jarring rush of light.

Something tugged on his cloak from behind.

He turned, slowly, and his blade clattered on the deck.

Sheira's face flashed before him.

"Gunnar, turn off Dark Sight!"

He obeyed, and his vision cleared considerably. But his Health was down to 20% and dropping fast.

"P-pooassh..." He felt like he was speaking underwater, and he couldn't remember the rest of the word.

Sailors rushed across the deck towards them, drawing their scimitars.

Sheira gripped his hand. "We've gotta go."

Gunnar could barely keep his feet under him, and without Sheira's hand at his back, he would have certainly toppled over. They staggered to the edge of the deck and leapt.

Cold water rushed around his head.

Sheira kept tugging at him, and behind them, Gunnar saw an explosion of flames. Shouts filled the night as they swam away into the engulfing darkness.

[*Congratulations! You have completed the quest* Break the Chains! *You have successfully rescued—*]

Gunnar's Health bar flashed red across his vision.

[*You have been killed by Cabin Boy Level 3! Wow! Just wow...*]

Gunnar began to drift out and above his body. The image of Nymoria hovered over the water, but her voice was muffled and indistinguishable.

Sheira was still struggling to swim before she realized she was dragging a dead body. She pounded the waves and cursed.

And Gunnar thought it was a nice change from the last time he had died in Sheira's arms.

Then, everything went black.

━━━

Flashing lights and the soft beep of technology drifted into his consciousness.

At first, he thought he was in a hospital. A blur crossed his vision and stayed there, slowly coming into focus.

Shad's grinning face loomed before him.

Jake grimaced.

"What the hell is wrong with you?" Shad asked, laughing.

"Whaaa?" His mouth couldn't quite finish the words. The console whirred as the robotic arms shifted and tubes retracted from Jake's body, and the momentary numbness faded away. He braced himself for the pain about to come.

"You look like a damn monkey wincing like that."

"Y-you're not gonna shock me?" Jake asked.

"Nah, kid, I ain't gonna shock you. You did good. Now, come on, time to get up."

"Time to work, you mean?"

Shad just would not stop grinning. "Hey, there's more to this place than tasers and shit shoveling. Why you so paranoid?"

Jake groaned as he sat up. "Must be from general experience."

"Maybe it's time for another type of experience."

"What are you talking about?" Jake's head was pounding and his whole body felt heavy. Almost like he'd just died.

"You did good, son. It's time to reap some rewards."

"From who?"

Shad leaned in close. "Whom. And that would ruin the surprise now, wouldn't it?"

Jake wasn't sure what to think. He was here in this place because of a horrendous crime. Moments before, he had seen someone in-game who looked just like the girl he had killed IRL.

He had so many questions, but he was pretty sure he wouldn't get any straight answers from Shad. He'd have to figure things out on his own. So, he kept quiet and followed Shad out of the room.

They didn't return to the main part of the prison, but followed the hallway to the other end. They stopped in front of a steel door for a few moments while a light scanned over their bodies. Well, Jake's body, since Shad was simply a hologram.

The door opened, and they walked down a long white-walled corridor. At the end was another door, and another hall, and another door after that. After three iterations of this sequence, they reached a staircase that winded up several floors. Following one last hall, lined with doors on only one side, they ended their journey in a holding room that looked out over the entire prison complex from high above.

The only furniture in the room was a long steel table with

two chairs. One of them was occupied by a woman with her back turned to them. As the door closed, she turned.

Her brown skin radiated in the light pouring through from the prison complex. Frizzy black hair framed her head like a halo. She wore a black skirt and a white short-sleeved blouse, revealing long arms covered with tattoos.

To Jake's amazement, she looked much like she did in the game, minus the business attire.

"Hello, Gunnar," she said.

Her voice was soft and slow and seemed to seep into the core of his being.

He shook his head and stepped forward, more confused than ever.

"Hello, Nymoria."

50

CHAMPION

THE WOMAN—THE goddess—let out a soft laugh as she rose from her seat to greet him.

"Surprised to see me here?"

Jake turned but Shad was gone. Only he and Nymoria were in the room.

"Well, I'm getting used to weird shit," Jake said. "I figured you might exist somewhere, but I've only seen you in that recording each time I level up in-game."

"I truly hate that script."

"So I've heard."

Nymoria smiled. "I wanted to finally meet you in person."

"What exactly is going on here?"

"Not many pass the trials," Nymoria said sweetly. "Certainly few of my wards."

"Well, the deck is a bit stacked in there."

"You're not wrong, Mr. Darrow. You're not wrong." She turned toward the window, motioning him closer. "A dreary reality here, isn't it?"

Jake gazed out at the industrial dome. But his thoughts

drifted to the girl, Alex Keynes. He wracked his brain, trying to remember if he'd talked to her.

Why else would her voice have sounded familiar?

The memory was all pretty hazy.

Except for her face.

Covered in blood.

"I deserve it," he said at last. "At least I have the game, right?"

"Hmmm..." Nymoria's voice drifted. "Yes, the game is meant to serve as a sort of respite, isn't it... Tell me, is it a respite for you?"

Jake wondered if she meant something more than she was saying.

He shrugged. "It helps when I'm winning. Is that why you're here? To see how I'm holding up?"

"I suppose I should explain," Nymoria said. "I forget how little you know starting out. You and I have been paired in a way."

"By the game?"

"By the fate I am able to purchase, you might say."

"So, you're—what?—an investor in *Pantheon* or something?"

"Of a sort. I don't know if you realize it, but you are on the ground floor of something world-shattering. And I am one of many who wanted in on the action. And the ability to become a goddess offers a certain allure, as you might imagine."

"As a recording in a game," Jake said skeptically, noting that Nymoria did not have any of the same metal disks in her arms that he bore.

"This is no mere game. We are creating a new reality. Do you know the lengths people will go to in order to escape the reality they were born with? You prisoners are the ultimate example. But even I find an appeal to escaping our predictable world."

"Yes, we clearly have a lot in common," he muttered, sarcasm dripping from his words.

"I like your attitude, Mr. Darrow. But don't mistake the dynamic here. You're a felon who happened to wind up in prison at an opportune moment. I suggest you don't screw it up. You're right. I managed to attain the lowest level of goddess in the realms of *Pantheon*. And up to this point, for better or worse, you are my most promising servant."

"What does that mean exactly?"

"The higher you ascend, the higher I ascend. *Pantheon* offers opportunities beyond anything you can imagine. It is about to go live, and the world will be watching the first players. As you might imagine, considering the hardware in your neck, this level of reality subversion will come at a high ticket price, and not a little trepidation. Most of the world will see it streamed, at least at first. The best players will be famous, and their sponsors will gain incredible money and power. I am offering you an opportunity to be my champion, if you will."

"A lot of good fame is worth down here."

Nymoria smiled and drew closer to him.

Her hand brushed his shoulder, and he winced with surprise, realizing that she was actually sharing this room with him.

He hadn't realized how much he missed real physical touch.

"The beta is nearly over, Mr. Darrow. And most of these prisoners will exist as little better than NPCs when *Pantheon* goes live. Low-level players trod on by the greater gods and their greater players. You've already seen this play out. But you have an opportunity."

"To be a prisoner who works for you."

"Never underestimate the power of fame and money. You and I will be showcasing the greatest advancement in technology to the entire world."

Jake didn't believe what he thought she was suggesting. "You think you could... get me out of here?"

"If we rise high enough, anything is possible." Nymoria smiled broadly, but there was something about it that felt strange. As though she were not accustomed to smiling very often.

Jake was skeptical that she could actually get him free. But he couldn't imagine it would be a bad thing to be on the good side of someone rich and powerful. A champion.

"I'm off to a good start, then," Jake said.

"You've barely begun. However, you've proven the ability to see past the inequitable mechanisms of the game and overcome them. You've got grit and intelligence, and a stroke of luck. And you'll need more of that going forward."

There were so many things he wanted to know, but he knew he couldn't risk spoiling this opportunity. "What do you need me to do?"

"I need you to ascend, Jake. You've created an intriguing origin story. An elf betrayed by his mentors and forced to walk his own path. You've got the makings of a guild of your own in this crypt of yours, but I think we're getting ahead of ourselves. You're not ready for that yet."

"I'm not?"

Nymoria smiled maternally. "I loved the way you refused the Nighthawks. I think it will all play well. You've been a hit with the focus groups."

"Focus groups?" Now, that was *really* intriguing.

Nymoria grinned. "I think the Nighthawks understand the potential you have, just as I do. They'll come back calling, and when they do, I want you to say yes."

"You're sure about that?" Jake asked.

"I need you to trust me, Jake. I know a thing or two about how this thing works."

Jake shrugged. "All right."

"I think we have the makings of a heavenly partnership, Mr. Darrow. But there are still plenty of people who want to bring you down. The real game is about to begin. And the world will be watching. I hope you're ready."

Jake did not say so, but he was desperately hoping the same thing.

There was more going on. More than Nymoria was letting on. Perhaps more than she knew.

But for now, all he could do was play along.

"I'll be ready," he said.

"Good."

Nymoria crossed the room and pressed a keypad on the wall. A compartment opened, and she removed a silver-lidded platter. The goddess brought it over to the table and removed the lid, revealing a sizzling cast iron plate filled with food.

"I hear you like rib eye."

He smiled and took a seat.

The meal tasted divine. The steak was tender and juicy, with just the right amount of marbled fat, and Jake Darrow did not let a single bite of it go to waste this time.

━━

When Gunnar respawned, he nearly screamed at the hideous face hovering in front of him. Yellow snaggle-fangs jutted from a leathery black mouth mere inches from his face. Its breath smelled like rotting flesh.

Azmar cackled in his gravelly voice. "Never gets old."

Gunnar shook his head. In truth, he was glad to see him. "I guess I'll just have to get over it."

"That's the spirit."

"It's sweet of you to wait up. Did you miss me?"

"I do the bidding of my mistress. And so I am here on this gods-forsaken roof, in this gods-forsaken city, waiting for a house cat who thinks himself a king of the jungle."

"You can say it. I did all right, didn't I?"

"You're a house cat with claws. That's as far as I'll go."

Gunnar grinned. "I'll take what I can get. Anything important happen while I was away?"

"After you so impressively died at the end of your quest?"

That reminded Gunnar that he hadn't actually seen the reward from his quest. He pulled the notification back up.

[*Congratulations! You have completed the quest* Break the Chains! *You have successfully rescued ten prisoners from the clutches of evil. Here's* 150 XP!]

[*Congratulations! You've reached Level* 12 *in Stealth. You've reached Level* 17 *in Throwing Blade. You've reached Level* 7 *in Slashing Blow. You've reached Level* 11 *in Parry Blow. You've reached Level* 12 *in Lockpicking. Hey, you're not totally horrendous at this Rogue thing.*]

[*You sacrificed yourself so that others could live. You've earned the Bleeding Heart badge! Now, everyone will know how to tug on your heartstrings and take advantage of you:* +1 *to Agility,* +1 *to Strength.*]

[*Congratulations! You have reached Level* 12 *in Glory!*]

Nymoria did not appear this time, and Gunnar guessed it was because she had already appeared right after he died. But a quick check of his HUD confirmed he had another attribute point to distribute.

Considering all he'd been through and all that lay ahead, he applied it immediately to Wisdom, distributing the skill points between Mindful Moment and Perception.

It was hard to believe how much had changed in one night. He'd infiltrated a noble's party and been betrayed by his friend. He'd completed his trial, saved some dwarves and a whole shipload of slaves, and potentially set the stage to form his own faction in this damn city. He'd garnered the favor of his goddess, who was actually some wealthy titan back in the real world.

And now, he had an opportunity to be one of the first heroes —*or is it villains?*—in the most advanced and immersive virtual game the world had ever seen.

Gunnar smiled. "Yep, Azmar, I've done pretty well for myself considering I've only been here a few days."

Azmar rolled his dark eyes. "Well, before you get a hard-on for yourself, need I remind you that you completely botched your initiation into the Nighthawks?"

"I think that will work itself out," Gunnar said.

"We'll see. Your freed prisoners reached safety for the moment," Azmar continued, and then his expression shifted into a dark smirk. "Oh, I should probably tell you that Sykes was not pleased with the way things panned out at Dravingdel's party. He is rounding up his forces."

"A lot of good that will do him."

"Your pal Kohli is with him."

"Sykes let him live?"

Azmar nodded. "Your old friend may have failed to sabotage your guild trial, but he did still have some useful information."

Gunnar thought for a minute. "Ah, shit. The crypt!"

"I don't think Sykes will rest until he has your head mounted on the wall of the Mermaid," Azmar said. "So I wouldn't dally."

But Gunnar was already crossing the roof. As he ran, a notification appeared.

Quest Alert - Mermaid's Vendetta

Description: You've gotten on the wrong side of a powerful crook in the underbelly of this decrepit city. And he knows the location of your new safe haven.

Objective: Protect your new sort-of faction from a ruthless barkeep and his minions.

Reward: A chance at a future in this game.

Do you wish to accept? Yes/No

Gunnar glanced up at the sky. The deck was stacked against him again, but he couldn't help but think, *I bet this will play great IRL.*

He grinned and accepted the quest.

INTERLUDE

THE GODDESS NYMORIA strode through the towering halls of the fortress of Elysium, basking in the swaths of darkness that shrouded her passage. Shadows fell upon her skin tangibly, cold and bitter and intoxicating.

Nymoria detested the daylight. The way its warmth pressed upon her chest as though trying to suffocate her. The way it illuminated every blemish, every secret.

But the dark...

It could make even the most loathsome place tolerable. Even the illustrious halls of Elysium.

She supported her steps with a sleek black staff with a silver lioness's head at the crest. The body of the staff was etched in runes, which had once shone brilliantly, an immediate symbol of her power. Now, the staff barely glowed at all, and Nymoria's spells were equally weak.

It would not be permanent. She would not let it be.

Every day, she was growing stronger. She could feel the warmth of magic pulsing through her body once more. And even more, this night.

Nymoria slowly ascended the long and winding steps to the

tower at the western end of the fortress, where she found the goddess Ariadne waiting for her.

The spritely woman's long dark hair was pulled back, and her pale skin flashed in the moonlight as she turned and greeted her with a delightfully sinister smile.

Nymoria clasped Ariadne's hand and pulled her into the shadows and into an embrace.

"It has been long since you've graced these halls," Ariadne said.

Nymoria had hoped never to return. All the more since she'd been brought low, humiliated before the entire Elysian Court. The memory ate at her gut.

In the daylight, the shimmering spires of this place only reinforced her revulsion, but at night, the towers reminded her of sharp spearheads plunging into the heart of the night sky.

"Well, thankfully, little changes here," Nymoria murmured. "It appears I've missed precious little these past years."

"For now," Ariadne said.

Nymoria smiled softly and nodded.

The two goddesses met one another's gaze. There was a pregnant pause as they contemplated the gravity of what lay before them.

Ariadne broached the subject. "This new realm holds promise."

"We've thought that with others. Yet the Elysian Court remains as it always has."

"But this is different."

Nymoria nodded. "I wouldn't be here if it wasn't. This realm is fixed as always. But there seem to be forces conspiring in our favor."

"Perhaps it is fate."

"I believe in no such thing. But something—someone—is

also trying to tip the scales. And we can bend that to our will. If we are patient."

"At last," Ariadne said, "a chance to forge our own destiny."

Nymoria raised her fingers toward the sky, relishing the thought, picturing this entire fortress in flames. Crimson magic coalesced at her fingertips for a moment, and then, vanished.

"For now," Nymoria whispered, "we must wait and see."

They, and so many others, had waited years for such a chance to shift the balance of power.

It was probably only the fraction of a chance. And it would take little for it to be obliterated entirely.

Nymoria feared it was only a fool's hope. But she could not deny the change in herself, even if it was only a taste of her former strength.

Hope is a cruel, tantalizing seduction, she thought.

But she could not help herself.

She clasped Ariadne's fingers once more.

"Let the games begin."

End of Book One

Gunnar's story continues in Rogue Assassin...

Gunnar Ashwood

Glory: Level 12

Servant of Nymoria

Coins: 167

Character Traits

Race: Dusk Elf

Clan: Maldan

Class: Rogue (Rank - Initiate)

Faction: Well, this is a bit of a cluster right now...

Renown: There's a Small Price on Your Head

Character Stats

Health - 120/120

Stamina - 110/110

Mana - 140/140

Physical Attributes

Strength - 9

Dexterity - 14

Agility - 9

Constitution - 9

Mental Attributes

Intellect - 9

Wisdom - 11

Charisma - 10

Creativity - 5

Physical Skills

Endurance - Level 10 (+25 Stamina Buff)

Throwing Blade - Level 17
Slashing Blow - Level 7
Parry Blow - Level 11
Head-Butt - Level 6
Enhanced Blow - Level 9
Sheer Strength - Level 8
Wall Climbing - Level 10
Leap of Faith - Level 8
Pickpocketing - Level 14
Lockpicking - Level 12
Stealth - Level 12
Stealth Attack - Level 6

Mental Skills

Perception - Level 26
Mindful Breathing - Level 7
Art of Diplomacy - Level 15

Active Items

Basic Dark Cloak (+10% Stealth)
Stealth Boots (+10% Stealth)
Leather Vambraces (+10% Resistance to Damage)
Leather Greaves (+10% Resistance to Damage)

Inactive Items

Lock Picks (2)

Spells

Scan - Level 26
Dark Sight - Level 8
Mindful Moment - Level 13
Call of the Wild - Novice-level Bond

ACKNOWLEDGMENTS

This book is dedicated to the members of my writing group—David, Jason, Blake, Zack, and Danielle. I am almost certain this book would not exist had I not started meeting with you guys every week. Your critiques made this book so much better, and your encouragement and excitement for this project kept me at it.

An especial thanks to Blake for feedback on the game mechanics, and for literally introducing me to this incredible genre.

My wife, Kaitlin, has supported my writing career every step of the way, and she always enthusiastically reads and critiques my books, even when they are often far outside her normal genres.

Thanks to all my family for their love and support, and especially to my boys, Logan and Parker, for their constant source of joy.

A final thanks to the first readers of this series over on Royal Road. You all helped me spot logistical and mechanical errors, and encouraged me that I had something good going here.

Can't wait for Book 2? Come join my Patreon for first access to new chapters as they are written.

Don't miss S.A. Klopfenstein's complete epic fantasy series,

The Shadow Watch Saga!

MORE LITRPG

If you loved this book, find more LitRPG in some of these thriving online communities:

LitRPG Rebels
LitRPG Forum
Gamelit Society
LitRPG Books
LitRPG
Gamelit, litRPG, Xianxia and Wuxia - Fun Group
Fantasy Nation - Urban, Epic, LitRPG/Gamelit
Fantasy, Fiction, Litrpg books and Audible
LitRPG Adventures: Reviews and Discussions
LitRPG Reviews Group
LitRPG Reads
Spoiled Rotten Readers (RPG+Game Book)
LitRPG Releases
Progression Fiction Addicts

ABOUT THE AUTHOR

S.A. Klopfenstein grew up on a steady dose of Tolkien and Star Wars. As a child, he wrote his first story about a sleep-walking serial killer. He lives in the American West with his wife and sons, and their dog, Iorek Byrnison. He can be found exploring the peaks of the Rocky Mountains, or daring the halls of the high school where he teaches mythology and English.

For the latest information on his writing:

Visit authorsaklopfenstein.com
and sign up for his newsletter.

Made in United States
Orlando, FL
14 December 2024

55319649R00224